Bayou Bound

by

Linda Joyce

Fleur de Lis Series, Book Two

Bayou Bound

Cover Art by *Kim Mendoza*

The Wild Rose Press, Inc.
PO Box 708
Adams Basin, NY 14410-0708
Visit us at www.thewildrosepress.com

Publishing History
First Champagne Rose Edition, 2014
Print ISBN 978-1-62830-232-5
Digital ISBN 978-1-62830-233-2

Fleur de Lis Series, Book Two
Published in the United States of America

Under the shroud of darkness, minutes clicked away slowly. When the driver's door opened, the overhead light snapped on and startled her. The stranger climbed into the driver's seat. He yanked on a sleeve and started to remove his large coat. Biloxi strained to get a better look at his face.

Just in case she ever needed to identify him.

Like in a line-up.

"Take it off." He motioned to the blanket.

Her mouth gaped. He sounded like a man used to giving orders—and having others follow them, doing exactly as he said. Well, he could wait forever. She didn't take orders from anyone. That's why she worked for herself. Besides, she'd freeze without the blanket.

"No."

"C'mon now, you're cold and wet."

He must have read shock on her face. He sighed, but the sigh was tinged with disgust.

"Okay, here goes."

She froze statue still. The man straddled the console, a knee in each front seat, then he faced her. He reached toward her and yanked the blanket.

Clearly he was the stronger one. Their tug-o-war lasted less than a minute. He pulled the blanket away, wadded it up, and tossed it on the floor.

She pulled her legs tight to her body, prepared to fight, kick, even claw. To her surprise, he gently draped his long coat over her. The lingering heat from his body covered her shiver. The coat would protect her, if from nothing else, from him.

Praise for *BAYOU BOUND*

BAYOU BOUND received First Place in Romance from the Southeastern Writers Association in 2011

~*~

"A raging storm has nothing on the steamy and fierce passion of Nick and Biloxi. Linda Joyce is the new author to watch!"

~Kathy L Wheeler, author of *The Color of Betrayal*

~*~

"As if the bayou needed more heat and steam! Step aside, Shakespeare. Linda Joyce adds southern charm, and a much happier ending, to this modern day Romeo and Juliet."

~Claire Croxton, author of *Santorini Sunset*

~*~

"Family feud turns up the heat between jet-setting photographer Biloxi Dutrey and family-oriented veterinarian Nick Trahan. *BAYOU BOUND* is a keeper."

~Marilyn Baron, author of *Under the Moon Gate*

Dedication

This book is dedicated to my voracious reading nieces,
Julia, Latasha, and Maya.
May you always find joy in reading books.

Acknowledgments

It takes a village to raise a child. My novels are no different. The story is mine, as are the words, yet made better through the support of friends, critique partners, family, and my editor, Ally Robertson. I extend my deepest appreciation to all.

The public unveiling of *Bayou Bound* took place at the Writer's Academy in Jodi Thomas' inaugural class. I am especially grateful to Kathy L Wheeler, Claire Croxton, Jan Morrill, Gina Hooten Popp, and Romney Nesbitt for their input and support with this book.

I am thankful to the Southeastern Writers Association for the boost in confidence that propped me up and kept me pushing forward. They awarded this manuscript First Place in Romance in 2011.

Encouragement and support come in many forms. I offer a big "Thank you!" to Michael H. Harper, and Kelly and David Silverman. When I'm sitting with self-doubt, you offer a hand up. I appreciate you.

A special "Thank you" to Dr. Amy Reich for her healing hands and her "second pair of eyes," to Adam Throne for his scholarly consultation, and Pamela Mason for teaching me much, including Twitter.

As always, my world is possible through the encouragement, love, and support of the hero in my life. My darling husband, Donald, thank you for sharing this journey with me.

And like all authors, my stories are for you, the reader. Thank you for taking a chance on a new author. Your support is invaluable. I hope to hear from you. Please enjoy the story of Biloxi and Nick.

Chapter 1

Nick Trahan squatted next to the whelping box and tucked more hay around the sides. He never would have thought he'd choose a date with a dog over a date with a hot looking woman. After giving the litter of puppies one last glance, he rose and stood next to Captain Jack in the doorway of the old barn.

"Doc, I sure do appreciate you com'n out on a night like this. Rain enough to choke a frog," the old man hollered over the rain pounding the tin roof.

Nick nodded. "Anytime, Capt'n Jack. Anytime."

Captain Jack's emergency provided a graceful exit. The perfect excuse to escape his date.

"What did I pull you away from?"

"Nothing really." He hoped that would end the direction of the conversation, but the old man's gaze went to Nick's black Lucchese boots. Fresh from the box, they shined. Not his usual veterinary footwear for mucking around in barns. "Just your run-of-the-mill date."

He focused on the puppies again, hoping to distract Captain Jack's prying curiosity. Five orange and white newborns huddled close to their mother. Hay and strips torn from an old wool blanket surrounded them while a heat lamp warmed the damp January night air.

"They're gonna be just fine," Nick assured the old man.

"Sugar here, she's a special one." Captain Jack radiated pride and affection.

"The perfect mother," Nick agreed, thankful for the change in the conversation.

"Back to your date." Captain Jack cast a suspicious glance. "Don't know what's run-of-the-mill about any pretty young thing."

Nick coughed back a chuckle. No mistaking the glint in the old man's eye, the tilt of his head, and raised wiry eyebrows. With hands shoved deep into the pockets of his bib overalls, the old man nudged Nick's side with his elbow.

"Okay, okay," Nick said, putting up his hands in surrender. "Sugar's a better date than the woman I left behind at the Seafood Shak." He never ever kissed and told, though in this case, no kissing had taken place.

"You're gonna be a gentleman, eh?" The old man rubbed his thumbs down the sides of the overall's suspenders, then nodded toward the litter. "Sure you don't want one? I'll make you a present of the pick of the litter for comin' out to help Sugar birth her pups."

"No, sir," Nick replied. "I don't have time to take care of a puppy. I'm not home enough to housebreak a dog."

"What you wanna go and ruin a good huntin' dog by making a lap puppy outta it for?" The old man's frown said it all—housebreaking a hunting dog was sacrilegious.

"Well, sir, to tell you the truth, as Grandpère would say, tonight's a two-dog night—"

"Your granddaddy's an upstanding Cajun gentleman, if ever there is one." Captain Jack bobbed his head.

"—and a dog would be good company up at the house on a night like tonight," Nick finished.

The old man eyed him as if he'd grown two heads.

"Son, you need a woman. A dog'll love you always, but the right woman'll give you the real warmth you need." Captain Jack winked.

No disagreeing with the old jasper. However, the right woman hadn't wandered onto the horizon. Whoever she was, she'd have to have Gorilla Glue sticking power. Marriage required commitment. He'd dated nice girls, "proper young ladies" as his grandmother called them, mostly to keep her off his back whenever she went into her marriage mode. But he refused to walk in the wake of his parents, poster children for a bad marriage.

Not gonna happen to me.

He needed a graceful exit now. He wasn't about to discuss his lack of love life in any detail with Captain Jack, especially since the old man and Grandpère remained friends. Maybe a twist in the topic might shake the old man's dogged grip on the subject.

"Ya hear me, Doc? A woman."

"A woman. *Mais*, I don't have time to find one of them, let alone try to housebreak her, too. Maybe I'll consider a puppy after all."

Captain Jack's round body shook and heaved. He slapped Nick on the back. "Damn, son, you sound just like your granddaddy. I got to get by and see him soon. Say, how 'bout a beer up at the house?"

Nick checked his watch. Old Jack could shoot the shit for hours. An early morning surgery meant he needed sleep, especially after spending the day driving all over the county to visit patients. He needed his bed.

His patients deserved his best, even at six in the morning.

"Next time. I promise."

Nick slipped on his canvas duster. He waved good-bye, then darted out into the rainy night and climbed into his pickup. The diesel engine rumbled. He backed down the drive and drove toward home.

Nick hit the "hot" button for his seat and blasted the heater. Warmth flowed. Forty damn degrees in Mississippi was the same as freezing anyplace else. A hot shower and a stiff drink would remedy the chill before sleep.

He reflected on his date with the New Yorker who came south to visit family for Twelfth Night festivities. She demanded a *real* good time. Good looking. Tight skirt. Pointy shoes. However, the glint in her eyes sparked red-flag warnings. His sixth sense, developed after his less-than-discriminating college years, told him to run like hell.

They met in a hole in the wall. Her choice. Clearly, she chased a bona fide slumming experience. The odor of hot grease greeted them when they opened the door. Two local good ol' boys stumbled out—pickup-driving, shotgun-toting types. Their wheels sprayed gravel everywhere when they left the parking lot. Not the kind of place he'd choose for a date. Hell, not the kind of place he frequented.

Ms. New York drinking beer from a longneck bottle—not so bad. Her licking her fingers after eating hush puppies—disgusting. Then, she tried her come on, only her Scarlett O'Hara impression lacked...everything. In the end, her language ruined the date. He was an easy-going kind of guy, but a woman dropping F-bombs all over the place made him cringe.

Nor did he sleep with any woman on the first date.

She'd called him old-fashioned. He called it safe.

If the rain wasn't pounding the asphalt and if he were less tired, the drive home would run fifteen minutes. However, the weather forced him to drive slower. He flicked on the radio. The windshield wipers kept time with the bass of a bluesy tune. Stevie Ray Vaughn hit his licks, wailing on a guitar. Nick thumped the console in rhythm with the bass to stay awake.

Storm-swept clouds hid the full moon and rendered the landscape invisible. He watched the clock as he drove. While tracking his progress on a stormy night, he measured distance by time. His pickup lumbered through the weather oblivious to the pouring rain.

His house appeared through the trees when he rounded the bend. The gaslights mounted on the porch flickered and signaled the end of a long day. It had rained for hours. Small creeks and ponds flooded, but his home was safe, even if the nearby Pearl River overflowed her banks. His raised Creole cottage, a replica of an old plantation house on River Road, sat on the highest spot on a two-hundred acre spread of Trahan land.

He slowed, anticipating the curves. At least once a month, around the full moon, some fool would fly along the two-lane road as though the devil whipped his back and end up in the ditch—the one where his driveway intersected the road. He counted back. Yep, every month for the last six, he'd found some fool stuck in the ditch.

****

Biloxi Noël Dutrey's mind wandered. Her hold on

the steering wheel slipped when on-coming headlights suddenly blinded her. Someone had changed the path of the road. It used to roll left, then to the right, but not left again. She slammed on her brakes. Her BMW skidded on rain-slicked asphalt. Tires spun on gravel, sending rocks flying.

Crunch.

Thud.

The car stopped abruptly.

"Damn it!" She smacked the palms of her hands against the steering wheel. The horn's dying *ooh-ahhh* sounded ghostly in the rain-soggy night. She jumped. Around her rain poured down. She faced a water-filled ditch.

Not the homecoming she'd planned.

"Who changed the damn road?" She pounded her fist on the dash. First, Atlanta's I-285 was more parking lot than interstate. Then the accident in Montgomery brought traffic to a stop. Now this."

She knew this road like the back of her hand, had traveled it hundreds of times. Except no longer limestone and gravel, the freshly paved asphalt curved in a new spot, and her precious sports car faced a possible watery grave.

Turning the key off, then on again, caused the headlights to flash, yet the engine failed to turn over. The blue-green glow of the digital clock on the dash announced midnight had come and gone. She tapped her fingers at her temples hoping inspiration would break through the fog of fatigue.

She needed to inspect the car.

Light would illuminate any problem. She grabbed her purse and rummaged through the backpack-sized black hole. The flashlight app on her cell phone could provide a necessary tool to assess the damage. Turning her purse on its side, she felt around inside it again. No phone.

Turning the purse bottom up, she dumped the contents on the passenger seat, then gave the bag a hard shake. Out of patience, she flipped on the overhead map light.

After sorting out the lipsticks, light meter, chewing gum, and dental floss, she chucked the items back inside. Her wallet next, then her watch. No cell phone.

"Where is it?" she groaned.

She shoved slips of paper and business cards, contacts from her last photography show, into the side pocket of her purse, then scooped up the pens and dropped them in the cup holder on the console. Maybe the phone slipped to the floor on the far side of the passenger's seat.

"*Grrr!*" Karma must have deserted her when she left Atlanta. There was no way to avoid the unwanted shower that waited once she opened the car door. What did it matter? Who needed new Donna Karan silk pants? Or the splurge of Jimmy Choo shoes? She cringed anticipating her feet sinking into ooze and slimy muck. At least she could spare her new leather jacket.

"Buck up, baby. You're almost home," she muttered.

The rain lightened from pounding to misty. She reached for the golf umbrella. She yanked on it, trying to maneuver it out of its place on the floor next to her seat, but it refused to budge. The only way to dislodge it was to open the car door, which guaranteed a shower.

Determined, she unlatched her seatbelt. Grabbing the car door handle, she pulled the latch open. A force on the other side yanked.

She held onto the door. It pulled her from her seat. "Ahhh!"

Her butt hit the ground first, then her back. The hard landing beat the breath out of her.

"Are you all right, *chèr*?" a man's voice came out of the dark.

On her back, feet still inside the car, she managed to make out cowboy boots and the hem of blue jeans with the help of the meager light shining from inside the car.

"No. I'm *not* all right."

She sputtered and squirmed and tried to rise. Misty rain dampened her face. She wiggled more, but no success.

Strong hands grasped her under her arms, picked her up, and set her on her feet. Wetness soaked through her clothes to her skin. Her cashmere sweater was ruined.

With the car's headlights pointed into the ditch, dark water swallowed the light rather than reflected it. She looked up. A Stetson, pulled low, protected the man's head from the rain and shadowed most of his face. A long, oiled-canvas duster, something a cowboy riding the range might wear in an old western movie, covered the rest of him. In her mind's eye, a picture formed. Him on a dark horse riding through a field of white cotton.

She flinched at a flash of lightning. It brought her wandering mind back to the stranger.

"Branna Lind? What are you doing out here?"

With Marine-wide shoulders and standing a head taller than she, at least he spoke like a native. She heard Southern in his smoky deep voice, but he plucked her last nerve when he called her by her cousin's name. And what was he frowning about?

The brim of his hat moved with the tilt of his head. He appeared to give her the once-over. "No, you're not Branna. You're the other one."

She grunted and grabbed for the umbrella. It wouldn't save her from the rain, but it could protect her from him. Just in case he had ideas or he called her Branna again.

Three hard yanks pried the umbrella loose. She pushed a button. The umbrella flew open, forcing the man back. With him out of the way, she had three tasks to complete. Inspect the damage to her car and with luck, find her missing cell phone. She liked the third one best—get the hell away from him, whoever he was.

The man stood tall on the high side of the ditch's slope. She glanced up when he reached for her. She rocked back on her heels to scrutinize him further. Her spiky high heels plunged into the waterlogged earth. She'd sold three black-and-white prints to pay for the Choo shoes, and now they were ruined.

She blinked when heavy drops replaced the mist. "I'm not Branna," she shouted over the pelting cold rain.

"Already figured that out," came his slow, matter-of-fact reply. "You're the look-alike cousin I've heard about. You're also not injured. If you wait in my truck, I'll take you home."

"Huh?" Uneasiness rippled through her and she took a hard look at him. The angled planes of his cheeks made him look menacing. His beard was past a five o'clock shadow. He looked tough and hard. Looked like he could do harm.

The man wanted to take her home? To Fleur de Lis? Or where? Alone? In a truck with a stranger?

Bayou Petite might not be Miami or Atlanta, but that didn't mean she was safe. In the pouring rain. On a dark night. In the middle of nowhere.

Fear gripped her hard as she debated her options.

"Look, *chèr*, it's real late. I've got an early morning call. If you get in my truck, I'll get your toy car wrestled out before it drowns in the ditch. If there's damage, you can get it towed to town tomorrow. Gus is too old to come out in this weather this late at night."

At least he knew Gus. The old man ran the ancient "fill'n station," and the only tow-truck service for miles. She calculated the odds. Her rescuer meant her no harm, right?

Before she could speak, he turned and stormed up the slope while she remained with her heels stuck in the mud.

"Wait. Don't go!" She stepped and pulled her feet from her shoes. Barefooted, she started to climb under the shelter of the umbrella. The man stopped. He turned as she started her next step. Looming before her, he caught her off guard. Her arms flailed. Feet slid on wet grass. The umbrella took flight. She tumbled, then slid to a stop, half-in and half-out of the ditch.

"Aw, shit," the man grumbled when he reached her. Bending over, he scooped her up as easily as he might throw a bale of hay. He carried her up the rise to his truck, testing each step along the way.

"Open the door," he barked.

She complied.

The man plopped her on the back seat unceremoniously, like she were nothing more than a dirty burlap bag filled with oysters.

"Wrap yourself in that." He pointed to an old faded blanket. "It's clean…at least cleaner than you."

She struggled to right herself and grab a peek of her rescuer, but he closed the door. The interior light snapped off, leaving her in darkness. Shivering, no pride left, she yanked on the blanket and wrapped it around her. It smelled like dog.

Folding herself up on the back seat, aching and wet, she tried to hold her breath against the odor from the now-damp covering. The truck's heater blew warmth around her, but her toes tingled from the cold. She rubbed them to warm them, then curled up tight and hoped the dampness seeping through the blanket wouldn't damage the leather seats of his new, monstrous-sized crew-cab Ford.

She yawned. Exhaustion washed over her body. The droning clatter of the diesel engine lulled her and took the edge off her fear. If the man intended to harm her, her best plan of counter attack was one she learned in junior high—to kick him in the nuts.

Under the shroud of darkness, minutes clicked away slowly. When the driver's door opened, the overhead light snapped on and startled her. The stranger climbed into the driver's seat. He yanked on a sleeve and started to remove his large coat. She strained to get a better look at his face.

Just in case she ever needed to identify him.

Like in a line-up.

"Take it off." He motioned to the blanket.

Her mouth gaped. He sounded like a man used to giving orders—and having others follow them, doing exactly as he said. Well, he could wait forever. She didn't take orders from anyone. That's why she worked for herself. Besides, she'd freeze without the blanket.

"No."

"C'mon now, you're cold and wet."

He must have read shock on her face. He sighed, but the sigh was tinged with disgust.

"Okay, here goes."

She froze statue still. The man straddled the console, a knee in each front seat, then faced her. He reached toward her and yanked hard on the blanket.

Clearly he was the stronger one. Their tug-o-war lasted less than a minute. He pulled the blanket away, wadded it up and tossed it on the floor.

She pulled her legs tight to her body. Hunched her shoulders for more protection. Prepared to fight, kick, even claw. Every nerve on high alert. Her heart slammed into her throat making it hard to breathe.

To her shock and surprise, he gently draped his long coat over her. The lingering heat from his body covered her shiver. Her guard dropped a half-notch. The coat would protect her, if from nothing else, from him.

Quickly, she tucked the coat tighter around her. Apprehensions about the stranger began to slip as she warmed up.

"I can tow your car," he said, "But you'll have to get in it and steer. I've winched it up the slope." He proceeded to situate himself back behind the wheel.

The windshield wipers whisked away the downpour. The man sighed again. His weariness matched her own. That was one thing they had in common, but probably the only thing.

Who was he?

And when had the road changed? Was it that long since her last visit? She sighed. No matter how bad, things would look better in daylight. She considered tomorrow's possibilities. She'd worked too hard on her plan to give up on it now because of a minor setback.

Tremors of excitement competed with shivers from the miserable cold. As much as she loved her new car, it was replaceable.

Home. Land. Family endured, and she had finally arrived. Almost.

Chapter 2

"Um. Before we get started…" Biloxi winced at the timidity in her voice. "How do you do? I'm Biloxi Dutrey."

"Yes, I know."

She bristled at his tone. Of course he knew her, everyone in Bayou Petite knew of her family. Though he had mistaken her for Branna earlier, and then corrected himself, so of course he knew. Yet, that didn't explain *how*.

However, he had stopped to help her and used his polished Southern manners more than she had. But still she needed to know more about him before he dragged her and her car to Fleur de Lis, or to God-knows-where.

"I apologize for my lack of manners. Thank you for stopping to help me, Mister…?"

"Nick."

Nick who? And more importantly, how did he know her family? A community connection or maybe a business one? He didn't look like a local struggling fisherman or farmer. He didn't look like he struggled with anything at all.

"Well, Nick. Thanks again. And I appreciate the use of your coat, too."

No response. Not even a grunt. She shifted and leaned toward the console, trying to sneak a better look at him. She considered herself a good judge of character—usually—and tried to ascertain the nature of his. Nothing prevented him from leaving her in the ditch, but the fact that he had stopped to help on a night like tonight said something positive about him, right? Unlike some men she knew.

"So, Nick, how do you know where I live?" She tried sounding friendly.

"*J'ai passé par la maison.*"

Cajun French. She understood her mother's language. It sounded mesmerizing coming from him. She relaxed a little more. "You passed by the house?"

"Never been invited in."

His voice resonated somewhere between baritone and bass and vibrated calmness. His tone held no accusation. She waited for more explanation, but after a minute, his continued silence unsettled her. Somehow challenged her. To what? She didn't know.

Hadn't every local been to Fleur de Lis at one time or another? A wedding, an anniversary party or a ladies' tea? Not that he would ever attend a tea, but it was odd that he'd never been there.

"Thank you again for rescuing me. Since you know where I live, turn down Loblolly Lane and drive around to the *garçonnière*. Do *not* go to the main house."

"You look like Branna, but you're definitely not."

She frowned. That was his second reference to her cousin. They could pass for sisters, twins almost, and shared the same middle name because of their Christmas Eve birthday. However, Branna had always glided through life like a Saks-Fifth-Avenue and Jimmy-Choo girl, while she was more the everyday Macy's and Cole Haan shopper.

Had there been something between Branna and

15

Nick?

She hated the constant comparison to Branna. Had lived with it all her life. It was like a knife twisting in her gut. Now, the mention of her cousin irked her more than ever. She hated being number two. Returning home always meant living in Branna's shadow. She just hadn't expected it to be up in her face before she ever set foot on Fleur de Lis ground.

She could handle it. Had to.

Besides, she intended to nurture her deep family roots until they grew deep, to the center of the earth. Then nothing could shake her from this place. Home provided the security she craved. And with Branna gone, it was her time to shine as number one.

She had a mission.

The family needed a warp-speed jump from their nineteenth-century traditions to the modern era of the twenty-first. Her plan to keep the family from financial ruin would require gentle finesse, and could be so easy if Branna willingly turned over the job of Keeper. The one she hadn't shown any signs of wanting.

Biloxi sighed. The family's outdated notion of "that's the way we've always done it" would require patience to change. However, she hadn't counted on needing a heap of that patience before she reached the front door.

The stranger's comparison of her to Branna hit a sore spot the first time. The second time was as though he'd poured salt into the wound, but she wouldn't allow the irritation to fester.

"So *you* think Branna and I are definitely different? How so? After all, you mistook me for her."

"You're demanding. Pushy. Bossy. She's quietly

polite. A lady."

In the rearview mirror, Biloxi watched the corners of Nick's mouth curl, yet his voice sounded grave and serious. She wasn't in the mood for teasing.

"Well...Does that mean you won't turn on Loblolly Lane?"

"*Biloxi la reine est elle.*"

"I'm the queen?"

She ignored the comfort of his voice that wrapped around her like a velvet blanket as her blood simmered with frustration. First, he compared her to Branna. Now, he mocked her. If only she'd found her damn cell phone, she wouldn't have to endure insults from a stranger.

Just who the hell was this guy?

Crossing her arms over her chest, she sat back. "*Will* you or *won't* you drive around to the back of the house—to the *garçonnière*?"

Stubborn man. Just like Gregory. Men who tried to dominate. She'd had enough of them. Couldn't Nick just answer her question? She imagined glaring a hole into the back of his head.

"Okay," he chuckled. "I'll do it. Let's get you into your car. Steer gently. If you see my brake lights, ease on your brakes. It'll keep you from running into the back of my truck."

The rain had slowed to a misty spit when Nick opened the back door and lifted her out. Her bare feet rebelled against the cold rough road. She tiptoed while the heels of his boots thudded against the asphalt.

The accident had ruined her plans for tonight, but she could make a grand entrance tomorrow. At least she'd made it home and her bed was only a few minutes away.

Drunk on exhaustion and giddy about her dreams, she carefully tiptoed back to her car. Tomorrow the southern sun would shine brightly, and she'd soak it into her bones. Tomorrow held the promise of all possibilities. She would begin with "show and tell." Hard evidence in the form of a step-by-step business plan would prove she was best suited to be the estate's next Keeper. Out with the old and in with her.

If Nick dropped her at the *garçonnière*—the garage apartment where single male family members stayed— the rumble of his truck wouldn't wake the Old Aunts— Great-Grandmother Grace and her twin sister, Marie. But, Greta, the Old Aunts' companion, remained alert and attentive as any watchdog. If Greta's hawk-like ears heard the truck, it would squash any plans for a surprise grand splash tomorrow. Maybe she'd play the pity card and that would soften Greta up.

Maybe. Though it might take forever with Greta.

A midnight arrival—plus looking like something a raccoon dragged through the mud—would count as a black mark against her on the Old Aunts' scorecard. Not the best way to launch her campaign. Manners and decorum counted big with the two old women holding on to antebellum ideas.

Nick opened her car door and waited while she situated herself in the driver's seat. The bulk of his coat bunched around her when she sat. Squirming, she managed to un-bunch it from under her butt. Once the buckle on her seatbelt clicked, Nick leaned in close, forcing her back into the seat. He appeared to check the dash, then hit a button. The emergency flashers started to blink. Her head began to pound to the clicking rhythm.

Closing her eyes, she prayed quietly, "*Be patient, not too much longer now...a hot shower, Goody's Powder, and sleep.*"

Squatting down beside the open car door, Nick grasped her hands. "Put the car in neutral. Don't start the engine. I'll drive slowly." He smiled. "The tricky part will be the turn at Loblolly Lane."

She scowled, unimpressed with his humor, but his face took on an interesting appeal when the corners of his mouth rose, allowing dimples to form in the hard planes of his cheeks. His lips were full and uncomfortably close. His warm breath caressed her face. But that damn hat brim prevented a good look at his eyes.

"Steer. Brake gently. No engine," she recounted.

"Do you know how to work one of these?" Nick handed her a walkie-talkie. "I use them when I hunt. They'll help us communicate if there's a problem."

She would have preferred her cell phone. "Yes," she snapped. "*Of course,* I know how to use one."

"Good." He closed the door. A loud click sounded.

Clack. Clack. The *clack* of the flashers protruded through the silence. The thudding in her head matched the annoying rhythm.

"Thanks," she shouted. Did he hear her? Probably not. Already, he had retreated.

The truck rumbled, then pulled onto the road. The chain tugged and her car followed. Biloxi rested her hands on the steering wheel, guiding the car as Nick had directed. In just a few minutes, she'd be home. Fleur de Lis. She understood Katie Scarlett O'Hara's joy after the war when Scarlett returned to Tara. That same giddiness had a hold on her.

As she pulled away from the crash site, she settled in for the ride. Looking around, she noted the distinct changes in the scenery.

When had the road changed? Who paved over the shells and gravel? When was that Creole cottage built? Better yet, who lived in the new house that looked just like the restored antebellum over on River Road?

Everyone knew the property belonged to Trahans, Fleur de Lis' non-resident neighbors. The Dutrey-Trahan family feud continued, but she couldn't remember the details. Searching her memory made her head hurt more. Great-Grandmother would have told her if the Trahans had sold their land, particularly if they'd sold to strangers. As far as she could recall, the Trahans lived over in Baton Rouge and managed their land from there.

Oh God!

Was Nick one of them?

****

"I'm turning," Nick said after pushing the pager button on the walkie-talkie. He used his best announcer's voice and didn't hide his amusement. "Next stop, *Loblolly Lane.*"

"Thank you." Her reply was short and clipped.

Biloxi had pushed his buttons. Maybe all her worldly travels made her think she needed to appear tough and talk tough to get respect. He'd heard all about her and her photography talent, but nothing about a reputation for rudeness.

Drive around back. Do not stop. Humph. Who the hell did she think he was? Her order-taking lackey? Maybe she'd hurt her head in the accident after all.

"We'll be there in a few. By the way, I believe your car isn't damaged too badly." Maybe that would improve her sour attitude?

"Okay," she snapped.

Maybe he should reconsider Captain Jack's offer. A puppy. That'd be easier than dealing with an ill-humored, bossy woman, no matter how hot she looked in wet, clingy clothes.

But, he probably shouldn't have baited her. She sounded pissed. What woman wouldn't be on a night like tonight when they looked like they'd driven through a car wash in a convertible with the top down. A stab of guilt sliced his conscience. He hadn't exactly been polite. Bad date. Bad weather. An all-around bad night. Maybe it had been a bad night for her, too. He could relate to that. He shouldn't have taken his bad blind date out on her.

Pushing the button on the walkie-talkie, he called, "Biloxi?"

"Yes, Nick?"

Could he find a way to make things right? "You done good, *chèr*. Didn't mean to be so hard on you." After all, he didn't want to be on worse terms with his closest neighbor. But, was that even possible?

Flowers. Women loved them. Tomorrow, being neighborly of course, he'd bring a bouquet as a peace offering.

Besides, there was something about her...aside from the fact that she looked like Branna's twin, which he couldn't ignore. He had to give her credit. Biloxi hadn't flinched, and she showed no signs of intimidation, even when he answered in Cajun. Even when wet, muddy, and cold, she still exuded attitude.

Michael Bublè singing "Try a Little Tenderness" popped into his head. That was rich. If she knew, she'd probably slap him silly.

He passed the turn leading to the front of the antebellum mansion. He'd heard about Fleur de Lis' wide front and back galleries, large round columns, and the multiple red-brick chimneys. Antebellum architecture fascinated him. A daytime visit would provide a better view rather than squinting in the dark.

"Here we are. The *garçonnière*. Brake slowly." He pulled to one end of a six-bay garage with a living space above it. A floodlight blinked on when he nosed his truck close to one of the doors. A barefoot man dressed in blue sweat pants and an orange shirt bounded down the stairs.

Nick killed the engine. He glanced over his shoulder for a look at the woman he'd rescued. Sitting in her car, she made no effort to move.

"Hey, Linc," Nick called as he opened his door, and started to climb down.

"What the hell? Did you hit her?" Linc asked pointing to the front of the sports car.

"I found your sister in the ditch. She and her car missed the turn."

"Is she hurt?"

Linc's voice hitched and Nick saw concern on the younger man's face. He smiled at Linc's protectiveness.

"I think mostly her pride. She *insisted* I deliver her back here."

Linc pulled a cell phone from the pocket of his sweat pants and hit a button. "Greta? Sorry to wake you. My long-lost sister is here. Looks like she crashed her car. She's wet and—"

Floodlights clicked on. *Bang*, a screen door closed. A ghost-like figure charged ahead, a long white housecoat billowed behind like a superhero's cape.

Nick grinned. The night was growing more and more interesting.

Chapter 3

"Finally home," Biloxi sighed, then opened the car door. The inside lights glowed, but the guys with their backs to her didn't seem to notice. Shielding her eyes, she let them adjust. She considered sleeping in the car; however, a hot shower and dry clothes were far more appealing. Besides sleeping in her own bed could cure her ailments—bruised pride and bruised backside.

She wiggled out of Nick's duster and laid it on the passenger seat. She'd return it clean and dry, with Greta's help, of course. That was the least she could do after he'd rescued her. Without her phone, who knows how long she would've waited for someone else to travel that road. Given the way Linc chatted with Nick, he probably knew where the man lived. The two of them looked chummy. But how did Linc know him?

She grabbed her purse, hooked the strap over her shoulder and considered how much more embarrassment she could handle. The whole rescue thing was not something she'd live down anytime soon. She'd traveled the world taking photographs and had never been a damsel in distress. Leaving Nick to her brother would alleviate further humiliation. Linc could bring her bags upstairs when he finished his male bonding, and Nick could disappear into the night as though he'd never found her. She could focus on a hot steaming shower.

With Linc and Nick occupied, it seemed like a good a time for an escape. She could make a run for it. Closing the car door, her bare feet padded on the cold wet path. She followed it toward the main door at the opposite end of the garage. She started to jog, but her foot slid on mud covering the sidewalk. She managed to right herself. Clutching her purse, she continued on while trying to push away the image of bugs and worms squishing under her feet. The ick factor was high.

"Thanks, Nick. Good night," she shouted over her shoulder. Not her best effort at politeness, but she'd thank him properly when she returned his coat. Maybe then, she'd finally get a glimpse of his mysterious eyes.

"Stop!" Linc hollered as she trotted farther away, but she ignored him. She faltered mid-step when Carson, her cousin, shouted from the apartment's upstairs gallery.

What did he want?

"Biloxi!" Another voice yelled.

"Greta?" Crap. Now Greta knew she was home. The night couldn't get any worse.

"Biloxi! Stop!" Carson barked like a cop chasing a thief.

Panicked, she tried to stop, but spied the gaping hole too late. The mud covering the concrete provided no traction. She teetered on the edge of a hole the size of a small car. When she looked down, her balance shifted. Her arms flailed. Her feet slipped out from under her.

Whomp!

Her butt and backside hit the ground at the same time. Air left her lungs. She gasped for breath. Flat on her back, she fought to open her eyes, but kept them closed against the throbbing in the back of her head.

"Biloxi!" A multitude of voices shouted her name.

She groaned. Speaking was out of the question. Her feet moved, but only to a bent-knee position. She feared sitting up—her head hurt so badly, it just might roll off her neck.

Strong hands felt her body. Hands started at her neck, then gripped her arms, legs, and feet in a too-familiar way. Dazed, she couldn't swat them away. Her arms fell limp, heavy like lead. They refused to move to her mental commands. But she wanted whoever had touched every inch of her to stay. Not leave her alone in the muddy hole that could be mistaken for a grave.

"Ohhh." Had that moan escaped her lips? She fought to hear what her closed eyes couldn't see.

"I don't think anything major is broken," a male voice said. "Are there some boards around here? Let's make a ramp so I can carry her out. I don't want to jar her any more than necessary."

She couldn't place the voice of the man who took control. The voice sounded deep and commanding.

"Yeah, sure. Be right back," someone said from above her.

"Biloxi, are you okay?" An eager voice drifted into her consciousness. Linc? How far away? She opened her mouth to answer. No words formed. She tried to lick her lips. Pain gripped her body.

"Did you do this to my baby?"

She recognized Greta's voice.

"I need to call a *real* doctor," Greta said angrily.

Greta's suspiciousness was something she heaped on anyone she didn't know. Biloxi would have chuckled, but it hurt too much to move.

Warm hands gathered hers. She wasn't alone in the hole. That gave her comfort until a raindrop hit her cheek. Another hit her forehead. More drops fell.

"Hurry, Carson, hurry! She's gonna get soaked," Greta barked.

"She's *already* soaked."

There it was again. That warm deep voice she still couldn't place.

"And how'd she get that way?" Distrust threaded through Greta's accusation.

Lying in a hole, while above her people bickered, wouldn't solve her problem, Biloxi wanted to say. She groaned and tried to lift her head, but kept her eyes closed. If she tried to wipe the rain from her face, she'd smear it with the mud that covered her hands.

"Carson, angle those two boards like a ramp. Linc, grab that flashlight. I'll pick her up. Be ready to catch her if I start to slip."

Now she remembered the voice. Nick. The guy in the cowboy hat and boots who'd picked her up—after she fell out of her car—after the ditch—and he was picking her up again.

She fought against the pain. Her body, supported by strong arms, hovered in the air, but everything hurt with each step he took. She bounced when he walked. She wanted to wrap her arms around his neck, but couldn't lift them. She was nothing more than a limp ragdoll. A dirty wet one.

"I'm taking her to my truck."

A moment later, a bright light shone in her face. She flinched and jerked her head to one side.

"Oh my God!" Greta cried. "She's bleeding. She's bleeding."

Linda Joyce

"It's her head," Nick said. "It'll be faster if I take her to the emergency room in Picayune. She can't wait on an ambulance. Call ahead and tell 'em we're coming."

A soft rain drizzled over her face. She groaned when Nick shifted her weight. Each step he took put her in agony.

"I got the door," Carson said.

"Be careful with her," Greta ordered.

"I'm trying," Nick snapped. "Not hurting her on purpose. Carson, unhitch her car from my truck. We'll push it out of the way."

"Maybe we should wait for an ambulance?" Fear seeped into Greta's voice.

Biloxi tried again to open her eyes. She managed to squint.

A hard jolt sent pain racing through her body when Nick climbed into the truck. He lowered her gently onto the backseat and covered her with something warm. From touch, she recognized his duster. Someone must have pulled it from her car. He wrapped her feet with something damp.

That doggy-smelling blanket.

Blinking slowly, the world came into focus. Nick backed out of the truck and Greta scrambled inside. The older woman knelt on the floor beside the seat and grasped her hand as Nick closed the door.

"You're gonna be okay, baby girl," Greta cooed over and over and stroked Biloxi's hair.

If her body didn't hurt so much, Biloxi would've laughed. Those were the same exact words, in the exact same tone, Greta used to comfort her when she was a little girl.

Greta's hand moved to the base of her neck and supported her head. The physical contact soothed her, but when Greta jerked her hand away, the jolt startled her.

"Doc! Give me your shirt! I need to stop the bleeding. She's got a cut near the base of her skull."

A dark sticky substance covered Greta's raised palm. Biloxi's stomach lurched.

Darkness fell as she fainted.

Chapter 4

Was it a gurney or a slab of ice? A thin mattress resting on hard cold metal was unforgiving against her bruised backside. Her head hurt. Biloxi prayed for a mute button to silence the ER's clatter and chaos. The bright white light made her flinch, even with her eyes closed.

She hated hospitals and their harsh reality—the place where the living died.

Unlike her last hospital visit, this time she wasn't alone. A quick peek let her know that Nick stood by the side of the bed. When he squeezed her hand, she gripped his tighter, thankful for the comfort of his support. Her brother, solemn and pale, stared from the foot of the bed.

"I'll be all right, Linc," she whispered.

"Doc, you gotta step out," a nurse said. "You're not next of kin." She confronted Nick from the opposite side of the gurney.

The nurse pushed up the gray cashmere sleeve of Biloxi's wet sweater, then leaned over. Biloxi recognized Patricia Ann, an old childhood friend, whose eyes darted several times to Nick as she fumbled with the blood pressure cuff, trying to wrap it around Biloxi's arm. Nick's bare chest clearly distracted her.

"It's too tight," Biloxi cried when the cuff inflated.

When Patricia Ann released the pressure, her

stethoscope dropped to the floor.

"Darn it," she said through clenched teeth. "Look folks, you can't hover in here. My patient requires privacy."

"Nice to see you, too, Patricia Ann," Biloxi mumbled.

Nick took a step back, but she refused to let go of his hand. She wanted comforting reassurance that only human contact provided, no matter how pathetic she seemed.

"*Go!*" Patricia Ann pointed at Nick's broad chest, then toward the narrow break in the curtain. "Get out of here, now."

"I'm in good hands," Biloxi whispered. "Ya'll can go." She wanted the shouting to stop. As a child she had learned to cry at will, but never to faint. She regretted not developing that skill. Passing out would be as good an alternative to enduring the moment. And maybe the whole next hour.

Truth told, she wanted Nick and Linc to stay. It was bad enough that Greta wasn't there. Where had her childhood protector gone?

When Linc hesitated, she nodded at him, then dropped her hold on Nick's hand. He frowned, yet turned to leave. Linc followed, but as Nick parted the examining room curtain, their exit was blocked.

"Damn, Nick. You causing trouble again?" A doctor in a white lab coat chuckled. He rolled his eyes and snorted a laugh, then planted his fist on Nick's shirtless chest. The *slap* of skin against skin made her cringe.

Nick shook his head.

"Outta my way," Greta growled, shoving past the

two men. Her robe, no longer white, was streaked with dirt and blood.

"My blood?" Biloxi squeaked. The room around her wobbled. She fought to stop the faint that started to consume her. She'd grown in and out of many things in life, but still couldn't stand the sight of blood. Even dried blood made her queasy.

"Okay, that's it. Everyone out. *And I mean everyone*." Patricia Ann's low tone carried a threat, though she looked anything but serious. Her colorful hospital scrubs made her look more like a walking pink, yellow and green flower garden rather than a medical warden. Her soft Southern accent cooled all the heat in her stern threats.

"I've got to finish getting my patient cleaned up and out of these wet clothes," Patricia Ann announced. Biloxi almost laughed from picturing her friend as a child pitching a temper tantrum.

"Let's let the nurse do her job so I can do mine," the doctor said.

Linc stepped out immediately. Greta lowered her chin and looked up, wide-eyed, as though looking over half-rimmed glasses. Biloxi recognized the look. It didn't matter who gave what order—Greta took them from no one. It would take more than Nurse Patricia Ann, a lab-coated doctor, and General Lee's army to move Greta the Great. That was one of the things she loved most about the woman. Greta was loyal to a fault.

"Greta," Patricia Ann cajoled, "I'll take care of your girl. Go on, now. Let me do my job."

Nick gave a half-wave good-bye, then cupped Greta's elbow, taking her with him from the room while the doctor started telling Nick a joke.

"And you call *me* bossy," Biloxi whispered at Nick when he stepped out of sight.

Patricia Ann closed the door to the examining room, then pulled the curtain, blocking any view outside the glass cubicle.

"Roll to your side," Patricia Ann instructed.

Biloxi shuddered when the nurse moved her long, blood-soaked hair away from the wound at the base of her skull. Hair matted from blood gave her the creeps. She grimaced. Thankfully, she couldn't see the mess.

"Doesn't look like I'll have to shave your head," Patricia Ann announced.

Biloxi jerked when the nurse doused her neck with something cold. The acrid smell of iodine hit her noise. The wound began to burn.

"Ouch! Isn't it written in the nurse's code that you're supposed to lie and say, 'This won't hurt,' before you kill a patient?" she asked through clenched teeth.

Patricia Ann ignored her complaint and continued poking and prodding. "What in the world did you do to yourself?"

She wanted to shrug nonchalantly, but her body hurt too much. Instead, she grimaced.

"Have you taken up mud wrestling or something?" Patricia Ann asked, rolling her onto her back.

"Not yet, but I'll think about it," she mumbled. Her head pounded like a bass drum in a fast-paced solo. "Will you give me something for the pain?"

"Not until after the doctor sees you, and we get x-rays."

Snip. Snip. Snip.

The sound grabbed Biloxi's attention. She

struggled to sit up, but Patricia Ann levied firm pressure against her chest, keeping her prone with one hand. "What *the hell* are you doing?" Every open-and-close of the cold steel scissors against her damp skin was like a snake slithering up her leg. Her body convulsed.

"I've got to get these wet, muddy rags off you before I can help you further. Be still."

"But—" Biloxi whined. "They're brand new. I paid a lot for these pants."

"Maybe so, darl'n, but they've got to come off. You didn't walk in here under your own steam. While it's great to be wrapped in the arms of one of the most eligible bachelors in Bayou Petite, if you can't walk, we've got to figure out what's wrong." Patricia Ann continued cutting.

Stunned, Biloxi blinked. "What do you mean, I *can't* walk?"

Adrenaline surged. She flung her legs over the side of the gurney. Her foot struck a tray of supplies. Instruments clattered to the floor, sounding like bullets ricocheting off tile walls.

She landed squarely on her bare feet. Hot searing pain shot from her right ankle, up her leg, to her hip.

She gasped.

Then started to fall.

She grabbed for the gurney.

Patricia Ann rushed around to grab her. Biloxi braced her arms on the table to take the weight off her foot. Patricia Ann grasped her legs, lifted them, and helped her back onto the bed.

Patricia Ann glared. "*Humph*," she snorted. "Biloxi Dutrey! I declare, you're stubborn. I'm in charge. You're gonna do exactly what you're told." Her childhood friend, now with a drill-sergeant voice, leveled a deadly stare.

"Everything all right in there?" Two male voices asked at once from beyond the door.

"No!" Biloxi cried.

"Yes, Doctors." Patricia Ann sounded cotton-candy sweet. "Everything's *just* fine. The patient and I are getting reacquainted. After all, we haven't seen each other in quite a long while." Patricia Ann's smug smile silenced Biloxi.

"We'll be back in a moment. I'm going to find Nick a scrub shirt."

Biloxi's tears leaked out one at time. The pain shooting through her head and her leg was bad enough, but the loss of her new pants made it worse after the ruin of her most expensive shoes. She wanted to arrive with a "Branna-image." Her cousin always looked like she stepped from a fashion magazine.

Biloxi winced. Designer clothes had dented her checkbook, but she'd been convinced the expense was worth it. "Investment pieces," the clothing consultant had said. Who knew they'd be ruined in less than a week?

She shivered from pain and exhaustion. A soft sob escaped along with falling tears.

With a much gentler touch, Patricia Ann helped her remove the mud-soaked sweater, then offered a green hospital gown. She slid her arms through and Patricia Ann efficiently tied it crisscross closed in the front.

Biloxi trembled. The cold, the aloneness, and the hospital gown all triggered memories that blurred the present with the past.

Her last hospital stay haunted her still. A year ago,

a doctor and nurse stood beside her bed, smiled and said they had good news—a healthy young woman could get pregnant again. A miscarriage wasn't the end of the world. The news shocked her.

Nevertheless, Gregory left the hospital that night, and left their relationship. She saw him only one time afterward, an accidental meeting at a restaurant. He made it crystal clear that his lifestyle had no room for a baby. His shocking confession had been a one-eighty turn from the man she'd dated. Maybe she'd never really known him at all.

"Sorry. This will be cold." Patricia Ann sponged the cuts on Biloxi's legs.

She shivered so violently her teeth chattered.

"I need warm blankets in here!" Patricia Ann shouted.

Another nurse appeared with a stack. Patricia Ann grabbed the top one and tucked it around Biloxi's quaking body, fitting her into a tight cocoon.

"Ooohhh," Biloxi groaned.

Patricia Ann wiped her face with a damp cloth. "Hang in there, darlin'." She continued to whisper words of encouragement while the other nurse tossed another blanket on top of her.

"Get Doctor Efferson," Patricia Ann barked at the other nurse.

Sliding her hand out, Biloxi reached for her old friend. "Will I be okay?"

Patricia Ann's forced smile, one that a tolerant adult would give a child, chilled her more.

"Let's see what we find in X-ray. Doc Nick said nothing major was broken, and I believe him. That nasty cut on the back of your head is going to require a few stitches. But I didn't lie. We won't have to shave your whole head."

Patricia Ann held a tight grasp on her hand. "She's ready for you to examine her, Dr. Efferson."

Chapter 5

After all the poking and tests and X-rays, Biloxi waited quietly for the doctor's final word.

He arrived a few minutes later and announced, "Ms. Dutrey, possible mild concussion, multiple lacerations, bruising and sprains. We're keeping you the rest of the night for observation. Just in case." He didn't look up while he continued scribbling something in her chart. "In the ER until the morning shift starts. Then I'll decide if you can go home or move you upstairs to a room."

She started to protest, but everything moved in slow motion. The meds had kicked in. Her muscles had turned to Jell-O. Her aches faded like melted ice cream spreading out over hot pecan pie.

"Doctor, may I stay with her?" Greta asked, bustling into the examining room.

"No, I'll stay," Linc said, entering behind Greta. Nick followed Linc wearing a green scrub shirt.

"No," Patricia Ann cut in. "There isn't enough room. Besides, Biloxi needs rest. The best thing ya'll can do is go home. Trust us with her care."

"She's the boss," Dr. Efferson said. "Ms. Dutrey needs quiet right now. She has no life threatening injuries. I'll probably release her in the morning."

Greta's watchful eyes looked at the doctor warily.

Nick finally broke the silent standoff. "C'mon,

Greta, let me take you and Linc home."

"Go. I'll be fine," Biloxi croaked.

The group, gathered at the foot of her bed, ignored her. They continued their negotiations with Nurse Patricia Ann, who held her ground.

Finally warm, exhaustion kicked in and Biloxi's eyelids slowly drooped. On their way down, she caught Greta's frown, then tried to jerk herself awake.

Linc shifted his weight from one foot to the other. Though younger than her, he always wanted to protect her. Nick stared as though he willed his strength to her. He, too, looked unwilling to walk away while she lay in bed.

"Go," she urged, then closed her eyes, unable to fight the cocktail of medications.

Later, she wasn't sure of the time, she blinked her eyes into hazy focus unsure if she dreamed or was awake. Voices sounded beyond the curtain. Thoughts popped into her brain, only to disappear into obscurity. When she tried to sit up, misery came in a sharp wave. Each muscle snarled. She flopped back onto her pillow. Pain shot into her head. She fingered the bandage that wrapped it.

Definitely not a dream.

Breathing deeply to will the agony away, she focused on voices. A giggle erupted.

"Oh, yes! You should've seen it. Him, bare-chested and brawny, carrying her in here. Just like in the movies."

"Was it as romantic as it sounds? I can't wait to bid on his date at the Valentine auction."

"Yeah, Miss Macy does that charity event up right. She did a great job on my wedding. Seems like Branna and Biloxi are..." Patricia Ann's words trailed off. Biloxi recognized none of the other voices. The conversation of the women moved farther away, until completely out of earshot.

"Morning," someone spoke quietly.

Biloxi turned to look in the direction of the whisper. She blinked several times to bring the form into focus. Her brain fought the fog. "Huh? Nick?"

"Shhh." Nick put one finger to his lips. "I snuck past the nurses. I wanted to check on you, to be sure you're all right."

He pulled the only chair in the room close to the bed. She focused on him, then closed her eyes. Visions fluttered, then flashed frame-by-frame like an old-fashioned viewer, and then finally knitted together.

Car in ditch. Drive home. Fall into hell. Then hospital.

"You know, I think I prefer the *you* I met last night." His breath tickled the hair over her ear when he whispered.

"Huh?" She opened her eyes again.

"I prefer you full of sassy attitude, rather than lying so still in this bed."

Nick pulled back. The corners of his mouth rose into a crooked grin. His features softened when he smiled. No intimidation. And his eyes shone.

"Warm topaz brown," she whispered.

"What?" Nick leaned closer.

Last night, his hat had hidden his soulful eyes. She'd not seen them at all. Later, during the hospital frenzy, she hadn't noticed. The warmth of his hand had been more important. Now, his eyes glowed. Rich and warm with hints of shiny gold. Even through her haze, her photographer's eye focused on male beauty. A headshot of him formed in her head, then the perfect way to capture him in a photograph at his best.

"Topaz," she mumbled.

Then, nodded off back to sleep.

****

Screech. The sound of the curtain rings scraping across the metal rod startled her. Biloxi flinched when the bright overhead light switched on.

"She's doing fine this morning! Not a single complaint all night. I go off duty in a half hour. Greta is waiting to take her home." Patricia Ann spoke to a woman trailing behind her.

"Good morning, Sunshine!" the woman said. She stepped close to the bed. "The doctor will be in to check you over in a few, but word has it, you're sprung from this place." The silver-haired woman in the starched scrubs sounded cheery. Too cheery, in fact, so early in the morning.

"Biloxi, this is Roberta. She's taking over for me on the day shift. You'll only get a brief taste of her hospitality since you're going home."

"So how's our patient this morning?" Dr. Efferson appeared, as if on cue.

"Fine, Doctor," both nurses said at once.

"Biloxi, honey, call me when you're feeling up to company," Patricia Ann said. "We'll see what mischief we can cook up. Maybe we'll have dinner. You can invite Handsome." She flashed a bright smile, then wiggled her fingers good-bye as she left the room.

Confused, Biloxi shrugged. *Who's Handsome?*

Nurse Roberta helped her to sit up, then leaned close to Dr. Efferson and scrutinized every movement he made.

Biloxi tried to ignore the nurse's prying intrusion. Now she could relate to the monkeys at the zoo with people coming, going, and gawking.

"Take it easy for a few days. No driving. No getting the stitches in the back of your head wet. No heavy lifting, no lugging camera equipment around. No…"

The doctor continued rattling off his list of her curtailed activities. No way could she remember all of his "no's" though, and she considered snapping his finger off if he waved it one more time and flicked her nose. Hadn't his mother taught him better manners? Or hadn't he learned something about bedside behavior in medical school?

"…no driving…no…"

"What? Wait! No driving?" she blurted. "For how long? I've a contract to complete." Being mobility challenged wouldn't work at all. There had to be some negotiation about what she could and couldn't do.

"You can't go mucking through the swamps, shooting photographs with a sprained ankle. Nor can you get those lacerations wet," Nurse Roberta chastised.

"How did you know?"

"I'm a nurse."

"No," Biloxi narrowed her eyes. "About my assignment."

"Why, I told them," Greta said when she stepped into the crowded space looking fresh and rested. A far cry from the mess from last night. "Besides, it's in the newspaper," Greta continued, like that absolved her of any sin. "The whole idea was explained—to help promote tourism and bring more business to the area." Greta's voice lilted with pride.

"But…" she started, confused. The confidential contract, the publisher had said, originated from a grant from a private benefactor. Who else knew about the contract? When did the paper publish the news? Why?

"Greta," the doctor said. "See to it that she takes care of herself. I want to see her again in two weeks. We'll check out the dissolving stitches then."

Biloxi shifted her focus away from the doctor's instructions. She needed to make some phone calls. Who leaked the news? The hiring New York agency gave very specific details, and yet they said nothing about a newspaper story.

"Biloxi Dutrey?" An orderly arrived with a wheel chair.

"She's not quite ready," Nurse Roberta explained. "Just hang close and we'll let you know when you can wheel her out."

"I've got clothes for her in the car, I'll go and get them," Greta said, then bustled away.

Biloxi swung her legs over the side of the gurney with help from Nurse Roberta.

"Will you get her discharge instructions?" Dr. Efferson asked the nurse. After the woman departed, the doctor scratched more notes on a chart. When he finished, he pulled a chair up close to her and leaned in. "Ms. Dutrey, here's a prescription for muscle relaxers. I expect you to heed all my directions if you want to heal properly." He leveled a threatening look.

How in the world would she mesh her goals with his list of "don'ts"?

He started to rise, and then sat back down. "By the

way—"

She hated his tone. Hated that phrase. It was a predictor of doom. The other shoe was about to drop, some other devastating consequence waited. After all, it *was* a hospital. From the forced, thin smile on his lips, she guessed he was confident that he had her full attention.

"—take care with my friend."

"Huh?"

Dr. Efferson raised his eyebrows. "Dr. Trahan."

"Oh, is that Handsome's name?" Nurse Roberta asked, materializing from behind the curtain. Greta followed carrying folded clothes.

"Whenever you're ready, Miss Dutrey." The orderly sounded impatient, hidden behind the curtain.

The blast of voices from all sides topped with instruction after instruction, made her want to scream. The doctor in his clean white coat, the nurse with her too-cheerful smile, and Greta beaming like she'd found a pot of gold at the end of the rainbow, were all too damn much first thing in the morning. Her head throbbed. Her body ached. She wanted out, away from the harsh lighting and the hospital chaos.

Her bed at Fleur de Lis would be a welcome relief as long as her mother didn't show up.

Chapter 6

Taking in the view of Fleur de Lis, Biloxi relaxed for the first time since arriving in Bayou Petite. Greta drove the white Suburban around back and parked on the brick driveway.

The raised two-story antebellum home exuded strength. The tall white columns and cast iron railing added details of charm. Biloxi sighed. She'd take any kind of homecoming over none at all. Best of all, under southern sunshine, there was no place like home.

Linc and Carson stood ready at the top of the wide, wooden steps on the back gallery that spanned the length of the house. They waved, then ran to the rear of the Suburban and opened the hatch, pulling out a wheel chair, which they rolled beside the passenger's door. Carson pulled the left armrest off the chair. Linc opened her door, then set a board in place from the vehicle's seat to the wheelchair.

"Slide," Linc instructed, as though she were part of some assembly line.

A sprained ankle didn't require a wheel chair. Crutches would be enough, though once again, Greta had gone overboard in an effort to protect her. She wanted to humor the woman, but looking at the angled board, the steep pitch, it rivaled any amusement park slide. One wrong move, the board could twist, and she'd be dumped on the ground. Or worse. Splinters

45

would decorate her already bruised butt.

She eyed her brother's latest invention warily. "I don't know, Linc."

"I'll be right here, I promise."

"Yeah, and I'll stand behind you so you won't fall," Carson chimed in.

She looked up from the wooden slide when a maroon Ford pickup rolled into view. It pulled in beside the Suburban. Nick climbed down, his cowboy hat resting further back on his head. Standing next to the open door, he eyed Linc's wooden contraption with an expression that could not be mistaken for anything but wariness.

"Well," Nick drawled. "Interesting."

Her awareness of him inched up. Darkness no longer hid anything about him. Broad shoulders and masculine hands. Wrangler jeans and worn work boots. His topaz eyes danced with amusement, but the rest of his face held no expression. He exuded powerful energy. He was a man's man, solid and utterly calm. She swallowed and looked away.

"Pardon me, ya'll," Nick said to Linc and Carson. When they stepped back, Nick moved the board out of the way. "Grab the chair and take it upstairs." He instructed them as though he did it every day. "I'll carry the patient."

There it was. That commanding attitude. That smoky voice. It sounded even more familiar now. A ripple of delight raced up her spine. She was especially happy to be home.

Linc and Carson snapped to and acted on his orders. Greta grabbed the pair of crutches off the back seat and said, "Okay, this way."

Nick grasped her gently, but she winced when he slid her off the seat.

"Sorry," he said, but he avoided her eyes.

Once again, his strong arms carried her. She counted the number of times since they'd met. Four. This time, the nearness of him increased her pain. Her ever-present pain of embarrassment. She wasn't Branna and never played the damsel in distress...but she might grow to like it if Nick was the one who always came to her rescue.

"You're Dr. Trahan, aren't you?" she asked, searching for a safe subject to avoid the uncomfortableness of being carried.

He nodded.

She recalled his comment about never having been inside the house, remembering her manners, she smiled, then said, "Welcome to Fleur de Lis."

****

Nick carried Biloxi to the stairs leading up to the wide rear gallery. He began to climb, taking care with each step. Even with her arms wrapped around his neck for support, she winced at his slightest movement. He held her tighter to his chest hoping to lessen any jarring bounce. Though she looked pained, she never made a sound, never complained. Most women would whine or put on a Scarlett O'Hara faint. Her brave resolve said a lot about her character. He admired her fearlessness.

"This way." Greta held the kitchen door open while Linc and Carson waited outside with crutches and the wheelchair. The guys had looked relieved when he arrived and took command.

Nick stepped into the kitchen with Biloxi in his arms. He'd never carried a woman over a threshold

47

before. He liked that she was the first one. Maybe the gossip he'd heard about the Dutreys hating all Trahans came from exaggerated history. Or maybe his presence there would fuel the gossip mill more.

The aroma of freshly brewed coffee reached his nose and reminded him of home—his grandparents'. Greta's kitchen had a homey appeal. Lived in. A large calendar with scribbles on certain dates hung next to an antique-looking box phone. Upper and lower white cabinets lined one wall. A cookbook sat in a stand on the dark green, marble countertop. On the other wall, above the base cabinets, a bank of windows opened to the back gallery and natural light spilled in. This was nothing like the kitchen at his house, which was mostly unused, except for the coffee pot and occasionally the dishwasher. He ran it to wash mugs and silverware used for eating take-out.

"Do you want to go upstairs?" Greta asked gently, brushing a stray hair from Biloxi's face.

He waited for instructions.

"The sunroom." Biloxi pointed. "Through that doorway, past the dining room. It's on the east side of the house."

Greta strode ahead. He followed a few steps behind through the large dining room, his boots tapping on the polished wooden floor. He glanced at the cream colored paint on the walls with dark brown wainscoting. A long dinner table sat in the middle of the room surrounded by matching chairs.

Dutreys gather here, he mused.

He crossed through the dining room and entered a glass-enclosed sun porch filled with white wicker furniture covered with blue and white striped cushions.

Too many green potted plants adorned the space. Even the rug on the floor had a floral print. A feminine room, the frilliness of it made him itch.

"On the couch, please?" Biloxi asked, looking sheepish.

He nodded and waited while Greta quickly arranged a few small pillows for Biloxi's comfort. When she finished, he bent to place the woman in his arms gently on the couch. Her grimace and squinted eyes let him know of her pain. Stepping back, he removed his hat and held it in his hands while Greta fussed over her patient more. From an old worn, wooden steamer trunk, Greta pulled out a rose-colored blanket and snapped it open. She covered Biloxi from chin to toes, tucked the blanket along her patient's legs, then folded the ends under Biloxi's feet.

"There, now." Greta preened like a proud mother hen when she stepped back and perused her handiwork. Biloxi, however, looked one step away from being mummified by blankets.

"How about something to eat and some coffee to wash it down?" Greta asked.

He wasn't sure if she intended to include him, but knowing Greta's reputation for cooking, his mouth watered.

"Nick, won't you stay for lunch?" Greta asked. "Why don't you keep Biloxi company? Have a seat there." She pointed to a chair next to the couch. "I'll put together some food. That is, if your schedule will allow. The Old Aunts and the boys—I mean guys, they'll always be boys to me—will be eating with us."

Biloxi grinned at him, then winked.

It was all the encouragement he needed. "Yes,

ma'am. I'll stay."

Greta squared her shoulders and walked away humming a tune. She appeared extremely pleased with herself, or maybe pleased that he'd accepted the lunch invitation—or both. He hadn't imagined that his company, based on all the rumors he'd heard, could produce an invitation into the Dutrey household.

"I think she has a crush on you," Biloxi whispered.

"On me?"

"It's a really good thing to have Greta on your side."

Before he could respond, a matronly voice with a full southern lilt from beyond the room interrupted. "Biloxi? Is that you, dear? How wonderful to have you here. If you had arrived earlier, you could have attended church with us this morning."

"I know, G.G. Grace. I'm in the sunroom."

"You know how Marie and I hate it when you—" A white-haired woman ambled across the threshold. Despite the cane, she carried herself regally. Her blue silk dress and white sweater looked designer-made, even to his untrained eye. A long strand of pearls knotted at her chest hung almost to her waist. He'd rarely seen an elderly woman dressed in what had to be the finest fashion, even if she had just come from church. Out of respect, he rose.

"Oh, I was unaware that we were receiving company." Standing in front of him, she paused, looked him up and down, as if she measured the type of man he was. Her perfume wafted to his nose. He knew Chanel Number 5. His grandmother wore the same scent.

The old woman nodded, but her face remained

inscrutable. She made her way to a chair, opposite the couch, and seated herself like a regal queen.

"Welcome, sir." She motioned to him to sit.

Nick obeyed, taking the chair closest to where Biloxi rested her feet.

The woman turned her attention back to Biloxi. "Child, it's lovely to see you. Why are you lying on the couch when we have company? And what is that thing on your head?"

"G.G. Grace—"

"Start. Again."

"Great-Grandmother Grace, please let me introduce Dr. Nick Trahan. He rescued me last night after I had an accident. Doctor Trahan, this is my great-grandmother, Grace Dutrey."

Nick didn't miss Biloxi's demure tone, or the immediate deference to her grandmother whose formality reminded him of a bygone era, but if he lived to be in his nineties, he'd do what he damned pleased, too.

Grace turned to him. She lifted her chin and contemplated something.

Would she, *not if but when*, put two-and-two together? Would she ask him politely to leave? Or just have Linc and Carson unceremoniously throw him out?

"Biloxi, dear, what has happened?" Grace asked. "Are you going to be all right?" But the old woman's stare never left his gaze.

"Your gardening project got the best of me last night," Biloxi joked.

"Now in English that I can understand."

"I fell in the hole where the big magnolia used to be. Afterward, Nick took me to the hospital."

"But you're going to be fine, correct? And that thing on your head? I know it is not the latest style. Even I read fashion magazines."

Nick stifled a snort. He bet she did.

"I spent the night in the emergency room. I cut the back of my head when I fell. Only a few dozen stitches. The bandage is temporary."

Surprised at Biloxi's recounting of her injuries, he decided she must have a reason for the exaggerations.

"If you need to retire to your room, I will call for assistance."

"I'm fine here, Great-Grandmother. Greta's making lunch. Tell me, how are you and Auntie Marie?"

He recognized Biloxi's attempt to deflect the conversation away from herself, but would the matriarch allow the discussion to shift?

"Do you need a nurse? Did they give you a prescription for the pain?" Grace asked.

"I'll be fine. Sore right now. I need a few days of rest. Mild medication. Nothing for you to worry about. You were going to tell me about you and Great Grand Aunt Marie?"

It was a tennis-match of wills he hadn't witnessed in a long time. If the elderly woman started a line of probing questions with him, he'd have to find a distraction to avoid the topic of Trahans.

"I'm going to keep my eye on you, young lady. The accident could have happened anywhere. Thank goodness for you, it happened here, with your family to care for you. As for us old ladies, we are fine. We played nine holes of golf last week. Twice. That nice Mr. LaRue drove the cart for us."

"Where is Auntie Marie?"

Grace didn't answer. Instead, she narrowed her eyes.

"Trahan?" Graced asked him.

"Yes, ma'am."

"Young man, are you related to our neighbors who own that land across the way?"

"Yes, ma'am, I am."

Grace lifted her chin and pursed her lips. Nick hoped the story of the feud between the Dutreys and Trahans was more legend than fact. Since he was raised in Baton Rouge, rather than across the road from Fleur de Lis, he'd only heard of the feud six months ago when he moved to town and built his house. Construction workers, he'd learned, gossiped the same as a bunch of old women at church bingo, but he never paid any mind to most of the mumblings. Now he wished he hadn't ignored the snickers and rumors that placed blame on his family.

Being unaware of how to separate fact from fiction left him at a huge disadvantage. He'd have to pin his grandfather down on the specifics of the story still circulating.

"You are Charles Nicholas Trahan. Your father is Edward. Your grandfather is Claude." Grace's voice rang out strong and clear. A Shakespearian actor couldn't have delivered the lines better. Each word she spoke struck a dissonant, accusatory chord, like plucking strings of an out-of-tune guitar.

"Claude Trahan sought to *kill* my son. Claude's challenge came from twisted imaginations of a fool."

Nick blinked. Was that a sneer in the old woman's voice?

Biloxi's eyes narrowed. Her brow and nose wrinkled. Her mouth formed a small "O." Her grimace looked more pained than when he'd carried her up the stairs. Clearly she'd been raised on stories of the tribulations between the Trahans and the Dutreys.

While Grace certainly knew his family tree and her version of history, what did that have to do with him? He was generations removed from the rumored event. Besides, hadn't it all worked out for her son? All in Robert Dutrey's favor?

He willed his racing pulse to calm. The situation could explode if he didn't tread lightly. Or maybe a Come-to-Jesus meeting was what the two families needed. If he went that route, he'd bet good money that Linc and Carson would be escorting him from the property. That would add fuel to old gossip. No, the conversation needed a new direction, though he doubted Grace would let him off the hook easily. Old wounds and mistrust had simmered for a long stretch of years, one meeting wouldn't solve the issues. However, if he behaved like a gentleman, maybe her lit fuse would sputter out.

Before he could respond, Biloxi cut in, "Great-Grandmother. He's a guest in our home!"

"Girl, exactly *how* did that happen?" Grace snapped.

"He rescued me. I could have *died* without his help." A bright blush crept into Biloxi's cheeks.

"Quiet!"

He tried not to chuckle or Grace might think him impolite. Biloxi's dramatics were overdone, but under the circumstances, he appreciated her efforts. He'd heard stories about the Old Aunts and how in their advanced years they took carte blanche to voice *any* opinion, anytime, anywhere. An Army general couldn't look more imposing than Grace did with her back ramrod-straight and her pointed stare. Yet, the last thing he wanted was to further the ill opinion she obviously carried about all Trahans. At least until he'd wrangled a date with Biloxi.

"I learned my good manners from you and Great Aunt Marie. You taught me...And my mother." Biloxi struggled to sit. With her feet on the floor, she faced Grace.

"Oh, honey, do not get me started on your mother. I thank God every day that you are your father's daughter and just your mother's girl."

When Grace rolled her eyes, Nick barely contained a laugh. Grace's whole demeanor screamed *Whatever*. The eloquent old woman's display of ineloquent manners had him clamping his jaw shut and locking his fingers together in his lap. Biloxi apparently knew how to handle her family.

"That mother of yours..."

Biloxi shrank down on the couch while Grace continued listing complaints about the younger Mrs. Dutrey.

He winked at Biloxi and started to enjoy the interchange before him. Delicious aromas drifted from the kitchen and his mouth watered. Greta couldn't announce lunch soon enough.

As he listened to Grace's diatribe, a second elderly woman, equally well dressed, rolled her way into the sunroom on a walker. He looked from Grace to the newcomer and back to Grace. Twins? He'd thought they were just sisters.

Biloxi closely resembled Branna, but Grace and this woman looked exactly the same.

The older woman stopped in the open space between the foot of the couch and the chair where Nick sat.

Nick stood. No one would accuse him of poor manners.

"Good day," she said and nodded. She had a gentler tone than Grace.

"Marie, he's Charles Nicolas Trahan." Grace's disdain shouted over her words.

"Oh, my." She gazed first at Biloxi, then strained her neck upward to look at him.

The hair on the back of his neck stood up. Usually a signal that whatever was coming his way was something he wouldn't like.

Biloxi pulled the blanket closer to her chin and smiled weakly at him. "Dr. Trahan, this is Great-Grand Aunt Marie. She's Great-Grandmother Grace's twin sister."

Oh, no. Double trouble.

"How do you do, Miss Marie?"

Marie's hands flew to her cheeks. Bewilderment etched her wrinkled face. "Trahan?"

Nick nodded and smiled, deciding the best defense—a good offense.

"Miss Marie?" He motioned for her to take his seat in the chair he once occupied. After she sat, when he had her attention, he said, "I see you're well-acquainted with my family. I'm sure, given your generous nature, you've forgiven the love-struck young man who challenged your son to a duel. It was a shameful thing he did, my grandpère. But—" Nick shrugged. "You, yourself know, love makes fools out of men. Or, at least that's what my grandmother always says."

"Well!" Grace snapped.

If he didn't know better, he'd swear she had snorted her response.

"Grace, this young man is a guest in our home." Marie spoke calmly and evenly. She shot Grace a withering look. Grace's chin and shoulders stiffened, however, she remained quiet. If Grace was the general, then Marie was her second-in-command.

Thankful for the reprieve, Nick mentally scrambled for a plan to extricate himself politely from the ladies, one that would not offend Greta after her kind invitation for lunch. This wasn't the time to take a family stand against the past. However, mending broken old fences between the two families would give him a reason to visit with Biloxi again. Branna had caught his attention from afar, but Biloxi intrigued him more. With time and charm, he could heal the wounds his grandfather had caused. Or that was his hope. Biloxi was his incentive.

"Biloxi, child, we didn't know you were coming," Marie said. "We were happy to hear of your photography contract. You know how proud we are of you. Though I was dismayed to learn about it all in the newspaper. We expect you to deliver that type of good news yourself." Marie sounded disappointed.

Biloxi shook her head. "It wasn't supposed to be announced. I had hoped to arrive last night—a surprise—to tell you about my job. I also want to share other ideas I have for Fleur de Lis. I'll be here for a while. At least if that's okay with the two of you."

"Of course, sugar. Your room is always ready for

you. Same as all of the great-grandchildren," Grace said.

Linc pushed a wheel chair into the sunroom. Greta entered behind him.

"Lunch is ready."

Nick breathed a small sigh of relief. Things could've gone worse, could have dissolved into an ugly scene. Greta's interruption proved timely. Plus, Linc and the wheelchair were a great idea. After all, Grace probably wouldn't appreciate him picking up her great granddaughter and carrying her into the dining room. Grace might faint if she caught her great granddaughter in the arms of a Trahan.

He helped Biloxi from the couch into the wheelchair.

Grace rose. "Marie and I will take lunch in the sitting room upstairs."

Chapter 7

Aromas filling the dining room made Biloxi's mouth water. She spooned up seafood and andouille gumbo. The flavors swirled in her mouth, heaven in a single bite.

Greta spoiled her with her favorite meal—gumbo with crab, shrimp and okra. There had to be okra, otherwise it wasn't truly gumbo. Like always, Greta served hot-from-the-oven French bread.

A glass of sweet tea waited beside each place setting, and ever-thoughtful Greta had set a glass of water out for her, to wash down the medication. The pill bottle label read, "Take with food."

Biloxi smiled between bites. Linc kept the conversation lively by sharing funny stories about flying. Had he overheard any of the tense conversation in the sunroom? Did he agree with G.G. Grace? Was Nick persona non grata, with Linc now only being polite to a guest? Thankfully, Carson joined in and started with his "one-up" of Linc with other stories about sky-jockey antics, however, for her, the elephant in the room remained the conspicuous absence of the Old Aunts.

Her mind whirled like a large tropical storm. Anxiety flooded like rain flooding the bayou. What would Linc think about her plan to wrestle control of the estate from Branna? Carson surely wouldn't like it.

After all, Branna was his older sister.

Biloxi's stomach clenched. She had to make her plan work. Otherwise, once again she'd be looking for a new address. The vagabond life seemed glamorous at first. And at first it was, but after six years of living out of tote bags and backpacks, it turned into a monotonous hamster-on-wheel show.

Where would she go if she failed to change tradition? She hated entertaining that idea, but she couldn't stay and watch Fleur de Lis disintegrate from lack of care. Branna had gone to "find herself" leaving the family's tradition in limbo. No one seemed concerned.

Conversation swirled around her. Occasionally, Nick smiled and nodded. He answered Linc and Carson's questions in single word responses, but otherwise he hadn't engaged in the ongoing dialog. She did catch him sneaking glances at her. Maybe G.G Grace's inquisition had pissed him off.

The horror of that moment when her great-grandmother confronted Nick had shocked her. G.G. Grace had never behaved so rudely to a guest. Ever.

She caught Nick's gaze and smiled. Unlike her brother with his elbows on the table, or Carson with his napkin wadded up in one hand, Nick's napkin remained on his lap and his elbows never touched the table's top. Under other circumstances, G.G. Grace would be impressed with a man like Nick. Fine manners were something raved about, often used as examples to scold Linc and Carson for their own less-than-stellar display.

"Sweet potato pecan pie for dessert," Greta said, rising. She began to clear the plates from the table.

"We'll help." Carson stood and nudged Linc. The

two grabbed the remaining dishes and left the dining room.

"Nick, I'm sorry about that scene earlier. G.G. Grace isn't usually like that," Biloxi said quietly.

"Don't worry about it. How do they get upstairs without assistance?" Nick asked. He appeared unconcerned by the earlier rudeness. Maybe he expected hostile treatment in enemy territory. After all, history noted their families as enemies.

"What looks like an old cistern on the end of the house, is actually an elevator."

"Hmm, interesting. That keeps the authenticity of the old house."

Carson and Linc returned to the dining room. "Hate to eat and run, but Carson and I have to get back to school. He's PIC this time, so I can study for my next exam. I've got Greta's pie to go."

"PIC?" Biloxi asked.

"Pilot-in-command," Nick answered. "That's how Linc, Carson and I met. At the airport. I'm a pilot, too."

"Bye ya'll. C'mon Linc, we gotta go." Carson waved and headed out of the room.

Biloxi pointed to her cheek. Linc made a grand gesture of kissing the air beside it. Something they once saw in an old movie and made it their own. She couldn't ask for a better brother.

"Hang in there, sis," Linc said. "I'll call you later. We both know Greta will wait on you hand and foot. Spoil you silly. Hey, Nick. Thanks for the help. She's not always such a spaz." He waved and followed the path Carson took. From the kitchen, she heard Greta shouting good-byes to the guys.

Biloxi waited with Nick. Silence ticked away with

each "tock" of the Grandfather clock. They waited for Greta to serve dessert. Nick's gaze rested on her. Weary, sore and bruised, fatigue washed over her, and she fought to stay awake. Propping her elbows on the table—G.G. Grace would be aghast—and resting her chin in her palms, she stopped herself from falling asleep. She wouldn't let Nick leave without a proper apology, but with the medication taking effect, she couldn't quite form all the words in her head.

She bobbed awake at the sound of Greta's footsteps against the wood floor.

"Nick, I have pie with your name on it," Greta said. She carried a large tray with three plates and three cups of coffee. "Why don't you wheel Biloxi back to the sunroom? We'll enjoy dessert in there. She's looking peaked to me."

Biloxi started to argue, but Nick was out of his chair and standing behind her before she could voice her exception.

"Wait. Let me try to do this on my own."

The chair moved backward before her hands touched the wheels. She looked up. Nick smiled down at her, then guided the wheelchair toward the sunroom. She had wanted to work the unnecessary contraption; however, she gratefully accepted his help.

"Nick, if I recall correctly, you had an early morning appointment. Do all veterinarians work on Sunday mornings?" Biloxi asked as he wheeled her toward the sunroom.

"Not unless there's an emergency. This morning, I had a specific purpose. I'm taking on another vet in my practice. I wanted to check out their surgical skills. I found a home for a stray, but it needed a procedure before I could send it to its new family. It was the perfect opportunity to help the stray and observe Dr. Gilbeau's expertise."

Too tired to inquire further, she remained quiet. Once in the sunroom, Nick picked her up and placed her on the couch as gently as he had earlier. She laid back and sighed. Greta covered her again. Biloxi's eyelids drooped closed and she snuggled under the blanket.

"I think I'll be going," Nick said.

"No," she mumbled. "I'm just resting. Eat your pie and talk to Greta. Please Nick, don't go yet. Greta, don't let him leave until I've had a chance to apologize. I just need to rest for minute."

"Doctor Trahan, thank you for all of your help. I know I shouldn't play favorites, but—" Greta's cup clinked against the saucer. "Biloxi has always been special to me. I came to Fleur de Lis when her momma had her and Miss Macy had Branna. Did you know those girls were born on the same day, fighting to see which one would come first? Always a competition between them since the day they were born."

"The same day." Nick repeated Greta's words.

"After their mommas didn't need me anymore, I stayed on as a companion to the Old Aunts."

"I wasn't aware of that."

"Yes, well, you being raised someplace other than Bayou Petite…anyway, Branna grew up mostly here, although the Linds live down at the coast now. But, Biloxi, her daddy's an Air Force man, he drug the family all over the country. Biloxi came home to visit on holidays and spent her summers here. Every time she had to leave—the crying jag that girl would have."

"I'm resting. Not dead," Biloxi said, irritated at Greta's gossiping. "I've heard everything you said."

"And nothing I've said is untrue."

"No, but it's private." Biloxi opened one eye and scowled.

Greta shook her head. "All I can say is that she grew up a lucky girl. Her family cares about her, though she's always off chasing the next big photography assignment. Did you know she's famous? A photographer. She's even done portraits of rock stars and a few models."

"I heard that," Biloxi whispered.

Nick chuckled, "*I* hadn't heard that."

"She's one of a kind."

"I imagine holidays with this bunch are fun." Nick grinned. Dimples transformed his face. His eyes twinkled with amusement, like he enjoyed life. His strong arms and hands had held her gently and she hadn't missed the strength of his muscled body. Very sexy.

Greta and Nick continued their mutual admiration tête-à-tête, which allowed her to observe Nick relaxed and unguarded. A shiver of excitement washed away her weariness when creativity took over. She pictured Nick as a calendar model.

What would he think of that?

Chapter 8

Through the slats of the white wooden shutters in her bedroom, the moon's glow bathed everything in clear magical light. Biloxi rolled onto her side in the four-poster bed with her body shouting protests, but the luxury of waking up in her own room at home made the pain worth it. She faced the tall windows. Long silk, watery-blue drapes cascaded down their sides like flowing water. She took comfort from the familiarity of the view.

Last night had been a perfect night—storm clouds hiding the moon and stars—for the legendary Cajun werewolf, Loup-Garou, to appear. Except he didn't. Nor had he ever. Whenever visiting at Fleur de Lis, after-dinner storytelling was a highlight. However, it meant that at bedtime, sleep often eluded her. She huddled in fear of the creature's appearance. Yet, he only came to life in paintings created from George Rodrigue's vivid imagination. She'd seen the paintings at galleries in the French Quarter and when she visited Bittersweet Plantation.

Her other childhood dreams were about leprechauns and fairies. Grandma Elise had whispered stories about elves that danced on the windowsills at night to protect Fleur de Lis, probably to settle fears about Loup-Garou coming to carry off children. Her grandfather scoffed, saying Grandma Elise shouldn't fill her head with old Irish nonsense. Her grandmother had smiled and paid him no mind.

Biloxi wrapped herself in memories. She'd believed in magic as a child and never wanted to leave Fleur de Lis. Even now with her aches and pains, along with the ugly bandage that could not be mistaken for chic, her injuries were powerless over her deep-rooted contentment of being home. Safe. Protected. If she never left this place—that was exactly what she wanted.

Reaching for her favorite childhood stuffed toy, Mr. Rabbit, she pulled him from his perch on the pillow beside her and laid him with his head resting on the pillow. She'd be mortified if anyone knew how much she loved the old thing. Made from velvet with loose hanging limbs, much like a sock-monkey, the old-fashioned toy looked slightly worn after twenty-nine years.

"You're happy that I'm home for good, aren't you boy? I'll dress you in a tux with a big red bowtie and take your picture for a kid's poster for the Valentines Ball."

Mr. Rabbit always welcomed her whenever she visited. She'd left him there, knowing he'd always be protected and waiting.

Growing up on military bases, places so different from Bayou Petite, had spurred her interest in photography. She learned to capture the beauty of her surroundings, but those places never felt like home. New places provided the adventure she wanted, but always left her longing for the permanency of Fleur de Lis. Her heart and soul resided within the property markers where her roots ran deep. Maybe her connection had to do with the house standing strong for over two hundred years, the vibration of her ancestors resonated there.

"G.G. Grace always wanted all of us to live here. Claimed there was no need to live all over the world. Fleur de Lis was all the home any of us ever needed."

But could they keep the walls standing? The list of repairs was growing.

She came to share with the Old Aunts *all* of her plans. Would they even consider a change? Could they accept a break in tradition? Logic had to win over convention if Fleur de Lis was expected to stand through time.

Tomorrow was initiation day of her plan.

"What time is it, Mr. Rabbit?"

Scanning the room, she noticed a glass of water and her cell phone on the antique marble-top table beside her bed. Who found the darn thing?

She reached for it to check the time. "Nine-thirty?"

She'd slept all afternoon and into the evening. Foggy memories returned. Nick had picked her up and followed Greta to the elevator. Once upstairs, he placed her in bed. Then, Greta had fussed over her, a gentle nurturing her mother never managed to provide.

Biloxi nestled in the covers, pulling them over her shoulder. Her stomach rumbled. After no breakfast and a half-eaten lunch, she wanted comfort food.

She hugged the toy to her chest. "Mr. Rabbit, could you hop on down to the kitchen and ask Greta for something to eat. What? Carrot? Food for me, silly, not you."

She could call Greta from her cell phone. Maybe, if she asked nicely, Greta would bring a dinner tray? Everyone else would have eaten. The kitchen already

Linda Joyce

cleaned for the night. The Old Aunts kept to a schedule. Dinner at five p.m., television until nine, then to bed. She hated to disturb Greta's quiet time, but her rumbling stomach refused to be ignored.

"Knock, knock."

She rolled slowly to her other side. "Come in."

"How's the patient feeling?" Greta whispered as she entered.

"Famished. Sore. I think adrenaline kept me going through lunch." She yawned, then scooted to make room for Greta to sit on the bed.

"Would you like something to eat?"

"Yes, I woke up hungry. I didn't want to holler and disturb the Old Aunts. I don't have the strength to go downstairs. By the way, who found my cell phone?"

"That handsome man." Greta plucked Mr. Rabbit from her arms. She set him in her lap and stroked his long ears.

"Nick?"

Even in the moonlight, she caught Greta's blush.

"Yes, he brought your bags from your car," Greta continued. "They're downstairs. Then he called Gus and waited for him to arrive. The two of them looked at your car. Why is it you drive that little thing? Their diagnosis—it needs to go to the dealership over in Kenner. The closest dealership in Mississippi is too far north, up in Meridian."

"That must mean there's more damage than I thought."

"Maybe. Gus said to give him a call when you want the tow."

"I love that car," she whined.

"No. You like things. You love people," Greta

68

corrected.

She'd heard that mantra from Greta all of her life.

"You love Nick?" she teased.

Greta shrugged her shoulders. "He's a nice young man. This family invented stubbornness. The Old Aunts don't have enough to occupy themselves. They dwell on that old Trahan story because it gives them something to talk about. Besides, it seems like fate."

"Huh?"

"You meeting Nick. His grandfather was willing to fight a duel over your grandmother Elise. I doubt he intended to kill anyone, but who knows...and now his grandson rides in here—"

Biloxi grinned. "No horse. A big, fancy, crew-cab Ford."

"—and rescues you. May have saved your life. Just seems that Nick's actions alone are enough to grant him some 'grace' around here." Greta raised an eyebrow.

"Traditions, even unhealthy ones, live long at Fleur de Lis. I'm sorry to ask, but may I have something to eat?" She offered a pitiful face, one that she hoped would buy her sympathy.

"Just don't tell your mother. You know what a fit she'll pitch. It was fine for me to take care of you when you were a baby, but now...I'll be back in a few."

"Thank you, Greta."

Greta tucked Mr. Rabbit half under the covers, then quietly left the room.

So Greta admired Nick, Biloxi mused. She sighed. He deserved a proper "thank-you" for all his help. Where was his coat? She needed to find it and wash it. Or buy him a new one. She owed him. He had willingly helped her, a virtual stranger. His chivalrous actions were commendable.

However, the warmth and safety that emanated from his embrace was more than a little unsettling. Each time he'd held her in his arms, a sense of strength surged from him. However, any attachment to strong arms and broad shoulders could lead to heartbreak.

"No need for you to be jealous, Mr. Rabbit."

She pondered. What was so special about Nick? How well did he know Branna? In time, she'd figure it all out.

He mentioned he was a pilot. Would he take her flying? She itched to start on her project. Aerial shots of the Pearl River and the Mississippi snaking through the countryside would impress the editors. With Nick's piloting skills, she might bring in money sooner than later to bring her visions to life.

The reward of doing what she loved could offer a means that Fleur de Lis needed—money. The plantation produced barely enough revenue for upkeep. Expenses were climbing, along with taxes, which meant family members were digging deeper into their pockets to sustain the property. Her plan could make Fleur de Lis entirely self-supporting.

An uphill battle awaited. She had prepared, but enough?

She fluffed a pillow and scooted to sit, her back against the carved wooden headboard. She wanted another read of Aunt Macy's monthly report, but it was downstairs in her computer bag. As she had understood the meeting minutes, the family voted to limit repairs to those that made the Old Aunts comfortable in their final days. With that plan of action, Fleur de Lis would die of neglect. She couldn't let that happen. Why did the rest of the family take their legacy for granted? Fleur de Lis oozed with history and could be a showplace in the south. It was just as grand as many of the houses on River Road or those over in Natchez. However, she would never reduce anyone to wearing a hooped skirt to make money. Way too cliché.

Maybe the family would see "home" differently once she finished her photo-essay book.

She turned back to her toy. "Mr. Rabbit, do you know Nick Trahan?"

Who remembered that Claude Trahan had a grandson? Or that G.G. Grace's failing memory would recall that Claude challenged Granddaddy Robert to a duel? Old timers gossiped about it, though the family rarely spoke of it.

"Just old folklore, like Loup-Garou."

Grandma Elise. She always flashed a secretive smile when the subject came up, yet never made any comment.

Biloxi sighed. If she understood history, the incident in question took place back when Grandma was still Elise Murphy. Granddaddy Robert always called her the prettiest girl around. She couldn't imagine him as a young man, let alone crazy in love. He did, however, always light up whenever her grandmother walked into a room. It was sweet, especially because he thought no one was looking.

The Dutrey-Trahan story reminded her of something from an old Hollywood black-and-white, long forgotten movie. Her grandfather had passed two years ago. Her grandmother grieved a long time, though had recently seemed content in widowhood.

But was she?

Was it coincidence that Trahans were back?

Was Claude Trahan still alive?

She drew a sharp breath. If G.G. Grace boiled at the sight of Nick, setting eyes on Claude would probably kill her.

Yet, if she ever behaved toward a guest as G.G. Grace had with Nick, not only would ancestors roll in their graves, but a permanent "F" would mark her social-graces report card. Long ago, G.G. Grace had taught her to mind her manners. Once when she mocked a neighbor kid, G.G. Grace punished her, made her go to mass every day for a week that summer. She claimed it was the only way for her to prove she was truly repentant. That lesson stuck.

Good manners were not contingent upon age. She'd never seen G.G. Grace react so rudely to anyone.

Until Nick.

She would apologize to him on behalf of the entire family. No sense in fueling the gossip mill and dredging up stuff from the past. She'd call Linc about how to contact Nick.

She yawned. Tomorrow. So much to do.

A list of tasks bounced in her brain like an out-of-control pinball game. Her new business card designs were ready for the printer. The contractor the family always used was scheduled to take measurements for construction she'd planned. It was premature, but she wanted to be prepared.

Injuries from the accident would not prevent her from working. In every spare moment since she inked her photography contract, she had added to the list of photographs she wanted. In her mind's eye, she pictured the first photo on her list. Pinecote Pavilion at the Crosby Arboretum. A night shot with the place ablaze, lights reflecting off the water would make it appear to rise up out of nothing.

Like Nick appearing out of nowhere to rescue her. Warm liquid brown eyes with flecks of gold. An odd excitement fluttered deep in her gut. Why did every other thought drift back to him?

Once she had her studio operational, would Nick sit for a portrait? A sepia tone that showed off his eyes and his dimples. One that his family would be proud to hang on the wall.

His eyes drew her. Made her feel as though she was the only woman in the world when she was with him. Made her insides liquid and warm.

Hopefully he hadn't been too insulted by G.G. Grace. Neither she, nor he, had anything to do with the disagreement their grandfathers had so long ago. Ancient history. The Old Aunts couldn't hold Nick accountable for something that happened before he was born. She'd talk with them about it tomorrow.

The clatter of china caught her attention.

"Here you go." Greta carried in a tray with a plate, pot of tea and two cups. She set the tray on Biloxi's lap, then poured tea into the cups. In the moonlit room, steam rose in curls.

Biloxi frowned at the plate. "The doctor gave a long list of "no-no's," but he didn't say I couldn't eat. Are you rationing me?"

"It's late, you need rest. A little cheese, apple slices, broth, and bread. It's all you need before you go back to sleep."

"Well, maybe so, but I'm home, Greta. I'm *home*. And I want comfort food. Gumbo or etouffee."

"Maybe so. But pace yourself. With that photography contract, you're going to be here a while. Rich food every meal, honey, you'll be wider than this house. Now eat and go to sleep."

Biloxi smiled. "Greta, you mark my words. I'm home for good. Branna better watch out."

Chapter 9

The clock on the wall ticked to ten-thirty a.m. Nick palpated the cat on the examination table and confirmed his visual diagnosis. This kind of oddball case showed up on Mondays. Remaining professional, with a straight face he said, "No, Miss Laulie. Oscar doesn't have cancer. He isn't sick. *She's* going to have kittens."

"No, Dr. Trahan. That can't be." Miss Laulie covered her red-lipsticked mouth with a bony, age-spotted hand. Her ancient deep blue eyes narrowed. "Oh, you're just josh'n me." She giggled.

Nick chuckled. "No, ma'am. *She's* going to have kittens. How long have you had Oscar?"

"A month. My cousin gave him—I mean her—to me. Said he was fixed—the cat, not my cousin. Well, I guess Oscar will have to be Oscar de la Renta. I'll call her De la Renta. It sounds much more feminine, don't you think? I couldn't *possibly* call her Oscar anymore." The tall, reed-thin woman fanned herself with her hand.

"Is that what you want me to put on the records?" Peaches, Nick's office manager asked. She stood next to him, a good foot shorter, and jotted information on a form. Her pink lab coat matched a shock of pink that striped her black hair. She'd pulled it into a severe bun at the nape of her neck, but he wasn't fooled by her attempt at conformity.

He looked from one woman to the next. The

contrast between the two was comical.

"That's her new name," Miss Laulie answered. She stroked the cat tenderly.

"I'm going to do a complete exam on De la Renta. She looks like a Himalayan. Do you know anything else about her?" Nick asked, placing the stethoscope on the cat's belly.

"She's great company. She stayed by my side most of the time while I recovered from that flu that made the rounds."

After finishing the exam and assuring Miss Laulie of her cat's excellent health, he washed his hands, then went to his office. Peaches would handle the rest of the business.

He pulled a large textbook into his lap with the idea of reading up on bovine reproduction. He leaned back in his chair, put his feet up on his desk and flipped to the bookmark.

"That'll ruin your posture."

He didn't look up when he heard Peaches' voice from the doorway directly behind him.

"For an office manager, you sure have your nose into everything. You didn't take me to raise."

"You, same as with your patients, I take them as I get them. Give'em what they need. If you need reminding about what's good for you, I'm the one to do it. Besides, I'm not old enough to be your mother. Maybe a big sister."

He snorted.

"So, you never said. You gonna hire that Dr. Gilbeau? If so, I want you to know right now, I'm not taking orders from her. I expect you to be the one to tell me what to do."

Peaches' defensive tone made him swivel in his chair to look at her. "She's a very competent vet."

"Maybe. Maybe not. One thing I know for sure. That one—she'd eat her young to get what she wanted."

"What's that supposed to mean?"

"You watch yourself, Doc. I admit, I'm on the bandwagon to find you a wife, but I have a sense about her. She's bad news. And...*news flash*—she wants you."

"Naw. Peaches, you're wrong about that. I'm too countrified for Chantel. We're old family friends. Besides, she wants...I don't know. Something that I'm not."

"She may be great with animals. People? Not so much. All I'm tell'n you is, I'm gonna make sure she doesn't take a bite out of you. I'm gonna find you the right woman. You just wait and see."

"Yes, ma'am." Grinning, he saluted. Peaches treated him more like a son than a boss. Most of the time, he didn't mind. He trusted her to run the clinic, especially when he made house calls. But he wanted her—and everyone else—to leave his love life alone.

"Now, you've got an appointment after lunch over at the Michaels' place to look at the new horse Mr. Michaels bought for his daughter. That girl's so spoiled. My Cody built their new stable, but I gotta tell—"

"Peaches," he interrupted.

"Hmm?"

He closed the book in his lap and moved his feet to the floor, setting the book on his desk. "I'm going to check on another patient. I'll be back in the clinic for the afternoon appointments, after I see the Michaels' horse."

"But, there's no appointment on the books and it's too early for lunch. What are you up to?"

"Just looking in on another patient. One that's never been to the clinic."

"Well, I'll expect a full report to handle the billing."

Once outside, he zipped up his coat before climbing into the truck. The sun made it look warm, but the wind and the temperature shouted winter. Mondays were usually busy times at the clinic. Rarely could he slip away, but the lack of patients around lunchtime meant he had time to visit Biloxi.

Unusually busy, Main Street had a line of traffic when he turned on to it. He stopped at Flora's Flower Shop, the only one in town. Flora brought her Shih Tzu, Sam, to him for checkups and shots. He'd heard that Sam was as good a host at the florist as any Walmart greeter, only smaller.

When Nick stepped inside, perfume from the flowers assaulted his nose and Shih Tzu Sam assaulted his jeans.

"Sam! Stop that!" Flora scolded. "Dr. Trahan, how may I assist you?"

After Sam slunk off to the corner, Flora helped him pick out three herb pots—basil, rosemary, and thyme—in a basket for Greta.

"Now, who do you want this bouquet for?" Flora asked, while studying the refrigerated case full of flowers.

"Biloxi Dutrey."

"I read in the paper where she was coming home. Some sort of photography contract? But you say, you don't want roses?"

"No, ma'am, no roses. These are a get-well bouquet. Roses, well, they're too—"

"Ah…might send the wrong message." Flora nodded. "How about a mixture of orange Gerbera daisies, yellow poms, white mini carnations in that tall green vase over there?"

Nick nodded. "Whatever you think is best. Fine with me. Just no roses."

"Biloxi is sick?"

Flora, like all the other women in town, would want to know details. News in Bayou Petite traveled faster by word of mouth than through other channels. He refused to add anything new to the already chattering gossip line.

"I'm sure she's doing fine."

"Well, I heard Gus say this morning, over at Maucele's diner, she'd wrecked her car. You want me to deliver this?" Flora held up the empty vase.

"No. I'll wait and take them with me. Say, what about balloons?" Could he distract Flora from any further discussion about Biloxi? Who knew what comment he might make that would have everyone making assumptions. It had happened before. He'd learned his lesson. He didn't talk about his private life. Not to anyone.

Flora's eyes danced. "Balloons. They make a festive statement. Sort of Mardi-Gras-in-helium. How about six?"

Nick paid the bill, then loaded his purchases into his truck. He pushed a button and the sunroof rolled closed, a way to keep the balloons inside. He headed toward Fleur de Lis. Just before reaching Loblolly Lane, Gus passed him while going in the opposite direction and waved his cap out the window. Biloxi's BMW rested on the flatbed truck.

"She didn't waste any time. All business that one," he said aloud.

He continued down the road until he reached the front of the house. The brick drive circled around a three-tier fountain where water splashed in the sunlight. Fleur de Lis looked different during the day, a less Gothic feel than on a wet rainy night.

He'd thought about that night a lot. He'd thought a lot about Biloxi, too. The image of her soft hazel eyes intruded into his mind as though coming out of nowhere. Her eyes, sometimes more green than brown, looked serious too much of the time. And her hair. He could almost feel it, imagined running his fingers through the dark auburn strands. He loved long hair on a woman. Yet, his imagination usually landed on her lips. Sensual. Whenever they curved into a smile, she looked sexy. Definitely sexy. Yeah, he'd been thinking about her far too much.

After parking the truck, he gathered the gifts and began to climb. His boots thumped a rhythm against the wide wooden steps taking him up to Fleur de Lis' gallery. It ran the length of the front of the house and wrapped around the sides to the back. Six rocking chairs invited folks to relax there, three chairs on each side of the double front doors. Fleur de Lis showed off its insignia on a welcome mat.

Greta appeared at the door before he knocked.

"Hello, Nick." She opened the outside screen door and he stepped inside.

"*They're* playing golf or bridge at the country club," she said. "It's their Monday outing." It was clear to him that she referred to the Old Aunts.

"Good to know. This is for you." He presented her with the basket of potted herbs.

"For me?" She smiled. "I can't tell you the last time a man brought me a gift. Thank you. This is very thoughtful of you." Greta beamed. Had she fluttered her eyelashes?

"The flowers and balloons are for Biloxi."

"She's in the sunroom. You know the way. We're about to have lunch."

"I'm sorry for the intrusion."

"No, it's only Biloxi and I. Want to stay? It's Monday. Red beans and rice."

Greta didn't have to ask him twice. His only other dining option was a po'boy from the diner in town where he ate at least five times a week. Or he could go home and burn something in the microwave. Him turn down a Greta-home-cooked meal? Not ever. Not even Grace Dutrey could stop him from saying "yes."

"Sounds great."

When Greta headed for the kitchen, he turned toward for the sunroom with flowers in hand and balloons bouncing together. He stopped at the threshold. Biloxi reclined on the couch obviously asleep. Wake her up? No reason to disturb her peace and quiet.

How did a woman who acted tough as nails when they met manage to look so vulnerable when she slept? Her legs were tangled in a blanket. Her dark hair shone in the light. Gazing at her made his heart beat double time.

He set the flowers on the side table and the sandbag anchoring the bouquet of balloons on the floor in the corner.

Biloxi Dutrey didn't strike him as a diva. He had dated plenty of spoiled daddy's girls. Biloxi carried herself well. Appeared to take her independence seriously. A businesswoman would. Knowing she would go toe-to-toe with him or anyone, made him want to learn more about her. And though he hated to admit it, he'd been wrong. Branna hadn't cornered the market on gentility. Biloxi's polish looked different, more modern than Southern.

His heart thudded. He watched her sleep. He imagined kissing her, lips touching, hers warm and pliant.

Bending, he narrowed the space between them, his lips aiming for their target.

Her hazel eyes opened in surprise.

He froze.

"Hey, Nick." Biloxi yawned. "Are you in pain? Why don't you sit down before you fall down?"

Chapter 10

The next morning, standing in front of the cheval mirror, Biloxi practiced her speech. She was accustomed to being behind a camera and having people look at her *work* rather than at *her*. Pitching her ideas to Aunt Macy and the family council about how to revive Fleur de Lis' cash flow made her knocking knees, trembling hands, can't-catch-a-breath nervous. Her military father had instilled in her a battle-mindedness. Always prepare for what's coming, and always be prepared for the unexpected.

Inhaling deeply she let go of the breath and hoped to exhale her angst away. Her plan was solid. She could infuse a new energy that Fleur de Lis needed to survive.

"Biloxi, dear?"

"Come in, Great Grandmother Grace," she said, then sat on her bed and propped a pillow behind her back.

Grace ambled into the room. "Dear, we must talk about this situation." Taking a seat in the slipper chair, she adjusted a shawl around her shoulders.

"Situation? Did something happen?" Biloxi leaned forward, worried.

"That young man is not welcome in this house."

"I don't understand."

"Don't be obtuse. We do not associate with Trahans."

Biloxi waited for further explanations. When none came, she asked, "Why?"

"That unseemly business that happened long ago. Since then, that is how it has been. We have no need for their company."

"Great Grandmother Grace," she chose her words carefully, "you taught me never to carry a grudge. That's something this family is known for, along with being fair-minded."

Grace sniffed and shifted in the chair. "This family is bonded through our history, our love and laughter. We do not carry grudges. Wisdom comes from remembering the past and allowing ourselves to be guided by the lessons we have learned. History says that Trahans are not to be trusted."

"But—"

"No exceptions."

"Nick didn't do anything to us in the past."

"Young woman, I expect you to honor your family. I do not wish to entertain that man as a guest in this house."

"I get it. Your house, your rules."

"Think of it in terms of honor and duty—no compromise, instead of rules."

Biloxi nodded dutifully out of respect. "I understand."

Grace rose. "I am very proud of you. Of all you have accomplished in your life. I worried what type of woman you would grow into, what with your mother's influences and your father's wanderlust. I am pleased that you feel such a strong bond to this place. This is our home. Your home. I love you and I know you will make the necessary adjustments to our way of life at

Fleur de Lis."

Grace left the room, the tap of her cane echoing a reminder that tradition ruled everything at Fleur de Lis.

"Yes, G.G. Grace." Biloxi stared at the closed bedroom door and smiled. "Rules are made to be broken."

Chapter 11

Nick pulled his pickup into an open parking space at the rear of Fleur de Lis, spaces usually reserved for family. The cool morning dragged in a damp overcast noon, but Greta's cooking could soothe anything. Biloxi's sudden lunch invitation had brightened his entire mood. He hadn't seen her in several days.

"How's the patient?" he asked, climbing the stairs.

"Hi, yourself."

On the back gallery, Biloxi sat in a rocking chair with a blanket over her legs, the one they'd played tug-o-war with on the night of her accident. He'd assumed it was lost when Greta returned only his coat, laundered and stain-free. Interesting that Biloxi would choose *that* blanket when Greta had a trunk full of nice ones in the sunroom.

He squatted beside Biloxi. Her dimpled cheeks and glittering eyes let him know that she was glad to see him, but what was up with the sharp attitude?

"You sure you're okay?" he pressed.

"Thanks for asking. I'm fine. Happy to see you, too."

He continued his perusal of her. The bruises had faded. She projected a wholesome image, more like the girl-next-door than an edgy woman with the worthless shoes he'd pulled out of the mud a week ago. He preferred her this way. Bright and grumpy, instead of dark, brooding, and flashing glares at him every other minute.

"Nice blanket." He fingered the corner of it, rubbing softness between his fingers.

Biloxi blushed. "I intend to return it to its owner…" She paused as though she wanted to say more. Her lips pursed before she finally spoke.

"Lunch will be ready soon. We're waiting on someone to join us," she said, folding and unfolding her hands in her lap.

Whomever they waited for rattled her usual calm.

"If you're having guests, I should come back another time." He stood.

"You can't go!" She grabbed his hand tight. Then, as if realizing she'd raised her voice, she sweetly said, "Please stay," and promptly let go of his hand.

"Are the Old Aunts home?"

"Yes, and that's exactly why I want you to stay."

"I don't think that's a good idea. There's no need to aggravate the situation. I don't have to understand their problem, but I can respect their wishes."

Her eyes pleaded with him. "I might need your help in stopping a civil war."

Her plea produced a jolt of protectiveness that surprised him. Vulnerability always brought out his guardian nature. It was part of why he became a vet. Animals were helpless against nature and man. But those two old ladies weren't ogres. They loved her. Plus, she was Greta's favorite. Something else was going on.

By staying, what was he getting into?

He sat in a rocker next to her and stretched his legs out. Beside him, she pulled the collar of her gray jacket closer to her neck, adjusted the blanket over her legs and fixed her gaze on the bottom of the stairs.

He pondered while glancing at her profile. Her hair hung in long waves halfway to her waist. She wore makeup, though in his opinion, she didn't need it. The gloss on her lips made her mouth look even more kissable than he'd remembered. There was something hypnotic about her that mesmerized him, drew him like a bee to a flower.

She nervously ran the tip of her tongue over the peak of her top lip. He wanted to kiss that spot.

He'd first noticed her lips the night they'd met, when he sat her in her car and turned on the flashers before towing her home. Then, concern for her safety had been the priority. Besides, he made a habit of never kissing strange women.

But that hadn't stopped him from wanting a kiss.

He twined his fingers together in his lap. That was the safest place for them. That would control the urge to touch her.

When had he ever been so distracted by a woman?

He would've kissed her that morning when he snuck into her room at the hospital, but she'd fallen asleep. He considered it again when he carried her up the stairs after she returned home, but Linc's stares had stopped him. Then, when she lay in the sunroom—that time he'd almost done it. Alone with her now, the perfect opportunity invited a meeting of lips. If he leaned in and she moved closer...he would savor the moment.

However, when he did capture his first kiss with her, he wanted no interruptions. He might not stop once he started.

"Are you warm enough?" he asked as she fidgeted.

"I have to warn you…" Her voice rose barely above a whisper.

He waited for her to continue. His mind raced. Was she sick? An infection? Something worse?

"My mother's coming for lunch."

As though cued by a stage manager, a red Volvo sedan pulled in and blocked his truck. A woman with dark blonde hair, dark sunglasses, tailored red coat, and black high heels exited the car. He half expected her to snap her fingers and demand a valet to park it. She strode up the stairs, a powerhouse of restrained intensity in a feminine package.

"I cannot believe you did *not* call me sooner." The sharpness in the woman's voice added punch to the wave of energy rolling up the stairs with her. Her pointed heels struck hard against wood, reminding him of a jackhammer—dangerous in the wrong hands.

He sat up straighter, boot soles flat on the floor. This woman commanded attention. Everything about her said, "I am important," with an oversized capital "I."

"So good to see you, too, Momma."

He couldn't read Biloxi's tone. A hint of humor? Or was it sarcasm? He stood as the woman drew closer. Any witty greeting he might have considered fled from his brain. A king cobra snake charmer would be lucky to win over this woman.

"Oh, honey! You are hurt. You should've called me. I hope you haven't put Greta out too much." The woman leaned down and kissed the air beside Biloxi's cheeks, then stepped back and looked at him. She took a good, long look. Boots to hat and back again.

Removing her sunglasses, she planted them on top of her head. She raised one skeptical eyebrow, appearing to assess him as a man might warily examine a used car, or as though he were a horse—one up for auction. She seemed to consider him. Her expression conveyed that she wondered why a strange man sat with her daughter. On the back gallery. In their family's private domain.

"Momma, may I introduce *my friend*, Dr. Nick Trahan. Nick, this is my mother, Deidre Dutrey."

Deidre's eyebrows lifted. Her smile had brightened when Biloxi put "doctor" in front of his name.

He offered his hand.

"You make house calls?" she asked. Her manicured hand held his in a firm grip. He stood straighter under her cool scrutiny.

"Well, as a matter-of-fact, I do," he said with his best lazy drawl, then winked at Biloxi.

****

"Will I survive this day?" Biloxi groaned in a low mutter.

"Lunch is served," Greta called.

"Finally," Biloxi sighed. She deferred to her mother and hobbled on crutches in her wake, much like following in the wake of an ocean cruiser. Not that her mother intentionally pushed everyone off balance, but her immediate family often experienced the gale force winds of Hurricane Deidre's storms. Her mother's mission in life, her mother always reminded the family, was to move them up Bayou Petite's social ladder. Albeit a small ladder, but the only one in town. Mostly, she wanted her children to stand out from the other great grandchildren. She made everything a competition. That made dealing with Hurricane Deidre difficult at best.

Although, her father managed nicely. She understood her father's attraction. After three children and years of marriage, Deidre Dutrey remained a stunning-looking woman, who, if inclined, could take over the world. When she walked into a room everyone noticed.

Biloxi entered the dining room with Nick following behind. Marie and Grace nodded to him, but didn't speak. They showed no clear hostile intent, but she watched Grace's eyes dart her way, then back to Nick, before Grace set her jaw firmly.

"Deidre, I wondered when you would pay us a call. Biloxi has been home for a week."

Biloxi cringed. Great Aunt Marie enjoyed baiting her mother.

Deidre smiled cotton-candy sweet and placed her napkin in her lap. "I would've come sooner, but you forgot to call me after the excitement of Biloxi's grand entrance. I forgive you, though. You did say your memory was slipping."

Greta cleared her throat. "More sweet tea?"

Biloxi mouthed "Thank you" to Greta for the interruption.

Although the conversation turned civil, the tension increased. She tried to steer them to safe topics, but that was like dodging balls in a tennis match to the death. Marie refused to look at her mother after Deidre's earlier quip. Grace avoided Nick, answering his questions as though someone else had asked them. Her mother poked the Old Aunts at every opportunity. All the while, Biloxi moved her food around on her plate unable to eat.

Nick displayed impeccable manners. He spoke to each of them, worked the room with a charm she never guessed he had, far more gracious than the man she'd met in the storm.

"For dessert, I made your favorite, Deidre," Greta said.

"Beignets with blueberry filling dusted with powdered sugar! You spoil me, Greta. You always have. I'll take a half. But I know, you spoil others more."

Her mother reached and patted her hand. Biloxi rolled her eyes before she could stop herself. She glanced around to see if anyone at the table had caught the gesture. Nick raised his eyebrows, then winked.

"Greta, these are great. No wonder folks call you Greta the Great," Nick said taking another bite of dessert.

Greta beamed.

"You've outdone yourself." Grace praised Greta as though Nick had not just spoken.

Biloxi shifted in her chair. Her neck and shoulders ached from the thick-as-lead tension. She wished lunch to be over and her mother on her way. When her mother's eyes narrowed and aimed a hard stare at Nick, Biloxi saw round three coming, but could do nothing to stop the impending train-wreck.

"Trahan. Are you related to Claude Trahan?"

"Yes," Nick replied.

She couldn't tell by her mother's expression if "yes" or "no" was the right answer. To his credit, Nick calmly continued to consume his blueberry-filled beignets.

Her stomach clenched tighter. Nick couldn't know that the next lob her mother intended could hit him hard. He hadn't seen her mother's military-style perusal or the strategizing wheels turning in her mother's head.

"Your grandfather wanted to kill my father-in-law."

"Mother!" She couldn't believe it, but should have expected it. How could she protect Nick from being Hurricane Deidre's next victim? It was bad enough that Grace snubbed him, and then had lectured her about any connection to him. Their behavior may have worked in the last century, but it wasn't acceptable now.

Tossing aside all etiquette training, she propped her elbows on the table and buried her face in her hands. Her head pounded. Her body ached. Was she going to be sick?

"Grandpère told me about that. He said his intention was to declare his undying love." While Nick spoke casually, she filled with dread.

"Noble of you to defend him. Loyalty to family. A trait I highly admire. Now, tell me how you met my daughter."

She would never understand the mental gymnastics of her mother's mind, but when had bad manners become vogue? Did things change when she was trying to survive up North and dying from homesickness? What happened to gentility and politeness? All the graces she'd been raised on—the required behaviors demanded from her as a child and made second nature to breathing.

Over the mental chatter in her head, she missed Nick's response. The man was a friend. A guest for lunch. Not a target with a red bull's eye on his forehead for her mother to shoot at.

"Enough!" Biloxi cried. She slammed her palms flat against the table. Silverware jumped. Tea in her glass sloshed out and made a brown spot on the white tablecloth.

"Child!" Grace and Marie cried in unison.

"I apologize." She paused. "May we please have a polite finish to this lunch?"

"More coffee?" Greta asked, rising from the table.

"Hmm," Deidre said. She gave Nick a once-over, as if taking in every detail about him and coming to some new conclusion. Her mother surprised her by turning the conversation away from Nick. "So, tell us all about your new job, Biloxi."

"Yes, tell us more," Grace encouraged. Marie nodded in agreement.

The first knot in Biloxi's stomach released, now only twenty-four more to go. "Well, it came as a surprise. I'm taking photos for Tourism, Inc., a private company whose goal is to promote tourism for the state. The project is broken down into several parts. Brochures and a calendar. The best part—I'm doing a book. A coffee-table book of my photographs. That will take time. They want four-season shots and a new perspective. It looks like I'll be here for a while."

"Nice," her mother purred. The hair on the back of Biloxi's neck stood up. Years of stimulus-and-response clued her into her mother's ways. Deidre was up to something.

"I know you'll be a big help to the Old Aunts, Greta, and even your Aunt Macy while you're here."

"Thanks, Momma. I intend to be very useful."

Biloxi looked down, picking at the dessert on her plate. She hated the ongoing fight with her mother about the estate. Her mother wanted to control Fleur de Lis, but since she'd married into the family and wasn't a blood relative, she would never have her wish. Therefore, she pushed in all the ways she could to get what she wanted. The emotional rollercoaster left Biloxi's stomach in her throat.

Her mother would have her claim squatter's rights and boot Branna out if she could.

But still, she wanted her mother's support for the plans she'd made. They shared the same end-desire, but for completely different reasons.

Guilt blossomed and tickled her conscience. She coveted Branna's role of Keeper. Tradition dictated that Branna was the rightful heir to the role. Being born only minutes later made tradition a hard pill to swallow. Though Fleur de Lis legally belonged to all of them, the Keeper managed the estate, and recently, the balance sheet had tipped into the red. Aunt Macy's too conservative approach had put the estate in jeopardy, and Branna had shown no interest in taking on the job.

When the conversation finally stilled, Deidre rose. "Greta, as always, thank you for a wonderful meal. You're always doing special things for us." She placed her napkin beside her plate.

Nick rose when her mother stood, and remained standing while her mother made her way around the room. She kissed Grace, Marie, and Greta on the cheek.

When she stopped beside Biloxi's chair, she leaned down and kissed the air beside each cheek, then whispered. "Honey, I'm so happy for your success. Do us proud."

It was an order.

"Dr. Trahan, would you walk me to my car?"

Biloxi's stomach somersaulted like a slinky going down the stairs. How could she protect Nick from Hurricane Deidre?

Chapter 12

Nick took Deidre's coat from the hall tree and helped her on with it. He opened the door and let her pass, following her out to the gallery. "After you."

Deidre's heels thumped against the wooden stairs, quickly descending.

He followed, stopping beside her car.

"Dr. Trahan, I see that you've ingratiated yourself with my family."

"If you mean, I enjoy Biloxi's company, then yes."

Deidre fished her keys out of her coat pocket. The opening *click* of the lock punctuated the silence between them.

"I believe in getting straight to the point. You're handsome. Charming smile. Engaging ways. I see that Grace is not comfortable with your company. I'm sure it's because of that duel business. However, that's not my concern. Biloxi is my focus. My daughter is injured. Recovering. I think it would be a good thing if you practiced your charms somewhere else."

He coughed. The cobra did have fangs. "Interesting."

"I'll be more direct. My daughter is not for you."

"Not for me in what way?" He kept his voice even.

"You're wasting your time here. I've heard about you. The bachelor veterinarian. All the local mommas are trying to hook you for their daughters. Biloxi is destined for great things. After all, look at her latest professional contract. And she's only twenty-nine. I want what's best for her. I want her here at Fleur de Lis. And married to the *right* man."

"I see." He folded his arms on his chest and nodded.

"Good. We can add *savvy* to your list of characteristics."

Deidre reached for the car door handle, but he got there first, and opened it for her. She settled into the driver's seat and clicked the seatbelt in place. When she pulled on the door to close it, he held it firmly.

"Just one little problem," he said flatly.

Deidre drew back in surprise.

"With all due respect Mrs. Dutrey, you *don't* know me. I see that you're a no-nonsense kind of woman, so I'll be direct. Your daughter is a grown woman. By all outer appearances, you raised her right. She can decide what I am to her. Maybe we'll end up as friends. Maybe we'll share a few kisses here and there, but she's a Dutrey. And as long as *my* grandmother's alive, I won't rub salt in that old wound."

He closed the door.

Deidre pursed her lips and frowned, then drove away.

His gaze followed the red sedan, certain the woman behind the wheel had wanted the last word.

****

Biloxi watched from the kitchen window. Her mother had her back to the house during the exchange. Nick's expression gave away nothing. She couldn't hear their words, but Nick was a man her mother couldn't twist to suit her purposes.

That could prove to be a predictor of trouble.

And she was sure to get more of that soon. Grace would confront her later with a reprimand about Nick at the dinner table. For now, she had a reprieve. The Old Aunts were waiting out front for the community van to take them to the library.

Retreating to the sunroom, she sat on the couch, scrunched her shoulders, released them, and tried to calm down. Did she owe Nick yet another apology? She'd said "I'm sorry" more times in the last week than ever before in her life, about things she hadn't done or caused or said. Would dinner out make it up to him? The Creole Kitchen in Picayune? Nothing fancy, just good food.

Nick appeared in the doorway no worse than when he'd left.

"Greta said I'd find you in here." He took a seat on the couch beside her, close enough that she caught a faint whiff of his cologne, but far enough away to meet the proper standards of politeness.

"Nick, I'm sorry about my mother. What did she say?"

"Your mother's a...a captivating woman."

Biloxi sighed. "Hurricane Deidre."

"Hmm." He seemed to contemplate the correlation. "Probably a suitable nickname for her, *chèr*."

Goosebumps traveled up her spine. She loved the sound of his voice when he called her that. Just a friendly term, but she had imagined a lover shouting it with passion. It had been a long time since any man shouted with her in the heat of passion.

"It seems I'm either apologizing to you for something to do with my family, or I'm thanking you for your kindness."

"I'm happy to help a neighbor."

She continued, "Well, this morning while worrying about my mother's visit, I neglected to thank you. You're spoiling me. More flowers. Flora's delivered early. I love Stargazer lilies. I put them on the dresser in my bedroom. You've really done too much. How can I possibly I thank you?"

Nick's eyebrow rose. "Do you mean that?"

"Yes, I mean it. Thank you. Very much."

Sitting so near him—the closest they'd been in a week—he radiated with an energy, strong as the muscled strength she'd felt in his arms. Nick's touch made her feel as though she might be fragile and valuable.

"I have a favor to ask," they said at the same time.

"You first," she said.

Nick's mischievous smile tugged at her curiosity.

"Let me take you to dinner tomorrow tonight?"

Chapter 13

The next evening, Biloxi gingerly ran a brush through her hair, careful not to rake the bristles across the tender spot where her stitches had been. Her hair hung in soft waves thanks to Greta's skill with hot rollers.

She checked her makeup in the mirror. Smiled. No lipstick on her teeth. She turned from one side to the other and examined her reflection. Black tulip skirt. Coral-colored sweater. Just enough cleavage showed. The low-heeled Cole Haans wouldn't stress her recovery. Her ruined Jimmy Choo shoes would've completed the outfit perfectly, but her tender ankle couldn't tolerate stilettos yet. Out there, somewhere, a raccoon was probably wearing them on a date.

The idea of an evening out had created as much anticipation as the plans scattered across her bed. Notes and notebooks detailed changes for Fleur de Lis. She'd spent the day reading over them. Soon she would launch her operation. Greta, her confidant, provided validation and boosted her spirits. While the long-time companion to the Old Aunts didn't vote in family decisions, she did have her avenues of influence. They both agreed that the more opportunities for Fleur de Lis to pay for itself, the better. Upkeep wasn't cheap.

The entire exterior of Fleur de Lis needed new paint. Rot had attacked several windowsills. Continued exposure to the blistering southern sun and high humidity could damage the sturdiest of houses. Neglect of basic home repairs could mean more costly ones in the future.

But would the family agree to the plan or would it mean her ultimate exile?

She couldn't stay and watch the decline. Convincing the family to choose her and her plan was a risk she had to take.

She turned out the bedroom light and closed the door behind her. With a folder of information for the printer and her head swirling with numbers, lists of supplies, and advertising, she almost missed the first step at the top of the wide carpeted staircase.

"Oh-my-God!"

A navy blue suit hugged wide shoulders and a starched white shirt showed off an artsy, multi-colored tie. Black western boots shone beneath pants. This time, he'd left the cowboy hat and duster at home. When she thought he couldn't look sexier, he smiled.

She gulped.

Heat rose from her toes to the roots of her hair. She swayed dizzily, but couldn't cut her gaze away and clutched the stair rail for support. Descending slowly, she continued to stare. Nick's wide smile changed to a modest grin. Did her appreciative stares make him uncomfortable? Could he hear the slamming beat of her heart?

She held her breath until the last step. With an exhale, another flush hit her cheeks. She hated that he had the power to make her blush.

Nick stepped closer.

She couldn't meet his eyes, choosing instead to

focus on his lips. Kissable. She tried to shake off the attraction. They were only friends. Why ruin a promising friendship with a fleeting physical attraction? After all, he was the only male friend she had in Bayou Petite. And even as friends, Grace had objections.

Besides, was Nick really her type?

At the moment, totally.

She preferred men who spent their day in suits. The Brooks Brothers model type…like Gregory. Not anymore. Clearly, her taste had changed.

"You look amazing," Nick said seductively.

When she finally looked up, his eyes lit and locked on hers. His grin widened. His stare sent her stomach into a free-fall plunge from thirty thousand feet.

Gregory had never looked at her like that. Even when he'd said he loved her.

Behind Nick, Greta cleared her throat. Biloxi turned. Greta held out a gray cashmere coat, then opened the front door and silently motioned them out. She and Greta had conspired earlier for the Old Aunts to visit a neighbor when Nick arrived to avoid Grace's disapproval. She wasn't exactly lying to Grace, but she did feel a tad guilty.

Nick offered his arm. Biloxi draped her coat over it. She didn't trust herself to touch him. When he grasped her elbow, a warm current flowed through her. She wouldn't need a coat to protect her from the evening cold.

All she needed was Nick.

He helped her up into the truck, then walked to the driver's side. After the truck rumbled to a start, they drove around the fountain and started down the half-mile drive lined with arching branches of ancient oaks.

The truck was her pumpkin-turned-coach and for once, she, not Branna, was Cinderella.

"Damn, *chèr*," he exclaimed.

She caught Nick's sideways glance as he drove.

"You aren't half bad yourself," she said.

"What? Half bad?" He frowned. "Maybe that fall hurt your head worse than we thought."

"Huh?" Then, inwardly, she cringed. Could she be any more inarticulate?

"Take another look." He made it sound like a dare.

Embarrassed, she looked him up and down.

"That look on your face," he continued. "The one you had when you stood at the top of the stairs. It didn't say I look 'not half bad'. It said that you think I'm hot."

"Really?" At least that sounded more intelligent. She didn't trust herself to say more. She'd lived her life photographing beauty, which included male beauty, too. She was used to great looking men, and had never blushed like this in the company of one. Usually, she handled flattery with ease. After all, she dished it out like warm butter on toast when she shot models. Flattery worked on them.

Although she was used to Gregory's friends complimenting her hourglass figure, she recognized insincerity when she heard it. Gregory's cohorts preferred waif-thin models. They often tried to wrangle models' phone numbers from her. So, why would a compliment from Nick make her shiver?

At five-foot-five and curvy, Ann Taylor's "curvy" line fit her best. She would never be a size zero. However, while too short to model, lack of height didn't exclude her from taking fashion cues and learning to dress her shape. She never worried about sizes marked on clothes.

Yet, the direction of Nick's conversation made her uncomfortable. They were just friends. She wanted to employ him as a pilot. Therefore, best to keep things friendly, more on the professional side.

"After we drop off my print order at the office supply store and we finish at the tux shop, where do you want to eat?" She'd almost forgotten about their errands before dinner, and was dying to know why Nick needed a tux. Asking seemed too nosy.

"Do you eat hushpuppies with your fingers?" Nick asked.

"Huh?"

"Never mind." He grinned.

They listened to blues on their drive into town. She was thankful for the silence between them, especially since some sort of brain-tic had taken over and reduced her vocabulary to mush.

After stopping at the stationery store, they arrived at the tux shop. She watched from a chair while the tailor fussed over Nick with the care and concern of a mother hen.

"The tux will be ready on Friday, sir."

The tailor, a short balding man, draped his tape measure around his neck and stood up. Taking a few steps back, he crossed his arms over his chest and surveyed Nick in the tux, then turned and smiled broadly at her and asked, "When's the wedding?"

Baffled, she shrugged.

A look of horror replaced the man's smile, and that made her giggle. Why would he think they were getting married?

Nick stepped down from the dais in front of the

three-way mirror and walked toward her. His solemn expression set off alarms in her head. Heat in her cheeks flared when he knelt on one knee directly in front of her. He took her hand.

The tailor hovered nearby wringing his hands. Nick cast a sideways glance at the man. "Thanks, I'll be by to pick up the tux next Friday after work." Nick dismissed the man from what appeared would be a private conversation.

"Oh. Right," the tailor said. "Just leave the clothes in the fitting room when you change. I'll pick it up from there." The man scurried away.

Biloxi giggled, and then tried to sound less nervous. Nick dressed like a groom-to-be on one bent knee. If he intended to tell her he was engaged to someone, she'd hit him over the head with her purse.

She looked down. His thumbs stroked the tops of her hands. Pale and smooth fingers were caressed by tanned, roughened ones. She waited for him to speak. Her heart fluttered to the beat of a thousand butterfly wings. The silence grew. She held back a nervous giggle.

Nick cleared his throat. He lifted her chin. "Biloxi Dutrey." His whiskey-smooth voice produced a string of scintillating shivers racing up and down her spine. "Will you do me the honor"—he squeezed her hand— "of having dinner with me?"

"Huh?"

When he drew back in surprise, his question registered in her mushy brain. "Yes!" she cried.

In the background, the tailor applauded.

"Good, now that we're going on a real dinner date, let me get out of this tux."

Had Nick said *date*?

She enjoyed his company, but couldn't think about him romantically. Secretly she wanted him. The thought of him washed her in a warmth more luxurious than cashmere. His nearness brought out a giddiness she'd never experienced before. But she wanted his friendship more than any romantic commitment. Her plan and work had to remain the first priority. She might assuage G.G. Grace's objections to Nick if they remained friends, but anything beyond that would pave the path to being disowned. Since she *had* to have Branna's job, it remained her biggest dream, strict decorum guided her actions, though she wondered how Branna had managed the proverbial good-girl lifestyle so effortlessly all her life.

Nick reappeared from the dressing room in his suit. He escorted her from the store. When they crossed the threshold, he squeezed her hand. Tingles raced up her arm, across her shoulders and down through her other hand as though she'd been plugged into the electrical current of Nick. He appeared unaware of her reaction. He guided her toward the truck. She would never share with him about her sensitivity to his touch.

The sun had set and the little town's gas streetlights glowed. Warm air clashed with cold, then settled into a misty fog that blanketed the town. It made the world cocoon-like. Intimate and private. Hopefully he thought her shivers were due to the weather.

They rode in silence. Nick pulled onto Interstate 10. He headed west on the highway and turned on the radio. Stevie Wonder's "Signed, Sealed, Delivered, I'm Yours" filled the quiet between them. That gave her time to think.

In the past, the old song always got her on her feet to dance. When she traveled, it reminded her of home. Now it dredged up memories of battles with Branna, ones soon to be renewed. In a few days, she'd launch her campaign to remove Branna as Keeper. How wide a family rift would even the suggestion of her plan cause?

Beside her, Nick thumped out the beat with the piano, drums, and crying guitars. That shifted her thoughts away from Branna to him. Every nerve in her body tensed. She needed a serious distraction.

"Where are we having dinner?"

"The Chateau," Nick said.

"Oh. *The Chateau*. Do you eat there frequently?"

"No, I've never been there. I've heard it's good. An old church converted into a restaurant, not far from Slidell. Seafood with a French flair."

She hesitated. "But, isn't that most of New Orleans cooking? Wait, you're taking me across state lines?"

"*Mais*, it's not like I'm taking you to France. No laws against transporting you to Louisiana."

"This place is that special?" she asked.

"Could be."

This was only a dinner. Nick liked to tease. She would never take his flirting to heart. That would allow their friendship to deepen.

But would "friends with benefits" interest him?

No serious commitment?

How would he feel about that?

"Hello over there," Nick called.

"Sorry, just thinking."

"Do you want to share?"

Again, heat rose in her cheeks. She had to focus on her mission. Would he understand that work had to come first? Her contract, her business, and most importantly—Fleur de Lis. She had to wrangle control from Branna. All it required was focus. Any relationship with Nick, beyond friendship, would create too much distraction.

Or a family civil war.

Dating Nick could rock the world in a not-so-good way. And, it would impact her, too. In the past, she'd allowed men to distract her from her purpose. Gregory had proven that point. She had no control when it came to him. She nurtured him, his work, and his interests while he complained about her travel schedule. All the while, she had wanted to feel like she belonged…with him.

Only he'd never belonged to her.

"You *must* like seafood," Nick said.

"I like it grilled, fried, broiled, boiled, and sometimes raw," she said. "Sushi, anyone? Cajuns are more than jambalaya, etouffee, and southern-fried everything." She developed an appreciation for other types of foods during her trips.

"I like to try new places. Not that I don't appreciate Greta feeding me." Nick winked. "She knows her way around a kitchen, and she can bang out something tasty in any pot. However, given your worldly travels, I thought you might be one of those pampered women who only dine on fine food. I thought good ole home-style cooking at a restaurant might not impress you."

"I'm not sure if I should be flattered or insulted."

"No insult intended," Nick said. "You think of Bayou Petite as home, and I know you love Fleur de Lis, but let's face it, you've had far more exposure to the world than any local belle."

She cut a glance at him. "For me, it's about the food. Some of the best places I've eaten in are dives." She paused. "Hmm. Some of the worst food I've eaten was also at dives. Guess it just depends."

"I'm *not* partial to dives."

His tone was emphatic. Defensive almost. Over what? She'd figure it out later. His continued tapping to the rumbling bass made his good mood contagious.

"Oh, by the way," Nick said as he drove onto the exit ramp. "Do you think the tux will help my chances?"

"For?"

"I'm part of the show for the Valentine's Day auction. Will more people bid on me because I'm showing off in a tux?"

"Don't tell me Aunt Macy roped you into that! I can see you now, parading down the runway. Women will bid on you like crazy. Aunt Macy's smart about some things. You'll probably be the big-money draw this year. What's your auction item? Veterinary services?"

Poor Nick. Each year Aunt Macy recruited the best-looking bachelors for the auction. The family-friendly fundraising event had bachelors supplying their expertise to the highest bidder. A few men came from as far away as Gulfport and Baton Rouge. One charter-boat fishing captain even came up from Grand Isle to participate every year.

"Hey. It's not *that* funny. This is for a good cause," Nick said defensively.

"I know," she admitted. "It's *always* for a good cause. But you've never been to one of these things. It's not *just* an auction. Ask Linc. It's a social statement.

Everyone in town will be waiting to see if you bring the winning bidder from the auction to the Valentine's Ball the following week. Bayou Petite is full of hopeless romantics. Women will gossip. Men will take bets. And single women will berate themselves if your bidder turns out to be a romantic match—because then you'll be off the market."

"Does that include you?"

"Me?"

"Maybe I *will* invite my winning-bidder to the Valentine's Day Ball. As for the auction item from me…You'll have to wait to find out."

"Don't think so," she quipped. Had his challenge turned to subtle innuendo? The repartee was only friendly. Right?

Nick guided the truck into a parking space at the restaurant. "Well, what do you think?"

The front facade of the restaurant looked more like a stone castle, though the stained glass windows gave the place a church-like feel. If the food was as impressive as the setting, dinner would be a hit. She cocked her head, looking around through photographer's eyes. A charming old place with light blazing through stained glass windows into the low hanging fog would make a mysterious picture.

Once inside, Nick spoke to the hostess. They were early for their reservation and she pointed them to the bar.

"I'm going to the ladies' room to powder my nose." Biloxi headed for the hallway, then turned back. "I'll take a glass of *Vouvray*, since this place specializes in all things French."

Her heels clicked on the stone floor. The echo

bounced down the dimly lit hall. The eeriness made her hurry the last few steps to the ladies' room. She entered a restroom decorated to suit Marie Antoinette. A woman at the sink gazed into the mirror, her raven-black hair pulled into a perfect twist. The sleek hairstyle enhanced the length of her slender neck and showed off large diamond studs at her ear. A black cocktail dress, open in the back, clung to her body. The woman had to be a size zero.

"Hello," she said.

The woman didn't respond. Instead, she touched a finger to a corner of her mouth, patting a non-existent lipstick smudge, then exited the ladies' room.

"Am I invisible or what?" Biloxi spoke to her reflection in the mirror while washing her hands. For good measure, she ran a brush through her long hair, now mostly limp due to the foggy dampness. She hated rude women, especially women who looked like everything in the world came easily to them.

She applied lipstick and inspected her reflection. Her "curvy" rarely competed well with tall, thin, and elegant, but nothing about her deserved that type of behavior. She stewed over the woman's snub, though couldn't turn off her photographer's eye. A backdrop of an ancient-looking stone wall with the woman in her clingy black dress pressed against it, the woman's expression matching the hardness of the stone, yet the softness of her dress exuded sexiness and femininity.

A definite study in contrast.

She tried to abandon her envy as she made her way back to the bar. She would never stand taller than five-five except in heels. Never be a size zero or model gorgeous. It took hard work to maintain a size ten.

Lucky for her, then, that she preferred to be behind the camera rather than in front. Creating art gave her a great satisfaction. And she was good. Good enough to win the contest and land the contract.

Reaching the end of the hall where it opened to the restaurant's foyer and bar, she rounded the corner. Her eyes sought Nick. She intended to do a little flirting of her own over dinner. Get back at him for his teasing.

She spotted him…and *her*!

The woman from the ladies' room stood next to Nick. Her hand rested intimately on his arm. The woman gave a squeeze, like a shopper in a grocery store might test fruit for freshness. In this case, was she testing for male muscle mass? Or more?

Chapter 14

Humph!

She walked up behind Nick as he stared in the direction of the departing woman. Would stomping her feet break his concentration? She reached and gently squeezed his forearm, just like the woman had done. Startled, Nick looked down at her, the warm topaz pools of his eyes glinted and the corners of his mouth lifted. He patted her hand on his arm. She smiled back while her irritation simmered.

That willowy woman stood taller, especially in black stilettos, and could look Nick directly in the eyes. Biloxi did a mental inventory of her shoes. With the right platform heels, she could manage five-eight, but that wouldn't be tall enough to get eye to eye with Nick's six-foot frame. After seeing that woman with Nick, she wished to be taller, but even with added height, that black dress wouldn't drape the same sexy way over a body defined by curves.

She definitely hated that woman.

"Oh my," Biloxi said, batting her lashes for effect. "You are sooo strong, Dr. Trahan."

"What?"

"Sorry to interrupt your view."

Low blood sugar. That had to be it. The reason for her bitchiness. She couldn't help herself, at least that would be her defense. Though they were only friends, right now, she was a cat with long claws—and that woman had better beware, or else.

She shook her head. Goodness, what a fool she had almost made of herself.

"Your table's ready, sir." The hostess carried two leather-bound menus. "Please follow me."

She waited, but Nick gestured for her to go ahead of him. She followed the hostess through the dining room. White linens covered tables. Fresh flowers. Small crystal vases sparkled in soft glowing candlelight. The dining room was cozy. Intimate and private. And oh, so romantic.

Still following the hostess, Biloxi approached a table. The woman she'd encountered in the ladies' room glared up at her. She smiled, but the woman rolled her eyes. However, her smile widened, and she rubbed a diamond stud in her ear lobe as if to draw attention to her long neck and cleavage.

The act looked totally rehearsed.

Then she heard the woman purr. "Good evening again, Dr. Trahan."

When the hostess seated her, Nick was only several steps away. He hadn't lingered with the purring woman. The hostess waited for him to sit, then handed them both menus. A waiter arrived with an *amuse bouche* and made wine suggestions.

"*Vouvray*, your favorite, right?" Nick asked.

"Yes, it's sweet, but dry, and made from Chenin Blanc grapes." When he looked at her quizzically, she replied, "When I interned, I helped with a photo shoot for a print ad campaign for wine in France. I like to know about my subjects, so I learned about wine."

"You're all work, aren't you?"

Not sure how to take his comment, she perused the menu, trying to focus on the food selections. Curiosity about Nick and the woman had her wandering mind re-reading the menu several times. She resisted asking who the woman was.

The waiter poured a sip of chilled wine. Nick lifted the glass, tasted, then nodded, after which, the waiter filled each glass half full and left the bottle on ice in a stand. She noticed Nick's hands. Tanned. Strong. Warm, especially against her body.

"Cheers," Nick said, and clinked his glass to hers. "What shall we drink to?"

"Friendship." Yet, once the words left her mouth, her heart skipped a beat. She wanted more than just friendship with him. But, after Gregory…did she dare? What about G.G. Grace's objections?

Nick represented a disaster waiting to happen in her life.

"To friendship." Nick clinked his glass against hers again.

She sipped and listened to Nick talk about a childhood friend and the trouble they fell into, and about how his grandfather kept him on the straight and narrow.

A tinkling laugh drew her attention away. The purring woman had apparently found something her date said very amusing, leaned in, place her hand on the man's hand, the same as she had with Nick. Then she pursed her lips and blew a kiss to the man across the table.

Irritated, Biloxi turned back to Nick. His raised eyebrows appeared to question her distraction. After a sip of wine, she set the glass on the table and arranged the silverware, making sure each piece was perfectly straight and a thumbs width from the edge of the table. Anything to distract her from the warm flush caused by Nick's intense gaze.

A server delivered hot French bread and crab bisque. "The butter is from a dairy owned by a famous Cajun chef in Donaldsonville." Next, he poured a spot of sherry into each bowl before leaving.

"I could eat a gallon of bisque at one sitting," Nick said.

Biloxi tasted hers, then put down the spoon. She couldn't stand polite conversation while her emotions churned. If she didn't satisfy her curiosity, she'd never be able to eat.

"I thought you said you'd never been here before."

"I haven't." Nick sipped his wine.

"You make friends quickly." She sounded sarcastic and silly, but an odd possessiveness inched into her heart.

Denying her increasing interest in him would be plain stupid. After all, all women love attention from a good-looking man. And, he'd said this was a date.

"*Chèr*, there wasn't enough sherry in the bisque to make you drunk. What're you talking about? Or bothered about? If I didn't know better, I'd say you were jealous." He popped a piece of bread in his mouth and chewed.

She wanted to wipe the innocent look from his face along with the teasing in his eyes.

"That woman hanging on to you before we were seated," she explained, "I met her in the restroom. She *purred* at you when we walked by her table."

"Chantel?" Nick's brows furrowed.

"How French." It was the only thing she could think to say. Of course, the woman had to be gorgeous and have a lovely French name.

"Dutrey is French," Nick said. "Let's face it, most of us from around these parts have French blood in us. She's my new business associate. Moved over from Baton Rouge."

"Really?" She sounded entirely too hopeful. No reason for her to be jealous. That woman was a mere associate.

"A business associate?"

Nick had a veterinary practice, but she hadn't stopped to learn much about it. All this time, she'd been too focused on her own mission to ask questions about his work. She hadn't given a lot of thought to what he did, other than make animal house calls. He never brought up his work.

But, if Chantel was working with him, would she be purring for him, too?

Nick continued, "Just before you and I met, I put out feelers for an associate. I own the clinic, but need help. There's more work than just my tech and assistant and I can handle. Especially if I'm out in the field. In the beginning, I didn't want to take someone on until I had a sense of the volume of business," Nick explained. "I make house calls to half of my patients."

She conjured up a picture of farmers herding sick cows to town. That made her chuckle. It made sense that Nick traveled the county. Having an associate to handle the office appointments would be a benefit for his practice.

But did that person have to be tall and gorgeous?

"In fact, remember the night we met?" Nick asked.

"The next morning I had a surgery scheduled and Dr. Gilbeau came to assist. Peaches, my office manager, had rescued a dog from the side of the road. I told her we'd do the neutering for free. Dr. Gilbeau came to help. I made it part of her interview. I needed to know how she would get along with all the other females in the office. She and I went to vet school together. Besides, she's an old family friend."

"Really?" It was all she trusted herself to say, but better than "huh?"

The knot in her stomach, could it be that green-eyed-monster envy? The only person she'd ever been jealous of was Branna, and that was for an entirely different set of reasons. Jealousy this intense was new to her—along with the level of possessiveness over a man.

"Chantel starts on Monday. She's a good addition to my staff. I won't have to be a midwife to prize puppies at midnight anymore."

Biloxi tried to process all the information. Nick had said more about his work in those few sentences than he had in all their prior hours together. But, she didn't like Dr. Chantel Gilbeau. Beautiful and elegant. A lovely French name. A smart woman, clearly. Without a doubt, she didn't like Nick's new associate...but truthfully, why? Because she was rude in the ladies' room? Or maybe because her feelings for Nick were on a collision course with that woman's intentions?

"Say, how's Linc?" he asked. "Last time I saw him, he told me about his plane. Do you like to fly?" Nick asked.

"Absolutely."

"I was wondering...I have a Cessna. If the

weather's good, we could go up tomorrow. You mentioned you wanted to get some aerial shots. We could fly toward the coast. Scout things out. I know a great restaurant in Natchez. What do you think?"

"Wonderful." She lifted her glass to toast. It was the man, not the wine she saluted.

****

Nick couldn't miss Biloxi's glow when he mentioned flying. Could he hope that she wanted to spend more time with him?

He listened as she shared her ideas about the aerial shots. She explained which lens she used for what shots, about zooming and apertures, and things he knew nothing about. Yet, her enthusiasm was contagious. When she smiled, her eyes shone like Christmas lights on a dark night. She had a heart-warming grin and an accepting way about her. He'd seen it with the tailor. She'd flattered his abilities to form-fit a tuxedo and transform a country vet into a James Bond look-a-like, good enough to model for a wedding cake topper. That must have been the reason the man asked about their wedding date.

"Nick, are you listening?"

"Absolutely, *chèr*."

"Now there is one thing about flying—"

"Only one?"

"Well, there's probably more, but we'll start with this one. You *must* swear you won't do a stall. Cross-your-heart-and-hope-to-die kind of promise."

"I fly for the comfort of my passengers."

"Huh?"

"It's an important rule."

"Linc must have been absent from class the day

they taught that one. The last time he took me up, he did a stall. With no warning, I might add. That screaming, warning buzzer scared the living crap out of me! Later, my little brother explained how the plane was actually falling back to earth because of the pitch of the nose. Thank God he leveled it off."

Nick suppressed a grin. "That's awful. I guess brothers can be that way. But, you've been up with him since then?"

"Well, yes. I love flying. Except for the stalls. I promised to beat him if he ever did it again. A caning might do him some good."

"I promise, no stalls."

He liked her spunk. Her tenacity. Very different from his impressions of her cousin, Branna. He'd purposely never mentioned to her that he'd considered asking Branna out, back before she left Fleur de Lis. Damn good move on his part. Otherwise, Biloxi might not have given him the time of day. She was locked in some sort of competition with her look-a-like cousin. Still, he admired Branna's polite and demure ways. Attractive qualities. However, while Biloxi could pass for Branna's twin, the woman in front of him exuded fearlessness. A very sexy quality.

And, she smelled good, too.

When she'd passed out in his arms after the fall and Greta screamed because of the blood, his heart had beat so hard in his chest, it damn near killed him. Later when he snuck into the ER, she looked delicate and frail lying in that hospital bed. Since then, watching her settle in at Fleur de Lis and recover, she attacked life with gusto.

"Nick?"

"Hmm?"

"Am I boring you with my tales?"

"Not at all."

"Well, could you wipe that silly grin off your face and talk about you? I know about your grandparents, but what about your parents? Have any hateful siblings like mine?"

He grew quiet. He hadn't intended traveling down that path. Given his growing attraction for her, he didn't want anything to mar the connection.

"My parents. Well…"

"Yes?"

"They have their own lives. When their marriage broke up, I went to live with my grandparents." She didn't have to know that he hadn't seen or heard from his mother and father in years.

"I'm sorry to hear that," she said softly. "That must've been hard."

"It was what it was." Would his nonchalance satisfy her curiosity?

"Do you have brothers and sisters?"

"No. Only child here." He tensed at the subject of family.

"What I would give *sometimes* to be an only child. However, thank God I have Linc and Nola. Their imperfections distract my mother and that takes her focus off me."

Her gentle laugh surprised him. He relaxed a bit. "Your mother seemed nice."

"Ha," Biloxi laughed. "You saw her on her best behavior. My mother is very headstrong. She has this image of the world, and she tries to make it like she wants it…and everyone in it." She leaned close and winked. "If you ever repeat that, I swear I'll deny it."

Nick made the sign of the cross and held up three fingers in promise.

"We call her Hurricane Deidre for a reason. She's so focused, she doesn't see the wake of disaster behind her. She doesn't intend to be hurtful, but sometimes she's clueless."

"Be thankful for her. And your entire large, extended family." Someday, he wanted a large family of his own. That was something Biloxi could relate to. Most women he'd dated toed the two-child-only line. "And, I swear, I'll never repeat those words."

He appreciated her as a woman. A friend. The connection was heating up and not because of the wine. How would her family react if his feelings grew deeper? Would their relationship die before it had a real chance to begin?

"What words are you talking about?" She smiled innocently, then sipped wine.

Would she be surprised to know the other words rattling in his head? Words about her that made his heart trip down a path to a place he'd never ventured before.

After dinner, Nick drove Biloxi home.

"I trust by the way you cleaned your plate that you enjoyed dinner. I love it when a woman isn't afraid to show her appetite. Shall I turn down Loblolly Lane? Go around back?" He didn't wait for an answer, instead, he headed the truck down the long drive to the front drive of Fleur de Lis.

"Are you ever going to forgive me for my rudeness?"

"*Chèr*, I forgave you when Greta asked me to stay

for lunch."

"Imagine that. A man who loves Greta's food."

He'd bet money that she was blushing. Something in her voice clued him. After pulling the truck up near the front steps, he asked, "How about if I pick you up tomorrow morning at seven to go flying?"

"That early?"

He climbed out of the truck and walked around to open the door for her. "There's less wind earlier in the morning. Makes for better flying. It'll be great to see the sunrise. It should be right at the horizon when we take off." He walked her up the steps. Their breath created visible puffs in the cold night air.

While standing in front of the doors, he could see her eyes. He wished he'd invited her to his house for a drink and some music. He wasn't ready for the evening to end.

"Dinner was wonderful. Thank you, Nick. I had a great time. The Chateau is an interesting find." Biloxi held out her hand. She wanted a handshake?

Grasping her hand, he pulled her close. "Say 'yes, Nick,'" he whispered close to her ear.

"To flying?" she whispered back, her breath quickening.

"To flying. And this."

He cupped her face with his hands. His thumbs caressed the soft smoothness of her cheeks. He bent and touched his lips to hers. When she didn't resist, he deepened the kiss. Everything about her felt right. The form of her body molded to his. Her arms circled his waist. She kissed him back. She was warm and smooth and heaven in his arms.

A porch light flicked on. The door opened. Biloxi

pulled out of his reach.

"I don't mean to interrupt," Greta whispered. "Your great grandmother is asking for you." Greta closed the door. The porch light snapped off.

"Come here," he said.

Biloxi backed away. "I'm sorry. I've got to go. I'll meet you at the airport at seven."

She scooted inside, leaving him wanting more.

Chapter 15

Anticipation vibrated through Biloxi. While gazing out of the kitchen window, she tapped her foot waiting for Macy's arrival.

For a distraction, she allowed her thoughts to drift to Nick. Last night she'd lain awake, her mind chattering like a piano player pounding out boogie-woogie, Jerry Lee Lewis style. Every thought circled around to Nick and his kiss. She'd tried to shove the thoughts away and smother the unsettling feelings by focusing on business, but instead she'd dreamt of him. That flooded her with more top-spinning, out-of-control emotions. She couldn't risk infatuation over any man to interfere with her plans. She'd been down that path with Gregory.

A sliver of guilt ate at her. Early that morning, she'd called Nick and cancelled their flying date, explaining she'd had a rough night, not enough sleep. Nick had taken it in stride. A part of her was disappointed that she wouldn't see him, *and* another part was relieved. The man messed with her mental synapses. She hated being in that place of "and."

During the last hour, she'd practiced her speech. Nervous anticipation bloomed into genuine excitement. With one phone call, Aunt Macy had buoyed her spirits when she said she planned to visit. Finally, a door of opportunity opened. She would pitch the business plan to Fleur de Lis' Keeper. What Aunt Macy thought mattered.

As Biloxi continued her vigil at the window, Macy's car appeared in the rear drive. Moments later, Biloxi opened the door to the person who possibly held her future.

"I'm so happy to see you." She planted a peck on Macy's cheek and helped her off with her coat.

"How's the patient today?" Macy asked, then hugged her tight.

"Excited."

She had planned the setting for the meeting carefully, like she'd planned the agenda. She ushered Macy into the front parlor, which was filled with well-kept family antiques and photos, and hoped the setting would remind Macy of their deep family connection. After lowering into the wingback chair, she crossed her legs and tried to relax. Macy took a seat on the camelback couch.

Did she look the part of a successful business woman? Back when she thought she wanted to shoot fashion, she bought designer clothes at consignment stores. While she wasn't going for a "banker" look, she'd donned a conservative pearl gray pantsuit and light pink silk blouse. She even managed short heels, the same ones she wore on her date with Nick on Saturday night.

"You're looking well, which I'm happy to see. It's always nice when you can visit Fleur de Lis."

Biloxi didn't miss the "visit" part. She folded her hands in her lap. Her shoulders tensed.

"It's been about three weeks since the accident. I'm better each day. Thanks for driving up to see me. I know you have a busy schedule, what with the Valentine's Auction and Ball coming up."

"I'll always make time for you, darl'n," replied Macy. "You know that. Besides, I'm intrigued. You sounded excited about this surprise. I couldn't refuse your enthusiasm. And by the looks of things, you mean serious business."

Greta entered the room. She carried a tray of hot chocolate and fresh-from-the-fryer beignets. She set the tray on the antique side table. "Macy, I have that recipe you want. Don't leave without it."

"Thanks, Greta, Are you joining us?"

"Not right now. Biloxi will call when she's ready for me."

Macy reached for a linen napkin, placed it in her lap, then took a plate and plucked a beignet from the platter.

The sweets would start the meeting on a positive note. After all, beignets were Macy's favorite dessert. After another bite of pastry and a sip of hot chocolate, Macy looked toward the easel. Her curiosity prompted Biloxi to dive in.

"Aunt Macy. I hope you'll consider my proposal carefully." Biloxi sipped hot chocolate hoping for a last minute caffeine and sugar fortification. Would Macy hate the plan she'd devised? Or just hate that it included her taking over Branna's role? Would mother spurn daughter for niece?

This wouldn't be a case of blood being thicker than water…after all, they were all blood kin.

Technically, she and Macy were cousins. They were from branches of the Old Aunts family tree. Grace Dutrey was her great-grandmother. Whereas, Marie

Covington was Branna's great-grandmother. Macy ran the estate as the current Keeper, which gave her power over decisions that involved Fleur de Lis. Macy had groomed Branna to take up the Keeper's role. After all, it belonged to Branna because tradition made the rules. She hated that she'd been born only a few minutes late, especially since Branna showed no signs of wanting the job.

"Speaking of the Valentine's auction," Macy said, "I again want to thank *you* for donating your time and your talent to a worthy cause. Your reputation adds extra interest to the charity auction. Next year, let's do a showing of your photographs at the event."

"That's the perfect segue into one of the topics I want to discuss. My career. You've always been supportive of my talents." She took a slow deep breath. Would Macy take a risk? Ten years ago, Macy's endeavors to offset upkeep costs for Fleur de Lis led to opening the house for weddings, bridal and baby showers, and ladies' teas. The events brought in extra money, but now with costs climbing, family members still dipped into their pockets to meet taxes and cover upkeep expenses, costs that would continue to increase as the house aged.

The biggest hurdle to her plan—Aunt Macy—who had to stamp it with a seal of approval before a presentation to the family council. Branna remained the second major obstacle.

She handed a folder to Macy. "My photography contract will take me at least a year to complete."

"I see."

"I want to open my own photography studio at Fleur de Lis. I'll pay rent, and that will be income for the estate. But I want more. I want to grow the estate's revenues. I believe I can make the property self-sustaining in years to come."

Macy cocked her head, but remained silent.

Biloxi hoped she sounded confident, yet respectful. The last thing she wanted was to offend. If Macy flatly disagreed with the plan, there'd be no hope of getting the family to accept it. One of the long-entrenched traditions that needed excavating.

Biloxi's stomach churned. She pulled on the cloth covering the easel and revealed charts with graphs and digitally enhanced photos. A picture paints a thousand words and she wanted these to paint dollar signs with her name listed next to "Keeper."

"I have the specification for the remodel to create a space for Fleur de Lis Photography in the *garçonnière*. Carson and Linc would each still have bedrooms, but the living room would essentially be my studio. No more video games for them, except when I'm not working." She laughed, trying to lessen the tension and tried to read Macy, but the woman's inscrutable expression gave nothing away.

"The studio would be large enough to do group or family shots. One bedroom would be my office, another a dressing room. Again, leaving bedrooms for Carson and Linc. The guys are rarely here anymore." She threw that last part in for good measure. The garçonnière would remain bachelor quarters, just as tradition dictated, but with slightly less room.

"Hmm," Macy said.

She rushed onward. "I already do the photos for the Valentine's auction for free. I'd like to parley that into free publicity for my new studio. I think the Valentine's

Ball also needs a photo concession. Couples and families who attend have asked me to take their photos for the last two years. I've listened about how folks dress up, then wish for professional shots to remember the moment. For some wives, it's the only time their husbands wear a tux."

"My," said Macy. "You've really given this a lot of thought."

Excitement raced through her, but she remembered to slow her pace, this wasn't a New York gig.

"With my studio onsite at Fleur de Lis, I believe brides will hire me to do their wedding photography. I will offer packages for bridal and baby showers, too. Plus, we could expand the type of events we host—like plant shows for orchid and African violet lovers. Things like that, and in turn those events will create more photo opportunities for me."

While explaining her plan, the success of it seemed certain. The plan would work for her and for the estate. She could bring this vision to life.

But would Macy agree?

"I can see the photography studio working really well. But are you sure with all the success you've had, you want to resort to wedding photography?"

"I don't think I'll be limiting myself," Biloxi countered. "I expect other contracts to grow out of this. Weddings are just a place to start. Here's where the rest of my plan is so great. We could turn the sunroom into a café. In time, build a banquet facility rather than renting tents for weddings and such. We can fix up the old barn and the other structures, then offer educational tours."

"Whoa. Slow down, darlin'. And the cost of these

changes?"

Macy, always the businesswoman, ran her own nursery and supplied plants to her husband's hardware store. Plus she provided potted plants for weddings at Fleur de Lis. Surely Macy would understand how the plan would enhance the property's appeal and in turn, add revenue to help it pay for itself.

"I have a breakdown of the costs for the changes to create the studio," Biloxi explained. "My equipment costs are separate. I've calculated what I'll have left from my current contract and how much more equipment I can afford."

"Estimate? You've already had someone look at the space?"

"Well," Biloxi paused. Would Macy think she'd overstepped her bounds? "When I landed this photo contract for Tourism Inc., I knew it was a sign. I've had this dream to come home..." It sounded dramatic even to her ears, but that didn't change the truth. Besides, this wasn't the time for keeping secrets or telling lies. "I did have a construction company come out and give me a bid. Three different ones actually."

She worried when Macy didn't respond.

"Aunt Macy, I've always envied Branna for living here. This place is the one constant address in my entire life. Now, I have a choice, one that I didn't have growing up. I can live anywhere in the world I want. This is the *only* place I want to be."

She also wanted to point out that Branna moved out of state for a job and tossed the care of the estate back in Macy's lap.

Macy lowered her gaze and sighed.

Biloxi waited before launching the next wave of

her campaign to win a "yes" for her plan.

"I didn't realize you felt this way. I thought you planned to move back to New York. You'd mentioned that when your parents moved back to New Orleans. Weren't you dating someone from New York?"

The last thing she wanted was a discussion of Gregory.

"Biloxi, darl'n, you know everyone in the family is always welcome here. All of us think of this as our home. So, about your plan—"

"Greta," Biloxi called out. She handed Macy another plan she'd spent days working on. One with specs for the build-out and the proposed advertising costs for the café.

"Ready for me?" Greta asked, appearing in the doorway with a portfolio. When Greta placed the artwork on the easel, Macy's eyebrows went up. She grinned and rose from her seat, crossing the room to examine the colored sketches for Fleur de Lis Café. Biloxi handed her a sample copy of the menu Greta created.

"Well, all I can say is—" Macy paused. Her dimples showed. "—this is quite a surprise. I see your enthusiasm for this project. Greta could absolutely run the kitchen."

Biloxi crossed her fingers, held her breath, and waited. Where did Macy stand on the project? Would she give it her seal of approval? Would she give it a "yes" vote?

"But before you get too excited…" Macy's expression softened.

Fear fluttered in Biloxi's gut. She clenched her teeth.

"You've done an excellent job at putting this together. The photography studio will work fine. I vote yes for that." She paused. "But, I'm not sure if the rest of this is the best way to increase revenues at Fleur de Lis. However, let's sit down and discuss it with Branna. Let's get her opinion before we consider whether or not to take it to the council."

"But this is my plan, not Branna's," Biloxi blurted out. "I want to be the next Keeper." She covered her mouth with her hand. The words had left her lips before she could check her brain.

Macy frowned. "You know we don't go against tradition. You can help Branna, give her your ideas, but...there can be only one Keeper. You can help Branna with execution. *If* she agrees."

Her heart plummeted. Fell to her feet and through the floor, and dropped to the center of the earth. Branna would be her executioner. Why wouldn't Macy give her a chance? These were her ideas, not Branna's. She knew how to implement the plan. She'd built a career and started a business. Branna may have been groomed to be the next Keeper, however, she'd done nothing *but* run from the responsibility. Branna had no dreams for Fleur de Lis. To her, it was a noose around her neck. At this rate, Branna would hang the family along with herself.

Macy tilted her head. "I know it's early in the day, but we won't let the Old Aunts know. Let's open a bottle of champagne and drink to the new photography studio. You've won my vote on that! Let's celebrate!"

Biloxi barely managed a smile.

Chapter 16

Nick looked at his watch. His stomach grumbled. He looked forward to lunch. The thought of one of Greta's home-cooked meals made his mouth water. Since Chantel started working in the practice, carving out time for lunch was easier.

He tossed the note Peaches left on his desk into the trash. A phone number of someone's cousin who was visiting town held no interest for him. He would never have wished the accident on Biloxi, yet he couldn't deny certain benefits came from rescuing her that night. His dating life had improved.

But he still hadn't met Biloxi's grandmother Elise. He wanted to see the woman who had altered the course of his grandfather's life, and in turn, his own.

Greta had called and said the Old Aunts were at the senior center playing bridge and encouraged him to come to lunch. While pulling into a parking spot at the rear of the house, he spotted a van parked in his usual place. The sign on the van's door advertised *Lind Hardware* with a Biloxi, Mississippi, address. Someone from Branna's family up for a visit? Maybe Branna? It would be interesting to see the cousins side-by-side.

Nick trudged up the wooden stairs. Greta greeted him at the back door waving a bottle of champagne.

"Hey, handsome. Come on in. We're celebrating."

How much had she had to drink? It wasn't even

noon yet.

Greta opened the screened door and he followed her to the formal parlor where Biloxi sat rigid in a chair. The parlor resembled a boardroom with all the props. Another woman sat on the couch. He noticed the family resemblance immediately. Branna and Biloxi looked like her, only she was older.

"Nick!" Biloxi raised a glass of champagne. "Come meet my Aunt Macy. Branna's mother."

Nick swore her enthusiasm sounded forced. As he crossed the room, Macy stood and extended her hand, her other held a glass of champagne.

"Nice to meet you, Nick. I've heard about you."

"Nice to meet you, ma'am."

"Oh, don't scowl. It's all good. My son, Carson, and my nephew, Linc, love flying with you."

"Greta? A glass for Nick?" Biloxi asked.

"What are we drinking to?" he asked as Greta filled a champagne flute.

"To new beginnings," Biloxi said. She raised her glass. Everyone else followed. She clinked her crystal with the others, then drank down the remaining liquid in her glass. Setting the glass on the table, she looked up. Her eyes burned bright.

"Nick. Things are going my way."

Did she mean today, or when? Whichever, her enthusiasm seemed contrived. He raised his glass in salute, then took a sip. Champagne wasn't so bad, but Abita beer would really hit the spot.

"I'll get lunch." Greta headed toward the kitchen with her glass of champagne.

"Nick." Macy turned to face him. "Thank you for rescuing my niece. But, um, I hear you're chivalrous to a fault." Macy winked. Her gesture embarrassed him.

"How am I so chivalrous?" he finally asked when Macy didn't continue. He dropped into a wingback chair and waited for her response.

"Well, as I hear it, if you hadn't yanked on the door, Biloxi would have never fallen out of the car. Never would have gotten wet. Never fallen in the hole. But what she doesn't know is that the extra curve in the road is there because of your house. So you see, it was *all your fault.*"

Biloxi threw a startled looked at her aunt, then at him. She grew pale. She looked as colorless as when he'd carried her out of the hole.

"Aunt Macy!" She squeezed her eyes shut. A bright flush crept up her cheeks. Slowly, she turned and narrowed her eyes on him. "You said you lived down the road, not across the road."

Tick. Tock. Tick. The grandfather clock ticked off seconds of silence. He wasn't sure why it mattered exactly where he lived. He didn't understand her accusation.

"Lunch," Greta announced, charging into the room. When no one moved, she said, "In the dining room. Now. Please."

"Shrimp po'boys. Sweet potato fries. Fruit. Sweet tea," Biloxi rattled off the menu like nothing had just taken place.

Nick rose.

"Nick," Macy chuckled, linking arms with him. "Don't look so shocked. The painkillers were talking when she told me the story over the phone. I don't think she meant it." Macy cast a look over her shoulder. "Did you, Biloxi?"

Nick glanced back at Biloxi, but Macy tugged on his arm. What did the woman hope to gain by embarrassing her niece?

"Now, Nick," Macy said and patted his arm. "I've also heard a rumor that you're one of those *Trahans*."

****

Though murder swirled in her mind, Biloxi still noticed the care Greta took in preparing for the luncheon. The lace-covered dining room table looked like a page from *Southern Living* magazine. Shrimp po'boys waited on china plates with crisp sweet-potato fries. A bowl of fresh fruit and a crystal goblet filled with ice waited in front of each of six chairs. The aroma of baking bread pudding drifted in from the kitchen. She doubted that she could swallow a bite after Macy's devastating words, "We don't go against tradition."

Champagne and celebrating…when she wanted anything but. The moment Macy uttered Branna's name and invoked the "family tradition" rule, she had wanted to cry. Shout. Scream. Anything *but* drink a toast with a fake-happy face and appear satisfied while frustration seethed in her gut.

The photography studio was only a small part of those means to the end result she sought. There had to be a way to make Branna give up her job of Keeper. Otherwise, what reason would she have to stay? To watch the place continue to decline? That would kill her. Fleur de Lis deserved better. What more could she do to prove herself worthy of being the Keeper than by unburdening family members' bank accounts?

She had to convince Branna. Aunt Macy couldn't say "no" then. Besides, if Branna really wanted the job, why had she moved to Florida?

"Yes, you're absolutely one of those Trahans," Macy repeated.

"I'm not sure what you mean by *those Trahans*," Nick said, pulling out a chair for Macy at the dining room table. He appeared unconcerned about the accusation. Macy, on the other hand, appeared to have left her good manners outside the door standing next to G.G. Graces'.

"You *know* the story of Grandma Elise and Nick's grandfather," Biloxi scolded, hoping Macy would take the hint and drop the subject.

Were the Old Aunts joining them? Why hadn't Greta warned her? From the dining room window, she noticed a car pulled alongside the elevator entrance to the house. The Old Aunts got out.

After a few minutes, they ambled into the dining room. Grace scowled. She and Marie took their seats. Marie sat at the head of the table with Grace and Greta on her right and Macy and Nick across from them. Biloxi sat next to Greta.

"Young man," said Grace. "Clearly, my great-granddaughter is healing nicely. As a doctor, how do you have time to make frequent house calls? I thought with HMOs and PPOs that doctors were tied to their office. They schedule patients every fifteen minutes. Herd them in and out like cattle."

Macy chuckled. "He's not *that* type of cattle doctor."

"Pardon?"

"Nick's not that type of doctor—" Biloxi started to explain.

"Well, he must be the type of doctor that says grace before a meal," Marie insisted. "We don't often entertain a man at lunch. Please begin."

"Nick, you don't have to," Biloxi whispered. Could her family be any more embarrassing?

Nick bowed his head and offered a prayer. His rich voice carried with confidence. A group of women didn't bother him. When Biloxi looked up, she could tell the Old Aunts were suitably impressed.

"Well, I'm waiting." Grace said, placing her napkin on her lap.

"He's an animal doctor." Macy laughed.

"But, I thought he was Branna's physician." Grace reached with her fork for some sliced melon.

Greta and Macy stopped laughing mid-chuckle when Grace frowned at them.

"Great Grandmother Grace, Nick is a veterinarian," Biloxi explained.

"Oh."

"Did you intend to deceive two old women?" Marie asked frowning.

Confusion shadowed Nick's face. "Deceive?"

"Yes," Marie continued. "You arrived when Biloxi returned home from the hospital. You've been here most days for lunch. We assumed you were her physician, which is why—"

"—why we overlooked the fact that you are a Trahan and allowed you in the house," Grace finished.

Biloxi's shoulders hunched. If ever she wished to play possum, this was it. She could crawl under the table and play dead.

"That is enough," Greta snapped, standing up she slapped the table hard enough to make the silverware dance and the ice slosh in the crystal goblets. "There are far more important things in life than old worn-out news. Miss Grace, I'm sorry that Nick's grandfather called your son out for a duel, but it never took place. Elise married your Robert. Robert and Elise had a happy life together. Raised a son! Robert's gone two years now. Let it all rest in peace with him." Greta stormed away, leaving all of them stunned.

Marie sipped her tea, then plunked the glass on the table. "Well, I'll speak to Greta later. That was an uncomfortable display. We intended no insult, Dr. Trahan. In my day, when a young man visited a young lady every day, it was called wooing, but that was 1920. In the vernacular of the younger generation, you call it dating. Or as my youngest great-grandchild would say, *'hangin'.'"*

Grace nodded. "Can you understand how we misunderstood and took you for a people-doctor, not an animal one? After all, Biloxi is not a heifer. However, that does not excuse you, Biloxi, for ignoring my wishes."

Biloxi nodded. "Yes, Great-Grandmother. Please pass the salt." *Or just kill me know.*

"We would not turn Dr. Trahan away if he were treating you. However, since he is not a physician, I hope you will regain your manners and honor my request."

"Yes, ma'am," she mumbled. Embarrassment rose like a rocket, and heat exploded into her cheeks. She could only blame herself. Any discomfort on Nick's part rested totally at her feet. How could she make it up to him?

She snuck a glance at him. He smiled back. The man had the nerve to be amused?

Lunch continued with polite conversation about the

weather and other benign topics. After lunch, she changed out of her suit into jeans and a sweater, then met Nick at the far end of the gallery, away from the kitchen door.

"That was…interesting," he said.

"I'm sorry about all of that." She grimaced and slumped into a rocking chair. "Remember, I told you it was a good thing that Greta likes you? The scene at lunch was proof enough. She puts the Old Aunts in their place better than anyone in the family."

Nick chuckled. "I have to admit, before now, I would've had a hard time imagining silence at lunch with five women at the table."

She crossed one knee over the other and pulled Nick's old blanket over her lap. "I don't get it. The whole thing was so long ago. How much did you know about the duel? We didn't talk about it when I was growing up. My grandmother pretended it never happened. She just smiled and got this far-away look in her eyes. My mother refers to it as *the scandal* when someone brings up old family history."

Nick leaned back, locked his fingers behind his head, and stretched his legs long. "As I hear it, Grandpère was quite taken with a woman. She, however, was Irish. Not Cajun. In the 1940's folks didn't mix much." He smiled. "It's an old tale. Two men in love with the same woman."

He made it sound as though it had happened to him. Was Chantel part of an old triangle? Had he been in love with her? "Never a happy ending."

She rocked and looked out over the formal back garden while waiting for Nick to offer more history. The hole where she'd fallen was a faint memory now.

142

The old tree had been there all of her life. She'd carved her initials in it. Now a younger version stood in its place. All part of the cycle of life at Fleur de Lis.

"Did you know my Grandmother Elise's side of the family owned a place down on River Road? The Yankees spared it during the Civil War. My however-many great-grandfather claimed neutrality during the war, since he was Irish, not American. Not a slave owner. The Yankees left his property alone. Smooth move on his part, but the old Southern guard didn't approve of him, a sea captain who'd won a mansion in a card game. He wasn't a planter schooled in the social graces of the time, but he became very rich after the war."

"What do you think? Were they fighting for love or money?" Nick asked.

"Our grandfathers? Some say my grandfather pursued my grandmother because she had connections and he had political aspirations. But that's not true. He never went into politics. I think he accepted the challenge of the duel to discover if my grandmother really loved him. He was a romantic. He wouldn't marry a woman who didn't truly love him. It wasn't about her money. How did all of it affect him? Claude Trahan, your grandfather."

Nick stopped rocking. A pause turned into a long silence. His face remained impassive, but his eyes betrayed a deep sadness. That sadness touched her as physically as if he'd placed a finger on her heart then pricked the spot with a pin.

"She broke his heart."

"Oh," Biloxi frowned. "I'm sorry."

"Why? You didn't do anything." Nick cocked his

head to the side. His stare bore into her soul.

"What?" she demanded and squirmed in her seat.

"Is that what the women of Fleur de Lis do?"

"What?"

"Break men's hearts?"

"Huh?"

"You promised to go flying with me, then cancelled at the last minute."

"I'm sorry. Work carried me away. I made final touches on the presentation for Aunt Macy. It took longer than I expected. I do want to go, I need to go, but this work had to come first. Besides, it's more efficient if all the shots are planned in advance."

"I thought aerial shots were work. However, congratulations. Your efforts must have paid off."

"You don't understand," Biloxi protested. "It's more complicated than that."

"But we drank a toast to the opening of your new studio. Isn't that what you wanted?"

"That, Dr. Trahan, is only the tip of the iceberg."

She wasn't going to explain it to him. He probably wouldn't understand. He received all the attention in his family. An only child, he never had to compete with an outdated pecking order. This was her problem to handle, and now she needed another plan.

It would be too simple to demand that Branna relinquish her role. But how could she persuade her cousin?

She sighed and shrugged. "But speaking of the studio, I want to photograph you. Will you sit for me?"

"*Chèr*, I take care of dogs. I don't take commands. Who are you asking to sit?"

"Very funny."

"That's right. It's funny. But don't smile. Whatever you do, don't crack a grin. I mean it. No smiling. Stop it."

Who knew Nick, with the handsome face and smiling dimples, had such a quirky sense of humor? His teasing made smiling irresistible.

"Well, my work here is done," he sighed, looking away. "I mend animals and cheer up the sick. Maybe that will be my epitaph." He leaned toward her. "So how about another date?"

Chapter 17

Nick drove back to his clinic. He'd left Biloxi smiling rather than down in the mouth, which made him happy.

Who would've thought attraction would pull him to the granddaughter of his grandfather's unrequited love? The irony of the connections struck him. Yet old history didn't matter to him. He and Biloxi were friends—and if he had his way, soon would be more. Greta had taken a special shine to him. And unless he was wrong, he was growing on the Old Aunts.

Maybe.

"I'm home!" he called, walking through the back door of the clinic.

"In here," Peaches said.

He wandered into the kitchen. Chantel and Peaches sat at a table in the small kitchen, where Peaches cradled a tiny dog in her arms. She stroked the little thing and cooed to it like a mother with a newborn baby.

"Isn't that Mrs. LeJeune's Yorkie, Anisette?

"My, Doctor, aren't you smart. It's one and the same." Peaches made a clucking sound and the dog licked her chin.

"Mrs. LeJeune died today," Chantel explained. "The EMS didn't know what to do with this little girl. They dropped her here rather than take her to the animal shelter. It seems you have quite a reputation of finding good homes for pets."

"I'm sorry to hear about Mrs. LeJeune. They've contacted her son?"

"Yes," Peaches explained, "But he doesn't want the dog. I think he's jealous of this little thing."

"Do you know someone who might want it?" Chantel asked.

He thought for a moment. "Maybe Biloxi."

"And she would be?" Chantel's tone sounded suspicious.

"A friend of mine."

"That's not what *I* heard." Peaches' singsong voice suggested she'd been listening to local gossip.

He narrowed his eyes and threatened with a glare. She knew how he felt about gossip. He'd been the big topic when he built his house and a clinic. He didn't want that dubious distinction again.

"Well, I'll take Anisette with me until you decide if she's a present for Ms. Dutrey or not." Peaches rose from her chair and scooted around him with the dog cradled in her arms. He didn't miss her amused chuckle when she slipped out the door behind him.

"Someone named Captain Jack called and wants you to come out," Chantel said, flipping absently through a dog magazine. "He said, Sugar's doing well. He wants you to look at the puppies again, to make sure you don't want one of them. If you go after work, I'd like to go."

Chantel lifted her gaze to him. "Maybe we could have dinner afterwards? Like old times." She rose from her chair and came toward him. Rather than passing, she stopped when they were shoulder to shoulder. She searched his face, as though looking for something. "It could be like old times, Nicky."

He shook his head. "No. We work together, that's it. You're a great vet, Chantel. But that's all that's between us. I'm not your transition guy."

She stared at him, stone-faced. "So this Biloxi. Are you sure you're just friends?"

"For now. You saw her. I had dinner with her at the Chateau."

She closed her eyes, as if searching her mind for the memory. Imaginary wheels turned in her head. However, she shrugged, like she didn't remember.

It was a risky move to bring Chantel into his practice, but after her last trust-fund-rich playboy dumped her, she had begged to work with him. She needed a change of scenery from Baton Rouge, and she needed a job.

She worked hard and played hard. Her male playmates had never prevented her from performing her veterinarian duties.

Grandpère had asked him, as a favor, to take her on as an associate in the clinic. While Nick respected her skill—she was good with animals and could charm their owners—he hesitated having her around all the time. He agreed to the deal for his grandfather's sake, but wondered if he'd end up regretting the decision.

"Well, Nicky." Chantel's silky voice washed over him. He expected a cutting remark to follow and waited for her to speak.

"All I can say," she said slowly, "is that you haven't changed that much since college. Just like with Sugar and Anisette, you've got more than one bitch wanting your attention." Then, she stepped into the hall, out of reach of his grasp.

He hated trashy talk from a woman. And, he knew far more about Chantel's ways than he wanted. It excited her when men talked dirty to her in bed, like a sailor on shore leave paying for his first prostitute. But, their friendship went back to childhood. He'd learned that she used her foul mouth as a defensive attack whenever she didn't get her way. Like shock therapy. It turned some men on. It had the complete opposite effect on him.

"*Mais*, good to know some things remain the same," he muttered and raked his fingers through his hair. If Chantel remained on the defensive, she'd keep her distance from him. That's exactly where he wanted her.

"Doc?" Peaches called down the hall. "Captain Jack is expectin' you around six p.m. Mrs. Babin will be here in a minute with Coco. The afternoon is booked. And remember—tomorrow is surgery day. Take a look at the schedule."

He heard Anisette's little bark and thought about Biloxi. Would a new dog make her feel more at home? Maybe cheer her up. He wondered what part of her plan—she was the most organized woman he'd ever met—Macy hadn't agreed to. Best if he consulted with Greta before presenting Anisette to Biloxi. "Let me know when Mrs. Babin is here. I'll be in my office making a call."

He entered the small space and settled into a chair, then planted his feet up on the desk. His work boots needed polishing. He'd put that on the list. Damn. Biloxi and her organization had him making lists.

He picked up the phone and punched in the

number, but before anyone at Fleur de Lis answered, he disconnected the call when Chantel carried Anisette into his office. His private business was none of her concern.

"I want her, Nicky."

"You want who?"

"I want Anisette. I'm living alone. A dog would be good company for me. I could bring her to work. It might help the folks of Bayou Petite trust me, like they trust you, if they see me taking care of Mrs. LeJeune's beloved dog."

"Using a dog as a marketing tool? Not the best idea."

Tears welled in Chantel's eyes. The emotion surprised him.

"Nicky, this little girl needs a home. We're perfect for each other." Tears rolled down her cheeks. "She's so cute and cuddly. I can't help but love her. And she'll give me unconditional love. I need that right now."

Hell. Now what to do? Her tears were real enough, but he knew she could turn them off and on. Usually they were aimed at a man, not a dog. Something told him he'd regret saying "yes," but he couldn't think of a good reason to say "no."

"If you're sure?"

Her eyes lit up. She beamed. "Oh, Nicky! I love you. Thank you! I knew you wouldn't let me down."

Before he knew it, she planted her lips on his, ran her tongue over them and sucked on his bottom lip.

"Ahem. Dr. Trahan? Coco is here."

Peaches stood in the office doorway with one fist on her cocked hip. "I'll put her in exam room one while you finish your...exam of Dr. Gilbeau." She turned and slammed the door.

Chantel batted her lashes while clutching the little dog, then left the room.

He raked his fingers through his hair and sighed. Chantel was up to her old tricks.

Chapter 18

Only weeks since the accident and her injuries had healed. Time had raced like a tornado on land, bringing change Biloxi never planned.

"It's already February fifth." She sighed and examined her reflection in the mirror. With all eyes on her in the bidder's circle, could she pull off the dress? Was it both glamorous and respectable? She'd never bid at the auction before. Being in the spotlight brought unwanted attention, but in order to give her business a boost of exposure, she had to come from behind the camera and stand front and center.

She reached for *Attraction*, her favorite perfume, and spritzed it around her neck. She turned for a better look in the mirror. The soft silk of her dress rustled. It reminded her of stories about grand, old Southern balls. She used to daydream in front of Grandma Elise's mirror about being a belle in a hooped skirt and attending a fancy party. Then, her grandmother surprised her with a mirror of her own on her thirteenth birthday.

The mirror hadn't made all the moves the military had required of her father. Instead, it stayed in her bedroom at Fleur de Lis. Each time she came home and looked in the mirror, she dreamed of living a fairytale. Fleur de Lis was to her what Tara was to Scarlett O'Hara. This time around, she might stand a chance of making that dream come true.

When she turned to see all of the dress, gratitude flooded her heart. It fit as if it had been stitched to her body with tucks and seams in the perfect places. She had resisted such a daring dress, especially one made of raw silk, but Greta had taken matters into her own hands. While they'd picked out a pattern together, Greta chose the fabric. That woman possessed magical skills with a sewing machine. She added special touches— garnets and tiny crystals adorned the bodice in an intricate hand-stitched pattern. When light caught the jewels, they twinkled like tiny stars. Greta had created an elegant, one-of-a-kind couture gown.

She never imagined she could look so good. She had agonized over whether or not the dress would suit her curvy body. It looked good on paper and on a mannequin, but she worried that on her it wouldn't look red-carpet amazing. After all, she could never be construed as statuesque.

It was the type of gown she had photographed on models when apprenticing with José in New York, but not the kind of gown she'd ever owned. She barely recognized the alluring reflection in the mirror.

Maybe the cheval mirror was somehow magical?

Her body had never before appeared flawless in a dress. She adored Greta for that. The dress meant even more because Greta sewed it with love.

What would Nick think? She couldn't wait to see his face. Turnabout would be fair play. She'd seen how handsome he looked in his tux. Would he be equally impressed with her?

Picturing him in his navy blue suit, then in the tux, made her breath catch in the back of her throat. Her heart fluttered and her palms perspired. And his kisses scared her as much as they excited her.

She adjusted the wrist corsage of miniature white roses. Feeling generous, she'd ordered one for all of the Fleur de Lis women, and at the last minute, ordered a boutonniere for Nick. Since they were only friends and she didn't want him to feel uncomfortable, she decided to order several more. Nick would match her brother, cousin, father, and uncles. He'd be one of them.

A boutonniere was the perfect accessory for a country vet dressed like a wedding-cake topper. Probably every woman at the auction tonight would agree. Nick would get the significance, their shared joke between friends.

Flora's Florist had delivered the order before lunch and she'd planned to give it to him then. However, he hadn't joined them today. He'd called and said he couldn't intrude on family time. She resisted his reasoning, but he refused to budge. Maybe he wanted to avoid a full-scale Dutrey inquisition.

Thoughts of him sent shivers rippling through her. She tried to ignore them and stared critically at her reflection. Maybe the red dress was too much? The front deep V trimmed in a flounce of soft white silk gave more of an illusion of cleavage than it actually showed. Self-consciousness bubbled up only to descend as insecurities into the pit of her gut.

If she looked good, she might attract attention during the bidding, and in turn, draw attention to her new business. At least that was the plan. All eyes would be focused on the bidders, especially if there was a bidding frenzy. She expected it when Nick took the stage, madness was sure to happen. After all, he remained one of the most eligible bachelors in the entire county. Since he was new to town, he hadn't yet learned all the idiosyncrasies of all the single women, most of whom she'd known since grade school.

Another truth pained her like an achy loose tooth. The irritation centered on Chantel or *Her Haughty Highness* as she had taken to calling her. If that woman got to Nick, that would end her connection with him. No more lunchtime visits. Their flying days would definitely be over before they really began. She would not underestimate that woman. Chantel was the type to charm men out of their pants and relieve them of their money. She was exactly the kind of woman who thought men and women couldn't be friends.

She frowned. A woman like Chantel didn't keep a circle of female friends. Women like her gave all women a bad name.

A knock on the bedroom door brought her thoughts back. "Come in."

"Do you need any help? I'm headed downstairs to herd turtles." Macy stepped into the room and stared. "You look lovely, darl'n." Her eyes shone with genuine appreciation.

While they stood side by side and gazed into the mirror, she bet Macy didn't see her as a woman with strength, fortitude, and unwavering determination. One who believed triumph came through perseverance. Something she'd read in a Jodi Thomas novel and it resonated with her.

Macy didn't understand how methodically she'd researched and planned all the ways to make Fleur de Lis a financial success. She wouldn't fault Macy for holding onto family traditions. Besides, Macy hadn't purposely opposed the plan. And other than this one disagreement, Macy had always seen the very best in her and treated her with kindness. She had to find a way to sway Macy's way of thinking. But how?

"Would you do the hook at the top in the back?" Biloxi asked.

"The ruffle adds softness to the dress," Macy said while attending to the hook. "The whole effect is very sexy. Is the effect aimed at a particular man?"

"No." If ever she wished for a switch to turn off her blush, this was the time.

"Greta—our Renaissance woman—cooks, sews, gardens, and runs this house. Have you seen her dress?"

"Yes. Greta's too frugal to waste leftover fabric. I'm glad she's joining us tonight. And her new haircut makes her look younger."

Macy leaned in close and whispered, "Is Greta seeing someone?"

"Huh?"

"Don't look so shocked. She's been dedicated to this family since you and Branna were born. She helped your mother and me when we came here from the hospital. She cares for the Old Aunts, but sadly, someday they'll be gone. Greta has lived in this house longer than any of the rest of us. Maybe she's finally going to embrace a life of her own?"

"I'll be here to keep her company."

"What?"

"I'm staying. Greta can live with me. That's what makes the café such a perfect idea. It will make Greta feel useful and bring in revenue."

Macy sighed. "I didn't say it wasn't a good idea. I just want you and Branna to be on the same page. It'll be her decision since she'll run Fleur de Lis after me."

"But—"

"Darl'n, you look so nice in that dress. It enhances your figure. You often hide your cute shape. I never realized how much before."

"Thank you," Biloxi replied. It wouldn't pay to argue with Macy right now. It wasn't her style to engage in direct confrontation.

A knock sounded at the half-open door. She fought to keep from rolling her eyes when her mother stepped into the room in an expensive designer gown. Nola, her younger sister, followed. Her cousins Elvie and Melody followed her sister. They exchanged simultaneous "oohhs" over each other's dresses.

"Ladies, you look amazing," Biloxi announced. Each of them kissed the air beside her cheek, then admired themselves in her mirror.

"Okay. Okay!" she laughed. "Now, everyone scoot. Let me finish dressing. I'll be down in a jiff." She shooed the younger girls out.

"Do you need help, sugar?" her mother asked. She stood behind her and eyed their reflections in the mirror. Her mother offered no comment or compliment. She didn't expect any special praise. That was Aunt Macy's department.

"I heard you're getting along well," her mother said, matter-of-factly.

"Yes, Mother."

"Well, Greta was a dear to help you with your hair. You can't tell anything in the back was shaved."

Suddenly, Branna glided through the open door. "Hi!" She waved. Biloxi tensed as her cousin wrapped her in a hug. "Did ya'll decide to have a party and not invite me?"

"No," Biloxi replied coolly. "I sent you an invitation. Mental telepathy."

Branna smiled. "I came to help you dress. But looks like you've got lots of help. Are you taking advantage of this whole invalid thing?" She winked.

Their reflections in the mirror caught Biloxi's eye. The two of them looked like a pair of matching dolls, though they were very different. Branna possessed a quiet feminine grace that she'd always wanted. Growing up, always second to Branna, made her feel unattractive. She had accepted that fact along with the rest of her ordained life. But not tonight.

"Me? An invalid? Whatever gave you that idea?" She patted her hair in the back and swayed her hips from side to side. In the mirror, she watched her cascading curls bounce. Mae West had nothing on her…except that she was blonde…and sexy…and knew how to work it.

"Biloxi, are you sure you don't need help?" her mother asked again, concern hanging in her voice.

"I've got it covered, Aunt Deidre," Branna insisted. "Everyone else needs to head downstairs. Uncle Sean has the bus out front ready to go." Branna shooed their mothers out the door. As they departed, whoops and cheers drifted up from downstairs. Something good must have happened on TV. The men of the family had gathered in the library to watch basketball on the large screen and root for their team.

Biloxi turned to her cousin. "Branna, I'm glad we have a minute alone. There's something important I need to discuss with you, before you head out tomorrow. Tomorrow morning before church—we talk.

But right now I have to ask. Does James knowingly let you out of the house like that?"

Branna's long, clingy dress revealed more of her cousin than she'd ever seen. It transformed a usually modest cousin into an elegant femme fatale.

"Like what?" Branna batted her lashes.

"I've never seen you...I mean...My goodness. A backless black mermaid dress. Very daring."

Branna blushed deeply.

"Not conservative at all. Love does strange things to me...I feel absolutely beautiful when I look into James' eyes. I love that man beyond reason. When I see his love reflected back at me, it's...more than wonderful."

"I told you so. Love would take you over the top. How serious are the two of you about marriage?" She fastened a ruby teardrop earring and tried to contain her envy. Branna deserved happiness. Her last relationship had ended on a sour note, too. And afterward, Branna abandoned responsibility and Fleur de Lis, whereas, she'd run home for comfort.

"Speaking of love..." Branna glided to the bedroom door, then stepped into the hall and called, "She's ready."

A feather could have knocked Biloxi over when Nick entered the room. He looked more delectable than Godiva dark chocolate. Better than he had at the tailor shop. A red bowtie, the color of her dress, popped against his starched white shirt. Unable to form words, she stared. Butterflies flitted in her stomach. Their loop-de-loops made her dizzy. Speechless, she took in the full length of the man, then stifled a chuckle when black western boots peeked out under the hem of his pants.

"What, no Stetson?" she teased.

A lock of dark hair fell over Nick's forehead. His haircut was recent. She missed the shaggy way it had curled over his ears. This Nick looked like an Armani model.

Nick's eyes never left her. "Beau-ti-ful," he murmured.

Could he truly be impressed? He'd seen her in any number of things, including in a hospital gown, but never like this. She fluttered her lashes and a blush creep up all the way from her chest. Nick continued to stare, his eyes reflected wonder and awe. Did he really see her as beautiful?

"Thank you." She tried for a smooth tone hoping her voice wouldn't break.

"Given the way you and Branna are dressed, I'm guessing *this* event is not family-friendly." His eyes never left hers, as if he was memorizing each fleck of green in them. The self-consciousness she had pushed aside rolled back again.

"No, it's not. The Valentine Ball is the family thing. The auction is a formal, adult-only black-tie affair."

"Ah, Nick?" Branna interrupted. "We need to go. Uncle Sean has gone ahead with the others. We're the last to leave."

No voices. No television. Quiet surrounded them. How had Branna managed that?

Nick surprised her when he offered his arm, and then motioned for Branna to lead.

Biloxi placed her arm through his. He made her knees weak. At the top of the stairs, Nick paused. He surprised her by leaning down, then scooping her up. She would have worried about her dress, but her knees quivered as they draped over his arm. He hugged her close.

"I always wanted to do this. A Rhett Butler kind of thing, don't you think?" His grin was mischievous. He carried her down the stairs. He eyed her as though she were his favorite dessert. She'd seen that look before—when Greta fed him German chocolate cake.

A nervous giggle escaped, though her stomach quaked. Nick was too close. Everything moved too fast. Feelings rushed through her, feelings she wanted to ignore.

She and Nick were only friends.

"I can't remember when I've been carried so much," she laughed. "Must have been before I learned to walk. I *can* walk you know."

"I recall seeing evidence of that fact."

She searched for a new subject to cover her uncomfortableness. Something safe to minimize her rising anxiety.

"What type of date are you auctioning? Where will you go? How long will this date last? I think Mark Landry holds the record for an eighteen-hour date. They went gambling on a Gulf cruise. Are you going to let me in on the secret?"

"No."

His quiet reply silenced her. They had reached the open front door where Branna was already making her way down the front steps to a waiting sedan.

"No? No, what?"

In the shadow of the doorway, Nick stopped. He held her effortlessly. Anticipation had her searching his face for answers. As usual, his expression gave away nothing.

"I'm not going to tell you. You'll have to wait like everyone else."

His topaz eyes and his soothing voice hypnotized, but his quiet admonishment embarrassed her. She lowered her chin, but raised her eyes for a peek at him. Her blush heated up.

She wasn't in the market for a significant other. She needed him as a friend. Friendship lasted longer. She liked Nick too much to lose him over any frivolous infatuation.

But if he asked, right then and there, she would follow him to bed.

"*Chèr*," he whispered. "Look at me."

A shiver raced through her. She did as he asked.

"About my auction date…should it include a kiss?" Nick slid the tip of his tongue over her bottom lip, then his lips gave a little tug.

Her breath caught. She crinkled her eyes shut. When she opened them, his peered into hers. She watched his mouth curl into a grin. His dimples were back.

"You, sir—though I doubt I should call you that—are incorrigible." She motioned toward the table. "Over there is a present for your lapel. If I told you I had ordered it special for you, you probably couldn't get your ego through the door."

Was her brain trying to run interference for her heart, or had Nick already stolen it?

****

Nick waited while the car pulled away from the house with Biloxi, Branna, and James. He wanted to hop in his truck, tear up the front lawn, chase down the car, make it stop, and bring her back with him. He'd always heard that when people had near-death experiences, their whole lives flashed before them. Falling in love had the same effect on him.

When he ran his tongue over her lips, the light touch barely made contact. In his mind's eye, he recalled every moment he'd spent with her. Like a movie, all of the scenes linked together. When it came to the end, he wanted the movie to go on forever. Life would her could satisfy his every desire for the future.

Adrenaline pumped through his body, hammering through his veins double time. He could have sprinted the half-mile without breaking a sweat, then stopped the car before it reached the main road. Stopped it from taking her away. How had he ever confused Biloxi with Branna? Biloxi's hazel eyes fired with green when she was excited. Vulnerability brought out warm brown. The curves of her body made him crave touching her all over. He wanted to carry her off to bed.

Doubt poked through his bubble of happiness as he climbed into his truck and traced a cold finger down his spine.

How would her family react to Biloxi marrying a Trahan?

Chapter 19

Biloxi surveyed the banquet hall. Macy's decorating had transformed the room. A line of potted palms created walls within the cavernous space. Spotlights, positioned between each plant, shone upward through the fronds and cast lacy shadows. Pink and red satin hearts, the size of melons, dangled beneath a mass of white helium-filled balloons covering the ceiling. A red carpet on the raised stage created a runway down the middle of the room, while rows of chairs lined each side.

She headed in the direction of her makeshift studio. In the hallway outside the banquet room, a large sign on an easel pointed folks to the alcove where her makeshift studio waited. Each bachelor and winning bidder, along with a "blown-up" bank check showing the amount donated to charity, would have their picture taken. A few of the photographs would make their way into the local newspaper, some on the internet; the rest would be placed in Macy's growing scrapbook that recorded each Valentine Auction.

Macy had recruited her again to take pictures. She always did the job for free to support the charity. This year, she was excited to display a sign advertising her new photography studio.

Nola had whined at dinner and demanded to help at the auction, but she had a few years to grow before she could attend the adult-only affair. Twenty-one and older were allowed. Thankfully, Linc had flown home that morning and acted as her assistant. They'd set up the booth in her usual organized fashion. He understood how she managed things after helping her last year. Technically, he could handle the whole thing himself. These types of photographs required a technician, not an artistic touch.

The backdrop she chose had a setting sun blazing through a forest of loblolly pines. It resembled the landscape around Bayou Petite. She perched the tripod in the perfect spot, then together they adjusted the lighting and took a few sample digital shots of Linc, her reluctant subject. Everything had checked out fine.

"What are you doing here? Biloxi, go," Linc urged. "I can handle this."

"You just want an excuse to hide."

"After my disaster date last year, do you blame me? Lucianne thought the plane ride was the same thing as a marriage proposal. Never again will I volunteer to walk that red carpet. And since school and flying burn up all my money, I consider *this* my contribution to the cause. Now, go."

She grinned. "You're the best brother." She started to say she loved him, but knew he'd just shrug it off. Rather than embarrass him, she blew a kiss, then went in search of a program that listed the order of tonight's auction.

Pin pricks of excitement made her shiver. She was anxious to read the lineup and fine print about the date each bachelor offered. Of course, in truth, the only one she really wanted to know about was Nick's.

She walked through the door to the main hall and

spotted her cousin handing out programs.

"Here," said Branna. "In case you're wondering, Nick's near the end. Number twelve. I promised to help Mama backstage. Would you keep James company?" She turned and left them standing alone.

"James, is she always this bossy?" she asked in the wake of Branna's departure.

James shrugged. "You tell me. You've known her far longer than I." His grin spread wide as he led her to their seats. The man was truly in love with her cousin.

She could see how falling in love had changed Branna. Always the "goody-goody," once demure as a lily waiting to bloom, now Branna carried herself with new confidence. Biloxi hated the envy that bubbled up whenever she looked at her.

Surrounded by everything that screamed *LOVE* at the Valentine's auction, jealousy whacked her good.

She wanted giddy romance, too. But not just yet.

Soon.

After her business showed a profit. After she convinced the family to open the café. After the banquet facility added income. Then, she would earnestly look for a man who understood grits with eggs, the blues, and Southern traditions. Most of all, someone who shared her dream of never leaving Bayou Petite. For now, she needed a friend. And Nick fit the bill nicely.

When Macy stepped to the microphone, a hush fell over the room. "Thank you for coming tonight. I hope you brought deep pockets and generous hearts."

Biloxi chuckled and looked up at all the dangling satin hearts.

"Here's the list of the bachelors' dates."

Macy's overview included names like Jungle Cruise, Cooking Delights, and Tasting Tour. Dates not just for women anymore, these included charter fishing trips and hunting trips designed for families. She laughed when she noticed Captain Jack had donated a trained bird dog, one of Sugar's offspring, and offered quail-hunting services to be led by Sugar—Mademoiselle Sweet Tea.

She scanned the program list for number twelve.

Dr. Nicholas Trahan offers a Flyaway Lunch.

That morning, after a careful examination of her tight budget, she had calculated what she could afford to spend. She glanced around the room, surveying the potential competition. As usual, Macy attracted bidders from New Orleans and Baton Rouge to ensure a successful night. She had the Midas touch, but only when it came to fundraising.

Biloxi recognized someone from Mobile who would make the competition interesting. She let out a sigh after scanning the room and not finding Chantel. Everything would be okay.

"This is Charles Lind," Macy said. "Husband, and already taken"—she paused over the laughter and applause—"he's our auctioneer."

Biloxi turned to James. "Uncle Charles will make everyone hoot and howl. His deadpan humor does it every year," she whispered.

"This should be interesting," James said.

"Will you save my seat? I'll be back later." She rose and headed for the hallway. Now that she knew the order and when Nick's date would be auctioned, she'd send Linc to watch the show. She would manage the booth, and hopefully draw interest for her new business until Nick came up on the roster.

As she exited the banquet room, she heard Macy say, "Our first bachelor."

She could make it to her booth in plenty of time for the first round of photographs.

"Go enjoy the show," she told Linc, who wandered away after she shooed him.

A few minutes later, the first bachelor and bidder arrived. Biloxi arranged their stance in front of the backdrop.

"Smile!" she said. "Fifteen hundred for a fishing trip. That's a whole lot of fish."

She snapped several shots, then waved, signaling that she'd finished. She mentally earmarked the photo for local newspapers hoping it would encourage more men to attend the auction next year. Maybe Macy needed to change the focus away from bachelor dates.

"Can I get a copy of that?" asked the winning bidder. "Want it for my trophy book."

She handed him her new business card. "Sure, sign the information sheet over there. You will receive one free photo for being the winner. If you want more, please let me know. Contact information is on my card."

"Nice touch," a voice whispered near her ear. She stopped short. A warm breath tickled her neck and a shiver ran down her spine. She recognized the smooth whiskey voice and the musky cologne. "You smell so good." Nick's voice cooed in her ear.

"Hi." She attempted to appear unaffected, but delight curled in her core. She moved away and turned off one of the shadow-box lights to avoid looking at him. "Shouldn't you be inside, Nick, or backstage, or something?"

He shrugged. "They just finished number four. There are other poor suckers ahead of me. Besides, your cousin, or rather your cousin's dress, is drawing a crowd back there. I came to get some fresh air."

"Too much competition for you in the green room?" she teased.

He returned a look of mock horror. "I don't see how movie stars do it." Then, he looked at her, as though he noticed her differently somehow. She always had a hard time discerning his thoughts when he scrutinized her like that. Good thoughts or flaws? Which did he notice?

Cocking his head to one side, he held up his forefingers with his thumbs touching, creating a half-frame. He gazed at her intently.

"You'd make a beautiful cover model in that dress," he whispered.

"Not ever. I've photographed models before. I can tell you a hundred reasons why I'll never be a cover girl."

"You don't see what *I* see, *chèr*."

His voice was warm like slow oozing honey. Desire ran straight to her toes. The sensation magnified when he casually licked his lips. She tried to push the intense feeling away, but sticky like honey, what she resisted only persisted. He'd captured her full attention.

But where would the infatuation lead them?

"Are you going to bid?" he asked, dropping on to a stool, then rolling closer. She sidestepped him to sit at the small makeshift desk, then looked him in the eyes, she sensed his hesitation.

"Well…" She paused.

"C'mon, Biloxi. I need you in there. I need *someone* to bid on me."

She glanced away.

He leaned closer.

His breath caressed her ear again. "I'll be embarrassed if nobody bids on my date. It'll ruin my newfound reputation in Bayou Petite. You're my friend. You have to do this for me. Just get the bidding going. If no one else bids, and you have to pay, I promise to reimburse you."

She fought to suppress a giggle. Part of his charm. Nick had no clue how women looked at him. How they saw him as a catch. But he'd called her "friend," which should have been a relief, yet a wedge of regret refused to be squelched about the *friend* part. Tonight, she wanted to be a fairytale princess with Nick as her prince.

"I don't know," she whispered. "You reimbursing me? Doesn't seem quite right."

"Biloxi?" Linc called out before he rounded the corner. "You better get a move on it if you're going to bid on Nick. Man, thank God it's him up there and not me. I won't ever—"

Linc came into view. His grimace let her know that he realized he should've been watching his mouth rather than blurting things out.

She closed her eyes and counted to ten. Sometimes little brothers were a pain. Opening her eyes, she watched Nick roll away wearing a grin.

"Yeah, Biloxi," Nick mimicked Linc. "You need to get in there and bid on Nick's date." Then, he strolled away whistling, his hands in his pockets like he had nowhere special to be.

"Thanks a lot!" she cried. If looks could kill, her brother would drop dead at her feet.

"Go on," Linc urged. "I'll do the photos for the rest of the dates. You go have fun. The winners will find their way here. Most of them have stayed to watch the show."

She passed him, striding toward the main hall. Her heels echoed a staccato beat. The quick sharp sound mirrored her emotions.

When she reached the turn in the hallway, Linc called out, "Good luck, sis." His chuckle echoed in the hall.

What did he know?

****

Nick squinted against the blast of lights when he stepped out on the runway. A shouting frenzy began. Charles banged his gavel and opened the bidding at one hundred dollars. Women waved paddles and shouted out bids like popcorn kernels bursting in hot oil.

He made his way down the runway, with each step, the stage appeared to grow longer like in a scene from a cartoon. Would he ever reach the end?

"Simmer down now! I can't hear the bids," Charles shouted.

The noise lowered a decibel.

At the end of the runway, Nick paused, then turned and retraced his steps.

"Two thousand was the last bid."

Biloxi came through.

The crowd quieted.

"Going once…" Charles began a count down.

"Three thousand." A new voice entered a bid. Nick glanced over his shoulder and almost stumbled.

"Four thousand."

Silence swallowed the room.

What is she thinking?

"Five thousand dollars." The bidder spoke slow and even, emphasizing each syllable.

Nick froze. The high bid startled him, but not as much as who was doing the bidding. Standing on the stage under the bright lights, he couldn't see the audience beyond the front row. Where was she?

"Amazing!" Charles cried. "Anyone else? Five thousand, going once, twice…"

Whispers drifted through the silence, they rose to murmurs, then climbed higher.

"No other bids?" Charles shouted. "Five thousand. Going once. Going twice. Going, going, gone. Sold to paddle number thirty-five! Thank you little lady for that hefty contribution!"

Charles banged the gavel and beamed. Macy clapped her hands, applauding loudly. She ran to Nick and hugged his neck.

Stunned, he wondered why Chantel had willingly plunked down so much money. She was up to something.

Anxious, he made his way through the crowd to the photo booth. Finding Linc instead of Biloxi waiting there, he relaxed. But what would he say to say her when he finally saw her.

"Smile," said Linc to a couple holding an over-sized check.

"Thank you so much!" Macy gushed at Chantel. Macy scrawled five thousand dollars on the face of another oversized check. "Singularly, it's the largest bid ever at any Valentine's Auction."

In front of the camera, Nick forced a grin. Chantel held the other end of the large prop and beamed like a beauty queen. Biloxi had driven the price up, but Chantel had bid higher. Was Biloxi's strategy to see how high Chantel would go? She'd shown the "good business" side of her. Plus, Chantel couldn't stand to lose. The upside of it all—the money was for a good cause.

"Okay, we're done." Linc said.

Nick placed the prop on the table and waited for Chantel to write out a personal check.

"Chantel, I didn't know you were so civic minded."

"Nicky," she said, sidling up to him after she tore out the check and handed it to Macy. She linked her arm with his, then stroked her hand down his sleeve as if petting a cat. "We made history tonight in this little place."

The hair on the back of his neck stood up. Whatever Chantel was up to, he wanted no part of it. Her manipulative streak could appear out of nowhere. He'd witnessed the fallout whenever she didn't get her way. Usually it involved a man and his money. He always pitied that poor guy. This time, he needed to be sure that "poor guy" wasn't him.

He untangled from her grasp. "Hey, Linc. Know where your sister is?"

Linc rolled his eyes. "Nola's too young for you, dude."

"Very funny," he snorted. "The older one. Beauty with brains."

"Yeah."

"Well?" He waited, then added. "Where can I find

her?"

"I'm here."

He turned to see Biloxi standing a few feet away. He stepped toward her, but Chantel tried to block his path. She turned her back to him and faced Biloxi. "I hope there are no hard feelings." No one could miss the condescension in her voice. He hated it when she got like this.

Biloxi smiled at him, a dreamy sort of expression, then batted her lashes. "Honey, hush! Hard feelings? None a'tall. The money's for a good cause. Why, Nick takes me flying and to lunch often. It doesn't cost *me* five grand."

Puzzled he looked at her. If he didn't know better, the unfolding tug-o-war sounded much like the beginning of a catfight. He frowned, then pulled a white handkerchief from his breast pocket and waved it, putting his hands up in surrender. While either woman could hold her own in any verbal sparring, this wasn't the place for it.

"Nick!"

He turned around. A police officer came toward him.

"Chuck?" He saw the Louisiana State Patrol uniform. Something didn't fit. Chuck had no jurisdiction in Mississippi.

"Your grandmother couldn't raise you on your cell, so I came as a favor to her." Chuck's tone was serious.

"Grandpère?"

Chuck nodded.

Grandpère must have taken a turn for the worse. He'd been to see him only yesterday. The old man had talked and talked and tired himself out, and had argued at the suggestion of rest.

"I'm sorry to be the one to tell you. Your grandmother wants you to come now. The doctors don't know how long he has left. The old man is asking for you."

"What?" Nick scowled. "No. This can't be."

Had Grandpère hidden the graveness of his condition? Had he sensed the end coming? Had that prompted their odd discussion about the duel with Robert Dutrey?

With Biloxi and Chantel flanking him, his heart thudded hard in his chest. Fear curled in his gut. Grandpère had raised him. Had given him all the things his parents never had. The old man couldn't die.

"I'll leave now."

Chuck nodded and headed toward the exit.

Nick reached for Biloxi's hand. "Will you come along? I know it's a lot to ask."

"I'll go Nicky." Chantel stepped in and inserted herself in front of Biloxi. He sidestepped the intruder, reached for Biloxi's hand again, and ignored Chantel's angry scowl.

"I'd really like you to come, but I'll understand if you can't." He rubbed her hand in his and waited for her answer.

"I'm going," Chantel snapped.

"Thanks, but this is personal."

He grimaced when hesitation flashed in Biloxi's eyes.

"I'll go with you," she finally whispered.

He pulled off his jacket and draped it over her shoulders. "Wait inside where it's warm and I'll bring my truck around."

He started toward the exit, but the crowd spilled out from the main hall and blocked his path. He dodged a few folks, then while he waited for an elderly man on a walker to pass he overheard Chantel's snipe.

"So this is how things are going to be?"

"Meaning what?" Biloxi asked.

"Don't get your hopes up," Chantel replied coolly. "I came here for a reason. I'm practically a part of the Trahan family."

"Really?"

Helpless with the crowd blocking his exit and his path back to Biloxi, Nick watched Chantel plant herself inches from Biloxi's nose. "I don't know what game you're playing," Chantel said to Biloxi, "but I promise you, Nicky's mine."

He tried to push through the crowd toward Biloxi, but she stopped him with a wave and motioned him to continue to the door. He turned toward the exit, skirted the crowd and shoved open the door. Cool night air rushed in. Just before the door closed behind him, he heard Chantel's jab.

"You opportunistic bitch."

He'd never hit a woman before, but Chantel made him want to.

After pulling his truck around, he helped Biloxi up the tall step. Once on the road, he merged into westbound I-10 traffic, pushed the cruise control button and headed for Baton Rouge. Guilt rubbed his conscience. He reached across the console for Biloxi's hand.

The woman beside him had no idea about what waited for her. No idea about the desires of a sickly old man. No idea about the snarled lines between their families. She knew very little beyond the fact that the Trahans had moved away after the duel that never took place. In her words, when growing up, she'd paid no mind to old-folk gossip.

A low fog had settled along the bayous. It made driving dangerous. Multi-car pile-ups were common on nights like this. At the same time, the thick fog created a cocoon around them.

"Are you warm enough now?" he asked.

She nodded. Her lips in a firm straight line.

When he changed the heater fan speed to low, he caught the scent of her perfume, and drew it in deeply hoping it would surround them and keep them safe from whatever waited in Baton Rouge. When he started to turn on the radio, Biloxi touched his hand, then shook her head.

Quiet suited him, too.

He focused on the road ahead, however, he couldn't put aside the recent conversations he'd had with Grandpère.

A month back, they'd sat on the porch and the old man said there were things he needed to get off his chest. Grandpère talked about his impetuous youth and falling in love with a girl from the Irish Channel in New Orleans.

"Another man, Dutrey, loved that same shy, lovely young thing, too. We vied for her attention. When I thought Dutrey had the upper hand, I issued a gentleman's challenge. I would've killed Dutrey in that duel. The law would've had no way to prove I'd done it…Strange things happen in the bayous, out in the swamps where no one has eyes but gators…"

He had hated hearing those details. All his life he

looked up to him. He couldn't think of him as anything but a gentleman. That's how Grandpère had lived his life. The pained confession painted a picture of a complex man, but not the grandfather he'd known.

"I gave her up. She was my one true love. I let her go because I loved her so much—not because my family forbade me to marry an Irish. My mother wanted a good Cajun girl for a daughter-in-law, someone the family already knew. I refused. I wanted Elise Murphy. But, Elise got wind of the duel—I'd bet money my mother told her—she cried and begged me to call it off. She said if I really loved her, I'd let her go. Her heart belonged to another."

Grandpère had said it remained the hardest decision he'd ever made. Then he spoke as if giving an interview, rather than talking to him. He said when he finally married, he chose a docile Cajun girl, Suzette, and they had one son, Edward.

"I was a poor father and an even poorer husband."

Where he had failed his son, he wanted to succeed with Nick.

He remembered that Grandpère considered it his duty to shelter him and had raised him as a son when Edward, his father, started to drink, and became too inebriated to function.

The old man loved him. Even now, he didn't question that fact. The only harsh words they ever spoke was when he was twelve, when he and Chuck stole a johnboat to go fishing after ditching school.

Grandpère stressed education. Said he'd have no hoodlums in his household and made good on his promise of punishment. Nick slept on his stomach for several nights. Always a quick study, it only took once.

A hide-tanning had never happened again.

He continued pondering the past as he sped toward the hospital. During another recent visit, the conversation had taken many turns. The old man crawled down memory lane. Nick recalled each word…

"I hated watching Edward waste away from alcohol. He grew bitter and angry," Grandpère growled.

"Are my parents still married?" He finally had the courage to ask, though he hadn't seen his folks since he was ten.

"I don't know the legal status of their marriage. I never tried to find your mother after she abandoned you. I wanted that part of the past to stay buried."

"And my father?"

"I'm the only true father you've ever known." Grandpère paused then said, "Nicholas, follow your dreams. You need a wife. Get married. Settle down and have a bunch of kids. Son, you're thirty. I know that's what you want."

"I've got what I want, sir. The practice. The house. You haven't seen it since Grandmère and the decorator cut loose on it. Come on over, let's have barbeque shrimp."

"I'll come when you marry."

Yesterday, he saw frailty. Always rock-solid before, the old man had avoided questions about his health. Instead, demanded that any honor-bound grandson would get married and settle down.

"I've deeded you all of the Trahan land. There's enough to parcel out to several children so you'll always have family nearby. You'll never have to leave. Like me."

Those words haunted Nick as he drove. Had the

old man remembered their conversation from years ago?

Just before starting high school, his grandfather had found him drunk in the pool house. Nick confessed he didn't want to go away to a boarding school. He refused to leave home. He feared losing everyone, being completely abandoned. Ashamed, he'd cried like a baby.

After that, no further mention was made of shipping him off for his high school years. And no words had passed between them about that event until yesterday, when he mentioned Biloxi Noël Dutrey.

"What're you wasting time for? I want to meet her. Bring her for a visit. Do it! You never wanted to leave home. If you marry that girl, you won't ever leave Bayou Petite," the old man had roared. "I have to meet her before I die." Then he'd mumbled something about seeing the face of the only woman he'd ever loved.

It had been an odd visit, one he'd never forget.

He squeezed Biloxi's hand. A comfortable silence surrounded them. Most women would chatter away, asking a million questions. Thankfully, Biloxi wasn't one of those.

His thoughts drifted back to Grandpère.

The old man knew about the auction tonight. Knew about Biloxi's photography. Was this his opportunity to present the one woman in the world his grandfather wanted to meet? But how could he prepare her? He worried what secrets might come out. What else might the old man reveal?

"I'm sorry to hear your grandfather's so ill," Biloxi whispered. "When did you see him last?"

"Yesterday. I flew over in the afternoon. We had a

long talk."

"Maybe it isn't as bad as it sounds."

He heard hopefulness in her voice and compassion when she squeezed his hand.

"I think it's the beginning of the end."

"I'm sorry."

"I need to prepare you, *chèr*." How could he broach the subject? She didn't deserve to be blind-sided. But how would she feel about him after he revealed the story? The one her family never discussed.

"For?"

"Grandpère is known to be a gentleman, but more vocal in his old age. Ignores good manners, and I'm never sure what'll come out of his mouth."

Peripherally, he caught her startled expression and asked, "Do you look much like your grandmother Elise?"

"Hmm," she said then paused. "Well, barely. I mostly take after the Dutrey side of the family—Aunt Macy and Branna...and my dad, he's Macy's cousin. I don't have the porcelain white skin or wavy red hair like my grandmother. Thank God, no freckles. Grandmother is what some would consider an Irish beauty. No. Not much resemblance between us." She paused again. "Why?"

Nick nodded, his hands massaged the wheel. "I'm not sure how my grandfather will react when he sees you. There are parts of the story you don't know." He wished he didn't feel compelled to expose the underbelly of his family. "You know my grandfather loved Elise. That's why he issued the challenge."

"New Orleans wasn't a lawless town in the 1940's. I mean, I know about the duel, but I don't think it's true. More like gossip blown out of proportion to titillate. Besides, it would've been illegal and everyone says your grandfather is a true southern gentleman. One who wrote the book and provided the dictionary definition."

"Legal or not, he did issue the challenge. They were going to use pistols."

Biloxi turned in her seat. "Well?" She patted his hand. "Tell me what happened then. Don't leave me hanging."

"Your Grandmother Elise begged my grandfather not to go through with the duel. She cared about him, but she was in love with your grandfather. She'd said if Grandpère killed the one she loved, he might as well kill her, too. Heartbroken, he left Bayou Petite."

"And they said it was because he was a coward. So tragically romantic," she said softly.

"What will we do if my grandfather demands to see your grandmother before he dies?"

"We'll cross that bridge, *if* we ever get there."

After they arrived at the hospital and parked, the person at the information desk gave him the room number. Once there, he ushered Biloxi inside to face Grandpère on his bed.

Grandpère's hand trembled when he lifted his oxygen mask.

"She's lovely," he whispered.

Machines beeped and flashed, around the old man, monitoring his vital signs. The cold room radiated lifelessness, even though blips on a screen measured the old man's heartbeat. Nick stared at his once-energetic grandfather. In the last twenty-four hours, he must have aged a hundred years.

Grandpère's condition staggered him. He couldn't die. This man had taught him to fish, to hunt and drive—not just a car, but a shrimp boat, too. Grandpère had farmed him out in the summertime to make spending money by crewing on a shrimper with a friend who ran a boat out of Grand Isle. Then, the old man sent him to college. Paid for all his education. At every turn, Grandpère had encouraged him to follow his dream of becoming a veterinarian.

From his grandfather he'd learned to be a man. Something his father hadn't been around to handle. Now faced with the old man's imminent passing, he didn't know how to let go.

Grandpère had taught him many things, but not how to say good-bye. The once vibrant man lay sick and almost lifeless, dying to catch a breath.

He would do anything to provide a few moments of happiness to Grandpère. He'd grant his dying wish.

Would Biloxi understand?

He couldn't be sure, but he would risk it. He hated the half-lie he'd told her, but to give Grandpère one last pleasure, he'd live with the crime.

"Grandpère, may I introduce Biloxi Noël Dutrey."

Chapter 20

Biloxi shivered and hoped Claude didn't notice. She hated hospitals.

The frail old man motioned her over. She moved to the side of his bed. Her anxiety rose with each beep from a machine opposite where she stood.

"Hello," she managed to choke out. Seeing Claude was like meeting a ghost from old family stories. To find him pale and gaunt filled her with deep sadness. He no longer looked like a man who might fight to the death for a woman.

Her grandfather had died without revealing the whole truth of the situation. Her grandmother never spoke about it. Could the old family grudge finally die with Claude? Or would the Old Aunts work to keep it alive?

She reached for Claude's hand when he offered it. He grasped hers. The strength of his leathery grip surprised her. He tugged. She moved closer. He tried to sit up. His head wobbled, then lowered. She stifled a gasp when he put wrinkled lips to her hand and kissed it.

"Lovely," he said, his breathing labored. He rested back on his pillows.

Her palms began to sweat. She swallowed hard. His stare made her want to run. How could she avoid his probing eyes without seeming rude? His gaze took in everything, as though he looked beyond her clothes, her skin, and bore a hole into her soul.

What does he want from me?

She glanced at Nick and smiled weakly. She didn't move, even when every fiber in her body shouted, "Run!"

"I'll be right back," Nick said to his grandfather.

Nick reached for her hand, tugged her toward the door, then waved to his grandfather before leading her out of the room.

"Sorry about that." Nick's sheepish grin softened his face around his eyes. Eyes that usually danced with amusement now drowned in sadness. "He's not exactly himself right now."

"It's okay," she said, trying not to sound upset. Honestly, the old man had rattled her. "I lost my grandfather a few years back. I loved him, but we weren't like the two of you. No need to apologize. I'll wait out here. Give you two some private time." She prayed he didn't ask her to go back in there. She didn't think she could deny Nick, despite the anxiousness wrapping tight around her.

How did a sick, dying old man manage to look at a woman as though she were his lover?

"You're sure you'll be okay out here for a little while?" Nick asked. "I hope his doctor will arrive. I want the real scoop about Grandpère's condition."

She nodded. "Take all the time you need." She certainly wouldn't have him rush on her account. God forbid, if they left because of her and his grandfather died without him there...she didn't want that on her conscience.

Just before Nick reached his grandfather's room,

he turned back to her. "If you see a doctor—Dr. Fletcher is his name—please ask him to step in."

"Absolutely," she said when he walked away. She scanned the hall, up and down. Not a nurse in sight.

Where would she find help?

****

Back in the room, Grandpère looked asleep, but gnarled fingers motioned Nick closer. With his eyes still closed, the old man removed the oxygen mask and reached out with his arm. Nick locked hands with Grandpère. Young, strong, and virile clasped old, weak, and feeble.

"I wouldn't embarrass your grandmother by asking Elise to come, but it's heaven to see her granddaughter," whispered Grandpère. "She's the one."

"Old man, you'll hound me from the grave, won't you?"

He wanted to lighten the mood, beat back the hovering gloom. For the last six months Grandpère never missed an opportunity to express his wish of seeing his only grandson happily married. Any other time, he would've made light of the words, but the time for joking had passed. Now, only important words needed to be said. At least ones the old man wanted to hear. Given his frailty, it was only a matter of time before no further words would be spoken.

Where's Grandmère? She should be here with him.

He'd done all he could to please the old man. The move to Bayou Petite—for Grandpère. Built a house, a place for Grandpère to imagine playing with his great grandkids—for Grandpère. He would do *anything* to buy more time. To his grandfather, the house represented safety, security, and marriage. Signs of a successful life. Plus, the old man liked knowing that Trahans once again lived on their land.

He understood that Grandpère worried about him. Didn't want his only grandson to live alone forever. He wanted for Nick what he'd never had—to marry the one true love of his life. Grandpère had said, it wasn't that he hadn't loved Grandmère Suzette, but never like he loved another. That other—Biloxi's grandmother, Elise.

Delusions of a sick old man made no logical sense.

Claude Trahan had loved Elise Murphy, but how did the old man translate that into believing Nick needed to love Biloxi?

"Well?" Grandpère asked. "Tell me you love her and will marry her. Make a dying man happy."

"She's very special," Nick said. That wasn't a lie.

"Very...special." Grandpère nodded. His breath grew more ragged.

Had the old man referred to Biloxi, or was he really seeing Elise, the woman he'd pined for all of his life?

"Put the damn oxygen mask on, old man," he ordered. Grandpère's coloring looked ghostly.

"No...want...to...talk. Does...she know?" His grandfather struggled to speak.

"About you and her grandmother?"

Grandpère nodded.

"Yes, she knows."

"Love...her...yes?"

He had to say it. Had to alleviate the pain of a dying man. "Yes. I love her."

"I...brought her...here...for you," Grandpère whispered. "Pictures. Contract. Marriage." Grandpère's chest heaved as he spoke.

The meddling old fool.

"I'll do my best. Now, put the damn oxygen mask back on!"

He looked away, unable to watch. Life appeared to drain from his grandfather. What could he do? His mind churned like a hamster on a wheel.

"Marry...soon," the old man whispered, then blew a short, labored breath. "Give me...reason...to live."

Nick's heart skipped a beat. Had it come down to his grandfather's final days depending solely on him?

On half-truths?

Could news of an engagement keep him alive?

"I'm going to ask Biloxi to marry me," he said quickly. "You've got to stick around to see me through it. You'll get to see Elise at the wedding." He gripped his grandfather's hand and wanted to shout, "Don't leave me. You're the only family I've got." Instead he reached for the oxygen mask and covered his grandfather's mouth. "There's time to talk about the details. You have to get well and get out of here."

Grandpère opened his cloudy gray eyes and nodded. A tear spilled down his saggy cheek. He lifted the mask, then whispered. "Proud...of...you."

He squeezed Grandpère's hand, hoping to offer comfort, but it fell limp. Grandpère closed his eyes.

Machines in the room shouted high-pitched beeps. Lights flashed. Nurses ran into the room. They shoved him away. They yelled at the old man, shouting his name.

The machines announced what Nick already knew.

Grandpère was gone. Peacefully. Happily. He'd seen to that.

He stood in the doorway and watched the chaos as his grandfather's body lay perfectly still. Taking a deep breath, he exhaled, crossed the threshold, and left the one man who meant everything to him.

Outside his grandfather's hospital room, life seemed ordinary. Voices and hospital sounds rippled down the hall. Normal people going about their normal lives.

His feet, heavy like lead, took slow steps and emptiness echoed in his heart. He walked toward the waiting room.

Whispers called to him, then magnified before reaching his fog-filled brain. Dazed, he didn't see Biloxi at first. Her voice called to him. He turned toward her. Her eyes watering. Bottom lip quivering.

He opened his arms and she rushed to him, closing the short space between them. He hugged her tight. Her strength moved into him like an electrical current of life. She understood his pain. He didn't have to speak the terrible words. She knew.

He cupped her chin and looked down into liquid hazel eyes. Planting a kiss on her forehead he said, "Thanks for coming tonight. It meant the world to him."

He wanted to add, *and me too*, but the words stuck in his throat.

She lifted on her toes and kissed him. Her lips were warm. Comforting. Like a welcome home. And though her kiss surprised him, he clung to her, his lips seeking more. Together, they took and gave to one another.

Hand in hand, they walked to the elevator in silence, leaving behind the heaviness. Outside the crisp cold seemed to blanket the world in a hush. Overhead, stars shone brightly, silver dots against an inky-black sky. He heard her gasp and she pointed beyond the glare of parking-lot lights to a falling star. She closed her eyes. What had she wished?

He, too, wished on that falling star, wished that his grandfather's wish would come true. However, to make it happen, he was in for a fight, a different type of duel.

One that involved Biloxi's entire family.

Chapter 21

On the drive back to Fleur de Lis with Nick, Biloxi considered the exchange she'd heard between Nick and his grandfather. She hadn't meant to eavesdrop, but when she couldn't find a nurse or the doctor, she wanted to let Nick know. She started to enter Claude's room, but stopped at the threshold. Closed curtains separated the space and she remained hidden behind the makeshift wall. She waited for the right moment to interrupt. However, while she waited, an elderly woman waited also, in the hallway on the other side of the hospital room door.

The woman's gray hair was styled, teased, curled, and combed. Not one errant strand. Her black leather purse matched her shoes, down to the Chanel buckles. She dabbed her eyes with a lace handkerchief. Her shoulders shook beneath a royal blue wool coat.

Just before the machines started to blare and chaos broke out, the older woman walked away. Biloxi backed away from the door and waited on the other side of the hall when a nurse flew into the room followed by two others. She returned to the waiting room, awaiting any news.

A few minutes later, Nick stepped out of the hospital room and appeared to be in a trance. She called his name three times. He hadn't heard her at first.

That wasn't the time for questions, but she'd heard

his lie to Claude.

That made sirens in her head blare louder than the ones in Claude's room. She never would believe that Nick would be so dishonorable as to lie. To tell a bald-faced, burn-in-hell kind of lie.

Disappointment dripped to the bottom of her heart. Why had he used her to make a dying old man happy?

Reeling in disbelief, she had wanted to ask. But dealing with death was enough confrontation for anyone to handle.

Unlike Claude Trahan, she and Nick could fight it out tomorrow.

****

Biloxi rolled over in bed and stared up at the ceiling, her room no longer a sanctuary of peace and contentment. At some point last night, exhaustion claimed her. She'd slept fitfully, waking up often. She wrestled with all she learned. When rays of light filtered in through the shutters and pushed all shadows away, darkness retreated, but frustration stayed. She checked the time again. Only an hour had passed since she'd last looked. Restless, she reached for her cell phone and tapped in the number.

"Good morning, Biloxi," her grandmother's voice answered.

"How are you, Grandmother Elise?"

How should she break the news? What would make it less shocking?

"I don't know how to ask you this, other than to just say it, so here goes. Will you go to a funeral with me?"

Silence hung between them before her grandmother responded. "What a strange request on a

192

Sunday morning. Who died?"

Biloxi paused and clutched the phone tightly. "Claude Trahan."

"Who, dear?"

"Claude. Charles. Trahan."

"Oh, my. *Oh, my.*"

"Grandmother, are you okay?"

When her grandmother didn't respond, she imagined her slumped on the floor. Had she fainted?

"Grandmother?" Biloxi started to panic. "Grandmother!"

"How did you know him, dear?" Her grandmother spoke in a slow cautious tone. "How did you learn of this news?"

Biloxi swallowed. "I'm friends with his grandson, Nick."

She heard her Grandmother's sigh. "Why is it that no one in this family tells me anything anymore? Since your grandfather died, people don't tell me things. Does your father know this news?" It sounded like an accusation.

"I don't know if Daddy knows. Mama met Nick."

"Humph. Your mama married into this family. It's not the same for her."

She wanted to point out, in fact, that her mother wasn't the only one. Elise had married into the Dutrey family, too. However much her mother and grandmother tolerated each other, they had one thing in common—neither carried Dutrey blood. But there was no sense in starting an argument. It wouldn't accomplish anything.

"Grandmother...I know the rest of the story...about the duel." She paused to let the information sink in. "I would like you to accompany me to pay last respects. Claude died last night. While I was there with Nick."

"You met him!"

"Yes. After last night's auction. I went to Baton Rouge with Nick. I don't know anything about the details of the wake and funeral, but I'd like you to go with me."

"I don't know. I haven't seen the man in years."

All night she had rehearsed how to break the news to her grandmother, and then how to convince her to attend the wake and funeral. Paying last respects had to be the best way to bring closure to the old family wounds. She and Nick would have to deal with the new one he'd created last night—she hadn't taken him for a liar. For now, no one needed to know about that little problem.

"Please, come with me," Biloxi pleaded. "You influenced Claude's life. I haven't spoken to Nick this morning, but I'm guessing the viewing may take place as soon as Tuesday, and the funeral will follow."

"But a funeral isn't the time to meet someone, dearest."

Biloxi countered with one of her grandmother's favorite sayings. "There's no time like the present." Grandmother Elise prided herself on being a living example of decorum and good manners.

"I'll bet the Old Aunts are going." It wasn't a lie because she had no way of knowing one way or the other. However, that tidbit of information would hold clout.

Grandmother was devoted to G. G. Grace, even more so since Granddaddy Robert had died. If anything, his passing brought the two women closer together.

Their family operated around a structured pecking order with G.G. Grace and Auntie Marie, the Old Aunts, at the top. At ninety-five, Grace still technically ruled the family, being the oldest twin, much the same way Branna ruled over her as the next Keeper. And, G.G. Grace would expect the family to make a respectable showing at the funeral.

It was what Southerners did. Couldn't live with the living, but happy to send off the dead.

"You are a wicked girl, Biloxi," her Grandmother scolded. "Why didn't you just say that in the beginning? You know I'll have to go if Grace and Marie do. Now tell me, do you know anything about the special family meeting Macy's called for this afternoon?"

Biloxi's gut clenched like a vice clamping tight. Her brain screeched to a halt. Hearing "Macy" and "meeting," she refocused. She'd forgotten about the family council meeting that afternoon.

While the photography studio would pose no barrier, she urgently needed to talk to Branna this morning. She had to know Branna's objections to her plan.

"Grandmother, I love you. I've got to go. See you in church." She hung up without a "good-bye" and sprang out of bed. Was her look-a-like cousin awake?

She grabbed her purple robe in case James or her brother roamed the house, then thumped down the stairs. Branna might be in the kitchen. She'd volunteered to make breakfast to give Greta a break. If Branna intended to get them fed before the organist started the opening, Branna would be standing in front of the stove.

The aroma of fresh brewed coffee filled the empty kitchen, and Biloxi breathed deeply while passing through. She pulled the back door open, then quietly pushed on the screen door. Outside, Branna and James sat in the rocking chairs on the back gallery. She heard their soft murmurs, but not enough to make out conversation.

While pulling her robe closed, she scrunched her toes. She hated walking barefoot on the cold, wooden-planks. Hobbling up behind Branna's chair, she said, "Good morning, ya'll. Hope I'm not interrupting."

James gazed up at her. His expression turned odd. "No," he said slowly.

"Good morning, cousin." She heard amusement in Branna's voice.

When Branna raised her hand, Biloxi squeezed it before coming around from behind and parking herself in the empty rocker next to James.

James stared at her, then at Branna, then back again at her with a pronounced crease between his brows.

"What?" Biloxi finally asked.

"Branna told me you two looked alike," he said, nodding toward Branna. "Last night, I didn't notice it as much. Evening dresses and makeup, I guess. But in the light of day..." James paused. "Maybe I should kiss you both and make sure I've got the right cousin?"

Branna rolled her eyes. "Hmm? Maybe you should ask Dr. Nick first?"

"You've kissed him?" Biloxi demanded.

What had she thought? Branna lived here before moving to Florida, and before meeting James. Branna had met Nick first. It bothered her. A lot. She hated feeling second to anything Branna did. Especially with

Nick. But had they kissed? Or more?

Branna winked. "Let's see if these men kiss and tell."

"Kissing and telling is not why I hunted you down," Biloxi snapped. Branna raised an eyebrow.

"James, I don't mean to be rude, but would you mind if I borrowed Branna for a few minutes? We have some family business to discuss."

"I didn't mean any offense by my teasing," James said. He patted her hand. "I'll relinquish her to you. I need a second cup of coffee anyway."

James winked at Branna as he passed. Branna blew him a kiss. Biloxi rolled her eyes at the lovebirds, impatient for him to be gone.

Branna twisted in her chair and watched as James walked away. When she turned back, she said, "Really, Biloxi, we were just kidding."

"Sorry. Anyway, I really need to talk to you, but first I have to know. Did you ever kiss Nick?"

"What?

"Kiss Nick."

"Me? Kiss Nick? No. I didn't meet him until last night. I'd heard of him. Passed him on the road. Seen him around. But we were never properly introduced."

She believed her. Branna never lied.

Branna rocked back and forth in her chair while nodding her head as though she were a woman wise with years. "You've got what I said all wrong. I meant that before James kisses you, he should ask Nick for permission. I saw the way Nick looks at you. That man's got more than kissin' on his mind."

"I think you're wrong." She didn't want to discuss Nick, especially after last night. Instead she wanted to focus on the goal at hand, but somehow, she'd managed to get off on a wrong start.

"Nick's grandfather died last night."

"Oh." Branna's smile fell. "I'm sorry to hear that. They were close?"

"Yes. Very. However, I need to talk with you about something else. Something we've never talked about before."

Branna frowned. "You're worrying me."

How could she ask Branna without sounding like a beggar? Or even more, without sounding as if she demanded compliance? According to family tradition, she had no right to what she wanted, but she wanted it nonetheless. Needed it like she needed to breathe. Living at Fleur de Lis and preserving it for coming generations, well, it sounded pretty old-fashioned even to her. But there it was. Her biggest goal in life. With a roadblock of a hundred-plus years that said she couldn't have it.

"Branna, we've always been told, blood is thicker than water. You know I love you. We've always been close. We share a special bond. I don't need to remind you of our birthday. We're practically twins, as everyone says. Even James sees the resemblance."

She drummed her fingers on the chair's armrest, then took a sip of Branna's coffee. The hot coffee hit her churning stomach. Her emotions spun, like a washing machine on a fast spin cycle.

Fate had them born in the same hospital on the same day, only a few minutes apart. Then cursed her by making her look like her cousin. But, they weren't two peas in a pod.

"Go on," Branna urged.

"I want to know what your intentions are about Fleur de Lis."

Branna blinked. She tilted her head from one side, then to the other, as if she'd heard a foreign language. "I don't catch your meaning."

Biloxi took a deep breath and prayed for help.

It's now or never.

"I know Fleur de Lis is yours—"

"Ours!" Branna insisted.

"Yes," Biloxi started again. "But, yours by birthright. You're the Keeper—"

"My mother is. Not me. Not anymore for a while." Branna lowered her voice.

"—but it will pass to you. And...I want the job. The responsibility. I want you to relinquish your role to me." She rushed the words, fearful that if she held them back, they'd be sealed inside her forever.

"You want...the responsibility? *Forever?*" Branna said "forever" as if the idea was utterly repugnant.

Dread dropped into Biloxi's stomach like a rock sinking into the Pearl River, but she pushed on. "Yes. Forever."

Silence hung between them.

"I'm stunned. I never knew you felt this way. There are implications..." Branna chewed the side of her mouth as if she contemplated something. "Could we talk about this later? I need to start on breakfast now." She popped up out of the chair and headed toward the kitchen door.

"Branna, wait! Please give me a chance to explain further," she pleaded.

"Cousin, you knocked me over with a feather. I need time to think. I can't even describe how I feel right now." Branna lifted her chin, looking regal and poised.

Biloxi held up her hands in surrender. "I understand. I'm not asking this because I want to hurt you. You know that, right?"

But you hold my future in your hands.

Chapter 22

"Just a minute!" Nick shouted. He grabbed his jeans and hopped on one foot, trying to climb into them. The doorbell rang three more times. "Damn it! I'm coming."

He pulled his jeans over his hips. With the zipper down and button still open, he ran downstairs like the house was on fire.

Why did anyone feel the need to lay on the damn doorbell before eight in the morning? Sunday morning at that.

After his grandfather had died.

That fact sobered him.

Descending the stairs, he grimaced. Another bell clanged in his head. One from too much bourbon and too little sleep.

When he reached the door, he peeked through the side window, blinked, and looked again. Shocked, he recognized who'd come calling before eight in the morning.

He opened the door wide. He ran his fingers through his hair as if to clear his brain. When the man at the door stared back, Nick blinked in disbelief.

"Hello, son. Please put a shirt on. Your grandmother's waiting in the car. We need to talk."

Edward Trahan, his father, stood equally tall but thinner, with short dark hair tinged with gray at the temples. He looked distinguished and somber. While he recognized the man as his father, part of his brain refused to accept the news. After all, he hadn't seen the man in twenty years.

"Come in," Nick said slowly. "I'll be right back." He headed upstairs, leaving the door open for his father to find his way inside.

A few minutes later, fully clothed down to his socks and boots, he peeked around the corner from the kitchen seeking reassurance that he wasn't sleepwalking or in the middle of a dream while he waited for coffee to brew. Edward—he'd recognize him anywhere, the father he hadn't seen since forever—sat on the couch and comforted his grandmother. He half expected the doorbell to ring and find Mary Catherine—Cat—his mother, waiting on the porch. It would be an odd family reunion.

When the coffee maker finished dripping, he poured dark liquid into two mugs and one china cup, adding a splash of milk and sugar for his grandmother.

"Grandmère, for you." He offered the cup and saucer and watched her delicate hands tremble as she took it from him. He handed a mug to Edward, then headed back to the kitchen to grab his own. If ever there was a time for drinking before noon on a Sunday, this was it. A shot of Maker's Mark would do the trick, might stop the banging in his head. But he resisted.

The irony of his desire for a drink wasn't lost on him. Alcohol had destroyed his father, or so his grandfather had said, and had broken up their family, once tightly knit together. Still, he wanted to knock back a shot of whiskey. Needed the fortification.

The man in the living room had called him *son*.

The last time he saw Edward, he'd been told to wait in the back seat of the car and stay out of sight. An obedient child, he wrapped himself in a new wool blanket, one his mother sent him from her trip to Santa Fe. The bold colors and strange patterns fascinated him. Her note said, "Native Americans made it with their own hands." He liked it when his mother sent him presents, yet never understood why he couldn't see her. As child, he'd always wondered what he'd done to make her stay away.

Years ago, he huddled under that blanket, scared of his drunken father, and prayed for his mother to find him. He pretended the blanket was Superman's cape and it would keep him safe. On that night, dark as pitch, he laid on the backseat as his father parked on the edge of an unfamiliar swamp.

His dad climbed out of the car and slammed the door so hard the windows rattled. Trembling, he heard the swells of an accordion and the whine of a fiddle—Cajun music. When he gathered his courage, he peered out the window. Flashes of neon illuminated a shabby bayou shack and bounced off the parked cars, before disappearing into the black night.

Then he heard screams.

His mother.

He also heard the smack of fist on flesh. A big splash. But he wasn't able to see anything. Loud voices frightened him. Angry men shouted. Suddenly someone shoved his father up against the car. He ducked down, then peeked from beneath the blanket. He tried not to cry when the back of his father's head smacked hard against the car's window.

"I'm going! I'm going!" his dad shouted.

"Faithless bitch! Rot in hell."

How he prayed his dad didn't mean those words.

When his father started the car, before he drove away, he heard his mother's sobs as she beat on the car's window. Huddled under the blanket, afraid to peek, he wanted to go back and find her. But his father sped off.

"I'm gonna kill him. Shit, I'm gonna kill her first!"

He remembered thinking that his dad must have forgotten about him, so he laid still and silent, wrapped in fear and the blanket, and dared not to breathe.

A few minutes later, the car stopped again. His dad pounded on the steering wheel, then became very still. The silence deepened. After a few minutes passed, his dad opened the console. While Nick couldn't see anything, his hearing was sharp.

Spinning metal.

Click.

Click.

Click.

His dad had loaded a .44 Black Hawk. The one he was told never to play with.

"No! Daddy, no!"

It was the last thing he remembered.

Those were the last words he'd spoken before his father knocked him out cold.

Later, he woke to his grandfather calling his name. A strange woman sat in the back seat of his father's car and wiped his face while his grandfather watched from a few steps away.

"I think he needs to go to the hospital," the woman said. "A few stitches."

"Okay, but I'll take him. I refuse to have him out of

my sight."

A police officer walked up. "I need to talk to the boy."

"Christ, it can wait until tomorrow. The kid's hurt. I doubt he saw anything. He was unconscious when I found him."

"A man is dead."

The officer's tone had scared him. Did the man mean his father? He started to cry.

"Daddy?"

"Hush, Nicholas," his grandfather said. "Come on. Get out of this car. Let's go in mine."

He obeyed. He grabbed the blanket, the present from his mother, and choked back a sniffle. Ten-year-old boys were too old to cry.

"Grandpère, I want to see Daddy."

His grandfather looked as though he'd aged a hundred years. His eyes looked flat and tired. His clothes were dirty, like he'd been wrestling in the mud. Grandmère Suzette wouldn't like it one bit.

"I'm sorry, son," his grandfather said. It sounded as though it hurt him to speak, which frightened Nick even more.

"Your dad is lost to you, just like your mother." He flashed a faint-hearted smile that never reached his eyes. "It's you and me now, son," he had said.

He recalled, very clearly, thinking—*but I'm not your son.*

The rest, as they say, is ancient history.

Except now, Edward sat in the living room, the day after his grandfather had died.

Something was very wrong.

Chapter 23

"Nicholas, I was at the hospital last night," Grandmère said.

Ever composed, she didn't look like a woman who'd just lost her husband, but more like a woman on her way to Sunday brunch at Commander's Palace in the French Quarter. Her hair was curled into a perfect style, sprayed in place, her nails polished, and around her neck, her ever-present pearls draped and shone against a dark gray, wool suit. Chanel, if he was correct.

She cradled the china cup—the china she and the decorator decided he must have—and stared into it. Edward sat on the couch next to her. Still in shock, Nick shook his head to clear it.

"I stepped out of the room to make a few phone calls." Grandmère's trembling hands rattled the china cup in the saucer.

"I didn't see you." He shrugged.

Grandmère looked up. Tears trickled down her cheeks, which surprised him. She was the stern disciplinarian to his grandfather's loving, jovial guiding hand. She made him mind his manners, made sure he had clean clothes, good food to eat, but had never shown him any affection when he was a child. Since he'd become an adult, she barely spoke to him unless issuing an order. And, he'd only seen her cry once before, over a letter from his father.

More tears traced the path of the first ones. Who was this crying woman? Whom had she called last night? Edward? Where had the man been for the last twenty years? What the hell did he want? Money from Grandpère's estate?

He couldn't have been more astonished by the chain of events than if a fortuneteller from the Vieux Carrè had made predictions about the morning after his grandfather's death.

The whole thing was too bizarre. Starting with Grandpère's confessions. That surprised him. Shouldn't have, but it did. Then, when his grandfather died, he couldn't get out of the building fast enough. He hadn't bothered to look for his grandmother.

Under her composed exterior lay hardened steel. She always had everything under control. Control. The very thing Grandmère battled her husband for every day of their lives. Their tug-of-war relationship had taken its toll on all their lives.

Grandpère. His gut tightened. He didn't want the empty shell of a body to be the final vision he carried of the wise old man who mentored him, became his father, and raised him when no one else cared. The old man's death haunted him. In the grips of grief last night, he had searched his own soul. The unresolved pain of knowing, yet not truly knowing, his own grandfather, had dragged him into this morning and brought him face-to-face with changes he never expected. Then magnified them in ways he'd never imagined.

Grandpère had manipulated not only him, but Biloxi, too.

"Your grandmother says there was a girl at the hospital with you." Edward sounded anxious.

"*Mais*, I'd hardly call her a girl. Biloxi's my friend. And who the hell do you think you are? You show up, and call me 'son.' Other than the physical resemblance to Grandmère, I don't know who you are. You ran out on me a very long time ago. *And*, I'd be careful, if I were you. I don't owe you anything, least of all, an explanation of who I was with last night."

"She's not here, is she?" Edward asked. He squeezed his folded hands. The muscle in his jaw tensed.

"No. We're not that kind of friends." He stared hard at Edward.

"Nicholas," his father started, "you're right. At this point, I'm a stranger to you, though you're not to me. I'm concerned. However, before you play judge and jury, knowing the true facts might help. But we can talk about that later. Right now, your grandmother needs us both."

Disgusted by Edward's continued referral to them as family, he looked to Grandmère for an explanation. Had she known Edward's location all of these years? Was she in contact with his mother, too?

"Grandmère, what's going on?" He pressed for a revelation. A confession. Something.

Grandmère looked up. She gingerly set her cup on the coffee table that separated them. Her face looked aged and pained. Opening her purse, she pulled out a lace hankie and dabbed the corner of each eye. She clutched the hankie in her hand as though it were a lifeline. Appearing to summons her courage, she breathed in deeply, then slowly let go of that breath.

"Your grandfather planned his own memorial service down to the music and a separate burial service.

And he wants *that* girl to speak at the memorial."

Nick silently counted and stopped at five. "Grandmère, with all due respect, that girl has a name. Biloxi Noël Dutrey. She's my friend. A very good friend."

Late last night, during his monologue with Maker's Mark while trying to deaden his pain, he considered his grandfather's dying words about Biloxi and marriage. Grandpère had brought her home? Believed she was the woman for him? Before his grandfather's revelation, Biloxi had occupied his mind. The fullness of her lips. The curve of her mouth. She looked stunning last night in that dress. In the early dawn through the haze of booze, he'd seen Biloxi in a whole new light. A woman strong enough to stand on her own, and yet vulnerable at the same time.

Grandmère's attitude toward a woman she'd never met puzzled him. Biloxi's only crime was being born a Dutrey. But had he heard his grandmother right? Grandpère planned his own memorial service?

The old man thinks he can control us from the grave.

"I'm slow on the uptake this morning. Grandpère wants Biloxi to speak at his memorial service? Odd, but that's a problem because?"

"I will *not* have *that* girl at the service!"

Her dark eyes bore into his. The rage and hate emanating from his grandmother shocked him. He leaned forward, placed his elbows on his thighs and clasped his hands together. He wanted to choose his words carefully. He'd lived a lifetime with secrets and haunting memories, grown up without a father or mother. His grandparents tried their best. He loved them. But their doings, their decisions, along with his parents' actions played into his parentless life. He'd managed, but the loss had cut deep as a child. And once an adult, he vowed not to let anyone dictate his life. Not the local do-gooders who thought he needed a wife, not his grandfather, and certainly not his grandmother now that his grandfather had passed.

"I want to be sure I understand," Nick said. "You're going to violate Grandpère's last request? Because you hate someone you've never met?"

"I saw *her* last night."

He could almost see venom spewing from her lips.

"Did you speak to her?"

Trembling hands sheltered her face. His grandmother sobbed.

An unfair advantage.

The world had turned upside down. His grandmother was a weepy mess. Did his father cause this change? What would it take to make the man disappear again? Grandpère's will? If so, maybe afterwards things would go back to normal. At least as normal as possible with Grandpère gone.

"Is this *your* doing?" he asked Edward. "Where did you come from? You don't look like a drunk. I guessed you were dead by now. And where's my mother?"

"Calm down, son."

Nick rose to his feet, pulled up straight and tall. The room closed in around him. Too small. Too confined, as though it shrunk. "Don't call me that. I am not your son."

"Nicholas!" Grandmère cried.

"Okay, everyone breathe," Edward said.

"What are you?" Nick snapped. "Some kind of

210

shrink, or what?"

"Doctor. Medical. Still. I run a little clinic near Tallulah. I'm sober for almost twenty years."

"You didn't get your license yanked? I thought surely after all that happened…"

"No." Edward's expression turned wry. "Your grandfather didn't want to defend me. He greased a few palms to keep me from shaming the family—guilty or innocent—he didn't care. The price for his *help* was you."

"What the hell are you talking about?" Nick moved to the fireplace to put more distance between them. He leaned against the mantel, and crossed his arms over his chest, refusing to entertain any inane accusations about Grandpère, who was now unable to defend himself.

"That *great* gentleman forced me to leave and give you up. Or…he threatened to make sure I was guilty of a murder I didn't commit.

"Edward!" Grandmère grasped Edward's arm. "No. That's not true. He did what he did to protect you. Protect me. Protect poor little Nicholas. And he helped you build a new life."

"One without my family! What kind of life is that?"

Edward's bitterness blazed. Nick could feel the heat of it from across the room. That sentiment—exiled from family—he understood. The pain. Aloneness. Isolation created by secrets and iron will.

Maybe he had something in common with his father after all. They both had lost.

But, he couldn't accept that his grandfather intended to harm the family, or bring on this kind of pain and misery.

Chapter 24

Sitting in the church pew, Biloxi bowed her head. An elbow jabbed her side.

"What's going on between you and Branna?" Linc whispered.

"Nothing."

"The two of you are thick as thieves and you're not sitting with her. You're sitting with me."

"Can't a girl sit with her only brother? And why do you think it has something to do with me? Maybe she's..." Biloxi pointed to the "Order of Service" in the book.

"May the peace of God be with you," the priest intoned.

"And also with you." The congregation responded in unison.

"Did you ever think that maybe she's not sitting with me?" she muttered. "Or that maybe it has something to do with James? Our family can be overwhelming. Maybe that's why they're off by themselves." She had no definitive answer about Branna's behavior, but surmised it had everything to do with her.

Or rather, the request she'd made.

The shock in Branna's eyes had stunned her; however, she hadn't expected to be shunned, especially since Branna had fought against taking the job of

Keeper when Macy had pushed it on her.

If Branna didn't want it, then why were they fighting?

It made no sense.

After Mass ended, Biloxi shifted from one foot to the other while waiting to exit the church. Her face hurt from the plastered smile. She nodded to others and tried to appear pleasant to those she greeted.

Stepping into the aisle in front of Linc, she tossed her long hair and squared her shoulders while considering her "Branna" situation. There had to be a way for them to be happy without alienating everyone and causing a rift within the family. She had prayed for divine inspiration. She needed a win-win.

A soft shove in the back got her attention. Linc let her know that she was holding up the line.

Outside, the sun warmed the cool morning air. An early spring made the world look fresh in many shades of pale green. Azalea blooms waited to pop. They needed a little more warmth and time. Exactly what she needed, too.

She made her way to the spot where the rest of the family gathered.

"Lovely dress. Nice to have you home to stay." Aunt Joan opened her arms for a hug.

"Thanks." Biloxi hugged her back.

At least someone in this family is glad I'm home.

"Hello? All ya'll, please listen," Macy said. "Mother made a reservation at the Magnolia Terrace for brunch. Head count, please." She started the count. "One."

The count continued. Greta sounded off last. "Sixteen."

"We're all here," Macy said excitedly. "Let's see if we can arrive in a timely fashion. No stopping along the way. No detours for anything. Also, remember, we have a family meeting at three p.m. Everyone is expected to be there. See ya'll at the restaurant."

Biloxi mused. To an outsider, their large family probably looked highly disorganized. Yet, after years of herding their clan, Macy managed it with grace.

"How come you're not riding with Branna and James?" Carson asked suspiciously.

"I think they want some privacy."

"I might have to charge you for all this chauffeuring I'm doing," Carson kidded.

"What the—?" Linc snorted. "It's my car. I'm driving."

"Yeah, well, you always need a good navigator," Carson joked. "For someone who's traveled so much, your internal location finder works as good as a drunk homing pigeon. Without my services, you might not get Biloxi to brunch on time."

Linc scowled. "Just because I couldn't find that grass landing strip on our last flight."

"Ya'll come on." She linked arms with her brother and cousin and headed toward Linc's car. "I think I'm safer with you piloting rather than driving, but let's go."

In Biloxi's peripheral view, she saw Branna and James drive off in Branna's Mercedes. At some point she had to get Branna to relent, right?

How do I get what I want without destroying our family?

****

After brunch, Biloxi arrived home and rushed to change clothes. Out the front door, hitting each tread, she ran down the front steps of Fleur de Lis and followed in Branna's wake.

"Don't we look like a Land's End advertisement?" Branna said as she set a rhythmic pace. "Jeans, sneakers, and turtlenecks. Blue fleece jackets."

Biloxi lifted her face to catch the sun's rays cutting through the cool February air. She slowed to feel the warmth while Branna kept moving.

"Wait up," Biloxi called out. She squinted against the sun, wishing she'd grabbed her sunglasses as Branna quickened her pace, speed walking past the fountain, and heading toward the long shaded driveway.

"Slow down," Biloxi demanded.

Branna's quick walk turned into a trot. As Biloxi narrowed the gap between them, she winced. Her ankle ached. Branna quickened her pace again, moving into a fast jog.

Biloxi poured on the speed, broke into a full run. She'd been number two behind Branna for way too long. Passing Branna, she ran three-quarters the way down the mile-long drive. Panting, she slowed to a trot, her ankle screaming with pain as Branna took her own sweet time.

Her cousin's behavior hit a nerve. She should've expected Branna's actions. While she waited for Branna to catch up, she took a deep inhale and let it go slowly. It was that or roar in anger.

"What's with you?" She limped to the intersection where the drive and the main road met. She bent at the waist and put her hands on her thighs, breathing in cool, moist air.

"You're a little out of shape, cousin." Branna's gloat pinched her last nerve.

"Yeah, well, remember, I had a very badly sprained ankle. The doctor probably wouldn't be too pleased with the running I just did. My ankle is already complaining. I think I need PT."

"Oh," Branna cried, her eyes grew wide. "I'm so sorry. I forgot."

Branna rubbed Biloxi's back.

"It's my ankle that's in pain." As she straightened, Branna took a step back. "If it swells, you'll have to fetch hot water for me to soak it."

"I'm really sorry." Branna winced. "I'll fetch and tote whatever you need."

They walked slowly side by side toward the large, carved wooden sign that welcomed guests to Fleur de Lis. A brick planter filled with blooming crocuses, sprouting tulips, and vibrant daffodils surrounded the sign. The loamy earth, mixed with fresh sprouting plants, made her think of spring and new beginnings. They sat on the edge of the planter and dangled their feet, just as they had as kids.

"I can't remember the last time we fought," Branna said softly, breaking their silence.

"Are we fighting?"

"Well, I'm not sure. If you try to force me to give up my job as Keeper, I guess, *then* it'll be a fight." Branna clasped her hands together and looked down.

"Ahh." Biloxi read the message loud and clear. Branna didn't like the idea of abdicating her inherited role, though she kept avoiding it.

"You sprung this on me. Out of nowhere, Biloxi. Just because I'm not ready to move back...I have James to think about, too."

"You lived here all your life, then went away to

college to escape this place. You've avoided Fleur de Lis. Just like you're avoiding James' proposal. You wear his ring, but won't set a wedding date. How hard is it to make a decision?"

"Leave James out of this," Branna replied icily.

"I will if you will. Stop using him as an excuse. James isn't the barrier. Are you planning to come home and take up your responsibility? I'd die for the opportunity handed to you. Besides, repair costs are mounting and we've got to do something now."

Branna sighed. "I guess we are fighting. You're too strong willed. You've had all kinds of adventures. Now it's my turn. You've not been saddled with the responsibility of this place and family duty all your life. I made a deal with Momma. It's only two years."

"I know what I want, Branna. I'm willing to fight for it."

"I understand...You've always wanted to live here. But, there's room enough for both of us. I can see it now, this'll be our retirement home and all of us cousins will hobble about with our canes."

"Could we be that lucky? But we can't continue if there isn't money. If we don't make repairs, this place won't be here for our retirement."

"Look—" Branna narrowed her eyes. "I can't, even if I wanted, just say yes, and let you take Fleur de Lis. I was raised to run this place. It's always been planned for me!"

Biloxi hopped down from the brick ledge and started to pace. "Then come home and run it. Or let me do it. If you don't want to lead, get out of the way." Tired and frustrated, she wanted Branna to budge.

"It's not that simple," Branna wailed. "And I won't

let you force me into a decision. I'll think about it more, but if you demand an answer right now..." Branna rose and stood nose-to-nose with her. "The answer is no. You can't have what's mine. Is that definite enough for you?"

Biloxi glared at Branna and waited for her to blink first.

"Is this hostile-takeover attempt part of the family meeting agenda this afternoon?" Branna asked.

Biloxi shrugged. "I want you to know I'm staying. Having my stuff shipped down from Atlanta. I'm not going anywhere. In fact, I'm signing a lease for the studio today."

"You're serious? You're really giving up traveling and all the perks to move back here? What the heck are you going to do? I lived through your journeys! You're a great photographer. For goodness sake, you can't make a living here!"

Maybe if they kept their dialogue going, Branna would come around to her point of view? "That's where you're wrong. I've lived in so many places. Just since college, New York, Miami, and Atlanta. This is where I want to be. This place is my choice. Fleur de Lis is what I want."

"But your ownership is equal to mine," Branna stammered.

"Ownership, yes, but not the caretaking. The decision-making, the planning to make it better and greater. That's still your responsibility." She wished Branna could see her vision, or at the very least, had one of her own.

"I promise to think about it. I guess I haven't looked at this place in a long time as anything more than a dreaded burden."

A glimmer of hope blossomed in Biloxi's heart. It could work out like she wanted it—if she could make Branna commit to letting go.

"I'll race you back to the house." Branna grinned.

"No. Don't think so. Ankle injury, remember?"

They turned when rumbles of a diesel engine neared. A familiar pickup slowed.

"What a picture," Nick said huskily as he leaned out of the window. "The Fleur de Lis flowers waiting to greet me. How'd I get so lucky?"

"Hey, darl'n," Branna called, then flashed a flirty grin. "You here to spark with my cousin?"

Biloxi scowled. Heat from a blush rose from her chest to the roots of her hair. She wanted to kick Branna or evaporate into thin air.

"Well now, Miss Branna, seems to me that if any sparkin' is gonna take place, I ought to have her permission first." Nick's words rolled like soft butter.

Biloxi's blush deepened. "We're just friends, Branna," she hissed through clenched teeth.

"So you say, cousin. So you say. *I think* you doth protest too much," Branna whispered.

She had never wanted to slap Branna silly until then.

"Nick? How 'bout a ride up to the house?" Branna asked.

"Absolutely. My chariot waits."

As Branna wiggled into the front passenger seat, Biloxi climbed into the middle of the back seat and clicked her seatbelt in place. Nick adjusted the rear view mirror, and when their gazes locked, she recalled their first encounter—when she sat in the back seat of the truck. She would never forget the moment of terror from their tug-of-war that ended with her embarrassment for doubting Nick's intentions.

From the grin on his face, Nick had read her thoughts. He winked.

"*Chèr*, I have a request and needed to ask you face to face. Well, actually, it's my grandfather's request."

Branna turned in her seat to face Nick, then threw a look over her shoulder, a smug smile, like a cat after a bowl of cream.

Biloxi hated the smirk. "You know me, *chèr*," Biloxi said to Nick and glared, "I'm the quietly polite queen. I'll be happy to grant your request, or your grandfather's. Just please put that peasant in the front seat out at the next stop."

"Your command is my mission."

Branna shook her head and giggled.

Ignoring her cousin, Biloxi pondered Nick's request. What would his grandfather want with her? The way the man had looked at her made her shiver.

Keb' Mo' played a bluesy tune with a Dobro twang on the radio as they drove, windows down, to the house. A cool breeze fluttered against her face. She freed her hair from the ponytail, ran her fingers through it, then shook it loose as Nick pulled up to the fountain. Branna opened the door and hopped down the moment the truck stopped.

"Thanks Nick," Branna said. Looking toward the backseat she snorted, "And you think *I* can't make a decision?"

"A decision about what?" Nick asked.

"Nothing. Just cousin speak," Biloxi said blandly. She'd let Branna stew on their conversation, then in a couple of weeks, she'd call her and broach the subject again. She wouldn't give up. Branna didn't want to be Keeper. Her cousin just needed time for that idea to settle in.

As Biloxi stood next to Nick by the fountain, the cascading water danced. Droplets sparkled like diamonds in the afternoon sunlight.

"Am I intruding? Yesterday, Linc mentioned..." Nick shook his head as if to clear it. "That was only yesterday? Anyway, Linc mentioned a family tag-football game this afternoon, so I figured you'd be home."

"Well—" She paused, reaching for his arm and looked at the time on his watch. "I have about thirty minutes before our family meeting. The game will start after that. You can stay and wait, if you'll be on my team."

"Trying to force the winning advantage?"

She had grown accustomed to his contrasts—stern expression one moment and laughing the next. His own personal way of teasing. When they first met, the sharp angles of his cheeks and the hard set of his jaw matched his tough demeanor. Danger had emanated from him that night, and she had forced her fear away because he appeared to be her only way home in the storm. Now, the angles of his cheeks looked less severe and his jaw looked ruggedly handsome. Moreover, she liked that he wasn't as serious as his tough exterior suggested. Plus, to her, clothes made the man, especially on him. He looked as relaxed and handsome in a tux as he did in jeans. And that smoky voice of his...it got to her every time. Just hearing him read something as simple as a menu caused her bones to liquefy.

"Me? Try for an advantage?" She batted her eyelashes and dipped her chin.

Nick rolled his eyes, looked toward heaven, and appeared to beg for deliverance.

"Okay, enough queen-for-a-day. What did you want to talk about? Or did you really just come here to horn in on the family football game?" She wanted to bring up the conversation she'd overheard last night, but the timing didn't feel right. Her heart wanted to comfort him over the loss of his grandfather, but her mind shouted, "caution."

Nick appeared as though he hadn't heard her. Had he mentally gone to another place? His sudden change worried her. What had Claude set in motion? Seeing pain in Nick's eyes made her decide that any discussion about last night could wait.

"Is there somewhere we could talk in private?" Nick glanced up to the front gallery. Several family members waved.

"There's a bench in the garden out back. Near the tree, you know, the spot where you rescued me."

She turned and took his hand, leading him around the house and toward the bench. Nick's mood weighed heavy around her. As they walked, his somber expression grew dark like a tropical storm gaining strength. He contemplated something. He wasn't happy. But about what?

When they reached the bench, she sat and patted the seat next to her. Nick shook his head. The energy around him seemed to tighten.

"You're scaring me. More than you did the first time we met."

She folded her hands together and continued to

wait for him to speak. She'd thought about him all morning during church. About their growing friendship. About how much she loved spending time with him. About how Chantel might be very upset about a certain kiss last night. And about the lie he'd told to his dying grandfather.

What was on his mind?

****

Nick squatted in front of Biloxi with one knee on the ground for support. He reached for her hand and began to massage small circles over her knuckles while he contemplated where to begin.

After his grandmother and father had left, he spent the morning examining his life. Scattered thoughts coalesced into a complete picture in his mind only after his anger finally ebbed. In its place a driving desire to get on with his life took root. Bayou Petite was his home. The place where he'd established a business. He cared about the people, not just his clients. And, one person in particular. However, he had to live for himself, not to appease his grandfather.

"I wouldn't do anything to hurt you," he said. "I care way too much for that."

"And I for you."

Her hazel eyes reflected concern. He exhaled before continuing. Then, he said, "My grandfather planned his entire funeral."

Her brow furrowed. She cocked her head to one side, though remained silent.

"He requested that you read a passage he selected for his memorial service. The arrangements are very specific."

Her concern changed to surprise, then turned to

dismay. She frowned. "Me? I only met him for a few minutes."

"I know, but yes, you." How could he explain without making Grandpère sound crazy? "Did you know my grandfather followed your work? He knew all about you."

She snorted. Disbelief shone on her face.

"It's true," he said quietly. "He was the one that sent you flyers about contests and shows. When you won the prize for Best in Show last year, he was there when they pinned the blue ribbon on that photograph. He believed in your work, so much so that he funded the tourism contract."

He expected shock from her. He held tightly to her hands when she tried to pull them away.

"I'm sorry to spring this on you in this way," he said. "Grandpère confessed it to me last night. I thought it best if you heard it from me." He paused and tried to figure out how to deliver the next piece of news.

"If you agree to speak—and I hope you will—you need to know you'll be entering hostile territory. My father has reappeared, and my grandmother has his allegiance. She's dead set against you reading at the memorial service."

"*Interesting* choice of words."

Nick squeezed her hand. He rose, took the seat next to her, and gazed into eyes that reflected confusion.

"Biloxi, I'm sorry to say that my grandmother blames your family for our sadness, specifically your Grandmother Elise, and thusly you. She believes my grandfather never loved her as much as he loved Elise. She objects to your family being there—at the memorial service in Baton Rouge and at the burial in the Trahan cemetery."

She didn't need to hear the rest of the story just yet. News about his father and his still-absent mother could wait. Funeral arrangements for the service loomed and took priority over everything else. Keeping his grandfather's wishes was the honorable thing to do. Biloxi could refuse to participate, but he'd make sure her decision would be made without any undue influence from his grandmother or his father.

"You're *serious* about this?"

He nodded.

"You're telling me that a dying man lured me home with a contract, then had his grandson lure me into meeting him? And now you say your grandmother hates me—not really me, but my grandmother—and you want me to speak at your grandmother's dead husband's funeral?"

He paused. "When you put it like that, it does sound crazy."

"Do I look like I'm nuts?" she cried. "I may have fallen several times, hit my head, but I'm certain no permanent damage was done."

She jerked her hands from his and stood. "I've a presentation in a few minutes. I can't do this right now."

After taking several strides away from him, she stopped, then turned back. Her shoulders drooped in what he guessed was resignation.

"What if we talk later this evening, Nick? I don't understand all of this. Do you really *want* me to speak at his memorial service? Or did you come here to tell me about it, hoping I'd say no?"

"How about dinner? We can discuss it more?"

Then he could present the information with more finesse. After she knew the rest of the story, he'd live with her decision. He wouldn't try to cajole her into doing what he wanted.

At least about the service and the burial.

"Dinner, then." She started to leave again. She walked a few steps farther away, then turned back and stopped. "By the way, while we're discussing your grandfather's funeral at dinner, let's discuss his suggestion about a proposal of marriage."

It was his turn to be shocked.

Chapter 25

With her hands folded in her lap, Biloxi looked at each familiar face. Blood knitted them together. They all belonged to Fleur de Lis as if something in their DNA made them human homing pigeons and brought them back to roost each holiday and for special events. Or maybe contained within their family genes was an invisible tattoo that identified them and the old house knew. Either way, she was home, surrounded by loved ones. Peacefulness resonated next to her nervousness. It struck her odd that such conflicting emotions could exist in the same space.

"This meeting is called to order." Macy stood at the head of the long mahogany dining table and banged a gavel. Everyone quieted.

"Roll call. Please say your name for the record." Acting as secretary, Branna noted the names of everyone present into a laptop spreadsheet. Another addition to family history.

"Biloxi Dutrey." She scanned the faces of each of her relatives, seeing bits of herself. Each person at the table owned a share of the estate built by Chalise Thibeaudoux's grandfather, their shared ancestor, over a hundred and fifty years ago. Chalise had inherited the home from her parents, and after she married, she bore twin girls, Grace and Marie, both now close to a hundred years old.

"Good job, Macy," Marie said.

The Old Aunts flanked Macy like guards at Buckingham Palace. It was decided long ago, way before Biloxi's birth, that since Grace was born a few minutes before Marie, she had final veto in all decisions at Fleur de Lis. However, documented family history revealed that Grace usually sided with whoever reigned as the current Keeper. In this case, it was Macy.

"Before you is a balance sheet. The landscaping project is noted. It includes a specimen magnolia tree. Another item, we finally paid off the loan for the building addition and the elevator." Macy's tone shifted. She was getting down to business. "We, however, have several large expenditures coming up and our reserves are dwindling. Not enough money in the pot to make all the needed repairs."

Biloxi listened and contemplated the family tree. Grace Dutrey had three children. Her two daughters had remained childless. Robert, her only son, had a son—Sean Patrick, Biloxi's father. Thus, Grace's branch of the family accounted for seven people at the meeting, whereas Marie Covington's son, also named Robert, had three children, who in turn had children, thus Marie's side of the family seated around the table now totaled twelve.

Blood, marriage, and love bound them together. Biloxi believed they would treat her fairly—as long as she kept with tradition. Within the family, it didn't matter that she was related directly to Grace, or that Branna was related directly to Marie, everyone had an equal vote, technically an equal say—except that Macy had a way of influencing others, which meant that in order to change the rules, a majority of votes was needed.

Biloxi's nerves tingled. Anticipation danced in her gut. She would make the Old Aunts proud, if given a chance. They inspired her, offered unconditional love in their staid old-fashioned ways. She would mourn their passing. Clocks would be stopped. The house would be dressed in black. These traditions would be carried out to honor them.

"Thanks, sis," Linc whispered. "You helped that bottom line. Not only ours, but the library's."

With all of her musing, Biloxi missed the reporting of the amount raised for the library from last night's auction. She refocused her attention on Macy, who continued speaking.

"The Valentine's Ball is this Saturday night. I spoke to the fire marshal about capacity in the hall and the good news"—Macy paused and eyed them all—"we can sell another twenty-five tickets!"

"My head count of the family attending, including the kids not here, is twenty-three," Branna announced.

A small sting of regret pierced Biloxi's heart. The missing twenty-fourth person in the clan was Camilla, Branna's younger sister. Since Branna's broken engagement to Steven, Camilla took off wandering out west. Not exactly missing. Macy said Camilla had taken odd jobs since dropping out of grad school, and now worked somewhere in Wyoming. Biloxi vowed to call her cousin to reconnect, and to determine what she might offer to lure Camilla home.

Why had Camilla traveled so far away? Maybe the second Lind daughter needed some support? She could relate to that.

"I'm thinking of wearing black to the ball," Aunt

Joan interjected. "Something different from the auction."

"Yes, but with pants instead of skirts," Aunt Leigh said.

Two loud bangs sounded when Grace and Marie struck the floor with their canes.

"No," Grace said, her voice ringing clear as a crystal bell.

"Absolutely not," said Marie, shaking her head.

"Ladies wear dresses," the Old Aunts stated in unison.

Further suggestion by anyone after that decree was pointless.

"Yes, well..." Macy redirected the conversation. "We have one more piece of business to discuss."

Biloxi rose when Macy nodded in her direction. "As you know," Macy explained. "One of our own has returned. She says 'permanently,' and I hope to make it so."

Standing next to Macy, Biloxi shifted into business mode like she would for any professional presentation. The family needed to see her determination and confidence. The first step of her grand plan was the Fleur de Lis photography studio. In time, the rest of her plan would follow. Just as soon as Branna stopped flopping around like a fish on a dock and made a decision.

"I'm happy to announce that I would like to open Fleur de Lis Photography. Some of you saw my brochures at the auction." Biloxi handed out flyers. "With your vote of support, I want to set up shop there—" She pointed out the windows to the garçonnière. "I've had a builder draw up specs. My plan is to create a studio in the living room. I'll make an office and dressing room from two of the unused bedrooms." She smiled at Linc and Carson, "And I intend to accomplish this without permanently routing the guys out of their crib." She paused for effect, looking at the eyes focused on her. "The best part, the currently unused space will bring in revenue...when I pay rent. And having an onsite photographer and studio will mean more brides may book Fleur de Lis for their weddings. It's a win-win."

Murmurs swelled. The family talked amongst themselves.

"Are there questions for Biloxi?" Macy asked.

"Who's paying for the remodel?" an uncle asked.

"I will, through the rent. There's no cost incurred by the family for my studio." Biloxi handed out a budget for the renovation costs.

"Macy, you've gone over the proposal and the costs," Macy's father said. "You approve of this plan?"

"Yes."

The conversations continued a minute more. Biloxi sat down and smiled, however, her insides were anything but calm.

"If there are no further questions, I suggest we vote on it now," Macy urged the group.

"I agree." Grace stomped her cane.

"Branna has ballots. We'll do a secret ballot as usual."

Tradition dictated that each family member put a "plus" or "minus" sign on the slip of paper that Branna handed out to them, then drop their vote into a bowl for Branna to count.

With a firm hand, Biloxi wrote a bold "plus" on her

ballot to ensure she'd have at least one vote.

She waited. Her face hurt from smiling. Her neck and shoulders ached. Tension rolled down her back. Her fate rested in the hands of her family.

The votes were counted away from the table. She prayed for a unanimous decision.

When Branna returned and paused in the doorway, Biloxi expectantly looked over at her.

"It's a go." Branna gave a thumbs up.

Biloxi rooted herself to her chair, but she wanted to jump up and do a happy dance, twirl like a whirling dervish.

After a round of congratulations, Macy closed the meeting.

"Champagne!" Deidre cried.

Cheers of agreement went around the room.

Unable to contain her euphoria about her first success, Biloxi darted out of the house for air.

"That didn't take long." Nick rose from a rocking chair on the front gallery.

Biloxi stopped. She'd forgotten that he'd been waiting.

"Biloxi?"

A voice from behind caught her attention. She turned back toward the screened door. "Ah. Hi. Um..." She panicked and froze.

"Please introduce me to your friend." Grandmother Elise smiled warmly.

Glued to the spot, sandwiched between them, Biloxi couldn't decide which one she needed to protect more.

"Good afternoon, Madame." Nick offered his hand.

"How do you do?" Grandmother Elise tilted her

head and shook Nick's hand.

"Uhm...Grandmother Elise, this is Dr. Nicholas Trahan." She spoke quickly, then sucked in a breath. She turned to Nick and gave a weak smile. "Nick, this is my grandmother, Elise."

She held her breath.

Nick bent slightly. "I've heard stories about how beautiful you are. I see they're true. It's a pleasure to meet you."

"You're a good-looking man," Elise said softly, "but even more handsome are your manners. Very nice to meet the newest neighbor from across the road. Please excuse me now. Biloxi darlin', we'll talk later."

Biloxi let out a breath after her grandmother's hug. Elise left her and Nick standing together on the gallery.

"Awkward, but that went better than I expected," Nick said matter-of-factly.

"You're quite the charmer," Biloxi noted. He was always polite. Behaved like a gentleman in every situation. Held doors, offered his arm, or stood whenever a lady entered or left a room. She shouldn't have worried. She should have trusted him.

Trusted him?

But she did *trust* him. Even after she'd given up the idea of trusting any man after what Gregory had put her through.

"It's hard to see our grandparents as young people," Nick suggested.

"It baffles the mind that your grandfather would issue a challenge to mine, over...my grandmother. I love her dearly. Don't get me wrong. But what about her caused them to think killing was an option to solve the problem?"

"Men."

It sounded silly coming from him, yet his deadpan delivery made the whole thing funny. Just like him to break the tension with humor.

"I know I promised to be on your team," Nick said. "But instead, I need to talk to you. In private. Away from the house. Could you leave for dinner now?"

His eyes pleaded rather than his voice. Her heart thudded double time. "All right," she said. "Let me tell Linc that he's captain today."

Once inside the truck, she placed her hand in Nick's when he wiggled his fingers. He squeezed gently.

"It's all gonna be okay," he said quietly.

His warm hand and warm voice produced a warmer sensation in her. Her adrenaline high suddenly melted into peaceful contentment. She believed him when he said everything would be okay.

But they had a lot to talk about.

"Anything strike your fancy? What are you hungry for?"

"I'm easy. Surprise me."

Nick took the remaining spot in front of Maucele's Place at the edge of town. It lured locals with authentic Cajun home cooking. He had said it was his favorite place—which was true until he sampled Greta's cooking.

Nick waved when they entered the diner. "Hey, Capt'n."

In less than a year, Nick had woven himself into the fabric of the community. One that accepted newbies, if ever, only after an extended time that usually lasted a generation. But he was a Trahan, and old family ties ran deep. Maybe to the old timers, Nick was the prodigal grandson returned.

"Come on," he told her. "The po'boys are on me." He led her to a small table by a window framed with red and white checked curtains and a view of freshly planted flowerboxes filled with pansies, parked vehicles, and the quaint-looking street. The savory aromas of hot frying seafood made her stomach growl.

The moment they sat down, Captain Jack made his way over. A jeans and T-shirt clad waitress wearing a denim apron followed him. The waitress scooted in front of Captain Jack and placed menus before them on the table.

"Hey," she said, then smiled tentatively.

Biloxi nodded.

"What can I get you to drink?"

"Hello, Tia. Have you met Biloxi Dutrey?" Nick's eyes remained trained on the menu. "Sweet tea for me and the lady."

The petite, middle-aged blonde scribbled on a pad. "Be right back with drinks."

Captain Jack pulled up a chair from the empty table next to theirs and sat down with them, dominating the small space with his sizeable girth. "I don't mean to intrude." He looked as somber as he sounded. "I came to offer my condolences. I can't believe he's dead. Your grandmother called. I'm honored to be a pallbearer. If ya need anything, Doc, *anything at all*, call me. Ya hear?"

Nick nodded and shook Captain Jack's hand. "Thank you. Grandpère would be happy to have you there."

Biloxi gazed out the window and considered

escaping to the ladies' room rather than intrude on Nick's privacy. After a moment of silence between the two men, Captain Jack scooted the chair back and stood, then patted Nick on the shoulder.

The portly old man in bib overalls looked down at her. "Biloxi Dutrey, you take care o' him." Captain Jack's voice broke. "Real good care."

She blinked, surprised by the emotion the old man displayed.

"I will."

Nick stared out the window. He appeared to have forgotten she was there.

She leaned in toward him. "Is this a good idea? Too many people here. We could get a po'boy to go and eat down by the river."

"It'll be okay."

His calmness soothed her when she wanted to soothe him. No stranger to grief, she laid her hand on top of his and offered what comfort she could.

Tia appeared with their drinks. The glasses *clacked* when she set them on the table. Biloxi straightened and folded her hands in her lap.

"I need a few minutes to decide," Biloxi told the waitress.

"Sure thing. And welcome home, Biloxi. We haven't met, but I'm friends with Greta. Wow. You sure do look like Branna." Tia paused and turned to Nick. "I'm so very sorry to hear about your granddaddy. If I can do anything, please let me know."

Nick nodded. "I guess news really does travel fast in a place like this."

"Wave when you're ready to order, that way I won't pester you," Tia said, then headed toward the kitchen.

Nick placed his hands, palms up on the table, and wiggled his fingers, an invitation to hers. Her palms met his. Nick squeezed gently and stared into her eyes. Warmth radiated through his hands, running a current to her heart.

Was she losing her heart to a lying man? She'd been down that road already. Gregory had said he loved her—said it was forever. And clearly he meant a forever that only existed in his mind.

"And what about you?" Nick's quiet tone held her hostage.

"Pardon?"

"What about you?"

"What *about* me?" she asked hesitantly.

His intense perusal made her squirm.

He released one hand and crooked his finger, inviting her closer, as if he intended to whisper in her ear. She leaned forward. He leaned in more. Gently he captured her face in his hands, his fingers splayed. His thumbs caressed her cheeks. Nose-to-nose, he tenderly touched his lips to hers.

Warm.

So warm.

Hypnotic.

When Nick deepened the kiss, she melted. All tension left her body. His thumbs stroked the hollows of her cheeks. His teeth tugged tenderly on her bottom lip. His tongue grazed that spot, then nudged her lips apart.

Nick's warmth triggered a burn low in her gut, then washed over her like a hot wave.

Biloxi tried to pull back, but Nick held firm, not yielding to the interruption. She'd never had a man make love to her mouth in public—for that matter, never like that in private, either. A rush of excitement deafened all other sound. She floated somewhere. Maybe Heaven.

When Nick released her, coolness brushed her lips where his warm ones had been. She was reluctant to let him go, and even more reluctant for the kiss to stop. Usually, self-consciousness prevented her from public displays of affection. Nick changed that.

"Are ya'll ready to order now?" Tia called from behind the counter.

"Not yet," Nick replied, but his gaze remained locked on Biloxi.

"Biloxi, let me ask you again." Nick's voice was low. His smoldering eyes held her gaze. Was it lust or love? Either way, he scared her. "What about you? How do *you* feel about me?"

****

Nick hadn't intended for the kiss to go that far. Yet, for the first time in a very long time, going with his gut provided deep satisfaction. He stuffed the rules of propriety into some dark recess of his mind and slammed the door.

He wanted Biloxi Dutrey.

She occupied all of his attention.

Disappearing sunlight through the window made her hair look darker. It shined luxurious under the restaurant's harsh lights. Her cheeks glowed. Her mouth smiled and formed small dimples in her cheeks. Her hands fit with his as though made to be held by him.

"Nick, remember how I said you were scaring me when we talked in the garden this afternoon? Well, I'm more scared now."

Biloxi ran her fingers through her hair, pushing it away from her face. A stray piece fell across her cheek. She shoved it behind her ear.

Had her hand trembled?

"You're the least scared person I've ever met," he said. He meant it, too. From the night they'd met, he saw her strength and respected her independence. Somewhere along the way, the lines had blurred. Friendship, respect, lust, and desire all collided into love.

She was the one.

His forever.

"I," she started then stopped. "I am"—she blinked—"dumbfounded. Confused. *Lust* is what you wanted to talk about?"

"Ouch, that stings. Lust. We'll talk about that later. Don't change the subject. We came to discuss my grandfather's request, his funeral, and the rest of *my* life. I want to know how you feel about me."

Her puzzlement made him chuckle. For once, he had her off balance. Okay, maybe he had scared her a little. But there was no way she didn't have feelings for him. Strong ones. Otherwise, she wouldn't have let him kiss her like that, nor would she have kissed him back. She couldn't deny what passed between them. He wouldn't let her.

"Let's talk about your grandfather's memorial service and forget the personal stuff for now," she said. "You want me to do this reading against your grandmother's wishes?"

"No."

"No? No, what?"

"I can't forget about the personal stuff. However, we'll talk about that kiss you gave me last. But about the reading, it's a Bible passage from the book of Ruth. Strange, but that's what he wanted."

"Explain this to me. Why on earth would he want *me* to read at his funeral? You said he lured me home. Was responsible for my contract. Unbelievable! Now tell me the straight-up truth."

How did he explain the desires of an ailing old man? One who'd lived with passion, but never with the one woman he had passionately loved? Could he possibly explain his grandfather's delusions of believing that the granddaughter of his unrequited love was born to be his grandson's wife?

It sounded ridiculously lame.

Yet, how would he ever explain that the old man was right?

Chapter 26

"Nick, this is awkward." Biloxi covered her cheeks with her hands. "I can't attend a memorial service for your grandfather, let alone do a reading when the widow doesn't want me there. That would be in extremely bad taste on my part."

Nick's eye flashed. She wanted him to do something, say something. Fix the problem. After all, she believed him when he said everything would work out okay.

"Biloxi." His smooth voice always hypnotized her, but did it represent the calm before the storm?

"I want you at the memorial for *me*. I understand your reluctance, but I'll stand next to you. This is an opportunity to show a united front. Let both our families know that what happened in the past, is past. That part of their life has nothing to do with us."

Oh, he was good. Convincing. Calm. Committed. "*Yes*" was on the tip of her tongue. She wanted to agree, if for no other reason than to see him smile again, but the word didn't spill from her lips.

"Nick," she whispered. "Is there a compromise somewhere to be had?"

"You want a compromise? The woman who wants *everything* her way?"

"There has to be a middle ground."

"I'm listening."

"I'll attend with you," she agreed. "But I won't read the passage. It isn't right. It's upstanding that you want to honor your grandfather's wishes. But he's gone. Your grandmother lives. Funerals are ceremonies for the living. I won't heap more pain on a heart that's already bleeding."

A soft smile pulled at his mouth. He closed his eyes and lifted his face, as though he savored something.

"*Chèr*," he whispered. "My grandfather believed a man only got one chance at true love in this life. Your grandmother was it for him. Sadly, my grandfather was the only one for my grandmother. Yes, it's dysfunction at its height, however, I thank you for caring about an old woman's feelings."

"I'm glad you understand." She placed her elbows on the table and folded her fingers together, then rested her chin on them. How would she start the next topic? "Now, just how manipulative was your grandfather? You're saying he *brought* me home with a rigged contest. It had nothing to do with my talent? In his mind, he brought me home for you?"

"Oh. So you do understand."

"Whoa. You don't get off that easy, Mister. Start talking. I get that the old man had some sort of covert mission. Did he think by giving me the contract, I owed him? And how did he connect the dots between the contract, me, and you?"

Nick's chair scraped the floor when he slid back. He stretched his legs long and crossed them at the ankles, then clasped his hands behind his head.

She eyed his nonchalant pose. Just like a man. He had gotten what he wanted when she promised to attend the memorial service, but he'd better think again about avoiding her questions. He knew her well enough to know she wouldn't renege on her word, even if he failed to reveal the full purpose of his grandfather's manipulation, but she'd find a way to get it out of him. Determination, not Noël, should've been her middle name.

"You're all worked up about the wrong thing," Nick said.

"How's that?"

"You got what you wanted—a reason to come home. He helped you get your wish—again a reason to come home *and* get paid for it through the contract. Staying in Bayou Petite is up to you. But you're wrong about one thing. You earned the contract. He didn't have final say in the photographer chosen for the job. The tourist council reserved that right. He just put everything into action."

That made her feel a little bit better. But, how many photographers had submitted portfolios? Was it a one-trick pony show? She wanted to know, but at the same time, she didn't. She had a signed contract. How much did the past really matter?

"What about this 'you and me' thing?" She challenged him to deny his grandfather's devious behavior after what she had overhead.

"Oh, so we *are* going to talk about the kiss now. Or is this the *lust* conversation?"

"Stop grinning at me, Charles Nicholas Trahan. This is serious."

He cocked his head to one side, his expression sliding into that dangerous one. The one that melted her heart.

"*Chèr*, Blaise Pascal was a mathematician, but probably remembered most for his philosophical mind. He said it best. 'The heart has reasons, reason knows nothing about.'"

He chose *now* to spout philosophy? From a man dead for hundreds of years? At this rate, the funeral would be over and she'd be none the wiser about the true intent of Claude Trahan's plan.

"You've got me going in circles, Dr. Trahan. I want to know how your grandfather believed that by manipulating me, luring me home with a photography contract, we would end up together. I'm a photographer. Life is a visual through my lens. Kissing? Lust? Dead philosophers? Draw me a picture."

"Okay."

"Now!"

"First, say it again."

"Say what?"

"Say, Charles. Nicholas. Trahan."

His whisper seduced her. She shivered. His whisky voice and topaz eyes that looked deep into her soul could take her far off track if she didn't pay close attention to her goals. If she wasn't very careful, Nick was a man who could make her forget...everything.

And he did exactly that when he kissed her again.

Chapter 27

All day, the mental back-and-forth match between thoughts of Nick's kisses and Claude's claims made Biloxi's head hurt. That pain joined forces with her aching shoulder muscles. How many arm curls had she done while putting fresh paint on the walls of her new studio? The sun had set and the race against time pushed her work efforts into the night.

"Anyone home?" yelled a voice from behind her.

Biloxi turned with a paint roller in hand to find Greta standing on the threshold of her soon-to-be completed office carrying something that looked suspiciously like a dinner plate covered with a tea towel.

"Welcome! Come on in." She laid the roller in a paint tray, then turned down the volume on the radio, silencing her favorite blues man, Tab Benoit. "Welcome to Fleur de Lis Photography."

Greta stepped carefully through the debris—paint cans, drop cloths, ladders, and brushes—while trying to balance the offering in her hands.

Biloxi spied a longneck bottle tucked in Greta's apron pocket. That would take the edge off her thirst. After a while, water alternating with sweet tea just didn't cut it. While she had planned to work non-stop until she finished painting, her stomach had plans of its own, and rumbled its message.

"You didn't come for dinner, and everyone else's gone off to bed," Greta explained. "I didn't want you dirtying up my clean kitchen, so I brought you a plate."

"Thanks." Biloxi wiped her fingers on a rag, then pitched it on the heap, a growing mountain of soiled rags. She turned two large orange buckets upside down and offered Greta a seat on one of them.

"Looks nice in here," Greta said, gazing around.

"Painting myself is saving me money."

She eyed the meal. Her stomach rumbled again. Greta waved the plate under her nose. Red beans and rice with andouille sausage. The savory aroma filled her senses. She laughed when her rumbling stomach grumbled louder.

Red beans and rice. One of her favorites, especially if made by Greta's hands.

Biloxi laid the towel in her lap, then set the plate on top while Greta pulled a spoon from one apron pocket and a beer from the other.

"I don't know how you've remained unmarried, Greta. Just look at you, apron on, spoon in one hand, bottle in the other. You're the poster-wife for a man who likes to eat. Lord knows we've got enough of them around here."

Greta sniffed. "I'm very particular."

"And selfishly, I'm thankful." She took the offered bottle and spoon.

"You going to work all night?" Greta asked, scooting the bucket closer.

"Decided to work 'til I finish painting this room. Almost done. Only the baseboards left after that one wall." Biloxi twisted the top off the Abita beer, sipped, and savored the tang. "I plan on opening the doors next

Monday. My furniture is arriving tomorrow afternoon...Oh, you'll be here right? To tell the movers where things go?"

"Yes."

"I placed the ads this morning for Sunday's paper and I'll hand out business cards and flyers during the Valentine's Ball on Saturday." She saluted Greta with the spoon, then loaded it with rice and sausage before putting the heaping spoonful into her mouth.

"You're rock'n and roll'n right along on this business," Greta said. "You are still planning on going to Mr. Claude's service tomorrow?"

"Mmm, this is good, Greta." She savored the dish, then reached her spoon in for more. "Yes, I'm going. Seems G. G. Grace and Grandmother Elise are not too pleased about my decision since they found out Nick's grandmother doesn't want any of us there."

"And you're going to piss off a widow because?"

"I promised Nick I'd be there for him."

Greta shook her head. "This family never did anything against the Trahans. I don't want to speak ill of the dead, but the problem sits squarely on that old man's shoulders. Yet, I can understand why his widow wouldn't want any of us around."

"Believe me, I feel very weird about this. Mother even called me today to *chat* about my attendance. Lord knows she expects me to follow propriety to the letter, but she finally agreed that if Nick wanted me there with him, it was okay."

"If it's any consolation, I understand why you're going. Gotta stand by your man."

She blinked. "What?" A spoonful of red beans and rice hung suspended in mid-air.

"Your man," Greta repeated. "You forget, this is small town Bayou Petite, not some big city. I heard about it at the market today, how Nick proposed. But I haven't said anything to any of the family. I'll keep your secret. It's your good news to share."

Biloxi blinked and dropped the spoon. It clattered against the plate. "Greta...what the devil are you talking about?"

"I've got my sources."

A warm flush crept up Biloxi's neck and past her cheeks, until her scalp tingled. Setting the dinner plate on the floor, she grabbed the bottle, turned it bottoms up, chugging down the beer.

Where's tequila when I need it?

Greta was right. No more big-city anonymity. No way to hide news *or gossip* in a small town. The blessing and curse of being part of a big, old, established family in a town with a population of less than a thousand—her permanent residency status may have driven the population to one thousand and one—meant everyone knew everything about everyone. And, an increase in the town's population by one didn't change the way gossip traveled. When she saw that little tailor next, he'd need to be fitted for a funeral tux. She was going to kill him. He had to be the source of the problem.

"Nick is only a friend."

"Look, you can say that all day long, but folks now think otherwise. And the more you deny it, the more believable the gossip becomes." Greta's knowing rang loud and clear like the bell on the town square pealing the message for all to hear.

"But..." Biloxi stammered. "It's not true."

If Greta didn't believe her, then no one would. If this gossip made the rounds before Claude's memorial service—or worse still, reached her mother—there'd be hell to pay, and she was fresh out of get-out-of-hell-free cards.

"What, may I ask, isn't true?" Greta asked. "Didn't Dr. Nick Trahan propose to you when he took you to Maucele's last night?"

"No. Absolutely not."

So it wasn't the tailor...but who, then?

Greta frowned. "I don't believe it."

"You don't believe me?" Stunned, she stared at Greta. "I'm telling you the truth. He didn't propose. You know Nick, he looks all serious and says stuff, but he's mischievous. He was playing around. Who told you this crap? And better yet, have you repeated it to anyone? Have you?" She gritted her teeth and glared at Greta.

"Well, I didn't quite believe it at first. Joe told me when I pulled up at the grocery. But then I saw Nick come out of the jewelry store carrying a small velvet box. Lavelle's only puts one thing in those little boxes." Greta's voice held great conviction.

Biloxi set her feet apart, planted her elbows on her thighs, then rested her chin in her hands and groaned. Her thoughts rammed into each like a rush hour collision. Her temples throbbed. Her head hurt. Fleur de Lis. Her family. Her business. Her plans. All of it did *not* include becoming anybody's missus. Her focus remained on her projects and none of them included a full-time partner of any sort. At least not yet.

"Nick was joking at dinner. I guess someone eavesdropped on a private conversation. Maybe someone you know named Tia could have misconstrued our discussion. But, I'm setting the story straight. There was no proposal and, more importantly, no acceptance of one."

Greta twisted her mouth to one side and cocked her head in contemplation. Biloxi nodded, reassuring her she'd spoken the truth. Whoever provided Greta with the information had gotten it all wrong.

"Well, I'm disappointed. I've been expecting that man to propose. I see the way he looks at you. However, I'm glad to hear he's got more class than to ask you to marry him in that hole-in-the-wall diner. I expect something way more classy from him. I believe you. Nick hasn't proposed...yet."

Biloxi picked up her plate and took another bite of the now-cold food. Her initial objective had been to satisfy the hole in her stomach, but until she talked with Nick about the rumors, the hole wouldn't disappear, no matter how much she ate.

"Not going to happen, Greta. Don't get your hopes up. We're friends. Besides, Miss Veterinary Clinic's got eyes for your Nick."

"We'll see," Greta said as she crossed the threshold to leave.

Greta's unspoken challenge hung in the air.

Biloxi reached into her back pocket, then groaned when it was empty.

"Where are you now?"

She scanned the floor.

Her cell phone had disappeared again.

Just as well. It had to be close to midnight and respectable calling hours had ended, but if she found it in the next ten minutes, she'd call Dr. Charles Nicholas

Trahan, even if it meant waking him up. He'd really messed things up.

On her hands and knees, she searched the drop cloth on the floor for the phone. Several minutes passed and still no phone. Nick was lucky. Off the hook for now. Besides, paint wouldn't make it onto the walls by itself. She needed to get back to work. In an hour, she could finish the baseboards. The room had to be completed tonight. Tomorrow other tasks required attention to prepare for the opening.

Her bank account would soon be in the red, after the remodeling expenses and incidental business costs. The doors to Fleur de Lis Photography had to open on Monday if she expected to succeed. She would schedule her studio work around the outdoor shots for the tourism contract.

She slumped on the floor to rest, tired from painting. But she had to finish. She crawled to the radio and turned up the volume. Bonnie Raitt's ballad "I Will Not Be Broken" got her to her feet, snapping her fingers and swaying.

Grabbing the paint roller, she heaved it into the paint pan. Pale blue paint slipped over the edge and dripped on the cloth that covered the wood floor. She ran the roller back and forth in the pan, saturating the nap before rolling out her frustrations on the wall.

Her feet moved and her hips gyrated in time to the music floating through the air. She shoved away her irritation and let her thoughts wander to the man who spiked her anger, yet somehow managed to keep her reassured that her life was going in the right direction. She hummed along until the lyrics ended, then made up her own.

"Dr. Charles Nicholas Trahan, don't you dare ruin what we have. You know what it's like to lose someone. We're burying your grandfather tomorrow."

She slashed the paint roller across the wall. "I don't want to lose you, but darl'n there's a line I ain't crossing again."

A stab of sadness hit her. Gregory. He'd walked out. Just when she needed him the most. Nick wasn't him. Nick had said it best—*Men!*

Still swaying when the next blues tune began, she made up words about losing at love and going home. Before she knew it, her eyes blurred when lyrics about missing out on a baby's butterfly kisses rolled off her lips.

She wiped her eyes with the back of her hand, then stood back to examine her handiwork. Satisfaction settled over her. After working alone all evening, she was tired of her own company. While dinner with Greta was a short break, it had also served up a heap more than red beans and rice.

With slow rhythmic beats from a drum and licks on a guitar along with a fiddle to accompany her, she sang her frustrations. "Damn you Nick! What's the deal? I'm not ready to feel...anything too deeply yet. Not ready to take a chance. Not ready to do a love dance. I'll die if you turn to Chantel. But darl'n...dying ain't nothin' new to me."

She wished away her maudlin mood. "Focus, Biloxi. Focus."

She couldn't lose sight of her goal. The movers promised delivery of her office furniture tomorrow. She'd sold most of her belongings. No need for thrift-shop furniture when Fleur de Lis had antiques waiting to be used. Boxes of books and stacks of photos, along with old 35-millimeter negatives she'd cataloged in binders would arrive, CDs, other pieces of memorabilia, and the bulk of her clothes, too. Plus, tomorrow, she had to schedule the pick-up of her car.

She continued to mindlessly swish white paint on the baseboards. Dread bloomed and anchored in her chest at the thought of the funeral *and* a dinner at the church afterward. The uncomfortable sensation continued to grow with each stroke of the brush.

Her confrontational *tête-à-tête* with Nick would have to wait, though maybe Dutrey women weren't intended for Trahan men.

And what about Chantel? Nick hadn't mentioned if he planned to escort that woman to Saturday night's Valentine's Ball. He probably hadn't given it much thought, given the death of his grandfather. Then again, he might not want to attend at all.

Either way, the event was a must-do for her. Linc would be home and she could count on her brother, once again, to be a stand-in date. There could be worse ways to spend a Saturday night. Thankfully, she adored him.

But what about Nick? Thinking about him confused her head and her heart.

Her thoughts bubbled like a hot pot of gumbo. Could he be the man of her dreams? Her head said "no." Her heart argued "maybe."

How would her family react to that?

Chapter 28

"Coffee," Biloxi groaned as she opened the screen door to the kitchen the next morning.

"It's a good thing you're going to the service," Greta said, handing over a mug of dark coffee.

The scents of frying bacon, browning potatoes, bubbling grits and baking biscuits caused Biloxi's mouth to pucker and her stomach rumble.

"Do I look that bad?" She cupped her hands around the mug for warmth.

"Well, I won't lie," Greta said dryly.

"I fell asleep after I finished painting the studio dressing room last night. The alarm on my cell phone woke me. I hate chimes when I'm trying to sleep. Crawled around on my hands and knees to locate the darn thing on the floor in my office."

Her hands still bore spots of white from painting the trim. With only four hours of sleep, she imagined the dark circles under her eyes were less than attractive. Yanking the bandana off her head, she laid the paint-stained cloth on the counter, then gulped down the last bit of her coffee.

"I don't have time for breakfast," she explained. "Nick's picking me up in less than an hour. Could I beg for a bacon biscuit and more coffee to go?"

Greta nodded. "You go on. I'll have food ready when you're done."

"If I'm not down when Nick gets here, please call me on my cell phone. I'd prefer he not have to start his day with an inquisition from the Old Aunts." She poured another cup of coffee, but it wouldn't sit well in her grumbling stomach. She needed food, but for fortification, she poured a big dollop of milk in the mug.

She headed up the back steps, two at a time, to her second-floor bedroom while mentally taking inventory of her closet. She hadn't given much thought to what she'd wear, but thankfully, she had several options. Between her few things here and the clothes Branna left, there had to be something appropriate.

A hot shower revived her somewhat. She dried her hair and dressed. After pushing her hair back from her face, she checked her makeup in the mirror while trying to suppress a yawn. The unmistakable rumble of Nick's Ford truck nudged her to hurry.

Sliding into black heels, she smoothed the black skirt and adjusted the cuffs on the long-sleeved, black silk blouse. The string of white pearls around her neck and pearl studs in her ears added the only color to the somber outfit.

She adjusted her purse strap over her shoulder, then picked up the cashmere coat. She descended the backstairs on tiptoes hoping to greet Nick at the rear door to the kitchen. Greta would have biscuits and bacon wrapped to go, including several for Nick. She figured they could eat on the way, and she could make calls about furniture delivery times.

It seemed odd to be concerned with the ordinary, everyday details of life while they headed to a funeral.

Before her heels clacked on the wooden kitchen

floor, she overheard Greta and Nick around the corner.

"I'm sorry for your loss, Nick. But, are you sure you need to take her along? Your grandmother is entitled to grieve the loss of her husband without being aggrieved by Biloxi."

Biloxi turned the corner to see Nick leaning against the counter next to Greta, who stood in front of the sink with her arms crossed over her chest. She was frowning.

"Good morning," Biloxi said in a hush.

"I packed biscuits in waxed paper." Greta pointed to the bag on the kitchen island. "Coffee in the travel cups. Cream, sugar, and chocolate syrup. Take a couple of tea towels so you don't soil your clothes."

"Thanks, Greta. I appreciate your help." She leaned in and kissed Greta's cheek.

When Nick opened the door, Biloxi scooted past him and waited for him to follow. He stood in the kitchen for a moment longer and grasped Greta's hand. "I promise. It'll all be okay."

The morning sun seemed too bright as they entered the truck. Once on the interstate, they headed due west with the morning light at their backs. She cast a glance at Nick, wondering what occupied his mind. Her grandfather's passing had been so different. Not full of aggravation and angst.

Grandfather Robert had died peacefully after a short illness. What she remembered most was the family's bonding after the funeral, how it brought them together. They shared memories of how he had touched each of their lives. Her large extended family melded together, supporting one another. She cherished the happy memories.

Biloxi turned to Nick. She ran her hand down his arm, hoping to offer support and reassurance. Something he'd given her time and again since they'd met.

Who did Nick have? His absent mother? A grandmother dealing with her own grief? She respected Nick's grandmother's position about the funeral arrangements, and she'd stay clear of the woman. However, she wouldn't abandon Nick.

She would make sure he understood that he could depend on her.

****

Nick scanned the church sanctuary. There was barely standing room in the rear when the memorial service began. Thankfully, except for a brief minute of polite condolences, he'd managed to make it so his grandmother and Biloxi were never in each other's company.

Sitting in the second row, behind his grandmother and father, he felt the warmth of Biloxi's hand in his. He twined his fingers with hers and faced the large painted portrait of his grandfather, the one that had hung in the family room in the Baton Rouge house. He preferred not to look when the casket was closed, which signaled the start of the service.

The minister in his pastoral garb stood at the pulpit and asked everyone to bow their heads. While the minister prayed, Nick closed his eyes and let his mind wander through old memories, trying to arrange the jagged bits and pieces into order. He needed to make sense of his reaction to his father's reappearance. At ten, he'd thought he hated him, at thirteen, he turned ambivalent. Not knowing the truth about the last twenty years made it hard to trust the man he used to call "Dad."

And where was his mother? Was she even alive? His grandmother and father swore they didn't know. His parents bothered him equally, absent or not. Last night, the past had him tossing and turning until he gave up the idea of sleep. He'd lit a fire in the fireplace and sat with a highball glass two-fingers full of Maker's Mark, sipping as he pondered.

The trauma his parents had put him through made him an obedient child. He never gave his grandparents any trouble, but made up for it during his hell-raising college years. Drinking and partying and girls produced a merry-go-round of hangovers. He had to change his ways to finish at the top of his class in veterinary school. Since then, his boundaries had grown more defined, though they hadn't protected him from countless bad blind dates.

His growing-up years were blessed with his grandfather's support, yet the hollowness after his parents' abandonment failed to lessen. Did that set him on a path of too-rigid standards? Standards that left him without a wife and children. He hadn't had a serious long-term relationship in several years. As much as he always envied his friends with their big families, as much as he said he wanted that for himself, last night— with the help of another two fingers of Maker's Mark— he'd discovered the truth about his solitary existence. He believed he would never make a good husband or father.

The minister interrupted his thoughts when he called Nick to the pulpit.

Nick rose, walked to the front, and looked out at

those who gathered. "Thank you for coming. You know how Grandpère loved a great party." A chuckle rose through the crowd.

"My grandfather requested this Bible verse. Evidently it carried a significant meaning to him." He cleared his throat, lifting the book to read. "Proverbs 19:11. *A discretion of a man deferreth his anger; and it is his glory to pass over a transgression.* A modern translation: *A man's discretion makes him slow to anger, and it is his glory to overlook a transgression.*"

After he sat down, he read over the verse again.

Grandpère is asking for forgiveness from the grave?

The old man had played a lead role in bringing unhappiness to the family, had committed many transgressions. He rejected his son, held back true affection for his wife, deprived his grandson of a father. And he'd manipulated Biloxi to come home.

And now he wants absolution from us?

The rest of the service ran together in a blur before it finally ended. In deference to his grandmother, he didn't stay for the gathering in the fellowship hall. Instead, he drove Biloxi back to Bayou Petite. In the rearview mirror, he witnessed the sky change like pictures in a flashing digital frame. Pink and purple against scattered silver clouds. Hints of a storm. A reflection of his life.

A comfortable quiet cocooned them. Yet, clearly Biloxi's mind had wandered somewhere, though at the same time, he appreciated that she didn't feel the need to fill silence with idle chatter. Hoping to lift some of the day's heaviness before they parted, he squeezed her hand to get her attention.

"Shall I turn down Loblolly Lane?"

His tease produced the desired effect. Her mouth rose at the corners. Her dimples appeared.

His heart beat faster.

He parked in his usual spot at Fleur de Lis, near the rear steps leading to the long back gallery, then walked to her side of the truck and opened the door. She balanced her hand in his, then stepped onto the running board. Grasping her around the waist, he set her on the ground. The clack of her heels against the brick echoed in the night.

She looked up at him with questions in her eyes. He folded her into his arms. Pulled her closer. Bent his head and touched his lips tenderly to hers.

Sweet. Her lips were pliant. Her warm scent mixed with perfume reminded him of elegance and seduction. He deepened the kiss, going for thoroughness instead of just ravishing her mouth. He slowed, then started over again, tasting the warmth she offered. When he started to pull back, she ran her fingers up the back of his head, sealing them together in a lip-lock.

Then she did exactly what he had meant to avoid.

She ravished him with kisses. Warm and wet.

His heart beat like a runaway truck speeding off a cliff. His body hardened. He wanted her. If they'd been any place but at Fleur de Lis, he would press things further. Right then and there, or in the truck, or...

Without losing the warmth of their contact, his lips moved against hers. "Come home with me?"

She responded by pressing her pelvis against him. "I can't."

After her mind-numbing kiss and suggestive grinds had he misunderstood her signals? She couldn't have just said "no"?

He pulled away.

"Please don't look at me like that," Biloxi said. "I went to the memorial service. I wanted to be there for you, but I've business to attend to right now. Maybe later?"

Her rejection was like a cold bucket of ice water, her priorities made clear.

"Okay, *chèr*." He started to take another step back when she planted a peck on his cheek, then she leaned in close to his ear.

"Nick, I am your friend, but I won't be a distraction to get you through your grief."

He didn't trust himself to respond. How could she think that? He'd been a gentleman. An honorable man. What made her think he only wanted to use her?

Climbing into his truck and closing the door, he started the engine. It rumbled to life. He rolled down the window and held his hand out to her. She reached for it.

"You're not a distraction," he said, giving her hand a gentle squeeze. "If you make your way around, know that at my house, I play for keeps. None of this kiss-and-run."

Her perplexed expression satisfied his rapidly beating heart and his ego. He squeezed her hand again, sealing his promise.

Life looked clearer now. He'd go home, take a nap, and sleep like a baby. He had a plan, knew what he wanted. Despite the day's tension, the aggravation of his grandmother's irrational behavior, and the unexpected return of his errant father, his grandfather had given him the gift of love. Within him was the capacity to forgive his family and put aside the past. That would open his heart for the love of only one woman.

That was the one thing he had in common with Grandpère.

Chapter 29

Biloxi rang the doorbell once more and looked at her watch. Eleven p.m. Late, but she guessed Nick would be awake, after all, the gas porch lights were still lit.

She peeked through the side window next to the door. No Nick. Her arms ached from toting the heavy pot. If she didn't put it down soon, she'd drop it. Taking a step back just beyond the welcome mat, she bent over to place the pot on the porch and the door opened. Bare feet appeared.

"No need to bow, though it is a nice touch, *chèr*," Nick chuckled. "They say a man is king of his castle, but I don't require formal gestures."

She grunted. "Ha. Ha. Greta sent over a pot of seafood gumbo. It's heavy, so get your butt out here and pick it up, Your Highness." She pushed past him, walked through the open door, not bothering to look back to see if he grabbed the pot or not, though she'd bet money he would. Greta's cooking was his gold standard.

Her boot heels tapped on the wooden floor. She walked into the living room and into the strains of Stevie Ray Vaughn's guitar playing magic. The melodic hum created an intimate atmosphere. She couldn't have prevented her reaction to the soul-searing sound even if she wanted to. Flames in the fireplace danced a faster beat. Immediately she was at ease.

She removed her boots before stepping onto a wool rug. Its plushness cushioned her feet, tempting her to remove her socks and dance around. Two leather side chairs flanked a red brick hearth which faced a brown suede couch. Lamps that looked like sculptures of branches with pinecones perched on matching side tables. A large wooden chest, the top of which had seen better days, sat against the couch to make room in front of the hearth for a pile of large pillows scattered on the floor.

Amber liquid in a cut glass tumbler looked to be Nick's chosen company for the evening.

"Didn't anyone ever tell you, you're not supposed to drink alone?"

No response. Where had he disappeared to? When she turned, he stood before her. He'd moved too stealth-like with no socks or shoes or boots.

"I only drink with others."

"There's only one glass."

Nick grinned widely. His eyes twinkled and his dimples promised mischief. He spun her around, wrapped her in his arms, and pulled her back against his chest. "It's you and me now," he whispered.

His husky voice sent shivers through her.

"We can sip from the same glass."

It wasn't what he said, but the way he said it. Every nerve stood at full alert. She squirmed and tried to wiggle free. Nick held firm and strong. After a minute, she gave up. She liked it right where she was.

"Nick?" she asked cautiously. "How much have you had to drink?" She sniffed. No odor of overindulgence.

"I have only just begun."

He released her and turned her quickly to face him. She staggered a step before catching her balance. His hands steadied her at the shoulders, then moved to embrace the sides of her neck.

Her breath hitched. She closed her eyes the minute his lips touched hers. Her arms wrapped around him. She clung to him tightly.

The heat of his body radiated through his soft flannel shirt. The hardness of his chest matched the steel strength in his arms. Hard, well-formed thighs pressed against hers. His was a body any woman would want. Anytime.

Yet, her brain screamed "no." Her heart waivered on "maybe." Her body shouted "yes!" Without a doubt, she wanted him.

A deep sigh escaped from her lips. Did she just moan? It had been so long, so long since the last man she'd allowed to conquer her. And she really liked this man, and wanted his kisses to take them further.

He nipped at her bottom lip. She gave in to desire. She trusted him. Somehow, he'd racked up lots of trust-points in only a few weeks. They could be friends with benefits. No strings attached. Right?

Giving over, she turned her full attention to him. His mouth seduced. Hands explored. Her hormones raged, triggered by his masculine scent.

He must have read her tremble as "yes." His lips never left hers when his fingers unbuttoned her blouse. A slow agonizing strip. Once undone, he slid the silk open. Slowly her blouse fluttered off her shoulders. The warmth from the fireplace was nothing compared to the sear of his touch against her skin.

Starting at her bra strap, he traced a line down, then stopped at the V of her cleavage. Heat from his touch shot to her gut, then moved lower. Tension built in places she'd ignored for a long time. Balancing with one hand on him, she wrapped a leg around his and longed to be tangled up with him. On the floor. On the pillows.

She needed...Nick.

When he looked into her eyes, she saw lust. Desire. And...

Shaking her head, to clear it, she looked again. Intense desire, like the one building within her, could produce a mirage, same as when someone wandered lost in the desert for too long. There couldn't be anything more between them. As long as he satisfied her growing ache, she didn't expect more. She could live with a temporary illusion of love.

Nick tugged at her blouse until the sleeves pooled at her wrists. Turning her around, her back rested against his chest and hardened body. Chest. Arms. Legs. Manhood. All pressed against her while her arms hung limp at her side.

He explored her bare stomach like he was reading braille. Light feathery touches caressed. The exquisite tease was pleasure and pain. Her head lolled against his chest. When the sensations became too intense, she clenched her legs together out of need. Her blouse might cuff her hands, but they were still able to grasp. She reached for Nick, feeling her way. When she grabbed his inner thighs, he harden more.

"I swear, Nick, if you're just teasing me, you are going to die." Her voice came out in a hoarse whisper.

"*Chèr*, I told you. I play for keeps. I don't say

anything I don't mean."

"Well, darl'n, you better get to provin' it."

He unbuttoned her cuffs and her blouse drifted to the floor. Reaching his arms around her, he unbuttoned, then unzipped her jeans. When he stepped back, she started to stumble forward. He saved her by grabbing a belt loop on her jeans and pulled her back upright.

In front of the hearth, he stretched out on the floor as though he had all the time in the world, and appeared totally relaxed. Mesmerized by his moves, she stared when he pulled off his shirt, and tossed it on top of hers. He grabbed a pillow for his head, then slowly unzipped his jeans. His every movement captivated her. Staring was impolite, but she couldn't avoid it. She was like a kid with her nose pressed against the glass of a candy store.

He rested one hand behind his head. "Biloxi, come here." He patted the space beside him. "You tell me how far we go. When. How. It's up to you."

The light from the fireplace danced against his skin as heat danced in her belly. His invitation was one she wouldn't waste.

Peeling off her jeans, she wrestled out of them and kicked them away, then motioned for him to do the same. He raised a questioning eyebrow when she pulled on the hem of his pants. When he was naked, she stood proudly above him. He reached up for the edge of her panties. Agonizingly slow, he removed them, stroking her legs from her hips to her feet. She forced him back onto the pillow, then straddled him.

A moment of shyness washed over her as he removed her bra. Need won out over apprehension. When he arched his hips up in invitation, she settled over him. Claiming him as his heat branded her.

Delirious with need, she gave into the feeling. Nick was like a drug. With each thrust, she craved more.

The fire inside took her higher and higher. They rocked back and forth entwined together, until her body arched with spasms so intense her mind blanked and all other senses dulled. She flew close to the sun and around the moon. Then floated back to earth.

Her blaze of desire for Nick touched her heart as much as the heat from the fire touched her skin.

****

"God, woman, I can't move," Nick whispered. He cradled her head in the crook of his arm, pleased that she spooned her body next to his. "You're like a drug."

Biloxi cuddled closer and sighed. Beside him, limpness claimed her body, and he couldn't help but smile. After a moment, a puff of soft breath reached his ear. She'd fallen asleep.

He closed his eyes and surrendered. Budding new feelings pushed old doubts away. He came to Bayou Petite under protest after his grandfather gifted him Trahan land. Maybe the old man had visions that no one else could see? The idea that Grandpère had lured Biloxi back, because he wanted her for his grandson, sounded insane. But it appeared fate had a hand in play. Maybe all of this was exactly how it was supposed to be. It was certainly the way it had worked out. He wouldn't argue with fate.

In the warmth of the firelight, he watched her sleep. Every instinct he had kicked into high intensity. He'd do anything to protect this woman and everything to have her love. She might not love him yet, however, he was certain her intentions went beyond just being friends, especially after the way her body responded.

He kissed her nose, then whispered softly, "It's my turn to show you how it's done."

He traced large circles around her breasts. The circles he made got smaller. Her body undulated, even in sleep. He rolled her gently onto her back and started a line of kisses from her throat, moving down to her chest. She trembled and moaned as he tasted. Clearly, she wanted him as much he wanted her.

Again.

She arched her hips to him.

"Slow and steady, *chèr*. We've got all the time in the world."

She opened her sleepy eyes and raised an eyebrow. Her look said she had a different idea.

"No need to rush this time," he whispered against her skin.

His hands roamed her smooth body. She looked like a goddess beneath him. Her long auburn hair splayed against the pillow. Creamy skin, soft like velvet beneath his hands. He inched them down to her hips, kneading and stroking all the way down to her thighs.

"Please?" she whined.

"Shush, no need to rush. I let you lead the first time. Let me give to you."

He kissed her, then took their building passion further when he melded his body with hers. Joined, they moved beyond the point of reason. Moved in perfect unison. Up and back. Up and back.

When he thought he couldn't hold on a moment longer, her body went taut. Eyes shut tight. She moaned, a long, slow pleasurable cry.

He thrust deep inside her, then let go. His soulful

moans matched hers. Their release melted them together. Their bodies merged as one while strains from the blues continued to play around them.

After a few minutes, his breath slowed and finally began to return to normal. He snuggled Biloxi close to his side. He grabbed a blanket from the chair and pulled it up to cover them.

Her breath came in little puffs. She was already asleep. His body was sated and relaxed, but his mind raced with his heart. Against the odds of family bonds, he had to find a way to keep her with him forever. But, could she break with her family's tradition?

Chapter 30

The next morning, a ringing doorbell and pounding woke Nick. The chime sounded again and again and again. He guessed who prevailed upon him so early on a Wednesday morning, and didn't rush to get out of bed. This time he didn't dress in a hurry, instead put on his clothes leisurely, then sauntered downstairs to the furious noise.

Opening the front door, two people entered—Edward and his grandmother. He didn't offer a greeting. Grim faces stared at him. He took a hard look at them and decided he needed coffee.

"Nicholas, I just won't have it!" his grandmother cried. She paced in front of the fireplace. Her pearls bounced as she marched back and forth like a military general searching for options on how to win a war.

"Good morning to you, too. Don't you know a growing boy needs his sleep?" He wandered toward the kitchen.

Edward sat on the couch.

After handing a mug of coffee to Edward and placing a cup and saucer on the side table for his grandmother, Nick lounged in a chair with one leg dangled over the arm while his grandmother continued her angry pacing. Not a bad thing, he reckoned—at this rate, she'd wear a hole through the expensive carpet she'd insisted he have, and then he would replace it with something he liked more. He breathed in the aroma of his favorite brand of Louisiana coffee and chicory. A sip, the dark brew took the edge off his irritation.

"Nick, son, please reconsider. I'm sure the young lady would understand."

"I don't understand. Why do you want to humiliate me more?" Suzette cried.

"Grandmère, this is not about you." Nick kept his voice low.

The memorial service had turned into a society social event just like his grandmother wanted. He thought she would've been pleased about the compromise he'd worked out. Biloxi honored her wishes—she hadn't spoken at the memorial. However, his grandmother hadn't mentioned to him, until just before the start of the service, about the specifics for the graveside service. He hadn't been at all surprised to learn there were written instructions for that, too.

Grandpère had requested to be buried in the old family plot in Bayou Petite rather than in the Baton Rouge cemetery where all of Suzette's ancestors resided.

"Grandmère, there are only a few people alive who even remember *the duel*. Biloxi's family didn't attend the funeral out of respect for your wishes. As for the burial, well, if you don't want Biloxi there, I won't come. Since Grandpère will be buried, essentially in my backyard, I'll have my own service for him. You do what you need to do, and I will understand."

He shot up from the chair when Suzette placed her hand over her heart and patted it rapidly. She began to pant. Her brow wrinkled and her mouth dropped open.

Her face paled, then she fainted.

He caught her before she hit the floor. Her head missed the brick hearth.

Edward placed a pillow on one end of the couch. Nick laid his grandmother's head there before gently stretching out her legs. He sprinted to the bathroom and back, then placed a cool, damp cloth on his grandmother's forehead.

"She'll be okay." Edward looked grim.

"I hope so. I couldn't handle another funeral right after this one."

"That's morbid."

"Look, Edward, since you have inserted yourself into her life and taken on the role of caretaker or defender, or whatever you call it—"

"Son."

"Don't call me that," Nick snapped.

"I didn't mean you. I meant that I'm finally free to openly take my place as her son. Now that your grandfather's gone."

"Oh. Then as her *son*, you can see how ridiculous she's being. I've never known her to be so over emotional and unrelenting."

"Your grandfather always kept her in check. Kept everyone in check."

They sat in chairs on opposite sides of the coffee table and stared at each other. Nick refused to believe his grandfather was anything less than what he'd always been—a gentleman. A strong man with strong ideas and a strong work ethic who had loved him and raised him. Edward didn't appear to have inherited the Trahan tenacity, otherwise he wouldn't have abandoned him.

Silence hung between them. Nick resolved not to be the one to open the conversation again. He pondered and hated to admit that Edward had a point. His grandfather hadn't been able to control Elise Murphy. She'd married Robert Dutrey. Therefore, it appeared that his grandfather had then tried to control everything and everyone in his life. He hadn't known that side of his grandfather. Good Southern manners had masked the old man's tendencies.

After a long silence, when Edward failed to fill the void and his grandmother hadn't risen from her prone position, although he knew she played possum and heard every word, he announced, "I'm getting married."

Chapter 31

Early Thursday morning, Biloxi rode with Greta, who dropped her at the car dealership in Kenner. She picked up her car, then hopped on the interstate. Destination—Nick's house. With the windows down, wind tossed her hair. The sensation of freedom matched the lightness in her soul. She had Nick to thank for it.

She smiled remembering the curve in the road that marked the place where she'd met him.

He'd rescued her just in the "Nick of time." She chuckled at her own joke. He was no prince, but maybe a saint. Her own Saint Nick. No, not the Santa Claus one. But then again?

She laughed like Santa Claus, a deep belly laugh. She pictured Nick's lean, hard body in a red-velvet Santa suit trimmed in white fur and showing off his abs...and his darned old western boots. Warmth flushed her cheeks.

That was one Christmas package she'd open early.

She hadn't liked the man in the beginning. But, the moment she'd opened her eyes in the emergency room and learned she wasn't alone, he eased her panic. Genuine concern flickered in his gorgeous eyes. Smokey topaz. They captured her attention each time she gazed at him, they hypnotized and swept her away on a magic carpet ride. At least in her fertile imagination.

Her heart fluttered from the beat of a thousand butterfly wings. She gripped the steering wheel. Joy and panic mixed into one. A scary cocktail.

When had she morphed into a silly starry-eyed belle? Did the end of celibacy plop her onto a planet somewhere beyond the galaxy of "do not pass go and do not fulfill dreams"?

That's how it had always been with her and men. She got lost in their world. She'd be going along fine with her life, meet a man, fall in love, then suddenly, the scenery would change. Blue would become pink and green would be purple. A man became the planet she revolved around like a satellite caught in a gravitational pull.

Her therapist had said that she still searched for an anchor. She found that in Fleur de Lis. So would she lose her way this time?

Last night, the businesswoman's worries were set aside like a pillow tossed to the floor and the starry-eyed belle had fun, an inadequate word to describe the night.

But could goals co-exist with frolic and fun?

If past behavior predicted the future, she'd end up losing herself to please a man. Just like with Gregory.

As she neared the curves in the road that intersected with Nick's driveway, the ruts in the ditch made by her tires when she crashed were still obvious to anyone passing. She navigated the right-angle turn with ease, but could she navigate her life the same?

Surely after all she'd learned in her last relationship, she could handle a sidetrack with Nick while focusing on business. Friends with benefits. That suited her *fine*. Nick clearly wanted the same kind of connection.

Though they hadn't yet hashed out the lie he told his grandfather, Nick had not offered false terms of endearment, like saying he loved her. He never spoke about the future. And God forbid, no hint of a proposal. Last night ranked high on her list of dates, Nick and hot, sweaty pleasure. A lover like no other.

At a snail's pace, she drove on the long driveway. Was it really only last month when they'd met? The erratic pounding of her heart was proof enough of her attraction to him. They'd become very close in a short time.

He had no way of knowing she'd let down her guard, released her inhibitions in front of the fireplace last night. The heat radiating between them had nothing to do with the hot burning logs in the fireplace or the fire's dancing flames. The room buzzed hot with need. Her heart would've blipped at heart-attack mode on an EKG if she'd had a way to check, the energy was that intense.

And still it was just sex. For once, she gave as good as she got. No holding back. Nothing more. Pleasure between two people who luxuriated in each other. Nothing as serious as love, right?

Love?

LOVE!

She gasped. Her stomach flipped, then flopped. Her hands trembled, barely able to hold the wheel. It couldn't be love. A lot of *like*. A lot of *lust*. Not love.

She let out a deep breath. Her brain clucked "no-no" while her body purred "*again*." Her heart tumbled into "*yes.*" Oh, no. It must be aftershocks from the funeral. After all, they'd stared death in the face. It was natural for someone to grasp for that kind of connection to prove they were alive. To revel in life's vitality. And sex provided physical, nerve-tingling evidence of living.

Nick was a drug she craved.

"But that doesn't mean it's love," she insisted while looking at herself in the rearview mirror.

She would take things with Nick slow. Here she had an opportunity to explore deeper feelings since she no longer jetted from one airport to another chasing photos and contracts. If she worked on her goals and reached for her dreams, she could handle a little of Saint Nick. Most definitely.

Breathing out deeply, she cleared her mind, and gazed at the planted border along the long stretch of driveway. Buds on the azalea were about to pop. Neatly trimmed boxwoods added elegance to the manicured lawn. Magnolia trees produced shade. Yellow and purple pansies would dot the scene with color. Mass planting of flowering impatiens would give the illusion of cooling in the summer heat. There was something refreshing about white and pink on a background of green. She loved summer in the south. If she asked Nick about his favorite season, he'd probably say, football.

She tried forcing him from her mind, but every other thought came back to him. She slammed the palm of her hand against the steering wheel, then winced in pain.

Love? Really? What have I done?

Reaching the house, she coasted. Several vehicles were already parked in the drive. She pulled in behind one and stopped. She'd expected his grandmother and father, possibly the funeral-home workers who set up the graveside service, but who owned the Mercedes, the Jag, the BMW, and a Cadillac Escalade? Nick had said it would be a private burial for his grandfather.

In the rearview mirror, she paused to check her lipstick. For once, she hadn't chewed nervously on her bottom lip. She stalled for time. In the crowd at the memorial, she remained fairly anonymous, but with this small group, she would stick out.

Biloxi exited the car and approached the steps leading up to the gallery. The front door opened and Chantel appeared, wine glass in hand. She raised an eyebrow, otherwise, her expression remained bland.

"Well, well," Chantel purred. "The woman the world revolves around." Chantel sauntered to the front railing and lifted her glass in mock salute.

"Hello, Chantel." Biloxi climbed the steps while trying to hold on to her composure. Chantel's fitted black dress and polished pearls was the perfect mourning outfit. The camera would love her, though her perpetual scowl would ruin any photograph.

Biloxi took several short breaths. She needed to keep everything on an even keel, scales level, no tipping to one side or the other. Beyond the occasional accidental meeting in town, there would be no need to ever set eyes on Chantel after today. This was a solemn event and she would conduct herself accordingly, after all, she represented the entire Dutrey family.

"I finally figured it out." Chantel's voice rose just above a whisper. "The attraction, you know, is for your large family. It's not you. But the package. You're just a means to an end."

Biloxi stopped. For a second, she considered

ignoring the comment altogether, but curiosity spurred her on. "I'm not into riddles. What do you mean?"

Chantel stepped closer. When they were side-by-side, shoulder-to-shoulder, looking like close friends to an innocent eye, Chantel glanced through the open front door as though checking for eavesdroppers. "The one thing Nicky has always wanted is a large family. He grew up without his mother and father. Did you even know that? His grandfather loved him to death, but it was never enough for Nicky. He wanted more. But then, given how close the two of you are, so quickly I might add, you probably already know this about him."

Biloxi remained silent. She didn't know. But was it true? Nick wanted a big family? He'd spent some time around hers. He did love lunching with her and Greta. Liked her brother and Carson. He'd even charmed her mother, though Hurricane Deidre would never admit it. Could Chantel be right?

"It's not really *you* he wants."

Biloxi's gut clenched, but she maintained a smile. "Chantel, I can see you're looking out for your friend's best interest. However, he's a big boy. Why don't we let him speak for himself?"

"*Tut-Tut.* We've waited a long time for Nicky to settle down. It was always assumed by our families that we'd be together. We're alike, he and I—"

"Really?" Biloxi interrupted. "Then I should be absolutely no threat to you." She'd had enough. Bayou Petite was her hometown. Generations of her family were born and raised here. No out-of-town she-wolf would make things difficult for her. Not now. Not Ever.

Chantel cast a wary glance over her shoulder, then in a low voice, ground out, "As only children, there's a bond between us. You, with your family the size of a football team, just can't understand."

Biloxi fluttered her lashes. In her best, sweet-tea drawl, she said, "Hmm, darl'n, you just said Nick's got a fascination for large families. Seems I *do* have a special bond with him, too."

Lordy! They were fighting over a man on his doorstep just before planting his grandfather in the ground. Disgraceful behavior, but she couldn't help herself. Ever since she'd watched Chantel stroke Nick's arm at The Chateau, that woman always produced an angry twist in her gut. Biloxi took a step toward the front door. As far as she was concerned, the conversation had ended.

She strode into Nick's house. One look at him and her heart swelled with longing.

Oh God! Lord help me. I'm in love with him.

"You made it." Nick planted a chaste kiss on her cheek.

She eyed him coyly. His gray suit fit him perfectly. His eyes warmed when he caught her visual once-over.

The twist in her gut relaxed. A rapid flutter replaced it. The fluttering rose to pound in her chest when she walked with Nick into the living room. A couple stood in the spot where, yesterday, she and Nick had better acquainted themselves by getting buck naked together. To her, everyone in the room was invading their private cocoon.

Nick addressed the couple before them. "John and Betsy Westover, this is Miss Biloxi Noël Dutrey. Biloxi, John is Grandpère's attorney from Baton Rouge. We had the final reading of the will before you arrived."

"Hello," Biloxi answered, aware of the heat creeping up her neck. Thank goodness, no one but Nick knew what had taken place in the room last night.

Nick stood close, so close that the heat of his body wrapped around her. Every touch, taste, and kiss they'd shared last night played out in her mind. She could barely manage polite conversation now.

****

She blushed? Damn interesting. It couldn't be that she's intimidated by John or Betsy. They're everyday grandparent-types. Something else put that color in Biloxi's cheeks.

While they stood making small talk, Nick spied the empty whiskey glass on the floor in the corner by the hearth. A picture popped into his head. One with drizzles of amber liquid over Biloxi's breasts. He remembered her tight rosy buds, and his gut tightened. He wanted to wish everyone else away but her.

Making love with her topped anything he'd shared with any other woman. He grinned. Was she remembering everything about last night? Was that why she blushed?

He liked that idea.

He loved her.

And he couldn't wait for all of the others to vacate his house so he could show her how much, again.

His grandfather would be pleased at the turn of events. Damned old man. He was getting his wish despite his earthly departure.

Or at least most of his wish.

With his grandfather's decisions documented, there shouldn't have been any fighting over details. Yet, even with all of the plans spelled out legally, his grandmother refused to honor all of his grandfather's wishes. She never would have challenged the old man when he was alive.

In a twisted way, he understood. Unfortunately, Biloxi represented the single flaw in his grandmother's life. As a descendent of the one woman Grandpère had never forgotten, Biloxi was like a red flag to an agitated bull, and his grandmother's old wound continued to fester.

Would she ever accept the woman he loved?

"Excuse me a moment." Nick interrupted Betsy's detailed discussion of her new beach house. "I'm leaving you in good hands," he whispered to Biloxi before making his way to the back gallery. He needed a moment alone before everyone gathered for the burial.

That morning, the reading of the will proved difficult, like running an obstacle course of hazards where walls moved and guillotines dropped. His grandmother had felt betrayed by his grandfather's instructions to be buried in the old Trahan cemetery, rather than in Baton Rouge. The reading came at the time orchestrated with specific plans by his grandfather. It dictated who should be present at the burial—Nick, Suzette, Edward—whom his grandfather had known all about—Jake, their farm manager, and their friends the Gilbeaus—Michael, Jonelle, and Chantel. And of course, John and Betsy Westover.

"He provided for everyone," John told them after they'd gathered in the dining room. John stood, looking official, at one end of the long oak table with a folder of documents while everyone waited. When he had their complete attention, he spoke.

"Nick is now the executor of the trust and is

responsible for all final decisions. Claude gave Nick this land last year and left him the Baton Rouge house—to be claimed only upon the passing of Suzette. However, while Claude trusted Michael Gilbeau's financial expertise, Nick is free to make his own decisions with a few exceptions. The funds Claude set aside to support Edward's medical clinic will continue with Michael being responsible for the business aspects of that operation. He will receive a salary for his time and efforts. Jonelle, he asked that you continue with your fundraising efforts for the clinic. He appreciated your commitment. Money will be available to ensure that fundraising continues. Chantel, he left you money to buy into half of Nick's clinic, *if* Nick agrees. If not, then the money is still yours, but only to be invested in a clinic of your choice. Not for anything else.

"And since farming has always been the backbone of this family, farming will continue with Jake overseeing things until his retirement in five years. Then Nick will have to select a new farm manager.

"Last but not least, the land trust stays intact. The land must be protected. Claude wants the next executor position to pass to Nick's first born when Nick retires."

At that point, John chuckled. "Claude said he'd moved with the times. The next executor will be the first born child, even if it's a girl."

Nick thanked John when the attorney finished his legal duties. They toasted Grandpère with champagne, which everyone drank except Edward, who asked for sweet tea. His grandmother refused to raise a glass and, rather than demur, had left the room.

Nick ran his fingers through his hair. His grandfather's passing was still a hard concept to wrap his head around. Even after the reading of the will, he expected the old man to appear from around the corner. He didn't know how he would handle it when his grandfather's coffin was lowered into the ground. A mantle of sadness draped his heart.

"Mr. Trahan?" The funeral home director interrupted his thoughts. "If you're ready, we can gather. The graveside is set."

Nick nodded. "I'll let everyone know. We'll meet you there in a few minutes." Nick followed the man inside and searched for Biloxi. Finding her in the spot where he'd left her, he slid his hand into hers and tangled their fingers together, then turned to his guests, "They're ready for us. John and Betsy, would you like to ride with us?"

"That would be fine," John replied.

"If you'll wait on the gallery while I gather everyone else, we'll be with you in a minute." Nick headed toward the kitchen with Biloxi at his side. His grandmother and Chantel's mother, Jonelle, had their heads bent together and looked deep in a private conversation. His grandmother dabbed her eyes and looked up when they approached. Her sorrow was as palpable as his heartbeat.

"Ladies, sorry to intrude. They're ready for us. We'll assemble graveside. Will you please let the men know?"

"Thank you, Nicholas," said Jonelle. "Chantel will ride with us after all."

Nick started to turn away to inform the others, but Biloxi stepped forward with tenderness etching her face. She reached out and placed her hand on his grandmother's arm. "Mrs. Trahan? I'm sorry for your loss. Deeply sorry. And if I can help in any way, please let me know. I'd like to offer my support."

Surprise registered in his grandmother's eyes, then she quickly cast her gaze downward. Nick guessed she probably was a little ashamed of her own lack of manners.

"That's very kind of you," his grandmother said, though she didn't look up.

Walking Biloxi to the front door, he wrapped his arm around her waist. They made their way to the gallery where Chantel stood talking with John and Betsy. A lump formed in his throat. These folks were his family. Part of his history of memories. He cared for all of them, including Chantel. No one escapes the pain of their childhood, and Chantel was a part of his, but so also were holiday celebrations steeped in tradition. Was there a way to ease the tension between his childhood friend and Biloxi? He hoped so, though in the end, his allegiance would be with the woman he married.

"What are you smiling about?" Biloxi whispered.

"What you said to my grandmother," he said. "That was thoughtful. Thank you. Oh, and I have a surprise for you later."

"You've been full of surprises for the last twenty-four hours. Don't know if I can take any more."

"The surprises have just begun."

When the rest of the mourners filed into their cars, Nick led Biloxi down the steps to the driver's door of an Escalade. The Westovers followed behind. "Here," Nick said dangling the keys in front of Biloxi. "It's yours."

"Ah, what?"

"It was my grandfather's. Since you're going to be

hauling camera equipment all over God's half-acre, he wanted you to have something bigger. This is bigger than that toy car you drive." Nick grinned.

The Westovers discreetly climbed into the back seat of the large white vehicle, leaving Biloxi standing alone with Nick.

"Nick, no. I can't drive this…this beast."

"Sure you can. I already had the title changed to your name. Hop in. We gotta go."

Biloxi huffed, walked around to the passenger's side, and climbed in.

Nick tossed the keys in the air and caught them. Smiling, he climbed behind the wheel. The woman next to him made life look brighter despite the sadness of the day. "Tell her, John. She doesn't believe me."

"Yes, well, not the most auspicious way of offering a lady a gift. Miss Biloxi, the vehicle is almost new. Claude bought it, then became too sick to drive any longer. He wanted you to have it. It's been garaged at the farm. While it wasn't mandated in the will, he did instruct Nick to transfer the title before he died. Claude knew you'd need a stalwart vehicle to haul around camera equipment."

Biloxi turned when the engine purred to start. "You're not Saint Nick, but are you sure your grandfather wasn't Claus—instead of Claude?"

Chapter 32

Claude had to be crazy or the biggest romantic she'd ever met, Biloxi mused. His fascination made her feel like a Pollyanna heroine in a spy movie. To meet a man in the hospital on his deathbed and discover he'd lured her home by dangling a lucrative photography contract under her nose *because* he wanted his grandson to marry her? Truth was stranger than fiction. Was this a case of stranger-danger? How did Claude know she would even bid on the job? Did he know about Nick's desire for a large family? Where would she find the truth now that Claude was dead?

"I think he'd hoped to show you some remote spots for photos," Nick said. "He liked the mist hovering over the river at dawn. Sunsets through the planted pines. A full moon rising over a cotton field with the white bolls shining." Nick spoke of the sights with affection. "And...I could get used to being a photographer's assistant."

Her cell vibrated, distracting her from his suggestion. She opened her purse and pulled out her phone. Aunt Macy's number registered on caller ID.

Nick stopped the SUV near the ornate wrought iron gates at the entrance to the old Trahan cemetery. An overcast sky painted the day in gray. Tendrils of Spanish moss hung from ancient gnarled oaks, creating a canopy over the gravesites. The beauty was not lost to her photographer's eye.

"Nick, I'll be along in a moment. Aunt Macy's calling." She opened the door, stepping onto the running board of the vehicle she'd already dubbed 'The Beast,' then gingerly stepped to the ground to avoid any ankle pain. Dry oak leaves crunched under foot. She tiptoed to prevent her heels from plunging into the soft, sandy soil while people made their way to the canopy and chairs set up graveside.

She pressed the talk button. "Hello?"

"Biloxi, thank goodness I found you," Macy exhaled. "I've got a wedding booked for Saturday at eleven a.m. and the bride's photographer just cancelled. Unfortunately, he was in an accident and can't work. Here's your chance to launch Fleur de Lis Photography with your first wedding. I know you're doing the Valentine's Ball that night, but can you squeeze this in? The wedding is small, maybe thirty people. The reception is a luncheon in the ballroom at Fleur de Lis."

Her first official wedding job! It would make Saturday a very long day with the Valentine's Ball that night. Organization and timing would be everything, but she could handle it for her first paying customer. "Yes. Tell the bride I'll do it."

"Great! I'll drive up. We'll meet with the bride and groom at 4:30 this afternoon to finalize the details."

"That's cutting it really close for me, but okay. I'm at the burial service for Nick's grandfather."

"Oh, Biloxi. I'm sorry to interrupt. I didn't know. Please give Nick my regards. See you soon."

Biloxi snapped the phone shut and turned off the ringer. Her first paid bridal contract! She wiggled a happy dance on her tiptoes and hoped no one watched.

She wouldn't want Nick to think her irreverent.

She composed herself and wiped away her grin. She smoothed the front of her black dress, held her head high and stepped from around the vehicle, then walked—glided really—to join the group. The somber occasion required calm order. She held her cell phone tightly in one hand and squeezed her other into a fist. Her manicured nails bit into the flesh of her palm, however, it would look silly if she pinched herself. She released her fist and took Nick's outstretched hand.

She sat next to him on the last seat in the back row. She bowed her head with the others at the minister's request, but she barely heard his words. Her focus kept drifting back to Macy's call. The goal of her own studio had become real. Now she needed to check backdrops for a formal bride and groom portrait. A chorus of "Amen" brought her attention back, and she caught Nick's curious glance.

"I want to give each of you the opportunity to say a few words about Claude Trahan," the minister said.

Though unusual for a widow to speak, the minister motioned for Suzette to begin.

Biloxi panicked. The request put her in an awkward position. What could she do? She mouthed "help" to Nick. She didn't want her words to be the last ones everyone remembered from the service. Nick patted her hand reassuringly. Her Saint Nick would find a way to save the day.

Suzette stood. She was a true Southern matron in a dark gray dress, black wool coat, and dignified pearls. Her tears started. She never managed a word. Jonelle hugged the older woman while she cried and helped her back to her seat. Edward rose and stepped to the podium. He made eye contact, and it was as though he peered into her soul. Maybe he had.

Edward began to speak. "I wish I had known—understood—all that my father did to help me. He's gone. I can't work out old issues with him. But I hope it's not too late for me and my son." Edward turned from the podium and placed a rose on top of the casket. "Father, thank you for raising my son to be a good man." Then he sat down.

Edward's words touched her. How did Nick feel about his father's desire to reconnect? It must have been awful for Nick to grow up without knowing his family. All her life, she believed Fleur de Lis and family were the most important things, yet she'd taken the family part for granted. Nick's experience had shined a light on her own need for family.

One by one the others spoke, each saying a few words about Claude. Then everyone turned to Nick. He stood, but stayed by his chair instead of moving to the podium. He held out his hand to her, and she put hers in his. He smiled, and the tenderness of it made her insides flutter and melt.

"Grandpère wants forgiveness," Nick stated. "He asks for it from the grave. That was made clear to me from the memorial service and the passage he wanted read. He was a more complicated man than I ever realized. I've learned a lot about him in the last couple of weeks. A lot of it he revealed himself. Yet, I want him to know, I forgive. Whatever his reasons might have been, he loved me. Loved us all, in his own way. He did what he did out of love...for that, I will always remember him kindly." He paused and looked thoughtfully at his grandmother. "Grandpère brought me together with Biloxi. He knew how stubborn I could be, but he had my best interests at heart. I am indebted."

Nick sat down and squeezed her hand. He'd spoken for the both of them.

The minister closed the service with a prayer. Biloxi had not known Claude, except in his last living moments. Having buried her own grandfather and then observed the changes in her grandmother following his passing, she whispered a prayer of hope for Nick's grandmother. Of everyone present, Suzette's loss was the most significant.

When the funeral home workers tossed the first shovel of dirt over the lowered coffin, Suzette let out a haunting wail, then collapsed into Edward's arms. He held her tightly and walked her toward the car.

Nick hung back while the others departed. He reached for her hand and at the same time called to the Westovers headed toward the car, "The Escalade's open."

He wrapped his arms around her, pulling her into a tight hug. He kissed her forehead. "Thank you for being here. I know none of this was easy for you. I appreciate the compassion you've shown when my grandmother hasn't been pleasant to you."

She hugged him back and held on. He felt so darn good. Strong. Solid. Her Saint Nick.

"I'm glad I could be here with you. I'm sad for your pain and your grandmother's, too. I feel sorry for her. I understand better now about why she doesn't like me. Conflicts are magnified at a time like this."

"She'll come around." Nick shrugged. "Just give her time. Everything will be okay."

She stood with him for a moment while the

cadence of two shovels worked in tandem. The rhythmic sound reminded her of the cadence and rhythm she and Nick were developing together.

Thank you, Claude.

A chill touched her. She shivered. It was as though someone ran a cold hand from the top of her head to the nape of her neck. She shivered again, and Nick pulled her close.

"There's a buffet being set up at the house. Everyone will leave after they've eaten. Will you stay with me tonight?"

Her heart sank. There had been no time to share with him about the business meeting. It was her first official job. She couldn't cancel on the bride.

"Nick, I'm sorry. I can't." She hated disappointing him. "I need to leave now. I have a client coming at 4:30. She's getting married at Fleur de Lis on Saturday at noon. I'm the fill-in photographer. I need to wow my first client. After that, I have to get the studio ready and plan the layout of shots. I have the wedding shoot, and then the Valentine's Ball Saturday night." She searched his eyes for understanding. Nick, a master at covering his feelings, appeared completely impassive.

"Nick? You do understand, don't you?" she asked hesitantly.

"You do what you feel is right." He dropped his hold on her and stepped away.

"Nick, I have to work," she pleaded. Hadn't she done everything he asked? Well, except for the Bible reading at the funeral, everything but that.

"Let's go back to the house. I'll have the Escalade delivered to you later." He turned and stalked to the vehicle, not bothering to wait for her.

"Nick?" She followed him, picking spots where her heels wouldn't sink into the sand. No point in making a scene. After all, they'd just buried his grandfather. Everyone reacted differently to grief. She'd give him some space and time.

Nick waited by the car to help her inside while the Westovers buckled their seatbelts. Once underway, he flipped on the stereo. Classical music filled the suffocating silence. Could the Westovers sense the tension? She wanted to be plenty angry with him, but couldn't. Given the events of the last week, he needed time to process and deal with the magnitude of the changes in his life. When it seemed like he needed her the most, like other folks in his life, she had plans.

After arriving at his house, Nick parked in the drive, and then opened the door for Mrs. Westover. Biloxi managed the two steps down in heels, then walked around the vehicle to Nick as the Westovers disappeared into the house.

"Maybe we could talk in the morning? Would you like to come for breakfast?" She hoped to lighten his mood. If anything could, it was Greta's cooking.

"Maybe."

It sounded like a brush-off.

"What about the Valentine's Day Ball? Are you still going? I'll be working most of the time, but save me a dance?"

"Hmm. You told me it was tradition to escort the winning bidder, so let's just play it by ear."

Hurt and confused, she turned toward her car. She had hoped he'd ask her to the Ball, but maybe he, too, intended to follow tradition. After all, Chantel had outbid her at the auction.

Before she walked to her car, Nick stopped her. He cupped the side of her face with his hand, rubbed his thumb across her lips, then added a slight pressure. A kiss. His eyes were as closed as was his expression.

"I'll see you later," he murmured, then turned and walked up the front steps.

Last night he'd made love to her, shouted out her name. Now nothing. No *chèr*. Her gaze followed him up the stairs. Chantel met him at the gallery with a glass of wine. Nick refused the glass and continued into the house. Chantel followed his retreat, but not before she flashed a haughty grin.

Deflated, Biloxi sighed. She couldn't ignore her work. And Nick was surrounded by his family. He probably wouldn't miss her, right? Damn it! She wanted to run after him. Make him understand. She couldn't be angry with him. Tricky business, grief. It settled over everyone differently. Nick just needed time. That, she had an abundance of.

Like Nick, she wasn't leaving Bayou Petite.

Chapter 33

Nick stormed his way to the kitchen, yanked the Maker's Mark bottle out of the cabinet, and plunked down a glass. It clinked against the countertop, then he filled the glass half-full. If he had to endure unwanted company, he'd do it with a little company of his own.

While the others milled about and the caterers finished their setup for the buffet supper, he pulled the knot of his tie loose, then yanked it off. Parking on the tall barstool at the kitchen counter, he wanted to brood. Alone.

She'd said "no."

He tensed. His jaw locked. His grandfather had died. His father returned. He'd argued with his grandmother about honoring his grandfather's wishes. About Biloxi reading a Bible passage. Endured the damn memorial, and the burial today. He'd had enough of being the calm voice of reason. Not once had anyone asked what he wanted.

Except Biloxi.

She'd asked the right questions. Said all the right things. Held him close and made love to him. Tonight he needed to be with her, and she chose work over him.

"Nicky?" Chantel stood beside him. "How 'bout some company? I don't think you should be alone." When he didn't answer, she pulled the other stool next to him and sat.

"I swear, I don't know what Claude was thinking. Giving that Escalade to *her*. She's not part of the family."

He didn't respond. He wasn't going to debate the subject. Sure as hell wasn't about to agree with her, just because he felt like a wounded pup.

"Nicky—"

"Don't call me that." He hated when Chantel whined, and hated it worse when she did it using his childhood nickname.

"All right. Nicholas. We need to talk about the practice. I do want to buy in. Actually, I would like to think of it as an infusion of capital."

Nick knocked back a gulp of whiskey. It burned his throat. When it hit his gut, warmth spread.

He turned to Chantel, his frustration and anger simmering. "You'll have to convince me that we can survive a business partnership. It's my clinic. I hired you to work with me, and I might be open to further negotiations. But Peaches and Biloxi might have the last say."

Nick rose without looking at her. He poured more whiskey into his empty glass and headed for his bedroom to rid himself of the too-confining suit. He needed jeans and a T-shirt.

He didn't give a damn about what anyone else thought. It was his house. He would do as he damned well pleased.

Including getting drunk.

****

The doorbell woke him. Shaking his head, Nick tried to sit up. His feet managed to find the floor. The carpet was warm. He rested his elbows on his knees and held his head in his hands. The ringing went on and on and on.

A gun would work right now. Put that bell out of my misery.

It rang again.

"What?"

When he rose unsteadily, he staggered and caught his balance. His feet bumped something.

Looking down, he gazed at Chantel asleep on the floor next to the couch. Her head rested on a big pillow. A blanket covered half of her, exposing a black lace bra against her white skin. Her prone model-like pose looked like a macabre scene from a film noir. She slept through the noise, or maybe she was passed out.

"I'm coming!" he shouted, then winced. What time was it anyway? Surely, his father or grandmother hadn't returned.

Flickers from the gas porch lights cast a glow through the window. The sun had set when? His body creaked like an old man's as he stumbled again on his way the door. An empty bottle skidded across the wooden floor. An empty Marker's Mark bottle.

"Who is it?" he croaked, his throat was dry and raspy like sandpaper. He opened the door.

"It's me. Little Red Riding Hood?" Biloxi grinned sheepishly.

He shook his head to clear the fog. What was she doing there? "What time is it?" He blinked to focus his eyes when he stepped out onto the gallery and into the cool night.

"Nick? Are you okay? It's 11:30. I tried to call, but you never answered, so I decided to drop by." Concern shone in Biloxi's eyes.

"Nicky?" Chantel groaned from inside the house. "Close that damn door. It's cold."

Biloxi's eyes widened. Her look of concern turned to shock. Her eyes narrowed. She glared. Even angry she was beautiful. He shook his head again hoping his foggy brain would clear. He and Maker's Mark had to break up.

"Yes, Nick, you probably *should* close the door. We wouldn't want your guest to catch a chill." He caught the frosty edge in Biloxi's voice, but before he could form words or make his lips to move, Biloxi jogged down the stairs.

Shit.

"Wait—"

"I'm not into threesomes, Dr. Trahan. You and Dr. Gilbeau—"

Biloxi yanked on her car door, but it didn't budge. She yanked harder and it opened. To him, she seemed to move in slow motion, like a special effect from a movie. Yet the chill in the night air began to move the brain-fog away. What had he done? Why was she erupting with anger?

"—can play doctor, or whatever else. But I don't play that way!"

"You got it wrong." He shouted at her closed door. Her taillights were already moving down the long drive.

"Are you sure about that, darl'n?" Chantel asked.

He turned to find her lounging against the doorframe. Back arched. One knee raised with her foot resting against the doorjamb. Flickering gaslights illuminated white skin while scant black lace barely covered her. No doubt, she looked sexy to most men. To him, she looked like trouble.

"Don't flatter yourself, Chantel," he said bluntly. "Even drunk, I wouldn't sleep with you. Tomorrow you're going to go with me, and we're going to straighten this out. Now get your clothes on and get out of my house."

Chapter 34

"Smile!" Biloxi told the bride and groom while she wanted to do anything but. Her face hurt from smiling, and thankfully, that was the last outdoor shot she needed. She'd already taken a hundred pictures of the couple with various members of their large extended family, along with the entire wedding party.

She snapped the last photo. "Okay, thank you. We're done for now. Go rejoin the reception. Make it look like you're having fun!" she teased the bubbly bride and stoic groom. "I'll be there in a moment."

The perfect spring weather made everyone drunk, that and the bubbling pink champagne. Everyone but her glowed with happiness. She squinted in the sunlight, then dropped her sunglasses into place. Even the sun cooperated for the bride by offering warm, clear morning light for all the outdoor shots. Flawless conditions for a February wedding with a Valentine's theme. The bride, a sweet rich girl from Covington, Louisiana, wore a lacey sweetheart neckline dress. Tiny crystals and seed pearls made the bodice sparkle, and she looked beside-herself-giddy standing next to her groom, a somber doctor-in-training. The groom wore a cut-away gray jacket with dark gray, pinstripe pants. They were the perfect wedding-cake-topper couple.

That thought made her gut clench.

With each picture she'd snapped, Nick invaded her

thoughts. She tried to ignore the welling nausea swashing back and forth in her gut when an image of Chantel with Nick flashed in her head. But she wasn't succeeding.

She refocused on the business at hand. The young bride desired the whole *Gone With the Wind* antebellum-house effect. The bride had whispered to the groom about how she dreamed of living in a house like Fleur de Lis and how, at least on her wedding day, she could pretend it was all hers. The hint wasn't subtle. The soon-to-be-doctor groom would probably be affording an antebellum home in his future.

The envy in the bride's voice touched Biloxi. She loved sharing the grandeur and beauty of her home. Weddings and other events produced income for maintenance on the estate, yet the scale and number of events had to be increased to cover costly upkeep. Her plans to make Fleur de Lis financially sound would succeed if the family would only give her a chance.

Just this morning, the HVAC system went on the blink. The repairman got it running in time for the wedding, but a full replacement system was needed and that price tag gave her sticker shock. She'd dealt with the repairman, which was Branna's job, while Aunt Macy attended to wedding details. Maybe now Aunt Macy would listen to reason, after all, Macy would've been in a bind if she hadn't been there to help.

Flipping through the memory card on her camera, Biloxi perused the action shots. The groom twirled the bride, then folded her into a dip. She'd snapped the last picture as the groom gently grasped the bride and bent her backward against a backdrop of the tall fountain's sparkling water droplets. She'd transform them to look like glinting diamonds. The photograph would capture memories the bride would remember forever.

And it was the one shot she'd always imagined in her bridal album.

That could have been Nick and me someday.

She had to stop torturing herself.

Adjusting sunglasses on her nose, a prop to hide her swollen bloodshot eyes, she wiped away trickling tears. The navy blue slacks and white tailored blouse might look professional, but for her, they were mourning clothes.

She bounced between fury and tears over the one man she thought perfect in every way. Her heart grieved for what might have been.

Walking up the steps, she headed in the direction of the wedding reception. When her cell phone vibrated in her pocket, she paused, set her camera and light meter on the table by the front door and dropped into the white rocking chair to check caller ID.

Him. Again.

The whole mess was her fault, yet knowing that didn't stop the hurt. Getting emotionally involved with the most sought-after bachelor in town proved to be the second worst thing she could've done. The worst was dreaming about a future with him. So much for her "friends with benefits" plan.

Chantel had helped in one way. She had to give credit where credit was due. Chantel made her face the realization that she believed in "one-man-one-woman" when it came to giving her heart away. She could never be just friends with Nick.

Chime. Her phone sounded again. She hit the *ignore* button. Yesterday, she'd hid from Nick by driving to New Orleans for the day. A tarot reader in front of St. Louis Cathedral tempted her with a fortune reading, but she'd refused. She couldn't bear to know the truth about her and Nick.

He'd called almost every hour on the hour, starting at eight the morning after. He stopped around suppertime. She swore she heard his truck rumble out on the main road about nine last night. He'd even called Greta under the guise of "casually inquiring" about everyone. Greta told him about the abrupt trip to New Orleans.

What did it matter? Even if she loved Nick, what future could she have with him if her family refused to accept him? And lest she forget, his grandmother hated her.

After gathering her gear, she headed for the noisy reception. Inside the ballroom, the disc jockey announced the next dance and guests clinked spoons against their glasses, demanding the groom kiss the bride. Young love. She had to remain professional, she couldn't back out of a job just because she had a relationship that ran amuck. However, taking wedding pictures after what happened with Nick was like burning acid in open wounds.

She was a fool. Chantel had warned her that she always got what she wanted. In this case, the object of Chantel's desire was Nick. When Nick said he had no interest in the woman, she'd believed him. At the time, the equation seemed simple enough. Chantel wanted Nick. Nick didn't want Chantel. End of story.

Nick's interest in her, she believed, was sincere, especially after they'd made love. Then, she'd foolishly thought there would be time to explore deepening emotions. That notion turned out to be...nothing more than a notion.

Once again, her old wound had opened. The pain doubled like yeast rising in Greta's bread-making bowl, making it almost unbearable. Because of Branna, she'd always been number two in the family. Always coming up short. Never number one. Well, she vowed not to love without being number one in someone's life. But, why couldn't that someone be Nick?

He was the steadiest man she'd ever met. The death of a grandfather compounded with the arrival of a long-absent father, could knock anyone for a loop. Add a budding relationship on top of that with a woman his grandmother despised. That sum equaled disaster. Hers.

She refused to be a rebound-girl. Nick wasn't rebounding from a relationship with another woman, but rebounding from life, a much bigger issue. But did he have to bounce into Chantel's arms the night after hers? It hurt too much to think about it.

She squared her shoulders. She was a professional. The reception photographs weren't going to leap into her camera. With a forced smile, she joined the festivities. She could fake happiness for a few more hours in the company of the newly married.

But what about tonight?

How could she bear to see Nick and Chantel together?

****

That evening, Biloxi twirled for her brother.

"Wow, you look great! For a sister, that is," Linc added. Appreciation shone in his eyes as Biloxi pivoted in her strappy black heels and form-fitting black cocktail dress. She offered a curtsy for his compliment.

"You clean up nicely yourself," she said, then stepped closer and tugged on both sides of his red bow tie.

"The Old Aunts said formal attire. Formal attire it is."

"I can't wait to take a picture of Mama and Daddy. *They* are the perfect pair," she told him.

Linc's eyes widened. "Did you see them together? For old folks, they sure look great. Hard to believe Hurricane Deidre's a mother of three."

Biloxi suppressed a smile. "Mother looks fabulous. Always does. It's hard to compete when you've got a mother who's hot."

"Just ignore her."

"Hard to do. The first thing she said when she arrived downstairs was, 'Did he break up with you?' Without even knowing anything about it, she assumed the worst of me."

Linc looked thoughtful. "Well," he started, then paused. "What exactly *is* up with you and Nick?" Linc's look nailed her. She couldn't fool him like she had when they were younger.

"Nothing. Absolutely nothing. We're friends." Biloxi picked up her black velvet wrap and started toward the front door. She stopped and turned back to him. "It's too personal to talk about."

"Somethin's up. Otherwise, you'd be goin' to this Valentine's Ball with *him* instead of me."

"You forget. I wasn't the highest bidder. I've got a job to do. Which is why we're going two hours early. I don't intend to work all night, just through the first hour of the Ball. Then, little brother, I'm going to dance with every available man there. My way of getting back in

306

the saddle."

With one eyebrow raised, Linc cocked his head. "In that dress, you'll dance with anyone you want."

Just like him to boost her confidence. She'd bought the dress on her last trip to New York with the sole intention of turning heads and had saved it for the right occasion. It fit like it had been sewn to her body. Wearing a fabulous black dress promoted the illusion she wanted to project. Elegant confidence. While she'd dreamed of coming home and her own studio, dreamed of making Fleur de Lis a show place that paid for itself, and dreamed of being anchored with family, she forgot the flip side of small-town living—bumping elbows with neighbors every day and gossip.

"Let's go to the Ball and find you a man with a saddle," Linc chuckled.

Chapter 35

"Chantel," Nick growled.

"Oh for the love of God!" Chantel shouted. "I'll find a way to talk to her. For the umpteenth time, I'm sorry."

"You should be," he snapped. "I don't understand what possessed you to purposely want to hurt her." He kept his eyes on the road and hands on the wheel to keep from wrapping them around Chantel's neck and choking the life out of her. Her behavior disgusted him, but if he hoped to convince Chantel to do what he wanted, he needed to remain calm. "Try as I might, that is exactly why you and I could never make it as anything more than friends. And right now, 'friend' is used sparingly. I might revoke that, too."

Chantel huffed.

"Explain it to me again?" Nick shook his head. He would never understand feminine logic.

"Again?" Chantel whined. "Look, a woman wants to know a man is totally devoted to her, that she can wrap him around her finger because he is so...besotted. *That* you are. But, she also wants to know that he's her knight in shining armor."

"And what is it that I am?"

"You Nicky, are not a romantic at heart. You're dependable. Somber. Safe. Always doing the right thing. A Boy Scout."

"Then, why did you give Biloxi the impression you were interested in me? And that display last Saturday at the auction, what was that about?"

"I don't know," Chantel shrugged. "I was bored. Wanted to shake things up." She sighed. "I did have some hope that you'd changed and we might actually get together after I left Alex. He turned into a bore, which is why I moved here. You were always my Mr. Dependable."

The root of her problem was Alex, yet that didn't excuse her hurtful behavior. Chantel hadn't broken things off with Alex willingly. She'd found him in bed with a mutual friend. When Alex's excuse for his infidelity was that she lacked certain amorous skills, Chantel had left him. But to turn around and pull a similar stunt to hurt an innocent person? Chantel proved to be as immature as he'd always thought.

"I can understand you being pissed at Alex, but to hurt Biloxi—and me?"

"I said I was sorry. Besides, if you really want this woman, you're going to have to step up your game. Dinner at The Chateau is nice, but you've got to do more."

Chantel perked up in the seat beside him. The look she wore made him wary.

"I'm going to be your coach! You want the girl? She's the one? I'm going to help you get her. But if I do this, you have to be ready to propose."

Nick fought back a grin. Chantel didn't know about the ring in his pocket. And, at this point, he'd take her help. At least this time he'd put Chantel's manipulative ways to good use. If she could help him successfully maneuver Biloxi right where he wanted—walking down the stairs of Fleur de Lis dressed in white, walking toward him and a minister—then he'd put up with Chantel's crap for one more night.

Nick grinned. They'd have to find a wedding photographer. It would be the one time he'd refuse to hire Biloxi.

Chapter 36

Biloxi made her way to the ladies' lounge, a quiet place to escape after an hour of taking photos of families. Also, the best place to avoid Nick and Chantel. She needed a private moment to gather her thoughts and put more rod in her backbone. She'd sent Linc off in search of a good time and came to hide...just for a few minutes before she braved the main hall. She couldn't avoid Nick and Chantel all night.

Her heart had lurched the first moment she'd spied them together. The pit of her stomach churned. Her palms dampened. Thank goodness a line of folks had formed waiting for her to take their pictures. Otherwise, she would have fallen apart, right then and there. Working helped her to pull it together, to maintain her composure, and—to ignore Nick. Would anyone miss her if she hid in the ladies' room like a junior-high girl for the rest of the night?

She pushed on the door and entered.

"Hi."

Startled, she stopped. Chantel sat in a chair in the lounge with one long leg crossed over a knee and artfully applied lipstick.

"Hello," Biloxi replied cautiously, then smoothed the front of her dress. A way to calm her shaking hands. There was no possibility of avoiding the woman. They were the only two in the room. Professional and polite,

311

that's all the situation required. She wouldn't give Chantel the opportunity to spread hateful gossip by making a scene.

She turned to leave before anything more was said, or before anyone came in and found them together. That would certainly fuel more gossip.

"Stay!" Chantel barked.

"Excuse me?"

"I mean, please stay. Biloxi, I really want to explain."

"No need," she replied, angrily. "I don't need you to draw pictures for me. I get it. You told me you wanted Nick. You got what you wanted."

Chantel snapped the compact shut and rested her hands in her lap. A mix of emotions danced across her face. What more could the woman possibly have to say?

"I'm here to make things right."

"Right?" Biloxi's irritation flared.

"Please, give me a minute. I promised Nick I'd talk to you."

"Chantel, I really don't see the point in this."

Chantel lifted her chin. She opened her black patent-leather clutch and dropped her compact inside. When she looked up, she frowned. Her eyes narrowed.

"Now look. I'm going to have my say. You're going to listen."

"Excuse me?"

"No," Chantel lashed out. "Absolutely not. I know how it feels to be in your shoes. Was there. Well sort of. Not very long ago. I walked in on two people who were *in flagrante delicto*. And that's *exactly* how I wanted it to look when you arrived at Nick's."

Nothing Chantel had to say mattered. What did the woman want? Sympathy? "I don't need to know any more. You want Nick. Clearly, he wants you. He and I are just friends. You're making too much out of this."

The door to the ladies' room opened, and Biloxi stepped out of the way.

"Biloxi? Daddy's been looking for you," her sister Nola said, walking into the room. "He's already danced with me." She paused and frowned. "Pardon me. Am I interrupting?"

"Yes!" Chantel cried.

"No," Biloxi said calmly. "I'm leaving." She turned back to Chantel. "I hope you have a lovely time at your first Valentine's Ball in Bayou Petite."

Biloxi exited the ladies' room with Nola, linking her arm through her sister's. "Thanks," she whispered. Nola gave her a puzzled look and shrugged, but continued with her.

When they turned the corner, Nick stood by the photo booth. Biloxi's heart jumped. How handsome he was in his black tux and silver bow tie, though his hair looked mussed, like he'd raked his fingers through it several times. A nervous habit of his when he wasn't wearing a hat.

"Hello, Miss Nola," Nick said. Biloxi rolled her eyes, hoping she managed to convey her complete annoyance.

"Hello, Dr. Trahan. Are you having a good time this evening?"

"No."

Beside her, Nola tensed.

People usually gave polite responses to such questions. To suggest that things were less than fine opened the door for speculation and gossip.

"Nola, go find Daddy and tell him I'll be along," Biloxi encouraged. "Give me a minute to speak with Nick."

Nola frowned. Her *humph* hung in the air. "Fine." She turned and stormed away.

"Has Chantel spoken with you?" Nick asked the minute Nola opened the door to the ballroom.

"We exchanged pleasantries."

"Oh good. Then everything is okay." Relief washed over his face. "May I have the dance after your father's?"

Clack. Clack. Behind them, high heels beat against the terrazzo floor. The sound floated from down the hall, pounding like a banging judge's gavel. Panic rose in Biloxi's chest. The last thing she wanted was a face-to-face with Nick and Chantel. Even if they were fully dressed.

"Pardon me." She strode away intending to disappear in the same direction as her sister.

"But wait. I want to talk to you," Nick called.

The clacking stopped. Chantel joined Nick. Biloxi's heart pounded. Her breath caught in the back of her throat. She'd stupidly fallen in love with Nick. She never wanted to hear anything Nick might say about his reunion with that woman. She pulled on the ballroom door and entered, leaving Nick and his date in the hall.

In the future, social gatherings would force them into each other's company. She dreaded those moments. They'd require all her good-mannered upbringing to get through those times. How long would it take before seeing them together wouldn't make her physically ill?

Forever?

She danced with her father and pretended everything was fine, though nausea bloomed in the pit her stomach and her face hurt from smiling. How beauty queens managed that for hours was beyond her.

"Nice dress," her father said. "You take after your mother that way. Elegant style."

"Thanks, Daddy. I don't know if one can inherit a sense of style." Her father had a purpose for his comment. He often used polite conversation to segue into a not so subtle point. He ruminated on something. The look in his eyes said he had a question she didn't want to answer, and it would come before the band finished their song.

"You look pale." Her father twirled her through a dance step closer toward the stage. A trumpet player stepped up to the microphone under a blue spotlight. He shrugged his shoulders, then puckered his lips, readying to play.

Hopefully, the music would take a decided turn to something more upbeat. More lighthearted jazz than blues. Whoever said music was tonic for the soul had lied, she mused.

"Biloxi?" Her father was back to prodding.

"I'm fine, Daddy." She offered a demure grin and hoped it satisfied his concern. He twirled her away from him, then tugged on her hand, pulling her back to him. His firm hands kept her from slipping when she missed the next step. She was an excellent dancer, but her feet weren't cooperating tonight.

"The band is good."

"Uh huh." She looked toward the stage at the

formally dressed men. Aunt Macy had hired a ten-piece band to perform for the Valentine's Ball. They played contemporary jazz and a wide range of blues. The trumpet player's talent rivaled Chris Botti's. His soulful notes sounded hauntingly beautiful. Each note matched her sadness, measure for measure. She batted her eyes to beat back the welling tears.

"It's him. Isn't it?" Her father tilted his head as they continued their dance.

Her gaze landed on Nick and Chantel dancing together like the perfect couple from a diamond-engagement-ring advertisement. Jealousy bit harder than ever. Even her long-standing jealousy of Branna didn't compare. Nick had hurt her way more than Gregory had.

"I don't want to discuss it."

"That tells me all that I want to know."

Her father led her through several quick steps, then stopped beside the other couple. The horn player finished his solo. Her father dropped his grasp on her and turned to Nick. "I'm cutting in." He politely offered his hand to Chantel. "Sean Dutrey," he said. "Father of the...mad-as-a-wet-hen."

When the band began another tune, her father danced away with the woman of her nightmares. Not just the last few nights. Always. Forever. She couldn't imagine what her father might say to Chantel. What did more humiliation matter?

Biloxi turned to leave the dance floor, but before she could get away, Nick grabbed her hand and placed it on his shoulder. He pulled her close, then resting one hand in the small of her back, he nudged her closer. Her heart slammed in her chest, once, twice, and again.

"You look beautiful." His breath tickled her ear.

She ignored the flattery, intent to remain stiff and unresponsive, hoping he'd give up. More people joined them on the dance floor forcing them to dance with smaller steps. Trapped by the crowd, she was forced closer to Nick, creating intimacy she fought against.

"You're a stubborn woman."

"What charming dance conversation, Dr. Trahan." When she started to pull away, Nick held firm. Rather than fight, she laid her cheek against his so he couldn't see her eyes. When she finally looked around, she discovered several couples staring at her and Nick.

She smiled politely at Captain Jack and his wife, then at Flora and her husband, and Tia with the guy who worked at Gus' filling station.

Continuing to dance with Nick would avoid a scene. She would not embarrass herself or her entire family. The band would stop playing any moment. Until then, she'd offer the world the illusion that she and Nick were fine.

Just small talk and pleasantries between old lovers.

After making love with Nick, the idea of friends with benefits became ridiculous. Her heart longed for commitment, and more. *More* was the biggest part. The forever part. How could she be so good at art and business, yet be so dumb when it came to men? After all, she gave advice to Branna about the opposite sex. Compared to her cousin, she had men figured out, or so she thought. Where she failed—her limited understanding of herself.

When it came to love, there were no runners-up, only winners and losers. It was first or nothing at all, and Chantel had grabbed that spot.

The band ended one song and immediately began another. A slow, bluesy tune. Nick refused to let go and he kept time to the music as he moved her across the floor. A smooth dancer. Just like her father.

"*Chèr*, you have to listen to me," he said. "Nothing happened between Chantel and me that meant anything."

"Oh, please. Maybe I'm naïve, but I'm not stupid."

"No, just hard-headed."

"Nick—"

"No, you listen," he said sternly. "I had a couple of drinks after the service. Okay, maybe more than a couple. At some point, I fell asleep on the couch. My grandmother and father were still there when I lay down. Chantel concocted the whole scene."

She wanted to believe him. Chantel had made an effort to tell her something earlier, but she'd been too defensive to listen. He said nothing happened. But Nick had lied before—to his grandfather—the one person who meant the world to him. Anxiety almost stole her breath. How could she trust him to tell the truth now?

Looking into his eyes, she wanted to search his soul. Something flickered deep inside. She blinked and looked again. So maybe he deserved a chance to explain. He couldn't hurt her any worse. Maybe she needed to be honest about her feelings as well.

"Nick—"

He released her. When she took a half-step back, her brother stood close by. Linc held out his hands.

"Linc?"

"I'm cutting in."

"Not now," Nick growled. He grabbed her hand and pulled her from the dance floor. Taking short quick steps, she struggled to remain upright in her heels.

"You're hurting me," she winced, and jerked to break free from his manacle-tight grasp.

Nick stopped dead in his tracks, causing her to bump into him. He turned and glared. Half-closed eyes, brown with gold flecks, shouted his anger. She swore his clenched jaw twitched and his nostrils flared. "Come here."

It could only be construed as an order.

Part of her wanted to bolt. Run the other way to escape with her broken heart. Nick loomed menacing and dangerous. Like the first night they'd met. She hadn't shown any fear then. She refused to now.

Mustering all her calmness, she held her head high and squared her shoulders. Five short steps closed the distance between them. She lifted her chin in defiance and glared, mentally calling him every foul name she'd ever heard. If she ever spoke to him again—some other place, some other time—she'd make certain he knew exactly what was on her mind. But not here, not now— the Ball was a family affair.

Nick reached for her. He grabbed her around the waist, then hauled her to his chest. Could he hear her heart pounding? Erratic rhythms sent her pulse racing. He made a sound. A grunt? Dazed, she couldn't be sure.

He grasped the sides of her face in his hands. Bent his head. When his lips met hers, she gulped. He held her there, suspended in time. Increasing the pressure on her lips gently at first, then ravished her mouth as if hungry for her. His lips, warm and firm, continued their assault, loving and intense.

She tried to catch her breath. Nick's tongue nudged

her lips and against her will, they parted. He tasted her mouth. His heat seared her heart.

Her heart gave in.

Her mind surrendered.

Her body went limp.

What to do? She totally loved this man.

****

Nick felt her yield. She tasted of sweetness and champagne. He wrapped his arms around Biloxi and pulled her farther into the secluded space behind the columns created by potted palms. He wanted their bodies to merge into one. He tensed with need. If more secluded by plants and less light, he'd have her back against the wall. They'd explore each other together. He'd raise the hem of her black dress, feel the length of her thighs and cradle her hips taut against him and kiss her senseless. If she'd let him, he'd do more.

"Nick," Biloxi gasped. "Stop."

He heard nothing but the single word. He froze with his fingers still in her hair. His lips barely a breath away from hers. The pulse of the music drifted into his consciousness, as if awakening him from a dream he wanted to go on forever. Punctuated laughter made it through to his brain along with clinking glasses. Dazed, he looked at her, certain she was aware of the reaction of his...anatomy. A minute more, who knows what he might have done. She might not love him, but clearly, she liked him enough—hell, it was a lot more than like. Their secluded encounter had moved her, too. Her pulse pounded, danced at the base of her neck—her long, beautiful, kissable neck.

"They're calling the bachelors," Biloxi whispered. Her voice was breathless and raspy, and heated with a desire that, if it didn't yet match his, it would in a few short moments.

"Huh?"

"No, that's usually my line." She laughed nervously. She stepped beside him and smoothed unseen wrinkles from the front of her dress. "Aunt Macy called all the bachelors and their dates from last weekend's auction. Go backstage. She'll parade everyone out, then announce how much money was raised for charity."

When Biloxi turned to make room for him to pass back through the sheltering palms, he moved beside her, not wanting the heat of the moment to cool. "No," he said. "Let's go. Let's leave. I have something to say to you in private."

"You can't leave," she wailed. "*You* have to make an appearance. Your date raised the most money."

"No. I can leave. And you're coming with me. Chantel is the one who made the show. Let her go up and take a bow."

Biloxi shook her head. She disagreed with his plan? Her Aunt Macy and the rest of her damn family handed out too many rules. He did his part last week. Hell, he'd even paid Chantel for her donation so he wouldn't have to take her flying, but he didn't want anyone to know. Besides, there was no way he'd walk on that stage with the one woman who'd make Biloxi bolt.

She looked at him and her eyes softened. "Nick, this isn't Baton Rouge or any of the big cities I've lived in. This is Bayou Petite. You're a local hero around here. You can't run out on these folks."

She had a point. Damn. "I'll consider it, but only if

you come with me."

"Oh, no." Her reply came too quick.

"I didn't make a contribution. Chantel did. You need to find her and escort her up there."

"No. Not without you."

The ballroom lights brightened a bit, casting a soft glow. Feedback squealed from the sound system.

"Testing." Macy stood on stage and tapped the microphone. "Now it's time for our famous Bachelor Walk. Will all the bachelors and their winning bidders please go around back? Ladies and gentlemen, we owe these special people a loud round of applause. Through their efforts and generosity, we have a very impressive contribution for the library this year. It tops last year's donation by double."

Biloxi nudged him. "You have to go, Nick."

He reached for her wrist and clamped his hands tightly around it. "Yes, but you're coming with me. And this time, be quiet. Follow my lead. I'll explain."

That seemed to pacify her. They walked hand in hand toward the door leading backstage. Nick smiled at those they passed. If he could just get her alone for a few minutes, he could explain. All of it.

They lined up with the others waiting to make their grand entrance. The band struck up a number which drowned out all noise. He leaned in close to Biloxi's ear, hoping to explain. "I paid Chantel."

Biloxi immediately stiffened.

She stood on her tiptoes and shouted next to his ear, "You paid her? You paid her! You son of a bitch. You think that makes it okay?" She jerked free and stormed away.

"What the hell?"

He had promised to pay Biloxi, too, if she bid on his auction date. Nick knew pissed when he heard it, but her response stunned him. Not because she shouted. But *what* she shouted. He'd never before heard her utter a foul phrase.

"Nick, you're up." Charles called from the top of the stairs. Nick paused, torn between running after Biloxi and making an appearance. Duty called, that's what she had said. He sighed and climbed the few steps, then nodded to Charles before stepping out. The spotlight hit him. He faced blinding white and red colored lights. A wave of applause rolled toward him. The noise quieted when the band started playing a slow ballad, his cue to walk the runway and wave. At the back of the room, a door slammed. He'd bet money that noise meant Biloxi left the ballroom.

Nick bowed to the audience. Thankfully, Chantel had the good sense to remain hidden within the crowd. While he crossed the stage, he replayed the conversation in his head. Biloxi's response baffled him. He'd never seen her so unreasonable. Well, when she thought he'd slept with Chantel, that reaction was understandable, sort of. She should trust him. Maybe the fall *had* affected her senses? Either way, he was the one who ought to be pissed. She ran out on him. Twice.

After completing his duty, he reentered the ballroom. The band played a quick-beat blues. People crowded onto the dance floor once more. Slow swaying bodies in dim light made navigation across the room impossible. He had to find Biloxi. He spotted her brother by the double doors. Maybe Linc could provide enlightenment on exactly what set Biloxi off, however, Linc's grim expression suggested he might prefer to throw a punch rather than answer a question.

"Man, Nick. If you were that kind of guy, why'd you tell my sister?"

Nick shook his head. His patience hung by a thread. He willed himself to be calm. "What kind of guy is that, Linc?"

"You paid Chantel?"

"Yeah, I paid her."

"Then, stay away from my sister," Linc warned. "I mean it."

The younger man glared and leaned closer. He clenched his fist several times, like he itched for a fight.

"Wait. Whoa, Linc. What does my paying Chantel have to do with me dating your sister?"

Linc's eyes widened. His body turned rigid. "I don't care who you pay, but keep your distance from my sister. We always knew Trahans were trouble."

The guy wasn't making sense. Nick shoved his fingers through his hair. Biloxi's big family looked very different now. Interfering and meddling relatives. More trouble than the idyllic picture he'd carried in his mind of holidays, birthdays, and other events.

Nick sucked in a deep breath, counted to ten, then let it all out. "I paid Chantel back for the five-thousand-dollar donation she made at the auction," he said while trying to hold on to some patience. "I didn't want to take her flying. Why is that a problem? And what's it got to do with me dating Biloxi?"

"Oh." Linc's expression transformed.

"Damn, Linc. What did you think?"

"You know. *Paid* for it."

"Biloxi thinks I *paid* Chantel for sex? Where is she? I need to talk with—"

"Guys," Charles interrupted. His expression appeared grim.

Nick's frustration shot up. Was he going to have to actually fight his way out of the Ball? The history of the duel suddenly took on a different meaning.

"We have to round up the family and get to the hospital," Charles continued. "Grace fainted and fell. She's at the hospital. It's serious. I need both of you to help gather the family in the lobby."

Charles went in one direction. Nick followed Linc in another looking for Dutreys and Linds. Charles' grave tone spoke volumes. Nick wished the old lady only the best. Maybe offering support at the hospital would show Biloxi his loyalty. Then she had to listen to him. He had to find a way to make her.

Chapter 37

Nick waited with the Dutreys and Linds. Biloxi's family filled the hospital's waiting room. Murmurs carried concern for Grace. Their solidarity showed their bond. Everyone in the room was related.

Except him.

He knew of the Linds through Biloxi's stories. Branna, Carson, and Charles sat in chairs against one wall. Branna's sister, Camilla, Nick had learned, hadn't been reached. Charles mentioned she might be traveling somewhere where cell service was spotty. James, Branna's fiancé, went in search of sodas. Nick counted him as a Lind, since he was engaged to one. Macy whispered with her parents, Margarite and Bob, near the open waiting room door.

Nick had never seen the Old Aunts apart before. They were like a matching set of salt and pepper shakers. One without the other didn't seem right. Marie sat calmly amidst the throng of family and radiated an aura of strength. Occasionally, she twisted a lace hanky, the only clue to her emotions. A Grand Dame to be sure.

On either side of Marie, Macy's brothers appeared like Buckingham Palace guards. Their wives, Joan and Leigh, ostensibly took their daughters, Elvie and Melody, to find restrooms. The energy in the room dropped a notch when the energetic teenagers embarked on their quest.

Then he counted the Dutrey family—Elise, Sean, Deidre, Biloxi, Linc and Nola. They hovered and paced, with Sean doing more than the others. He was Grace's grandson and closest blood descendant. Grace had outlived her husband and her children. Grace's side of the family remained smaller in number than Marie's.

His own was even smaller.

He envied Biloxi. True, he could see her point about the complex dynamics of a large family. It was like a sweet potato-pecan pie, Karo syrup for sweetness, nuts to mix it up, along with savory and some spice. The family's sheer numbers overwhelmed. Yet to their credit, they closed ranks to support each other when one of them needed help.

He, on the other hand, had never experienced family devotion on that scale. In a weird way, while sitting amongst the extended family, he considered them his own. His all-too familiar loneliness lifted a bit. His connection to them originated from a convoluted bond between his grandfather and Elise Murphy Dutrey. At the very least, they were all Bayou Petite neighbors.

Tugging at his bow tie, Nick freed the knot and let the ends dangle. He unbuttoned the top button on his tuxedo shirt and took in the odd contrasts before him. With everyone still in formal attire, the waiting room looked more like a funeral home lobby than a hospital lounge.

A hand on Nick's shoulder squeezed firmly. He looked up.

"Will you step outside with me?" Linc asked quietly.

Nick rose and followed the younger man, their footsteps echoed around them. The hospital's hall was decorated with contemporary art as though from a fine art gallery, except that the smell of antiseptics and cleaning supplies painted a different picture. Nick checked his watch. Ten thirty p.m. The hospital appeared shut down for the night.

Nick stopped with Linc, they were beyond earshot of the waiting room. Linc quirked his mouth to one side, then shifted from one foot to the other. Nick waited for him to speak.

"Nick, sorry about the earlier confusion."

"It's okay."

"I tried to tell her on the way over, but..."

"Linc, don't sweat it. She has other things on her mind. This isn't the time or place."

A nurse sidestepped them, then entered the glass-enclosed waiting room. Everyone stood up except Marie. Nick hurried after Linc to hear the nurse's announcement.

"Miss Grace is holding her own. Her heart rate is steady and her blood pressure almost normal. She fractured her hip when she fell. It requires surgery. Given her advanced age, there are risks. But, the surgeon has agreed to operate. This is not a simple fracture, and before we prep her for surgery, she'd like a word with her sister."

All eyes turned to Marie. She rose by steadying herself on Sean's arm while she clutched tightly to the lace hanky.

"Sean will accompany me." She spoke like a ruling queen.

"Please come this way," the nurse said, leading

them from the room.

The moment they cleared the door, everyone in the room collapsed into chairs. The din rose as though someone had cranked up the volume on a radio.

"Will she make it?"

"How will Marie handle it if Grace dies?"

"What will we do without them?"

In the far corner, away from the commotion, Biloxi and Branna bent their heads together, locked in deep discussion. Nick tried to catch Biloxi's eye. He wanted a private minute to finish the apology he'd started earlier. Depending on her response, he would stay, or go. But he was determined not to sleep until his apology had been heard.

After waiting a minute more, he walked toward her.

"Hello, Nick." Branna greeted him. Hopefully her pleasantness was a positive sign. Maybe Biloxi hadn't made him out to be a total villain.

"Hey, Branna," he replied. Biloxi's gaze remained lowered. Would she talk with him?

"Everything's going to be fine," Branna said, cheerfully. "Auntie Grace will use this to her advantage. She'll have all of us at her beck and call. Including *you*, if you're not careful," she chuckled.

He wanted to believe in Branna's optimism. "Sure," he said, but focused his sights on the woman who'd captured his heart. Biloxi might not listen to reason. Might reject him. But he had nothing to lose. Only one woman made him upside-down crazy. The one woman in the world he never wanted to hurt. He had to say, "I love you" and prayed she'd say it back.

"May I speak with you for a moment, Biloxi?"

When she looked up, uncertainty filled her eyes. Would she refuse? Just ignore him? Reject him completely? Finally, she nodded and rose.

The urge to protect her was strong. He wanted to promise everything would be perfect, and convince her how much he loved her—that the two of them could weather anything, including misunderstandings and family emergencies, if only she would give him a chance.

They left the room. The harsh hall lighting washed away any coziness. Maybe his apology would remove a layer of pain from her eyes. He followed her to the very end of the hallway. She probably wanted to ensure that no one overheard their conversation. A pit of dread curled in his gut. Could she intend to end what they had barely started? He ached to show her all of his feelings. The little box with the diamond ring burned a hole in his pocket. Under the circumstances, restraint was required. If she accepted his apology and miraculously threw herself into his arms, a proposal might be overshadowed by any bad news about Grace.

But he wanted her to remember his proposal and smile.

"I'm—" they said in unison.

"Ladies first," he chuckled.

"I'm sorry I jumped to conclusions."

"I'm sorry, too, for the misunderstanding. Chantel acted her way through the whole scene. I swear I had no clue that night that she'd stayed, until you rang the doorbell."

He waited to see if she believed him. He loved her. He would never purposely hurt her. But she might not have figured that out yet, and right now, those words might scare her. Gazing at her under the glare of fluorescent lights, he'd never seen her look more beautiful. The softness in her eyes reflected kindness. The feminine curve of her face begged to be touched. And her lips. Having her lips against his was worth dying for.

"Nothing happened with Chantel," he said quietly. "When I said 'I paid her,' I meant I reimbursed her for the charity donation. I bought back the date so I didn't have to take her flying and to lunch."

"I realize that now. Linc told me. I'm sorry."

He held his arms open and held his breath. Would she accept or reject him?

When Biloxi stepped close, he gently pulled her closer. She wrapped her arms around his waist. He kissed the top of her head.

"Are we okay now?" she asked.

"Yes, we're fine. Biloxi, I can't believe I'm saying this, but *we* need to talk. I need to explain about me...about my family."

"Sounds serious, Dr. Trahan. Ominous almost. Is the diagnosis that bad? You just called me by my given name. I've grown rather fond of *Chèr*."

He hugged her tighter, savoring the warmth of her body. Any moment a storm could descend—if Grace didn't make it out of surgery.

"*Mais, chèr,*" he said, trying to lighten the mood. "You feel too damn good. Nothing but good. You're the best prescription for me."

She tilted her head and looked up into his eyes. "Nick, would you go with me to the hospital chapel? It's quiet there. I need some time away from my family. We could talk there, if you'd like. I don't know how long a hip replacement surgery takes, but I'll go crazy in there." She pointed to the glass-walled room and her large family.

"The surgery will probably take a few hours. Are you sure you want to be alone?"

"I won't be alone. You'll be there. Everyone shoved in a too-small room waiting for the other shoe to drop is the perfect recipe for drama. I need quiet. It's been a hard week."

"Whatever you need."

The corners of her mouth curved into a smile, "I like the sound of that, Dr. Trahan."

He wrapped his arm around her shoulder and together they searched for the chapel. Left at the corner, right at the next, then down a long hall, which brought them to the hospital's center, a modern multistory-lobby with crisscrossing escalators between mirrored walls. Across the lobby, tucked in a corner, the stained-glass chapel door stood out against the modern surroundings.

Nick opened the door for her. On the wall opposite the doors, stained glass windows were backlit and splashed jewel-colored light across four rows of polished pews. Thick carpet muffled their footsteps and added to the intimacy of the room.

He eased into the back pew beside Biloxi. She slipped off her high heels and wiggled her toes. With her foot, she pulled the kneeling rail down, slid to her knees, then leaned forward, resting her forearms on top of the pew in front, there she folded her hands.

A sudden peace washed over him.

Biloxi glanced over her shoulder, he smiled.

She returned to her prayers.

Were his about to be answered?

****

Please take care of Great Grandmother Grace. We need her with us still. Please let her get well. And I need your help. I need this man. I'm very thankful he's here, but will he leave me if I tell him I love him? Is it too much, too soon?

Biloxi sat back in the pew when she finished the prayer. Nick remained silent, though care and concern glowed in his topaz eyes. She reached for his hand, it was warm in hers. His smile comforting. His strong arm around her shoulders offered support and demanded nothing.

"Thank you for coming with me. What did you want to talk about?" she whispered.

"I hope your Great Grandmother Grace will come out of this fine."

"If G.G. Grace could hear you now, she'd be pleased."

Her mind churned. Her heart ached. How insensitive was she? Not long ago, they waited in another hospital. That night, Nick's grandfather died. Very thoughtless of her not to consider how tonight might affect him.

"Nick, are you okay?"

"Biloxi, do you recall the night we met?" His wry tone eased some of her tension. "We spent that night in a hospital, too. I hope this isn't going to be our thing. Saturday night hospital dates."

She stifled a chuckle. Was it irreverent to laugh in the chapel?

"I started to say that things always work out like they're supposed to," Nick said. "But I don't usually

333

follow that theory. Usually I force what I can in my favor, and continue to fight for what I can't."

She squeezed his hand for reassurance.

"Patience is a virtue. That sounds like a universal truth, but I never thought it applied to me." Nick sounded philosophical. "I've always tried to even the odds, make situations more to my liking. I liked to be in control, but it never gave me back my family. Grandpère held my life together when it crumbled around me. The irony is, if my grandfather had married your grandmother, we wouldn't be having this conversation." Nick paused and looked deep into her eyes. "I wouldn't have wanted to miss meeting you. So, things do work out like they're supposed to."

Her heart swelled. She loved this man. He was strong enough to share the deepness of his heart. He'd lived without his mother and father. The idea of not having family sent a stabbing pain through her heart. "I can't imagine a life without my mother or my dad."

"I shoved childhood memories away, but they're back with my father's return. The last time I saw him, he told me to wait for him in the car. Memories of that night—not so pleasant. Gun shots. My mother screaming. Then the police."

"Were you hurt?" She searched his face for traces of his pain.

"Not that way. My grandfather took me home with him. My father was gone. My mother, gone. I hadn't heard from either of them since I was ten, until my father reappeared."

"That has to be hard. My family has its share of problems, but life without them? Though sometimes I need a break. Like now."

"As a kid, I thought if I asked questions about my parents, my grandfather wouldn't want me around. I still don't know anything about my mother. Now all I have is Grandmère, and a stranger who says he's my father."

She slid her arms around his neck and placed a kiss on his cheek. "There are lots of Linds and Dutreys to go around. I'm happy to share them with you."

The corners of his mouth rose slowly. He leaned in until they were nose to nose. "You're a generous woman, Biloxi Noël Dutrey." He kissed her, slow and gentle. Her toes curled into the thick plush carpet. She hung on through his heart-stopping kiss, the heat of it like velvet and silk sliding over her body. His lips tugged on her bottom lip. She wanted to be closer than clothes would allow. Her bones became jelly, her insides liquid fire.

She ran her fingers through his hair, and then kissed him back. Anything he asked, she would've agreed to, offering complete surrender. This man pushed her beyond normal reason to a place of deep raw emotion. And he made her feel safe.

She loved him.

"Ahem," a voice sounded behind them.

Startled, she turned. Her cheeks blazed with heat. She'd been caught like a high school kid making out in the backseat of a car after a Friday night football game.

Nola stood behind the pew looking straight ahead. "Biloxi, Auntie Marie is in the waiting room. She wants to speak with you, Mother, Branna, and Aunt Macy." Nola stalked to the door, grasped the handle, then turned and threw a heated glare. "Now!" she hissed, then shot out the door.

"Oh, no," Biloxi groaned. "I forgot to tell her what really happened. She still thinks you're the devil incarnate because of Chantel."

"Tell her now. C'mon," he urged. "Let's go hear the good news."

"How do you know it's good news?" She slid her feet into her heels, stood, and smoothed her dress. Nick waited by the door.

"Because I won't hear anything else."

"I'll take all the good news I can get," she said, crossing the threshold. Nick laced his fingers through hers, then brought her hand to his lips for a kiss.

"And, I have good news to share with you. Very soon, *chèr*."

Chapter 38

Biloxi held Nick's hand. Her heart pounded double time. There had to be a way to balance everything. Work. Fleur de Lis. And Nick.

They made their way through the hospital's labyrinth back to the subdued waiting room. Most of the family gathered at one end, whispering. On the opposite side, the assembled women summoned by Marie appeared to be waiting for bad news.

Biloxi hung back. A tense energy emanated from the group. Her every nerve stood at attention. Dread washed over her like a cold shower. She wished to be any place else but there. If only Nola hadn't found her.

"There you are, missy," Great Aunt Marie said. "I want a word with you over there." Marie pointed to where Deidre, Macy, and Branna waited.

Biloxi flashed an imploring look at Branna, hoping for a shred of insight into what prompted the formal meeting. Branna shrugged.

Taking a seat next to her mother, Biloxi refused to make eye contact.

"Where have you been? You've been gone for almost an hour." Her mother chastised in a hushed tone.

"I needed a minute," she replied, settling back into the chair. In the past, her guilt meter would've spiked at the censure.

But that was the past.

"I went to the chapel to pray," she explained.

Her mother wouldn't question her further. Deidre Dutrey never feared a worthy battle, but even she didn't challenge God. Biloxi sighed. Thankfully, Nola had no time to tattle about what she witnessed in the chapel.

But Nick's kiss was worth any reprimand.

Next to her, Branna stiffened. Their respective mothers flanked their sides. Before them, Marie stood with the help of her black cane and pointedly looked down at them. Her long gray-white hair, arranged in a twist, had not a strand out of place. Her cheeks were flushed. She radiated a grand-dame aura in her strands of pearls, but also an aura of utter displeasure from the rigid stance, firm-set jaw, and intense gaze.

"This decision has been a long time in coming," Marie stated emphatically. "It's a decision that must be made. Grace and I are *old*. There are a few things important to us at this stage of our life. None more important than our family's well-being, and the future stability of Fleur de Lis. The plantation was our grandfather's legacy to us. It is our legacy to all of you." Marie clutched a lacy hanky and pointed a finger heavenward. "At any time Grace or I could go."

Biloxi's gasp was joined by ones from the women around her. She shook her head in denial. "No," she murmured. "No."

Marie ignored her interruption and continued, "Grace might not make it tonight. We want things settled before both of us are gone. For our peace of mind. We must know that Fleur de Lis will carry on."

Biloxi blinked and looked away with tears forming in the corners of her eyes.

"Branna," Marie barked. Everyone jumped. "You

have been gifted with a privilege over all of your cousins, yet, you do not embrace that gift. Instead, you drag it around like a burden. There is a reason for our method of succession. Each generation must do their part, however, a willing spirit is needed."

Biloxi drew back when Branna flinched. Macy frowned and refolded her hands in her lap. Deidre looked away, barely concealing a smile. Marie had never spoken so directly to any of them before.

"Branna"—Marie's voice softened—"we took you in last year because you didn't want to live with your parents at their beach house. Your mother had to force you to participate in running the estate. You found no pleasure in the work. At first, we thought it was because of the demise of your engagement to that awful Mr. Sterling." Marie paused and eyed them before continuing. "But we were wrong about all of your sadness. I assure you, we want you to be happy. Therefore, unless you tell us within the week you are ready to move home to Fleur de Lis and take an active role in the business, we have decided to appoint Biloxi as the next Keeper. She has given every indication she welcomes the challenge. And she's here."

Biloxi's mouth dropped. Branna stared at her with wide-eyed shock.

"Fleur de Lis will always be your home. You are welcome here." Marie nodded. "However, it is clear the twenty-first century requires a different approach."

Marie's cocked head and raised eyebrow made it perfectly clear there would be no argument, no debate.

Biloxi cringed. Humiliation of her cousin wasn't how she wanted to land the job. Maybe she'd been fooling herself. Maybe the situation was never hers to influence.

But could she stay if Branna said "yes" to the responsibilities and came home to be Keeper?

Marie's bark fizzled to a sighing whisper. "One week, Branna. No more. You must provide us with your decision by then." Marie coughed and tottered. Nick ran to her side, held her upright, while Linc grabbed a chair and slid it behind the old woman. The two helped Marie sink gently into the seat.

"Thank you," Marie whispered.

"I'll get you some water," Nick said. Linc squatted beside Marie and murmured words of encouragement.

Deidre and Macy rose from their seats and left the waiting room. Biloxi remained seated beside Branna. The silence deepened between them. Through watery eyes, Biloxi caught Branna's changing expressions. Anger, concern, and exasperation flashed like a changing kaleidoscope, then dissolved into hurt.

Biloxi blinked back the tears that threatened to fall. She'd been direct about her ambitions. Never went behind anyone's back, nor schemed to undermine her cousin with the Old Aunts.

"What have you done?" Branna ground out the accusation.

"Huh?"

"What have you done?"

"Nothing," Biloxi defended. "I didn't instigate this, if that's what you mean." She tried to keep her voice level. She would never purposely hurt Branna. Never stab her in the back.

"I told you I would think about it, and we'd talk about it more—"

"You're jumping to conclusions."

"Biloxi Dutrey, I always thought I could trust you and my sister. She betrayed me. Now you!"

"Wait. I swear," Biloxi pleaded, but Branna held up her hand and looked away. "Branna, I never brought up my ideas with the Old Aunts. Or even my mother or sister. The only one, besides you, who knew about my idea was..."

"My mother." Branna's voice fell flat.

"What?"

"Now I get it. She's trying to manipulate me and Camilla."

Biloxi shook her head. "What are you talking about? Camilla isn't even here. And exactly how did your sister betray you?"

"I don't want to talk about her. It took me a long time to forgive her. I couldn't set a wedding date with James until I had forgiven my sister. But I have. I'm ready to commit to marriage now. And this was my mother's way of forcing my hand."

"I still don't understand." Biloxi frowned. "You wouldn't marry James until you had forgiven Camilla? Is that why she's roaming the countryside and got everyone worried?"

"She's not here because she still can't face me." Branna's eyes turned sad.

"What did she do?"

"Never mind about that right now. I had already made my decision about Fleur de Lis. I was going to tell everyone tomorrow at breakfast, but my mother didn't know that piece of information. She's trying to force my hand—a wedding will bring Camilla home."

What heinous thing had Camilla done? Branna keeping secrets? A lot had changed since they were kids.

"Congratulations on deciding to set a wedding date," Biloxi said.

"Thank you. And I need to share about my other decisions. James and I have discussed this. Weighed all the pros and cons. He's firm that the final decision must be all mine. Therefore, I decided—"

"Hey, all ya'll," Nola hollered into the waiting room. "The nurse is coming down the hall. She's smiling. I hope it's good news about Great Grandmother Grace."

Deidre and Macy followed the nurse inside. Everyone else scrambled to find a seat, their rapt attention focused on the nurse, who went straight to Marie.

"Grace is doing well. I'll come back with another status when we move her to recovery." The nurse's smile eased the tension in the room.

Biloxi sighed with relief. Good news had never been so welcomed.

"Now, it's late. She needs rest. Only a few will be allowed to see her tonight. Others will have to wait until tomorrow to visit."

"Elise, Sean, Deidre, and I will see to her tonight," Marie said, her voice warbling. "We'll arrange a visiting schedule tomorrow so we don't tire her. We'll let her know of your love and good wishes. Go home and rest. You know what it'll be like to wait on her hand and foot."

Biloxi hung back while the family departed. Emotionally drained, she needed time to digest Marie's declaration. Her mother waved.

"I'm going with Nick," she said, waving back.

Until she had a plan, she dared not talk with her mother.

She stepped into the cool night air with Nick. His arm rested around her shoulder. He didn't press her to talk. She needed his silent support. Her brain hurt from thinking. Were the Old Aunts just too old to see Nick as a person and not a Trahan? How would Nick react if she told him that she would stay in Bayou Petite for him, even if she wouldn't be the next Keeper?

Chapter 39

Headed for Loblolly Lane, Nick clutched the steering wheel.

"The world changes without any warning. In a second it can happen." Biloxi's voice sounded far away, like she spoke to someone unseen.

She had it right. And because of that, he needed her tonight. Wanted her in his arms. His mouth on hers. Her body tangled together with his. He wanted her in his bed.

Before life had a chance to change again.

He'd lost his grandfather. His grandmother phoned daily, often in tears. His father remained a stranger. His mother hadn't been located yet, and then there was Chantel, plus the problems she created. Now Grace.

None of those changes, challenging as they were, changed the love he had for the woman in the seat next to him. Loving her overshadowed everything else. Only here and now with Biloxi mattered. Here and now he needed her. Tomorrow would take care of itself.

As long as all his tomorrows included her, too.

"I don't want to go home right now," she said. "If you take me to your house, I could pick up The Beast your grandfather left me."

She sounded hesitant. He tried to gauge what she needed. "We could go to the diner for coffee. I can drop you home after that." He didn't want her out driving alone tonight. Not after her ride on an emotional rollercoaster with so many loop-de-loops.

"No. No coffee," she said, distractedly. "I'm already caffeinated enough."

"How 'bout a drink?"

"The Bait Place is still open." She paused. "We could go there. But we're a little over done." She looked down at her dress, and then over at him.

"How 'bout a drink at my house?" If she agreed, he might have a chance at persuading her to stay the night. Like the song said, he could "try a little tenderness" with her. In the faint illumination from the truck's dash, he watched her mouth form into a small grin. His hopes rose.

"Now, why didn't I think of that?"

They drove in silence the rest of the way. His heart thudded when she reached to hold his hand. After arriving at his house, the porch lights beating back the darkness, he offered her a change of clothes, then disappeared upstairs to shed his suit. He returned in jeans and a flannel shirt to start a fire in the fireplace. Quickly the kindling caught and flames danced. Orange, yellow, red, blue. The movement hypnotized and relaxed him, although every nerve in his body tingled because of her.

"Tea?" he asked, pouring a glass when she appeared from the guest room. She shook her head.

Sinking into the couch, he rested his feet on the coffee table, then held up the glass. Through ice and amber liquid, fire light flickered. He rested his arm over Biloxi's shoulders and savored the moment.

Biloxi curled next to him in one of his old flannel shirts. A blanket covered her legs and hid the oversized sweat pants and thick socks she'd borrowed. She'd pulled the pins from her hair, letting the long, dark auburn fall. Her skin, smooth like polished marble and soft like velvet, captivated him. He ached to taste her lips again. To stroke her silky hair.

He wanted to devour her.

Wanted to hear her moan his name.

He wanted to hear her scream, "Yes!"

Instead, he sipped his drink and listened to Bach on the stereo, allowing the ease of the moment to wash over him. He marveled at how a body could feel so relaxed and energized at the same time.

"Ahhh," he breathed.

"Exactly how I feel," Biloxi whispered.

"How is that?" He traced circles on top of her far shoulder, and caution told him to tread lightly.

She gazed at him. The green in her hazel eyes flickered and glowed brighter. She lowered her eyes. Her mouth spread into a shy, seductive grin.

The woman produced a gut-wrenching reaction in him.

Scooting down, wiggling until her back rested on his thighs, she rested her head on the arm of the couch.

His body responded. She couldn't miss the hard rise in his jeans.

When she lightly touched the hair over his ear, then slid her fingers to the nape of his neck, her stare stayed locked with his.

His breath caught. He set down the glass of tea before he spilled it.

"Nick," she whispered. Seductive. Inviting. Then she wrapped her hands behind his neck and lifted to meet him face-to-face. Their lips hovered close, not quite touching. She tugged on his bottom lip.

Restraint fled like a hurricane roaring onto land.

He pulled her into a bear hug. His teeth nipped at her bottom lip. The tip of his tongue traced the shape of her mouth. And back again. Her lips parted. She kissed him, her mouth warm and pliant. If he died right then, he'd die a happy man.

Tenderly he spread kisses across her face, then reached for the first button on the flannel shirt she wore. Her hand covered his and stilled him, but not his pounding heart.

Biloxi gripped his shoulders for balance and sat up, straddling his lap, her thighs grasping the outside of his. With a slow movement, she began to unbutton the shirt. Captivated by her every move, his eyes followed her hands. The too-large shirt draped in folds over her chest. When she'd relieved all of the buttons from their holes, her creamy skin shone through the gap.

Oh God!

A shy smile formed. She looked down to the spot where his hands rested on her thighs. He gripped her tighter to hold her in place, but let go when she tugged, then placed his hands over her collarbones, her skin so warm to his touch. Her eyes fluttered closed. Her back arched slightly, and she guided his hands downward to her breasts.

Heaven!

Not wanting to rush, or have her pull away, he took care when sliding the shirt slowly off her creamy-white shoulders. No bra to hinder the view. She sighed wistfully and arched a little more, gripping the top of his shoulders for support. Her movement cried for action from him. He wanted to feast on her firm round breasts. Suckle them tenderly, then hard. Watch her grow flush from desire. He wanted her aching. Aching as much as he ached for her. Wanted her starving, the way he starved for her.

He stroked his hands over her breasts, then his thumbs made circles.

She moaned.

He took one rose-colored bud in his mouth. Flicked his tongue. Then twirled and sucked.

She moaned louder.

Her grip on his shoulders tightened, then relaxed. He tantalized each breast with kisses. When she shivered, he held her hips in place, but she refused to be stilled. She pulled the zipper on his jeans. It sounded like a starter pistol.

Nick lifted her and set her on her feet on the floor. She grunted in protest. Quickly, he shrugged off his jeans and boxers. Kicked them aside. Flung his shirt across the room.

Her heavy-lidded eyes smoldered. She stood perfectly still. He tugged her sweatpants off of her, taking her panties with them, and tossed them aside. Then, unbuttoning the cuffs on the shirt, let it slide to the floor in a puddle. He smoothed his hands over her chest and her breasts, tracing lines over her stomach. Electricity arced like lightning between them. She was velvet and honey and the breath of life.

"Nick, please," she pleaded.

Desire took control. He wanted nothing more than to please her.

When he laid her gently on the couch and covered her body with his, they melded into a perfect fit. He rose up on his arms as he entered her. She embraced his hardness with the wetness of her silky apex. After his first thrust, they matched each other's rhythm, finding the perfect tempo that shot their desire to a frenzied need.

Her moans grew louder.

Quicker.

Closer.

She matched him move for move.

A bump to his thrust.

Her imploring cries were a symphony of pleasure. He increased their pace to a crescendo. His hard release came at the same moment as her final shout. Blood rushing in his ears drowned out his moan. A moment later, he collapsed on top of her, chest to chest. Her quick panting breaths made him hard again. He wanted to give her more. So much more.

The evening held great possibilities.

****

Surrounded by big throw pillows with a blanket for cover, Biloxi snuggled closer to Nick in front of the fireplace. Could mere words express what she'd just experienced?

Love was the critical ingredient to creating an everlasting moment. Making love had never been like that with anyone else. Only Nick. Wonderful St. Nick.

The heat of her flush rose. At this rate, she'd have a tan from the inside out. Nick had pushed her buttons perfectly, then catapulted her into oblivion. His liberation and guttural cry harmonized with hers. She'd never been with a man who vocalized so loudly when reaching satisfaction.

She tasted heaven in his lips. She loved the manly smell of him after making love, loved the smooth and the hairy-rough parts of his body, so firm and masculine. Her heart fluttered, taking her all the way to heaven. Coming back to earth, she still floated.

Nick interrupted her mind-melt when he kissed her forehead.

"I have something to tell you," she murmured.

"Okay, just don't move."

She trailed a finger slowly down Nick's nose. She hesitated telling him. What if Branna decided to take over at Fleur de Lis? Could she survive as second best? If not, what would happen to her relationship with Nick? Or worse, what if her family refused to accept a Trahan into the fold?

What if? What if?

"Well?" Nick yawned. The glow about him reminded her of a lion, relaxed and lazing.

She turned on her side, then laid one arm across his waist, fitting the length of her body next to his and snuggling close to his chest. His chin rested on the top of her head. The heat from the fireplace warmed her backside. Lying beside Nick, luxury at its finest, after making love, settled her into deep relaxation. With her ear to his chest, she heard the rhythmic thud of his heart. Strong and steady. Just like him. She let go of a long sigh.

It's now or never. Lord help me if he doesn't feel the same.

"I love you, Charles Nicholas Trahan," she whispered.

No response. She waited. The rise and fall of his chest moved slow and even. Couldn't he think of an appropriate reply? Had she said it too soon? Would her confession ruin everything?

She hesitated to move, but if he intended to sidestep or reject her declaration, she had to see the truth in his eyes. Her apprehension climbed as silence stretched longer.

"Nick?" she whispered, fearing the worst.

The lazing lion hadn't heard a word.

He'd fallen asleep.

Chapter 40

Cold seeped into Nick's body, and a shiver woke him. He stretched. He'd slept like the dead, the long-dead, like those buried in tombs in New Orleans' cemeteries for generations.

Weak morning light filtered through the half-opened shutters. He ran his fingers through his hair. An old tired ache in his gut had dissolved. A new contentment had found him. When had he ever slept better?

He rolled to his side.

Biloxi gone? Where? Kitchen? Bathroom?

"*Chèr?*"

Nothing.

"Biloxi."

Silence.

"Woman!"

He pulled the blanket over himself for warmth. The fire had died in the hearth, but the heater hadn't kicked on. It was cold on the floor without her.

A notepad propped on the floor against the side of the coffee table caught his attention, and he grabbed it.

Good morning! I need to get an early start. Call me later. She had signed it *BND*.

He looked at the initials. BND. Would she drop the Dutrey or just add Trahan? She'd never give up the N for Noël. It linked her and Branna together. Their mothers' birthday gift to them for their shared Christmas Eve birthday. Biloxi Noël Dutrey-Trahan? It didn't matter as long as legally she'd be Mrs. Charles Nicholas Trahan.

He'd heard her admission of love last night. It took all he had not to jump up and propose then. The ring waited upstairs on his dresser, only a few short steps up and back. He could've knelt in front of the fireplace and witnessed joy dancing in her eyes. It would've been good. But he wanted great. And although it was an old-fashioned notion, he wanted to be the first to say "I love you."

"I love you, Charles Nicholas Trahan." Her words were the wealth of a kingdom he had waited years to claim. Nothing would rush the pleasure he wanted for her. He planned to ensure she never felt second best to anyone in their life together. She was all he wanted in a woman, a wife, and a partner. For him, she was sweetness with vitality. She had fought to make a place in her family, to feel like she really belonged. He understood that driving emotion.

And she loved him.

Last night after her confession, he'd heard his grandfather's voice whispering lessons from the past.

A gentleman makes the first overture, offers the first words of love. It makes a woman feel special and valued.

Traditions lived for a reason. Rules and lessons melded together. A man had to act like a man in order to be one.

Now he needed a plan. The best place. The most romantic way. The perfect time. His proposal had to be an experience she'd never forget.

Ideas flipped through his brain. With almost her entire family in residence at Fleur de Lis, and knowing how much her family meant to her, he had to include them.

He reached for his cell phone. "Good morning, Greta. How's my favorite chef?"

"Why, Nick, good morning. Come for breakfast and find out. We'd love to have your company."

"Thanks, Greta. Maybe. I need to talk to Sean Dutrey. Is he available?"

"Sean? He's probably up and out the door for a run, but let me check."

Nick could tell by the sounds and voices that Greta carried the cordless phone with her. She greeted Linc and Carson. Then he heard James' voice. "Down toward the S-curves."

"You heard that?" Greta asked.

"Yes, thanks. I need to talk to you, too. Need your special expertise."

"Git your handsome self over here by nine."

"Will do."

Nick hung up and scanned the room for his clothes. Socks stuck out from under the end table, his jeans draped a chair, and his shirt was wadded up on the coffee table. Grabbing them, he dressed, then hopped around pulling on his socks.

The coffeemaker finished brewing a pot and he poured black liquid into a mug. Opening a cabinet door, he pulled down a phonebook and flipped through the pages until he found the florist. He picked up the phone and punched in numbers.

"Flora, this is Dr. Nick Trahan. I know it's early. I know it's Sunday, but I need a big favor. Please call me back on my cell." He left his number, then set the phone back in the cradle.

After a quick gulp of hot coffee, he reached for his running shoes. Sitting on the stairs, he tied the laces. His favorite boots rested next to the front door. He'd worn them the night of the storm, the night Captain Jack's puppies were born, the night he pulled Biloxi from the ditch. They were his lucky charm.

He retrieved his cell phone from his back pocket, flipped through the directory, then pushed the call button and waited.

"Captain Jack?" he said. "Good morning! It's Doc Trahan. Look, I know it's early to call, but I need a favor. Will you lend me your carriage this evening?" He wanted everything perfect. Everything had to fall into place.

"Whoa, son," Captain Jack said. "What's the rush?"

"It's a special occasion. A proposal, old man. A proposal." He ended the call after Captain Jack approved of the plan.

"Okay, now to find Sean."

After jogging down the front steps, he headed for the road. This was *joie de vivre*. Sunny. Cool. An early southern spring. Everything said fresh. Renewal. Regeneration. Rebirth. He breathed in, buoyed by the start of his day. All the pieces were falling perfectly into place. A stormy night had entwined his life with Biloxi's. Would her father understand?

He'd only met the man last night, but Sean had to be a reasonable guy. After all, Sean had danced Biloxi back into his life, then waltzed Chantel to the other end of the dance floor. That had to mean something. Sean hadn't objected to his presence at the hospital when he joined the family holding vigil for Grace. Nor had Sean displayed the slightest dissatisfaction when Biloxi left the hospital with a Trahan last night.

He continued his jog down the long drive. No one would mar the perfection of his plan, not even his father and grandmother. He would deal with them. Could they have a change of heart about the Dutreys?

"Nick!" The shout brought him to attention. "Trahan, I want to talk to you."

Sean met him in the spot where he and Biloxi had first met, where the drive greeted the curve in the road. Nick offered his hand. Sean grasped it firmly and pumped three times.

"I called over to Fleur de Lis," Nick told him. "They said you were coming this way. I came to talk to you."

Sean paused. "So you came to meet the conflict head on?"

"Conflict?" Nick asked.

"You brought one woman to the ball. You left with another. You kept my daughter out all night. What's a father to think?"

"Well, when you put it that way..."

"It begs a question, and I'll get right to the point, Nick. What are your intentions toward my daughter?" The older man stood with his hands on his hips. He was barely breathing hard after his run, he looked military fit and strong. Would Sean demand a duel?

"Mr. Dutrey, I've got hot coffee up at the house. Would you mind if we take our discussion up there? I came looking for you because your daughter is exactly what I want to discuss."

The older man raised one eyebrow and nodded. "All right. We'll talk. Man to man." He reached over and slapped Nick on the shoulder. "But first we race. Up to your house. Let's see what you're really made of, Trahan."

Nick scrambled to keep up with Sean. He had to win the race.

After all, a race was a duel of sorts.

Chapter 41

Biloxi returned to her bedroom after a long hot shower. Dressed in jeans and a sweater, she towel-dried her hair. When she opened the bedroom door, she was surprised to find Branna seated in the hall side chair. Her cousin was already dressed and wearing a smile wide enough to break her face. Wary, Biloxi's defenses went up.

"Good morning." She tried for cheerful, then closed the door behind her. If they were going to fight, they'd do it in private, not in the hall.

"You're still up from last night?"

"No, I had a very good night's sleep, thank you."

Branna nodded, but Biloxi could tell her cousin wasn't buying the lie. "I assume you're here because we didn't get a chance to discuss the ultimatum Marie issued last night."

"Coffee on the back gallery?"

Biloxi hesitated. Why had she hinged her life's dreams on her cousin's decision? The notion had bothered her all night. Then, early this morning before sunrise, the answers grew crystal clear.

"Well, c'mon," Branna urged. "Put on some shoes. Let's have coffee."

She slipped on sneakers and then followed Branna, unable to read her cousin's strange mood. If Branna was up before nine on a Sunday *and* had been waiting, the conversation could very well take a turn for the worse.

When they reached the kitchen, mugs lined the counter along with accoutrements, compliments of Greta's organization. Biloxi poured cream and sugar into her cup and waited while Branna filled her mug with coffee. The aroma of brewed coffee perked her up. She wandered behind Branna through the screen door to the rocking chairs. Her sneakers squeaked against the back wooden gallery.

"Good morn'n!" Greta called. She rose from a chair. "Dr. Trahan called. He's going to join us for breakfast, so it will be a bit late." She shuffled past them in her new, white fluffy slippers and silk robe, not even looking back.

"I think Greta has a crush on that man," Branna whispered.

"I think you're right," Biloxi agreed. She sat and rocked gently forward and back, looking out at the garden, waiting for Branna to begin.

"Nick's coming to breakfast?" Branna asked.

Biloxi spotted the recently-planted tree. The hole where she fell the night she met Nick now held a stately magnolia.

It'll be tall when I'm old like G. G. Grace...I can't possibly leave this place.

Nick had sealed the deal. Keeper or not, Fleur de Lis and Bayou Petite were home. She might not live at Fleur de Lis if Branna returned as Keeper, but she'd maintain her photography business on the premises. She'd help Branna make a showcase out of their home. Make the Old Aunts proud. She would ensure the legacy continued in grand form for future generations.

For her children, and her children's children. That's how it would be. She would work it all out, only Branna had to make it happen. There would be no rift in this family.

"Biloxi," Branna interrupted her thoughts. "I'm sorry for the...edge between us. This isn't a new situation for me. The last year has been hard. I love it here, too. Same as you. It just took me longer to realize it."

"The need of this place is so strong in my blood, Branna. And I admit, jealousy is an ugly green on me."

"Have I ever done anything to cause it?"

"No. But you can't really know, and I don't expect you to know, that living in your shadow is tough work. Born only a few minutes after you, yet tradition dictates you're special. That's a hard thing to swallow, especially with a mother like mine."

Branna nodded. They both endured challenging relationships with their mothers.

"I've given this a lot of thought. I haven't yet discussed my final decision with James or my mother. They both said I had to decide on my own, then talk to you."

Biloxi gazed at her cousin—a face that looked so much like her own. She sensed Branna's struggle, and whatever her cousin planned to share, the final decision had not come easily. Biloxi reached and gave Branna's arm a squeeze. "I've made my own peace. Whatever your decision, I will abide. I've fought the rules. I came back to change everything, wanted to force your decision. But now it's different."

Branna eyed her, then grinned. "I started to ask, 'what changed,' but I realize I already know the answer. Nick."

A heated blush chafed Biloxi's cheeks.

"Well, that certainly confirms it," Branna teased.

"And I used to give *you* advice about love," Biloxi said. "It's really different with him. If I have Nick, I'm willing to share everything else with you."

"Well, I owe Nick my gratitude. You see, I'm not ready to come back yet. I do have a contract to fulfill. But I'm not willing to walk away completely and just hand the reins to you. I can't turn my back on the role I've been groomed for all of my life. So, I have a plan, if you agree, of course."

Biloxi shrugged. "I'm willing to listen."

"Cousin, we share a birthday, a home, and a legacy. Let's share the responsibility, too. We'll make an addendum to tradition. You and I have different skills, and if we work together, it will be easier, and I believe we'll accomplish more in the long run. What do you think?"

Biloxi leaned over and hugged her cousin. "I'm relieved. It feels really right—us doing this together. We'll make it work."

There were details to resolve and they needed another family meeting to present their plan, however, Branna's compromise gave them the best of both worlds. While Biloxi was making a mental list of changes at Fleur de Lis, the movement of two men distracted her. Nick bounded up the back steps. Her father jogged behind him, waved, and entered the kitchen.

"Nick? Greta said you were coming for breakfast, but—"

"Good morning, ladies." Nick smiled. He bent and

kissed the top of Biloxi's head.

"Breakfast will be ready in fifteen minutes," Greta hollered through the screen door. "Marie is on her way down. Don't keep us waiting."

"I could eat a gator." Nick rubbed his hand together as though excited by the prospect. He came around to the front of the rocker and grabbed her hands, pulling her to her feet.

"I've got to find James," Branna said, clearly leaving to give her and Nick privacy. She headed down the steps to the garçonnière.

"That poor guy sleeps over there?" Nick whispered.

"Well, you know tradition. All single men are housed there. Since Linc and Carson are home, they have their own rooms there, and James is sleeping in my office-turned-guest-room. But not for long." Biloxi winked. "I think Branna is ready to set the date."

"Oh, so the married-types sleep in the house?"

"Yes," Biloxi replied. "Marie would *never* allow single men to mingle at night with unmarried females in this big house." She used her best southern drawl. "They must be separate, otherwise imagine the scandal."

"What about single men with married females over there?"

"Oh, you!" She giggled. "You know what I mean. The Old Aunts are *old*-fashioned. It's just the way of things here."

"Lots to be said for tradition." He tucked her hand in the crook of his arm. "Shall we, my dear, go into breakfast?"

"Is that your poor and shameless impression of

Rhett Butler?"

"Why, my dear, I think you give a damn," Nick whispered and patted her arm.

She laughed all the way to the dining room.

Family members filtered in and gathered around the large table. Marie sat at one end. The rest of the family filled in the seats. Biloxi motioned for Nick to sit next to her. Everyone quieted when they sat. Marie nodded to Elise.

Elise stood. "Grace had a rough night. She's in some pain, but is doing as well as can be expected. She doesn't want a lot of visitors at one time. She fears it will tire her out."

"Thank you, Elise, for sharing the news," said Marie. "Carson, say grace for us and let's eat." They bowed their heads. Carson offered a brief, and irreverent, prayer.

Giggles circulated around the table before he finished.

"Amen," she and Nick said at the same time.

"I enjoy your family," Nick whispered while accepting a plate of food passed to him.

"Easy enough for you to say. You're an only child. Never had to fight for the last piece of bacon or another helping of grits." She snatched one of the platters of meat before one of her family members could get to it first. "Bacon or sausage, *sir*?"

"Oh, I like this." Nick's wry grin teased. "Two strips of bacon, *please*."

"Daddy's an only child. I guess it wasn't so bad for him," she told Nick.

"Bad for me, how?" Sean asked.

"You had Aunt Macy, Uncle Pete, and Uncle

Edward around most of the time."

The four of them laughed simultaneously.

"Yeah," Sean agreed. "But we were pretty hard on Macy. Three boys against one girl. She grew up to be a lady despite our best efforts to make a tomboy out of her."

Nola looked aghast. "Aunt Macy? You were a tomboy?"

"I loved playing in the dirt. I guess that's what led me to buy a nursery."

Nick interrupted. "I think there are more pros than cons to a big family after all."

Breakfast continued with storytelling. It was the exact kind of moment Biloxi had come to bask in.

When breakfast was finished, the youngest girls cleared the table, and Greta poured coffee for the adults.

"Excuse me," Nick called out. His raised voice gathered everyone's attention.

Biloxi eyed him suspiciously. What was he up to?

"Thank you for including me. Breakfast was wonderful. Not just the food, although I admit, if I could steal Greta away, I would. The company is great. I know some of you have reservations about me..."

As though cued, Nola walked back into the dining room and cast a wary glance at Nick before sliding into her seat.

"Yes," Nick continued. "Even Miss Nola has dubious opinions about me. However, to show my best intentions, now that all of you are present, I am asking Miss Biloxi for an official date. With your permission, of course."

Lingering silence hung in the air.

A rush of heat crept into Biloxi's cheeks. What was Nick up to?

"Well," her father said, finally breaking the long pause. "Do we need to take a family vote? It's not like he's asking her to marry him. All he wants is a date."

Chapter 42

Back at home, Nick looked at the clock on the fireplace mantel. Grandmère would be home from church. He hit speed dial.

"Hello?"

"Good morning. It's Nick." He pressed the speaker button on the key pad, then laid the phone on the counter and hoped for the best. His grandmother had been more than just civil—polite actually—to Biloxi at the burial service. Maybe now that his father had returned, she'd had a change of heart about past events.

"Good morning, Nicholas."

"Do you have plans for this evening, Grandmère? I'd like to invite you to my house."

"I do have plans. But for you, I will change them. What's the occasion?" He heard her suspicion and it was well-deserved. He'd never invited her to his house after the initial housewarming.

"Will you bring my...father, too?"

"Certainly," she replied with a lightness he hadn't heard in a while. "Now tell me, what is this all about?"

He imagined her smiling since he'd included Edward and had called him father.

"I'm going to propose."

"Propose what dear?"

"I'm going to ask Biloxi Dutrey to marry me."

He counted to ten. Then to twenty. The phone

showed that the connection remained. His grandmother was on the other end of the line.

Still silence.

She had to have heard him. She hadn't hung up. "Grandmère? Did you hear what I said?"

"Yes. Yes, I heard. Charles Nicholas Trahan, I love you." Her voice trembled. "And if you really love this girl—if you're sure she's the only one for you, then I will do my very best to find a way to love her, too."

That was more than he hoped for. "Just be nice to her. That's all I ask. I love her enough for the two of us."

****

Nick redid the silk tie for the third time. Earlier, he'd waited at the tailor shop for the one p.m. opening and bought a new suit. Once informed about the upcoming proposal, the tailor handpicked a tie and white shirt as a gift. Now, Nick's fingers had a mind of their own and the tie wasn't cooperating.

Behind him, Linc snickered. He caught the younger man's amused expression in the mirror.

"What?" he demanded.

"For a flying geek who takes care of animals, you'll make a pretty good brother-in-law," Linc said.

"Listen to you." He playfully thumped Linc on the back of the head. "From one flying geek to another. I've seen you dressed in a penguin suit. Women gave you the eye. One day, you'll be standing where I am."

"Yeah, right," Linc scoffed. "Well, maybe. So what's with the boots? You've gone to all this trouble—way over the top. The flowers must've cost a pretty penny, you practically bought out the florist. Who gets the bakery to make a cake on Sunday? And you borrowed a horse and carriage. You've gone all out for my sister. But, you're wearing Luccheses for Christ's sake. With a suit! Remember, my sister's a photographer. She's got an eye for detail, and she'll notice them right off."

Nick adjusted the knot on his tie, finally satisfied with the result. "That's what I'm counting on."

Linc slapped him on the back. "Then let's go."

Together they bounded downstairs where most of the family waited, mingling in the living room, dining room, and a few in the kitchen. All had dressed for the occasion. Though Grace remained hospitalized, she'd sent her blessing with Marie, which meant a lot to him. The only other person missing—his mother. Still no word on where she might be. Given more time, news of her whereabouts might develop into something positive. He remained optimistic.

He looked around at the show of heartwarming family support. Without batting an eye, they'd all pitched in to help him.

All of them had made up stories about their evening commitments.

All of them now congregated in his house.

Even his father and his grandmother.

He'd taken his grandmother on his arm and introduced her to everyone. He credited his grandmother's change to her Southern manners, she acted pleased to meet each one of the Linds and Dutreys. Including Elise Murphy Dutrey. Any hint of past scandal or hard feelings had disappeared, or at least remained artfully masked.

His moment of truth was minutes away. He'd planned every detail with Biloxi in mind, and he wanted her to remember the details of his proposal for years to come. He hoped she'd sigh with delight when retelling the story to their children and grandchildren of how he proposed.

Now if she'd only arrive.

He paced the floor and waited for Sean to deliver the bride-to-be.

"It smells like a florist in here," Linc complained.

"Yes, isn't it great?" Nola said, a far-away gleam in her eyes. "And so romantic, too."

Linc grunted, then stalked away.

Nick chuckled and headed toward the kitchen.

"Nicholas, everything looks *very* nice." Very high praise from Deidre. He won marks when she first saw the outrageous display of flowers. Her daughter was worth all of them and more, though it didn't hurt that he'd managed to impress his mother-in-law-to-be.

"I didn't know Biloxi's favorite flower," Nick admitted. "Roses? Tulips? Daisies? I decided it wasn't a big deal. I just bought most of what Flora had in her shop. She never grumbled about working on Sunday, but she wouldn't start arranging until after church. She plays the piano at First Baptist. She had her husband, Fred, over here blowing up the helium balloons."

"The arrangements are lovely," Macy said, fingering the greenery on a bouquet of stargazer lilies. She bent to sniff the pink and white flowers.

"I hope she likes those," Nick said.

"Nicholas always did have good taste," his grandmother said, joining them in the kitchen. She actually sounded proud of him. She placed a kiss on his cheek, then rubbed her thumb over the spot. "I would like a word with you in private." She linked her arm through his.

He led her from the kitchen through the French doors, out to the back gallery. The sun shining through the pine trees warmed the late afternoon air.

"Nicholas, I've brought something for you." Suzette opened her purse and pulled out a small box. The black velvet lay stark against her white skin. "This was my mother's engagement ring. It's set in platinum. I'm giving this to you for Biloxi. It was always intended for your wife."

Nick took the box and opened it.

"The center stone is one carat. The four surrounding stones are a quarter carat each."

He hesitated. "Grandmère, this is a lovely gesture. Please understand, I am touched by your generosity."

"But?"

"I picked out a ring especially for her. Something that will always be just hers. No family strings or ties. No history to deal with or forget. Something that is hers alone to wear."

"I see," Suzette said stiffly.

"When you really get to know her, when you really care for her, then you can give her the ring as a present from you. It would mean so much more to her that way." Nick closed the box. "Thank you for caring enough for me to offer a family heirloom." He hugged his grandmother. When she hugged him back, a new confidence planted in his heart. Everything would work itself out in the future.

They returned to the kitchen, and Greta assisted his grandmother into a chair just as Branna rushed in.

"The dining room table is set," Branna said breathlessly. "Cake, candles, champagne and glasses, plates, napkins, and more flowers. Momma, take a look. Did I forget anything?" she asked. "I've got the long tapers set in silver candelabras you brought from Fleur de Lis. I think the room looks fabulous. I think I'm more excited than she'll be!"

Nick snapped his attention to Branna.

"Oh, Nick. I'm teasing. I'm just so excited, for both of you. I savor the anticipation. I'm thrilled that you invited all of us. I get to see her face when you propose."

"She's gonna know something's up the minute she and dad drive up," Linc said blandly. "When was the last time your front railings were covered in flowers and ribbon?"

"Never. But don't worry," Nick said. "You just be sure to bring the carriage around the minute after she says, 'I do.'"

"Man, she'll be too busy looking at that ring. She won't notice the carriage. All of this for a marriage proposal. *If* I get married, I'm going to elope." Linc folded his arms. "No long engagement."

"Only if some woman can put up with you." Nola sounded as though the likelihood of Linc snagging a woman was as plausible as frogs walking on two legs.

"Oh!" squealed Branna. "May I see the ring?"

Nick reached for the little box in his pocket. Macy, Deidra, and Suzette leaned in, too. Why did a diamond ring bring out madness in women? How did a rock reduce a grown woman to a drooling Pavlovian dog?

He paused. "No offense ladies, but my bride-to-be gets the first peek at the ring."

"But—you let Linc see it," Branna protested.

"That was just a guy thing." Linc shrugged. "And

371

after all, I'm going to be Nick's best man."

Nick mimicked Linc's nonchalant shrug, then made his way to the living room. He liked Branna, had an interest in her once. He'd even mistakenly called Biloxi "Branna" the night they'd first met, but now, knowing both of them, he could never imagine confusing the two. Nick chuckled. Biloxi would cringe at his *Gone with the Wind* reference, but she had Melody Wilkes' heart and Scarlett O'Hara's determination. She was the perfect woman for him.

"Are you doing okay, Aunt Marie?" Nick asked, squatting beside the chair where the old woman sat. Her trademark cane leaned against the other side of the chair.

"I'm fine, Nicholas. I'm so glad Charles is going to video tape this event so we can show Grace when she comes home from the hospital."

"I've got the camera ready to go." Charles held up the video camera.

Nick patted her frail hand. "I appreciate your understanding. I just couldn't wait another day. I wanted Grace to be here, too. You could take the camera to the hospital this evening to show her. You don't have to wait for her to come home."

Marie crooked an aged finger at him. "Well, what do you know? Now, don't go off and get married without us there. Neither Grace nor I want to witness the nuptials secondhand on a viewing screen."

"Wouldn't think of it." He kissed her wrinkled cheek.

Rising, he paced from the living room, across to the foyer and into the dining room, checking everything out for the umpteenth time. So far, everything had moved according to plan. But his palms were sweating.

This morning he'd asked Sean for Biloxi's hand in marriage after winning the race to his house for coffee. Sean gave his blessing, then confided that he and Deidre had been pleased the relationship had taken a serious turn. Even though Nick might be a Trahan, his roots ran deep in Bayou Petite. They always feared their photo-snapping daughter would find someone up in New York or down in Miami, and then move away forever. They wanted the family close. They wouldn't want photographs in place of grandkids' squeals for holidays. Sean had, not so subtly, reminded Nick that if he didn't make Biloxi happy, there could always be another Dutrey-Trahan duel.

After breakfast when, in front of her family, he'd asked Biloxi for a date, she'd laughed at his silliness, yet agreed. Afterward, he'd confided in Greta about the planned proposal. She in turn recruited the local pastry chef to open his bakery on a Sunday, and she helped make a two-tier cake topped with replicas made from fondant of his Lucchese boots and the expensive "Jimmy—who?" shoes Biloxi had lost in the mud.

Biloxi would understand the significance.

Charles had carted over champagne for toasting from the reserves at Fleur de Lis. Linc stole one of Biloxi's cameras and a tripod. He had instructed Nola, who was ready to snap photos the minute Biloxi walked through the door, on how to use the equipment. Nola, oozing with giddiness, had gleefully accepted the role as event photographer. Then, Linc drove Biloxi's Escalade over to Captain Jack's and rode back in the loaned horse-drawn carriage, the one Jack used in parades. Nick planned to take his bride-to-be for a buggy ride to celebrate their engagement at sunset.

The last piece of the puzzle turned out to be the hardest—convincing Biloxi to allow her father to drive her to his house for their date.

"I don't need my father. Since *never* has he delivered me to a guy's house so that guy could take me out on a date. I can drive myself. Besides, what's wrong with your truck? You're pretty nervy, Dr. Trahan."

Thankfully, she had finally given in.

He vowed to never lie to her again. Well, almost never. There were a number of surprises he'd want to spring on her that would require little white lies. Surprises for her birthday and all of the holidays when they would gather with family to celebrate.

"They're coming up the drive!" Edward shouted.

Everyone scattered and hid.

Nick peeked through the window when Biloxi stepped out of the car. Her long auburn hair bounced in large flowing waves. She looked spring fresh in her flowered dress. A pink sash wrapped her waist and tied in a bow on the side. He even liked her lime-green heels. Were they Jimmy—who's?

Once out of the car, she reached for the stair railing, but stopped. She pulled back. Curiosity etched her face as she examined the flowers and ribbons. When she started again to climb the steps, she avoided touching the railing.

He opened the door when she reached the third step.

"You look beautiful." He ushered her the rest of the way. She smelled fresh like a spring rain.

"You look handsome yourself, but where's the truck? And what's with the flowers—"

"Just wait."

As they reached the threshold, he swung the front door open wide and snapped his fingers.

"Surprise!" Everyone yelled at once. They spilled down the stairs, from around the staircase, and out of the kitchen. Marie rose from a chair, then leaned on her cane to steady herself with Greta's support. Bewilderment fixed on Biloxi's face as everyone gathered around them.

Nick led her to a chair he'd placed near the stairs, then gestured for her to sit. She slid hesitantly into the seat, then clasped her hands in her lap as though clutching for life itself. She blinked several times. Was that mist in her eyes?

"Nick? It's not my birthday, and Valentine's Day is over." Her eyes darted warily to the flower-filled room. She scanned the faces of their family members. As though it were all too much for her to comprehend, she returned her focus to him.

The room grew quiet. The sound of strings from a CD in the stereo gently swirled around them. Nick bent on one knee in front of her, then took her hand in his. "Biloxi Noël Dutrey, I love you. With our families as witnesses, I'm asking you to be my wife. Will you marry me?"

****

Joy lifted Biloxi's heart. Surprise swirled in her brain until dizziness threatened to submerge her. Tingles ran up her spine. Her knees wobbled. She grasped the arm of the chair to stop the room from spinning. Last night, she'd dreamt of Nick, and when she woke, she'd been disoriented and confused. The dream seemed so darn real. Could she be dreaming now?

She squeezed Nick's hand tightly. He squeezed back. Though his warmth radiated into her, she still couldn't be certain it all wasn't a dream.

"Biloxi Noël Dutrey, will you do me the honor of being my wife?"

Her bottom lip quivered. Tremors roiled in her stomach, first like a wave and then a rollercoaster. The rushing sound in her ears drowned out the music. Then echoes of her heartbeat pounded. Loud. Rapid. Joyous.

His proposal surprised her. In a good way. A very good way. Speechless and breathless she fanned herself, fluttering air with her hand. She loved this man. Nothing in life had ever compared to this single moment.

Nothing.

And nothing else mattered. Just Nick.

If everything else in life faded away, the world would exist with just the two of them.

Before her, Nick knelt on one knee. His eyes blazed brightly, his grin widened. His usual inscrutable expression radiated love.

"Nick," she said softly. The rest of her intended response died on her lips. Instead of speaking she nodded, leaned in, and gently touched her lips to his. Frisson flowed like a waterfall, and filled her to her core.

She belonged.

Right there.

With him.

It didn't seem possible that his smile could grow wider or his eyes could burn brighter, but they did. She gazed at him with wonder when Nick kissed the top of her hand. He unbuttoned his suit coat and reached inside it. He pulled out a small leather box. With a steady hand, he flipped the lid open. She stared.

A diamond ring.

It glittered. Sparkled. Her heart fluttered with palpitations like wings of a million butterflies beating in her chest.

"Ooooh!" Cumulative gasps escaped from family onlookers. Biloxi's vision turned watery. Tears spilled, rolling down her cheeks. With a finger, she wiped them away.

Nick plucked out the ring. *Thunk!* The small box hit the floor.

Grasping her left hand, Nick slid the diamond onto her ring finger. His expression softened. He appeared mesmerized by the sight of her hand. He kissed her palm, then stood and helped her to her feet. She moved into his arms. His embrace was warm, safe, and perfect.

She ran her fingers upward into his neatly combed hair. Life couldn't get any better. When he touched his lips to hers again, she melted against him. Every muscle in her body turned slack. Was she floating?

His kisses took her to a place beyond. A place where they belonged. Together.

Loud cheering and clapping startled her and brought her focus back to the room. To earth, and to family. Rhythmic applause from her family sounded like the cheering section at an Ole Miss football game. Nick didn't let go. He continued his kisses.

When Nick finally drew back, her father stepped beside them. Nick's mouth displayed the telltale signs of a man who'd been well-kissed. She reached up to wipe away a smear of color from the corner of his mouth. He nipped at her thumb before she pulled her hand away.

When had an innocent act become so erotic?

As much as she loved that her family witnessed the proposal, she wished she could blink them gone. What she wanted now was Nick. Just Nick.

A picture popped into her head. A family. Theirs. Five children.

"Ah, hum." Her father coughed. "We all wish to congratulate the bride and groom to be."

Nick released her hand, and her father wrapped her in a bear hug.

"I am so happy for you," Sean said. "My first-born. You're not a little girl anymore, but you'll always be *my* girl."

Awash with happiness, she hugged her father. Not only was he pleased for her, he approved of Nick.

Her mother hugged Nick around his neck, then whispered something into his ear, which caused him to grin. He nodded in agreement. It worried her that her groom-to-be had just bonded with her mother, which was akin to siding with the devil.

Her father hugged her again before relinquishing his hold. Edward Trahan quickly moved in. He placed his hands on her shoulders. Sadness mixed with hope glittered in his eyes. She was surprised, though pleased, to see both him and Suzette, and prayed it was a good omen.

"Congratulations," Edward said. "You look radiant. I expect we'll get to know each other well. You've got a big family." He gulped and nodded, clearly holding back tears.

"I hope so, too." Biloxi leaned in and kissed his

cheek.

"I will be so proud to call you daughter."

Before Biloxi could respond, Suzette stepped up and grabbed her in a sudden awkward embrace. Startled, Biloxi stiffened when the old woman crushed her tight, unsure which surprised her more, the strength in the old woman's arms or the enthusiasm. Suzette pulled back, adjusted the long string of pearls around her neck, and smiled softly. "Call me Grandmère," she said.

"Thank you," Biloxi replied.

Deidra stepped close. "You did fine, honey. And the surprise on your face! I hope Nola caught that. I love seeing you so happy. It's all I ever really wanted. Living here, you'll be right down the road from Fleur de Lis. Almost as good as living there."

Over her mother's shoulder, she watched Edward guide Suzette to Nick through the crowd. The family parted and then enveloped Suzette when she moved into their sphere. Hopefully, Suzette's tears were tears of joy. The old woman had been through a lot in a very short time. Biloxi respected the older woman, and maybe in time, they'd grow close.

The hugs and wishes flowed. Family members embraced her one by one. She couldn't recall ever receiving so many hugs at one time.

Biloxi gazed at her family. Work had brought her home. Work, she'd believed, was her ticket to belonging, as if she needed to prove herself in order to remain at Fleur de Lis. Nick brought life into focus, just like she brought focus to her photographs. All of her pictures captured love. It was reflected in the eyes. Yet, it took falling in love with Nick for her to understand where she truly belonged.

She turned toward Nick when he draped his arm around her. "Happy, Biloxi?" He pulled her tight and gently kissed her.

"Deliriously," she whispered against his lips.

"A toast!" Sean shouted.

"Biloxi?" Branna interrupted and Biloxi wrapped her arm around Nick's waist and turned to face her cousin

"I didn't think it was possible."

"What do you mean? *You* were the one who told *me* that when I fell in love it would take me over the top."

"Yes, well, I meant love for you, dear cousin. I wasn't sure I'd ever find true love."

"Heavenly, isn't it?" Branna teased.

All Biloxi could do was nod.

Pop! Sean opened a bottle of champagne. Everyone cheered.

"Biloxi, Nick, come cut the cake." Deidre waved at them from the dining room.

Nick tugged on Biloxi's hand and pulled her behind him as Nola clicked the camera and Charles recorded everything. Her father passed around glasses of champagne.

At the head of the table, Biloxi and Nick stood side by side.

"Oh. My. God!" Biloxi cried. "This cake deserves a first prize blue ribbon."

Sean raised a glass. The room fell silent. "To Nick and Biloxi."

In unison, everyone echoed his words.

Chapter 43

Alone at last, Nick stretched out his jean-clad legs on the couch and wrapped his arms around Biloxi, settling her back against his chest. The fireplace glowed. John Boutte's sultry singing, "That's My Desire," floated around them, enveloping them in their own special cocoon. Outside, dusk had faded away. They would never have to face a long night alone again.

Biloxi lifted her hand and moved her engagement ring back and forth, admiring the glint in the firelight. "The carriage ride was fun. This is truly lovely."

He heard awe and love in her voice. He kissed her cheek. "Not as lovely as you."

"I can't believe how happy I am. I love you, Nick."

He hugged her tighter, loving the feel of her in his arms. "I love you, Biloxi Noël Dutrey."

"Did you know"—she purposely accentuated her drawl—"I thought you kept coming around because you loved Greta's cooking?"

When he didn't respond right away, she elbowed him in the ribs.

"Hey, now. I can't lie and say I don't love Greta's cooking. In fact, how are we going to lure her away from the Old Aunts? Let's face it, knowing I'll have an endless supply of Greta's gourmet eats is a lot of your appeal."

"Really? I heard my big family was the

fascination."

"What? No offense, *chèr*, but sometimes they're a royal pain in the backside."

"I can cook. Almost as good as Greta. Who do you think taught me?"

Nick sighed. "Thank goodness. I'd hate to break our engagement and propose to Greta just to get another home cooked meal."

She chuckled and rested her head on his chest.

They sat in silence and watched the flames dance. Stars glittered beyond the windows, lighting Bayou Petite's dark blue sky. The excitement of the day folded into peaceful contentment. He wanted nothing to change.

"Nick?"

"Hmm?"

"I had the strangest thing pop into my head during your proposal," Biloxi said. "It was from a dream I'd had, and then suddenly remembered again."

He nibbled her ear, then whispered, "Tell me."

"An image, a picture of us...with five kids. Weird."

If he'd ever had any doubts about this woman, which he didn't, they were immediately erased. "Five?" he coughed.

"Yeah. Five. We've never talked about children."

"I imagine now is as good a time as ever."

"I don't want to scare you, Nick. You're an only child. Have you ever considered how many children you want?"

"Uh-huh."

"How many is that?" Hesitation wrapped her question, but before he could answer, she rushed in. "I really like the picture in my head. I'm thinking that five sounds like a lot, but I also think we have lots of love to give."

Life with this woman would be full of love like he'd never experienced. A large family of his own. Fixing bicycles and going fishing. He'd build a stable. They'd get a pony, maybe even get a horse or two. Each kid would have a dog...or cat. As long as he had Biloxi, life's possibilities were as wide as the universe.

"We'll make the perfect family," he whispered.

A word about the author...

Award-winning writer and author Linda Joyce has deep southern roots intertwined with her Japanese heritage. She was born in Mississippi, though she considers New Orleans home. She has lived coast to coast in the United States and spent four years in Japan.

She married her college sweetheart and now lives in Atlanta with her husband and three dogs: General Beauregard, Gentleman Jack, and Masterpiece Renoir (Beau, Jack, and Reni). She's still trying to convince "the boys" that they are her pets, and not the other way around. Beau, in particular, is not buying it. Linda loves boiled peanuts, sushi, and grits. She and her husband share a passion for college football.

Linda is a member of Romance Writers of America, Georgia Romance Writers, the Atlanta Writer's Club, and the Southeastern Writers Association.

Her Fleur de Lis series captures her love of the south, the backdrop for each Fleur de Lis book as it brings to life the extended Lind and Dutrey family.

In 2011, the Southeastern Writers Association awarded *Bayou Bound* First Place in Romance.

Linda invites you to contact her at:
http://www.linda-joyce.com

Thank you for purchasing
this publication of The Wild Rose Press, Inc.
For other wonderful stories of romance,
please visit our on-line bookstore at
www.thewildrosepress.com.

For questions or more information
contact us at
info@thewildrosepress.com.

The Wild Rose Press, Inc.
www.thewildrosepress.com

To visit with authors of
The Wild Rose Press, Inc.
join our yahoo loop at
http://groups.yahoo.com/group/thewildrosepress/